WRETCHED

ABSOLUTELY AMAZING eBOOKS

Habent Sua Fata Libelli

ABSOLUTELY AMAZING eBOOKS

Manhanset House
Shelter Island Hts., New York 11965-0342

bricktower@aol.com • tech@absolutelyamazingebooks.com
• absolutelyamazingebooks.com

Library of Congress Cataloging-in-Publication Data
Bethel, John David
Wretched
p. cm.

1. FICTION / Thrillers / Psychological. 2. FICTION / Thrillers / Crime. 3. FICTION / Crime
Fiction, I. Title.
ISBN: 978-1-955036-34-4 Trade Paper

May 2022

WRETCHED

John David Bethel

To my sister Paulette. A kind, considerate and very strong person.

"All men hate the wretched; how then, must I be hated, who am miserable beyond all living things! Yet you, my creator, detest and spurn me, thy creature, to whom thou art bound by ties only dissoluble by the annihilation of one of us."

—Mary Wollstonecraft Godwin Shelley, *Frankenstein*

The very life of any creature is a quick-fading spark in fathomless darkness.

—Anthony Doerr, *All the Light We Cannot See*

Rave Reviews for *WRETCHED*

"Based on real-life crimes as the blueprint for this story, *Wretched* breaks solid ground in its intent. With John Bethel's dark and dramatic narrative, you get an engaging novel that is to be taken seriously as an art form in its genre. The mystery at the center of *Wretched* and how it impacts the tiny community of Oletha makes for a compelling crime story."

—Five Stars from Reader's Favorites

"J. David Bethel's latest novel once again focuses on the evil among us. This time he chooses a small town cursed with a bully who terrorizes those with whom he comes into contact. His murder in broad daylight in the middle of town attracts the attention of the FBI when those who were there claim to have seen nothing. What seems a straightforward plot soon takes a twist that makes the bully's actions tame. The sexual sadism that is uncovered is hard to read, but Bethel convinces you that such monsters do exist. The novel does a great job of developing a cast of small-town characters who have no idea such evil exists among them."

—Terry Wade, Author, *Only the Rich and the Dead*

"Wretched delivers the disturbing high-paced realism that John David Bethel is known for. What unfolds is a story of investigation in an Iowan town fraught with obstacles that gradually reveal a daringly complex tale rivaling true crime stories. I highly recommend *Wretched* to anyone who enjoys true crime, Based on true events!"

—Jill McCracken, Host of the Murder Shelf Book Club podcast

Glossary of Major Characters

Ken Plough: Oletha town bully
Crystal Truville: Plough's first wife
Lurleen Ames: Plough's second wife
Tricia Plough: Plough's third wife
John Esper: Sheriff of Oletha
Eileen Prado: FBI Special Agent
Ira Fisher: FBI Special Agent
"Marshal" Leo Staton: Sheriff of Maryville
Orin Truville: Brother of Crystal Truville
Robert McCay: Special Agent and Profiler with FBI's Behavioral Analysis Unit
Frankie Hebert: Local thug/Confidential Informant

Glossary of Recurring Characters

Jill: Owner of Jill's Place
Silas Moore: Father of Alice Moore
Alice Moore: Mother of Alice Moore
Alice Moore: Daughter of Silas and Alice Moore, Victim
Ida Geist: Victim
Rochelle Lee: Victim
Dina Rounds: Victim
Gretchen Donovan: Survivor
Wilhelmina Geist: Survivor
Lydia Slocum: Survivor
Rusty Weiler: Owner, Dummy's Tavern

SIX MONTHS AGO

Oletha, Iowa

Ken Plough did not enter a room so much as invade it, slamming the screen door open at Dummy's Tavern, the sound ricocheted off the back wall.

"Yeah," he said, declaring his presence.

Plough was still an impressive man even as age was clawing at his body. Slightly more than six feet tall, he swiveled his broad shoulders as he walked to the bar, where he turned around slowly and looked at the few occupied tables before sitting down heavily on a wooden stool. He rapped his knuckles on the ebony bar that took up one side of the spare concrete room. A can of Budweiser was placed in front of him by Rusty Weiler, owner of Dummy's.

"You ever gonna to spend a dime on this place?" he spat at Weiler and raised his chin toward the steel beams overhead. "Maybe put a coat of paint on those." He jerked his chin at the mirror behind the bar. "Or just clean that damn thing."

Weiler did not respond. He took his customary spot at the other end of the bar and picked up a paperback.

"What's all them cars doing in front of city hall?" Plough asked no one in particular.

An uncomfortable moment of silence later, Weiler answered, "Don't know."

Two men sitting at one of five tables in the room continued their quiet conversation.

Plough sat upright, his elbows on the bar. He brought the can of beer up to his lips in a slow motion. His shoulders were thickly muscled, and his arms filled his black short-sleeved cotton Tee. A once slim waistline was now hidden under an avalanche of fat that hung almost into his lap. His legs were still muscled and threatened the stitches in his blue jeans.

Plough turned on his stool until he was facing the open room. The tables, covered with red-checked plastic tablecloths and surrounded by cross-backed wooden chairs, were scattered haphazardly around the room; two were pushed together; another was sitting in a corner as if someone had tried to push it away from the others; one had four chairs surrounding it, another none.

"How's it going, Randy?" Plough directed at a man sitting alone, who nodded his answer.

Plough turned back toward the bar. His once-handsome face, which had been dominated by a taut jawline and a prominent sculpted Roman profile, was beginning to melt. The jawline was now jowly, and his chin was one with a waddle of fat that ran into his neckline.

"What's that," Plough pointed to a squat bottle of amber-colored liquid.

Weiler pushed himself up and stood in front of a line of bottles arranged single file on a glass shelf that ran the length of the wall. "This one?" he said, moving forward and touching one of the bottles.

"Yeah."

"Pilar Rum from Key West. Leo picked it up on a trip there. Supposed to be real good stuff."

"Marshal Leo Staton?" Plough asked contemptuously. "When was he in here?"

"Right after he got back from Key West," Weiler answered and returned to his stool.

"About the last time he was harassing me for no good reason," Plough said contemptuously. "Just went to Maryville to pick up something." Getting no response, he continued, "Fuckin' Key West rum. Ain't we gettin' fancy in our little local bar in our little hayseed town."

Weiler glanced at Randy Starks, who rolled his eyes. Before Plough stomped into the bar, Starks and Wynn Keaton had been talking across tables about the most recent rash of missing hogs suffered by a number of neighboring farmers. Nothing new. Every few months hogs disappeared and had been with regularity for a long time. And for just as long, people knew it was Plough. He was clever enough to never get caught in the act, but they knew it was him. On every occasion after the hogs went missing, Plough bragged about the new coon dogs he had bought, or the addition he was building at one of his houses. He was always pointing out that he had to keep up three homes: two for his ex-wives, and one for him and Tricia, the current mother of his two children. He had seven children, three boys and four girls.

As was his habit, Plough was bold, never concerned about consequences, which he had managed to avoid, the occasional accusation aside. His tone bragging, he announced to Weiler, Starks and Keaton that, "I came into some money. Good thing. Truck's been actin' up. I'm gonna buy a new one this week. I'll be sure and come by and show it to you all."

***

Plough was born and raised in neighboring Maryville. His father was a tenant farmer who worked leased land and paid for it by giving up some of his crops to his landlord. This relegated young Ken to a lower status than those whose parents owned their land. Growing up, he was fueled by resentment that bred an intense defensiveness. This bred a violent bully who felt entitled to do as he wanted. As he told anyone who would listen, "They're no better'n me and I show'em that every single day of my life."

Despite their suspicions, no one knew what Plough did to keep his brood fed and clothed, afford his always brand-new Dodge Ram pickup, and the Ford 150's his ex-wives drove around town. He made a point of flashing a thick wad of bills he kept tucked into a gold money clip while talking about buying and selling "priceless" antiques and breeding the "finest coon dogs in the state."

He was often seen driving up and down dirt roads that ran from the state highway onto local properties. "Plough was spying on my place," a farmer would declare in Dummy's. "He's countin' my hogs. I just got some new ones." It was a warning to others as well as a marker in case some of the man's hogs did disappear. Not that anyone was going to do anything about it.

The few times Plough was accused of stealing hogs, and even of breaking and entering homes, he harassed his accusers into withdrawing their complaints. He perfected a routine to accomplish this, spending hours driving back and forth in front of their homes, a shotgun resting on the open driver's side window. He parked in front of their houses at night, raised the hood of his truck and tinkered with the engine for hours. If confronted, he would either point out that he was stopped on a public road or simply ignore the challenge. He was even known to show up at the local elementary or high school and call out to the children of his accuser asking them to "Tell your mama and daddy I said hello." Plough's ex-wives would take up the drive-by routine in front of the homes of anyone who expressed support or sympathy for a victim.

The intimidation worked in most instances and on those rare occasions when a case made it to court, the intimidation was ramped up. Wives and children of the accuser were followed. Anyone who was listed as a witness was included in this routine. On more than one occasion, livestock were killed as were domestic pets. Once a barn mysteriously caught fire. If the case still proceeded, Plough hired the best legal minds in the area. Countless delays, continuing threats and harassment, and the lack of resources for the accuser resulted in dismissals.

Plough used the threat of violence skillfully without ever carrying through. Except once.

***

Ed Renicker passed Tricia on the dirt road that led to their houses. It was spring and the ruts filled with water creating a sticky mud. Tricia had driven into a deep pothole and was stuck. Renicker stopped and as he was getting out of his truck to see what he could do to help her, Plough drove up. Renicker raised his hand to greet Plough, who appeared from behind Tricia's truck with a shotgun pointed at the man's head.

"What the hell, Ken?" Renicker asked, more confused than scared.

"You've been talkin' shit about me for years. You and Alice, that prissy wife of yours, been talkin' down to me and I'm tired of it."

Renicker looked from Plough to Tricia expecting more of an explanation from one of them. He had no idea what Plough was talking about.

As if picking up on Renicker's confusion, Tricia said, "Alice was in Loughlin's the other day and she told Sue that Ken Jr. stole some candy."

Plough advanced, his face screwed up in anger. "And they tossed my boy out 'cause your cunt of a wife said my boy was stealin'. He never stole nothin'."

Renicker took a step back. "I don't know anything about that." Plough continued to walk toward him, his face turning redder with every step. "Ken," Renicker said evenly, his hands in the air. "I'll talk to Alice and if what you say is true, I'll square it with Sue."

"*If*?" Plough blurted. "*If*? So, you think my boy might've stolen somethin'?"

"I didn't say that" Renicker replied his voice now breaking with fear. "I meant…."

"Meant?"

Renicker bumped into the front of his truck and slid across it, then along the side to his door. The body of the vehicle now between him and Plough.

The explosion of the gun startled Tricia who screamed. Renicker jumped back not realizing some of the buckshot had torn a hole in his shoulder and pierced his neck. He leapt into the cab, started the truck, threw it into reverse and was thirty yards away before he felt blood running down the inside of his shirt and soaking him at his waistline. "Son of a bitch," he yelled and slowed long enough to peek at himself in the rearview mirror. His shirt was torn away from his shoulder to his neck. A large chunk of flesh was gone leaving a crater of red, gnarled meat where his upper left shoulder and collar bone had been. The seriousness of his injury made Renicker feel faint and nauseous. He looked out his windshield. Plough and Tricia were distant figures. The last thing he remembered before waking up in the hospital was calling his wife and asking: "Did you accuse Ken Jr. of stealin' somethin' at the store?"

***

A week after the shooting Plough stomped into Dummy's and declared his intention to buy a new truck. "This one is gonna have it all. A back-up camera, Wi-Fi so my kids can play their games, and maybe a TV screen so they can watch their shows."

Weiler grunted and nodded.

"Hear about Ed?" Plough asked. No one said a word. Plough repeated, "Hear about Renicker?" This time it was a challenge.

Weiler responded boldly, "Yeah, you shot him."

Over the years, the bar owner had assumed the role of buffer between his patrons and Plough, who accepted the man in this role, notwithstanding Weiler's obvious distaste for him. Plough made a habit of directing his initial remarks to Weiler since his attempts to initiate conversation with anyone else in the bar were generally met with silence or one-word responses. Weiler would engage him and generally this allowed Plough to bully and bluster. In exercising this role, Weiler also became a voice for those in the bar as he responded to Plough freely in ways the patrons would not. Could not.

Plough laughed deeply. "That's what you hear? That I shot him? Like I just walked up to him and shot him?"

"That's what we heard."

Plough waited a beat before continuing, "Well, that's bullshit." He swiveled on the stool and spoke toward the room announcing that Renicker had been harassing Tricia, berating her; telling her Jr. had stolen from the store and should be put in jail. Plough slipped from the stool and stood leaning sideways against the bar, gesturing with the hand holding the beer, which sloshed onto the floor. "Tricia was stuck in the mud and instead of stoppin' to help her, he was sittin' there doing nothin' but insultin' her and my family. When he saw me drive up, he tried to get his gun from his rack. I had to defend myself and my wife from that crazy fool."

Plough turned and put his elbows and forearms on the bar. "Bet you didn't hear about that part, did you, Rusty."

Knowing that Plough would continue asking the same question until he answered, Weiler said, "No, I didn't hear that part."

"Changes everything, doesn't it?"

Weiler let the question sit. He considered his response. Despite the latitude Plough allowed him as a referee in his own bar, he knew there were limits. If he crossed a line it would unhinge the man causing him to erupt. It was hard enough to keep people in Dummy's when Plough was in town. Instead of saying, "You're full of shit," Weiler went with, "Sure, that changes the story, but Renicker said he's gonna follow through on this. File charges."

Plough widened his eyes in mock concern. "Is that what he's sayin'? Charges for what? We all know how that's gonna turn out. His word against mine and Tricia's." He tapped his knuckles on the bar, signaling for another beer and saying, "Right, Rusty? We all know how that's gonna to turn out. Right?"

Plough narrowed his eyes and stared hard at Weiler; his look demanding a response, but before one came, Tricia appeared at his side, surprising Plough. "What the hell're you doin' in here? I told you to wait in the truck." He glanced at the door. "Lurleen's still out there, right?"

Tricia leaned in and whispered causing Plough to smile. "No, shit. A whole group of'em on their way over here." He patted the stool next to his. "Sit your fine ass down here and I'll show you how this is done." He motioned at Weiler and demanded loudly, "Another one for me and a Coke for Tricia. She's too young to drink."

A shiver tightened Weiler's shoulders, causing him to roll his neck. Did he hear right? *A group was coming this way?* He knew some people were meeting in the Town Hall about how they were going to make sure Renicker had protection and got to court in Maryville. There was talk about not letting it go this time.

Weiler bent over the ice chest and retrieved a Coke for Tricia. "This is not good," he mumbled as the cold air hit him in the face.

Plough laughed boisterously, slapped the bar and said to the room, "This oughta be fun."

Before Plough's laugh settled, the door to the tavern opened and a line of men filed in. They ignored Plough and slowly filled the chairs around the tables; when the chairs were taken, the rest leaned up against the walls. No one took the vacant stools at the bar.

Plough made a point of watching each of the three dozen or so men walk in and tried to make eye contact with as many as he could. When the door closed behind the final person, he nodded at Weiler and said loudly, "A round on me for all my friends."

A tall, almost painfully thin man standing against the wall facing the door said, "I ain't drinking, Rusty."

Plough eyed the man. "You too good to drink with me, Silas?" He folded his arms across his broad chest, which he pushed forward. "That lady of yours got you on a short leash or somethin'? She changed her name yet to like Tequethia or somethin'. One of those fake names all those people have nowadays." He laughed and gestured toward the others in the room. "You ever notice the stupid names these people have. Like D'Andre or J'Caesar? What a crock of shit. Like that's going to make them African or somethin'. They should be glad to be livin' right here in the U.S. of A. Fuckin' Africa is a shithole."

Silas Moore stared back at Plough before saying, "Her name is Alice. You know that better'n anyone in this room. So *was* our daughter." Moore pushed himself away from the wall. "Gentleman," he said with a nod, letting his eyes circle the room before walking out of the concrete bunker.

"Okay, then," Plough said and let his arms fall to his side. "Who's drinkin' with me?"

One by one the men refused.

"What a bunch of pussies," Plough said angrily and turned back toward the bar. "They're too good for us," he directed at Tricia. "Funny how my money is good enough when I want to buy groceries at Walt's store." He pivoted on the stool and stared at a man close to him. "I'll bet I spend more in your lousy store than anyone else in this room. Know why?"

Walt Aikens lifted his straw cowboy hat and wiped his bald pate while returning Plough's stare. "'Cause I've got the only store in town, and you need to eat. I do appreciate your business, Ken." "Damn right you do, but you won't share a drink with me." Plough waved his arm in a circle. "Worse, you and everyone else in here ignore Tricia, Lurleen and Crystal and the kids when they go to church." His face beginning to redden, he added, "Won't even treat'em with respect in the house of the Lord."

This seemed like a cue for Weiler to jump into the conversation. "It's early, Ken. Some don't like drinking so early."

"No," Plough said loudly, "I seen Roy over there have a beer before noon."

Roy Nester shook his head. "Only in the winter. Never when I have corn and beans in the ground. Won't be drinkin' before sundown until after harvest." Nester, a short, stocky man with a face like a fighter who had seen better days, stood. "Speakin' of which, I gotta' get to it."

"Wait up," Plough said, holding his arm out in front of an advancing Nester. "This is about Renicker, ain't it?" He lowered his arm and smiled. "Ain't it? You all was meetin' together 'bout that, weren't you?"

It was like one of those games of "statue." No one moved. They barely breathed. The only sound was the hum from a wall air conditioner.

"I was defending myself and Tricia for fuck's sake," Plough said through gritted teeth. "He was goin' for a gun in his truck."

"Why would Ed want to shoot you and Tricia?" someone asked.

Plough moved his head to see around Nester and find the man who asked the question. "You should ask him, Mike. If I had waited to do the askin', I wouldn't be here right now."

Mike Norris shook his head causing Plough to explode. "You don't believe me? You think I'm lyin' and Ed's tellin' the truth?"

Norris, almost Plough's size, but most of his was fat, looked pained. "I'm sayin'…." He paused and cleared his throat. "I'm sayin' it don't make any sense that if he was goin' to shoot you, why didn't he already have his gun in his hand?"

Plough considered the question before answering, "How the hell should I know? But if I'd waited, he'd a gotten that gun and shot me and Tricia. That's the gospel truth."

"Okay, then," Weiler said, "and that's why we have the law and the courts to settle our disagreements."

Plough slammed a fifty-dollar bill on the bar. "President Grant should cover it in case anyone wants a drink after I'm gone." He lifted his eyes to Tricia and gestured at the door.

Plough always traveled with a posse that included Tricia, at least one of his ex-wives, and sometimes one of his older boys. Wife number two, Lurleen Ames sat in a red Ford pickup parked next to Plough's Ram truck. She started the engine when he and Tricia came out of the tavern. Her face registered surprise when Ken and Tricia were followed out by the group of men. They lined up on the sidewalk that ran in front of Dummy's and watched Plough and Tricia get into the truck.

After starting the engine, Plough put a cigarette into his mouth and was about to light it when the rear window shattered, and Plough's head jerked forward and bounced off the steering wheel. An explosion of blood and flesh splattered across the windshield. Another shot took out the windshield after tearing off the top of Plough's head.

Weiler, who was standing just inside the doorway, ducked and waited until it went quiet. He ran, head down, to the passenger side door and pulled it open. Tricia was holding her blood-soaked arms away from her and looking into her lap where pieces of scalp, hair and teeth stuck to her jeans and shirt. She was mute, her eyes saucered. Weiler yanked Tricia from the car and pulled her around to the passenger door of the red Ford, pushed Tricia inside, screaming at Lurleen to "Get the hell outta here."

As the Ford squealed away from the curb a loud pop triggered Weiler to drop flat. By the time he dared to look up, the sidewalk was empty. He pushed himself off the ground and stared up and down the street. No one.

Plough's foot was jammed between the brake and gas pedals causing the engine to scream and smoke. Weiler stared at the remains of the man whose head was a bloody pulp. He wanted to get his phone, which was usually in his front pocket, but was not there when he searched. He studied the ground around him.

"Mr. Weiler," a high-pitched voice jolted him.

Weiler turned toward his tavern where a boy stood, his face pale, his shoulders shaking. The boy was staring at the truck. "Whaddya gonna do?"

Weiler took a deep breath, turned in a circle, saw his phone in the gutter, picked it up, and dialed 911 as he told the boy, "Go get the sheriff."

TODAY/MONDAY

They noticed the yellow sticky on the door as they approached the storefront. "Well, this is different," the man said reading, "Be back in five. Go on in and make yourself comfortable."

John Esper, Sheriff of Oletha was painted in white block letters on the glass door. A small bell positioned along the top edge of the door rang as they pushed into the small office. Three scarred, green file cabinets sat against the wall behind an ornate dark oak desk. A dry and cracked leather pad was positioned in the center of the desk. A heavy marble pen and ink set faced two wooden chairs. Two small trophies crowned with figures in a baseball batter's crouch, along with a few stacks of *Gun Owners* magazines and red-bound law books, sat in a bookcase to the left of the entrance.

The bell tolled behind them. "Sorry," the man said, a cup of coffee in his hand, which he raised. "Fuel." He gestured toward the chairs. "Please sit."

"I'm Special Agent Eileen Prado and this is Special Agent Ira Fisher," she said as they settled on the round-backed, scarred, cloth padded chairs. They displayed their credentials. She smiled at Esper, a small compact man with a brush cut that contributed to his youthful appearance. "We're looking into Mrs. Tricia Plough's claim that her husband's civil rights were violated under the cover of the law. She believes that…."

"I know what she believes," Esper interrupted. "I have a question for you before we get started. People 'round here have been trying to get you to come help us for 25 years, maybe more, when her husband was terrorizing every living being in town, and we got nothin'. But the minute she calls, you're here to protect his civil rights. What's the deal?"

Prado responded, "We're here to investigate whether Mrs. Plough has a legitimate case. We know that Mr. Plough has been a menace. *Was* a menace, but…."

"A menace?" Esper interjected, bouncing in his chair. "That sounds kind of like he was just an annoying guy." Esper bent over, opened a lower desk drawer, slapped a pile of papers on his desk, and pushed them toward Prado and Fisher. "This is just some of the *annoying* shit he did."

Prado nodded and resisted the urge to ask where local law enforcement was during this reign of terror. "We know the history. The Bureau looked into instances when asked to by your predecessor, and others, and was never ever able to establish that Mr. Plough broke any federal laws. We've been requested by the U.S. Attorney in Sioux City to investigate whether Mr. Plough was denied due process under the law by…."

"He's dead," Esper interrupted. "How does a dead man have any civil rights?"

"The right to due process extends beyond the grave." Prado moved forward on her chair. "We're only interested in finding out if his federally-protected rights were denied."

Esper blew out a sigh.

Prado added, "The FBI does not enforce local and state laws. And, if I'm remembering correctly, Mr. Plough was never convicted of any crimes."

"No, no," Esper responded angrily. "Back up a minute. Ken intimidated people into not testifying or into pulling back the charges brought against him. He was acquitted in cases that actually got to trial because he scared everyone half to death, and because he got good lawyers who knew the right people and got continuances that gave him time to change minds." Esper paused before adding, "If you get my point."

Fisher placed his hand on the pile of papers at the edge of the desk threatening to spill into his lap. "In the current instance, there is reason to investigate a federal civil rights violation. Mr. Plough was killed in front of dozens of people, and no one saw a thing. Strange, no?"

"You aren't even curious about what went on before?"

Fisher pushed the pile away from the edge of the desk. "A civil rights violation is a federal matter." He nodded at the pile. "These aren't."

"Mrs. Plough," Prado said, "has come to us with information we need to check out."

Esper opened the top drawer of his desk and lifted out an envelope. He made a show of slowly opening the envelope and unfolding the page inside. He displayed the FBI heading on the page and read: "There is reason to investigate whether official and legal means are being used to prevent a thorough investigation of the murder of Ken Plough." He folded the page, returned it to the envelope, and put it into the drawer, which he closed.

"Yes," Prado said. "That's why we're here."

Esper stared hard at Prado who returned his intensity, squinting her steel blue eyes, a stunning contrast to her caramel skin tone. She toyed with the jacket buttons on her dark pant suit that hid an attractive figure honed by hours in the gym and on the track. Her short, dark curls were cut short framing a thin face devoid of makeup.

Esper fell against the back of his chair. "What do you need from me?"

"A little guidance is all," Prado replied reassuringly. "That and all the investigative material and witness statements you've collected."

Esper nodded at the pile. "It's mixed in with that. A lot of nothing. I've talked to almost every single person in Oletha. No one saw a thing. Everyone there was busy duckin' and divin'."

"Mrs. Plough claims there are people who should be investigated and either haven't been or have been dismissed without adequate reason."

"That's what she says. Now, what else can I do for you?"

"Let's begin at the beginning. Who called you to the scene?"

"Bobby Willis." Esper sat forward. "He was sent over by Rusty Weiler."

Prado consulted a small black notebook she pulled from a beat up, soft leather briefcase. "Mr. Rusty Weiler is the owner of the tavern, where things got started."

"Got started? You haven't been listening to anything I've said. Plough's been a pain in the ass for years. As long as I can remember. That's how things got started."

Fisher raised a finger. "We're talking about the timeline leading up to the murder. What did you see when you arrived on the scene?"

"Besides a dead man with his brains blown all over the inside of the cab? I didn't see a thing."

Prado smiled thinly; it did not reach her eyes. "That's hard to believe. As we understand it at least two dozen men followed the victim out of the bar."

Esper corrected her. "More like 30 from what I was told."

"And no one saw a damn thing?" Fisher said, a challenge in his voice.

"That's what I've been told by everyone who was there."

"How did you find out about the shooting?" Prado asked.

"Like I said, Bobby Willis came to my office and told me Ken had been shot. By the time I got there, the street was as deserted as it is early on a Sunday morning."

"You didn't find that strange?" Fisher said. "A dead man in a truck and absolutely no one around? No one was curious about gunshots? No one came out of the stores, restaurants, or anywhere else to see what was going on? No one tried to help Mr. Plough?"

"I didn't say I didn't find it strange," Esper replied to Fisher and shifted his attention to Prado. "That's what I saw."

"Thank you," Prado said, her attention on the notebook. "You talked to this man Willis…."

"Bobby Willis is a boy."

"Okay, you talked to the boy, and to Mr. Weiler. What did they tell you?"

"Bobby was inside Dummy's when Ken was shot, so he didn't see a thing, and Rusty, like everyone else, was busy getting out of the way. That's pretty much it."

"And everyone else just disappeared?"

Esper nodded. "And everyone just disappeared. Rusty did say that he pulled Tricia out of the truck and Lurleen grabbed her and drove her home." Responding to Prado's look of question, Esper added, "Lurleen Ames was parked next to Ken and she took Tricia home."

Taking another peek at her notebook, Prado asked Esper to "Tell me about Silas Moore."

"Whaddya want to know?"

Prado let her hands drop into her lap, and after an extended moment of silence, said, "According to Mrs. Plough he was the one who killed her husband. What does he say about that?"

"He says she's bat shit crazy."

"But he did have problems with Mr. Plough. Serious ones. Right?"

Esper threw back his head and laughed. It took a few seconds for him to regain his composure. "I told you, *everybody* in town had problems with Ken. Serious ones." He shifted in his chair. "Ken pulled a gun on me more'n once."

"What?" Fisher blurted, his voice croaking up an octave. "Did you arrest him for threatening a police officer?"

"Yeah, I arrested him."

"And?" Prado and Fisher asked simultaneously.

"And, he managed to get out of it like he always did."

"You're saying he intimidated you into dropping the charges?" Fisher asked, leaning forward, his glasses sliding to the end of his long nose. A tall, thin man, Fisher was a poster boy for the clean-cut image of an FBI agent. He could have been a bit sturdier physically, but that would have been quibbling.

"No, I'm not saying that," Esper replied angrily. "He and his lawyers managed to convince the DA that there was no case. And I can go into the details on how he managed that if you want. Continuances. Confusing the issue. Appeals to the Second Amendment and like that, but we'd be here the rest of the day."

Prado shook her head. "We can come back to that if we need to. About Silas Moore, he claims that Mr. Plough kidnapped his daughter." She looked at Esper for confirmation and he nodded his head. "That's what Mrs. Plough said started everything between them."

"No," Esper said, "that's not it. Least ways not exactly like Tricia told you. Silas did accuse Ken of getting his daughter to go off with him a few times."

"You talked to both Mr. Plough and the daughter, right?" Fisher asked.

"'Course I did."

"What did the daughter say?"

"All'd she say was she talked to Ken a few times." Esper screwed up his face in a look of disgust. "Ken does have, or *did* have a thing for young girls. Tricia was about sixteen when she ran off with him."

Prado asked, "When you say Mr. Moore accused Mr. Plough of getting his daughter to 'go off with him', what does that mean exactly?"

"I don't know *exactly* what happened with Silas's daughter. All we know for sure is that now she's missing."

"Six months, right?" Fisher said. "*Missing* if you're being optimistic."

Prado waved Esper on and he continued. "Silas said Ken used to wait for his daughter at school and when she got out he'd pick her up and they'd go off together."

"Go off together?"

Esper nodded. "Yeah, go off together. Use your imagination."

Prado brought the notebook up from her lap and placed it on Esper's desk. "Not the first time Mr. Plough has done this, right?"

"Like I just said, he had a thing for young girls. Same kind of thing happened with Tricia, only she didn't go missing."

"I'd call it a pattern," Prado said, again back into her notebook. "Jo and Cal Nesbitt, Tricia's parents, complained that their daughter was being abused by Mr. Plough. What can you tell me about that?"

"This happened before me, before I became sheriff, but I know the sheriff back then, Larry Lawrence, did all the usual stuff. Talked to Ken, who said he was just friends with Tricia, and took her and her friends to get sodas after school. That it wasn't anything bad. Then Tricia married him. End of story."

Fisher leaned toward the desk. "They're friends. They're going for sodas and, poof, they're married?"

"Ken had to get divorced from Lurleen first…"

"Wait," Prado said. "Lurleen? Is that the Lurleen Ames who took Mrs. Plough home after Mr. Plough was shot?"

Esper nodded.

"That's interesting," Prado said, "and we'll get back to it, but for right now, tell me how it was that all this happened with Tricia. She was underage. She'd need permission from her parents to get married."

"Ken's lawyer got her emancipated, I think they call it. He somehow managed to show that Tricia was being mistreated at home, and Tricia said she wanted to live on her own. Then she didn't have to get permission from her parents to do what she wanted. There were two others before Tricia. Crystal Truville and then Lurleen. Same kind of thing."

"*Same kind of thing,*" Fisher said, his distaste front and center. "Underage girls being stalked by an older man and the authorities saw no reason to intervene? No wonder you had problems with this guy."

"I thought you were here to look into a civil rights violation," Esper said. "You have a strange way of going about that."

"We're just trying to get all the information we'll need to do our job," Prado said. "Tell us about Lurleen Ames. How was it that she was there that day?"

Esper smiled broadly and relaxed back in his chair. "Looks like you don't have everything in that notebook of yours. Let's start with Ken's first wife, Crystal Truville. Ken burned down the Truville's house when Crystal's parents said they didn't want him coming 'round to see their daughter."

"Burned down their house?" Fisher blurted.

Esper held up his hand. "We don't know that for sure, but it's what everyone thinks. The Truville's accused him of statutory rape. Crystal was fifteen. The fire almost killed the Truville boy, who was five. The parents left as soon as the boy could be moved, but before they did, they dropped the charges. They said if she wanted to be with him, they were okay with that."

"Was Lurleen also underage?"

Esper nodded. "Like I said, Ken has a thing for young girls. Replaces one with the other when they...." He paused. "How should I put it?"

"Age out," Fisher volunteered.

"Yeah, so he was married to Crystal when he started up with Lurleen. He actually brought Lurleen home with him, and those three, Ken, Crystal and Lurleen lived together while he built a house for Crystal and the kids he had with her. Then he divorced her and married Lurleen. Same thing with Lurleen when he brought Tricia home. Ken, Lurleen and Tricia lived together while he built a house for Lurleen, then he divorced her to marry Tricia. Each time the new one was pregnant before Ken moved the old one out."

"And what about the first wife? Fisher asked. "Is she still around?"

Esper nodded. "Oh, yeah, Crystal's around all right. She, Lurleen and Tricia are inseparable." He lifted his hands, palms out. "I have no idea how that works, but Ken always has Tricia and at least one of the other two with him. Like when Lurleen was with them that morning. Whichever one of 'em isn't with them, she's usually watchin' all the kids, but there's times when the four of 'em are together. Drive around in a convoy. Ken and Tricia followed by Crystal and Lurleen."

"Dysfunction at its most functional," Fisher quipped.

"How did he support them all?" Prado asked, adding quickly, "I'm interested in what he told people about how he made a living." She held up her notebook. "I know what he's supposed to have done. How did he deflect the talk about him stealing and whatever else he was suspected of doing?"

Esper blew out a laugh. "Ken didn't explain himself to anyone. I can tell you he never worked a day in his life. Well, that's not fair. He worked hard at thieving and not getting caught. He never did an honest day's work in his life."

"So," Fisher said, "he's a life-long crook and bully, and everyone knew it, but no one said anything."

"I told you that anyone who confronted him got the Ken Plough treatment. It was bad, but you couldn't possibly know how bad unless you lived here; unless he walked up to you with one of his Bowie knives stuck in his beltline and warned you to stop lying about him, or else. Or you saw him sitting in your driveway in his truck with a gun pointed at your front door, and when you called the cops, he left and said he was nowhere near the house; and no matter what the neighbors would say, he had Lurleen, Crystal and Tricia to alibi for him." Esper shook his head. "No, you have no idea how bad it was."

"Can we get back to Mr. Moore?" Prado asked.

"What do you want to know?"

"Do you think it's possible he shot Mr. Plough?"

"Sure, it's possible, just like it's possible most anyone in this town could have done it."

"What did you find when you looked into the disappearance of the Moore's daughter?"

"I talked to her friends and some of the teachers at school. It was the same thing as with Tricia. He'd come around after school and she'd go off with him."

"What did Mr. Plough say about this?" Prado asked.

"He laughed about it, said Silas was just mad 'cause he didn't pay him for some kind of work he did on his car. Ken said he didn't pay 'cause the car still wouldn't work right."

Prado leafed through her notebook and felt Esper's eyes on her. "Mrs. Plough says there's a lot more to why she thinks Mr. Moore killed her husband." She went back into her briefcase and lifted out a sheaf of papers, which she reviewed. "She says Mr. Moore was cooking meth and he was afraid her husband was going to turn him in." Prado looked up at Esper. "She says that's one reason she thinks Mr. Moore is a good suspect."

"Really?" Esper said with a snort of laughter. "So Tricia's saying Silas killed Ken 'cause Ken wanted to protect our community from meth. That's rich."

"We do know Mr. Moore has a record of arrests for producing meth," Fisher said. "He also served time for assault and battery on someone he thought turned him in for dealing. Considering that, Mrs. Plough's allegations aren't that farfetched."

Esper confirmed that, "Silas was cooking in Maryville a few years back. One of his labs blew up and almost killed him. Scared him straight…."

"To coin a phrase," Fisher mumbled.

"…and he moved here. He runs a car repair business and he's a damn good mechanic. Been nothing but a hard-working guy who causes no one any trouble at all. I don't know anything about those assault charges, but you're missing a big chunk of history between him and Ken."

"Really?" Prado said, scooting forward in her chair. "Like?"

"Like about twenty years ago when Silas's wife Alice was maybe fifteen, Ken went after her."

"When did he find the time?" Fisher said. "Was this after Lurleen but before Tricia?"

"He was with Lurleen and looking around. Alice is from this area. She fell in with Ken, but it didn't take. Rumor has it he tried to do the 'play house' thing with her and Lurleen but she wouldn't have it. Also heard she told her parents that Ken started to beat on her, and he beat on Lurleen all the time She took off and Ken had it in for her ever since."

Prado asked, disbelief in her voice, "People knew he beat them?"

"Have you two not been listening to anything I've been saying?"

"You didn't say anything about...."

"And it probably isn't in your damn notebook, or in that report, or whatever all those other pages are. We're talking 'bout a bad person. An evil SOB. There isn't a person in this town who shed a tear when he got his head blown off. And anyone could have done it; might well have done it. And no one is gonna tell you a thing. You're wasting your time."

"Anything else we should know?" Prado asked calmly.

"Yeah, some say the daughter is Ken's not Silas's."

"Alice, the mother, had a child when she was fifteen?"

Esper stared at Prado. "That's what troubles you 'bout this?" He took a breath. "Most people 'round here get married young and have kids right away. Alice was sixteen. One other thing you should know, Ken was as racist as a man can be. He would leave a bar or restaurant if a black person was there, but not before announcing why he was leaving. When I confronted him 'bout young Alice, he said there was nothin' goin' on, but if there was, since Silas never fixed his car, he had every right to 'take it out in trade' if he wanted, but wouldn't because she was a 'stinkin'..." He hesitated. "He used the N-word."

"Alice Morris is African American?" Prado said, surprise in her voice.

Esper nodded his answer.

Prado shook her head. "This isn't making a whole lot of sense."

"No, shit," Fisher said, adding, "especially since the girl could've been his daughter."

"I don't put a lot of stock in that," Esper said. "But on the other stuff, Ken wanted what he wanted. That's who he is…*was*. You ever hear the one about the frog and the scorpion?"

Prado and Fisher both nodded, Fisher saying, "Like the scorpion, Plough couldn't help himself. He did what he did because that's who he was."

Prado objected. "No, I'm not on board with that. Plough might've fucked her" — Prado's words came angrily – "but he sure as hell wasn't going to take her in the way he did the other two."

Esper countered, "Let's just say Ken wanted to bend everything to his will. Going after young Alice was a way to humiliate her and her family. As I said, he had it in for the mother for a long time."

"One other thing," Esper said. "Ken was shot with two different weapons. First with some kind of high-power rifle, and then with a smaller caliber. A handgun."

Prado and Fisher sat stock still and stared at Esper, who pointed at Prado's notebook. "Didn't know that?"

Prado declared, "That means two people were involved."

"Yeah, it does, unless whoever shot him with the rifle ran real quick and shot him again with the handgun."

"The autopsy showed there were two weapons?"

"Showed there were two different kinds of wounds. The larger caliber bullets from the long gun were recovered."

"And the handgun?"

"No. Must've been through and through and the passenger window was shattered so the bullets must've exited and by the time I knew about there being two weapons and went to look for the bullets…" Esper shrugged. "Didn't find anything."

"Shell casings from the handgun?" Prado asked.

Esper shook his head. "No. Likely a revolver."

"How do you know what order the shots came in?" Fisher asked.

"I don't for sure, but I'm thinking whoever used the handgun would have had to be right up close. They'd only chance that after the first shots and everyone was running or ducking and not looking right at Ken."

"You haven't said anything about this to anyone?" Fisher asked. "I'm guessing that since Moore is the only one mentioned by Mrs. Plough."

Esper nodded. "Yeah, I figured I'd keep that close so I had something to use to help me find the right person. Well, right people."

"Two shooters" Prado said as she closed her notebook. "Someone had to notice the difference between the sound of a long gun and a handgun."

"I'm sure someone did," Esper answered, "but no one's said anything."

"Thanks for seeing us," Prado said and stood.

As she and Fisher started toward the door, Fisher turned. "Is this it?" he asked, looking around the office. "Do you have facilities for prisoners?"

Esper laughed. "Facilities? I get a salary and a car." He gestured at his surroundings. "And the rent is paid. That's it. No jail. If I ever have to arrest someone, and I haven't in the two years I've been in the job, we have an arrangement with the sheriff in Maryville so we can use his *facilities*."

TUESDAY

Ira Fisher walked down the breezeway of the Sweet Slumber Lodge. Eileen Prado's door was ajar. He tapped lightly. "Ready?"

Prado stepped from the dark of her room and pulled the door closed behind her. "Well, that was hellish."

"What, you don't like flea bitten rooms in a flea-bitten motel in the middle of nowhere?"

Prado ran her hands through wet hair. "And the water is brown and smells."

"I showered in the swill but I used bottled water to wash my face after the shower and to brush my teeth."

"I've got to buy some sheets and a pillowcase," Prado said. She shivered. "I know I'm going to come down with some horrible skin disease. Towels too. I need towels and a wash cloth."

They crossed the street and headed to Jill's Place where the motel manager said they could get breakfast. Prado stopped in the middle of the two-lane road dividing low slung buildings on either side, which were fronted by elevated wood sidewalks. "This isn't even a 'one stoplight' town," she said, letting her eyes roam from a small bank building to a hardware store to Walt's Grocery on one side, and Jill's Place, a gas station and Don's Farm Supply Store on the other.

"It's a 'one stop sign town,'" Fisher said and pulled at his partner's elbow nodding at a large blue combine lumbering toward them. "Rush hour."

They pushed open a squeaky screen door into a crowded room that smelled of grease and bacon. A long counter dominated the wall opposite the entrance with booths running along the facing wall, and at either end of the restaurant. The kitchen behind the counter was obscured by a cloud of white smoke that leaked into the dining area.

The place went dead quiet when Prado and Fisher walked in.

"Counter?" Fisher suggested.

"Booth," Prado said, pointing to the far end of the restaurant. She leaned close to Fisher. "I don't want to expose my back."

Fisher gave her a look. Prado smiled and winked.

As they walked between the counter and booths, the conversation slowly picked up behind them, and by the time they slid across the red vinyl bench seat, the level had returned to a steady hum.

"You'd think they'd never seen a stranger before," Fisher whispered.

"*Strange* strangers," Prado said. "Given the complexion of this room, I'll go out on a limb and say that Alice Moore might be the only African American for miles around."

"You think the boys in the big office thought they'd be cute and team us up for this visit to WASP central? I'm guessing the only time a Jew is mentioned around here is in church. As in 'the Jews killed Jesus.'"

"I doubt anyone gave it any thought, but maybe they should have. You're Jewish?"

"I'd have worn my Yarmulke, but I left it home. Now that would have been a fun accessory."

Prado and Fisher sat a moment and absorbed their surroundings. The dark blue countertop was trimmed with stainless steel as were the sides of round, backless, red vinyl-topped stools. This theme extended to the booths. The floor was black-and-white checkered linoleum.

Fisher said, "This is a very typical example of an early American diner. Nice place. I never expected this."

"You're an expert on diners?"

"I went to architecture school. Well, I started there." He waved his hand. "Long story. My first design project was to re-create an American standard. I chose the diner. I'm from a suburb near Philadelphia where diners are a big thing. The family went to one after Temple every Saturday. Had the best Matzoh Ball soup and corned beef sandwiches. Anyway, I learned a lot about diners from that project." Fisher said proudly, "Did you know that the original diners were converted railroad cars?"

"No," Prado responded and turned to face Fisher. "You went to architecture school?"

"Not for long. It took me all of one semester to realize I didn't have any creative talent and, besides, I couldn't handle all the math that went with studying to be an architect. Ended up going to law school. You?"

"Me, what?"

"College? What did you study?"

"I studied very little of anything, but ended up majoring in English." Prado looked toward the counter. "Are we being ignored?"

As if on cue, a tall, heavyset woman, a soiled towel tucked into cloth pants, pushed through a nearby swinging door. Smoke carrying the smell of onions followed her. "Sorry, busy morning," she said with a shrug. "Truth told, every morning's busy after 'bout 6:30." She nodded at the crowded dining room. "They get their first bunch of chores done and come in, talk about the weather, the crops, what seed they're using, eat up, and go back for more." She turned her shoulders toward the kitchen. "Coffee?"

"That would be wonderful," Prado said and looked at Fisher who added to the coffee order, and asked for a menu.

The woman smiled. "No menus. Anything you want that involves eggs, bacon, sausage, ham, toast, wheat and white, jam, butter and… ." She stopped and yelled at the top of her voice. "Randy, we got cheese this morning?"

"No," came back from the kitchen.

"Okay, what I just said is what we got. I can add onions to the eggs if you want."

"A lot of people are having those onions this morning," Fisher said with a smile that was not returned by the woman.

"I'll take two eggs scrambled, sausage, wheat toast and jam," Prado said.

"Me, too," Fisher said, "except I'll have bacon instead of the sausage, and make the eggs over easy."

The woman stared down at them. "You the FBI people?"

"We are," Fisher answered and gave Prado a look. "That explains the warm welcome."

The woman leaned on the table and took in both Prado and Fisher. Her violet eyes were the only distinguishing characteristic in a face distinctive only in its absolute ordinariness; round and encircled with brown hair. If asked to describe her after a single meeting, the mind would register nothing but the color of her eyes. "A little unsolicited advice. You're wasting your time." She straightened slowly and walked away.

"Welcome to Oletha," Fisher said to Prado, who felt the attention of all eyes in the restaurant.

She turned slightly in his direction, saying, "I'm thinking that's the message from everyone in here."

"Including the sheriff," Fisher said. "Speaking of which, we agreed to sleep on what he told us and share our thoughts this morning. You first."

"A man is murdered in the middle of town in the middle of the day in front of half the population and no one sees a thing. More to the point for us, no one cares. That's a hell of an indictment. Plough must have been a gold-plated asshole."

"Now what?"

"Based on what the sheriff told us and…" Prado paused and nodded at the waitress who was approaching with two plates piled high with food.

"We had some cheese after all," she said, "so Randy added it to your eggs."

"Coffee?" Fisher asked as the plates were placed in front of them.

"On its way," she said as she retreated.

Fisher surveyed the eggs which were spread across three strips of bacon and two pieces of toast. The aroma of butter wafted from the food. "You were saying?" he asked as he pulled the toast from under the eggs and took a bite.

"I think we need to be very strategic about who we talk to and how we go about talking to them."

"Meaning?"

"Thank you," Prado said, interrupting the conversation as the woman placed two thick white mugs and an urn in the middle of the table.

"Anything else?" she asked.

"We're good," Fisher replied.

Prado watched the woman walk away before continuing. "Word is going to get out very quickly about what questions we're asking, and I'm guessing a sort of hive mind will coalesce around what answers should be passed along to us. Before that happens we have to get to the people who matter most. Those who can provide us with what we need before all the answers begin to sound the same."

"Makes sense. Where do we start?"

"I say we start with Silas Moore and work our way out," Prado said, spreading blueberry jam onto her toast. "His daughter's missing. He thinks Plough was responsible. Plough's wife points at him as the person who shot her husband. Square one."

Fisher nodded. "Couple that with the bit about Plough and Moore's wife, and the meth angle, and there's a lot going on in that square."

Prado skillfully twirled her fork to wrap a dripping of cheese around some egg. "I knew Plough was a bad dude just from the briefing materials we were given, but I had no idea how bad. Worse by an order of ten."

"'Take the girl out in trade.' Can you believe anyone would talk like that?"

"Not to play the race card here, but, yeah, I can believe that bit of background." Prado raised her fork to make a point. "I'm talking about the attitude. It's an attitude that most people of color have experienced at some point in their lives. In this case, it sounds like Plough directed that kind of thinking, to one degree or another, to everyone he came into contact with. A real jewel of a human being," she said, tilting her head in the direction of the crowded restaurant. "Which explains why all the silence about what happened to him. Good riddance seems to be the order of the day."

Jill stopped at the table. "All good?"

"We are," Prado answered, placed her fork and knife on the plate and wiped her mouth. "You think we're wasting our time," she said, leaving her thought hanging.

Jill stared down at her. "If you think you're going to find out anything that hasn't already been found out…."

"Which is nothing," Fisher volunteered.

"…then, yeah. You're wasting your time."

"Because no one cares that a man was murdered in cold blood?"

The woman wiped her hands on the towel tucked into the high waist of her mom pants. "I don't think anyone sees it like that."

"How do they see it?"

"I can't speak for everyone, but the way I see it, the man had it comin'." She smiled without showing any joy. "I'll save you some time. I didn't see a thing. I was here workin'."

"We'll cross you off our list," Prado said, looking around the crowded room. "You have a good cross section of Oletha in here, I'll bet. Until this morning, we hadn't seen a soul other than the sheriff and the motel manager."

"You must've gotten into town in the middle of the day when everyone was out workin'." She turned toward the din. "No, I don't think anyone in here can help you."

"Can't help us, or won't?" Fisher asked.

The woman took a step closer to the table. "Like I already said, they come in here, eat their breakfast, and go back to the fields. They did the same that morning."

"Morning," Prado stated. "Mr. Plough was killed closer to mid-day."

"You never seen your food bein' grown, have you?"

Both Prado and Fisher shook their heads and answered "No."

"Farming is pretty much a job of routine. They ain't gonna break their routines by doin' nothin' other than going back to doin' what they do every day, and most have been doin' it for 20 or 30 years." The woman spoke evenly, without any inflection. "They ain't gonna want to take a time out to talk to you, and" – she put her hands on her hips and broadened her stance – "would be real upset if you tried to pull some sort of strongarm shit on'em."

Fisher asked, "How about if we work around their routines?"

"Routine controls their lives from the time they get up to when they go to bed. No free time."

"Don't you want to see justice done in this case?" Prado asked.

"You ain't been listening," the woman pronounced and left.

"We've been getting that 'you ain't been listening' thing a lot." Fisher said.

"I think we would've made more headway if you had softened her up by telling her all about diners," Prado deadpanned.

Fisher carefully cleaned the remnants of egg yolk from his plate with a slice of toast, took a bite of the bread, and asked around chewing, "Back to what you were saying about Silas Moore."

"I think we should go talk to him first. See what he has to say and how he says it. Get more on what went on between Plough and his wife. Talk to her. Push them both a little."

"Sounds like a plan."

Prado put her fork on the now empty plate and wiped her mouth. She sat heavily against the back of the booth and stared into the middle distance. "We have to get Alice Moore on record saying Plough raped her. Then we take that and confront Tricia Plough with it. Also ask her about the girl maybe being her husband's daughter."

"Which means he was hitting on his own daughter," Fisher said, his tone a mix of disbelief and disgust.

"Insert cheap shot at small communities here."

"Too easy," Fisher responded. "Big picture. How does any of this square with what we're supposed to be doing here?"

"After what the sheriff told us" – Prado let her eyes scan the room – "and what we just heard, it occurs to me that Plough's wife might have an ulterior motive. Hatfields and McCoys. Plough and Oletha. What better way to get back at everyone than bringing in the FBI to settle a score."

Fisher took a sip of his coffee. "That's a helluva leap don't you think?"

"I would've thought an entire town shutting up like a clam about a murder on Main Street in the middle of the day with thirty or more people on the scene was a leap, but not anymore."

"Okay, let's say we do come to the conclusion that we're being used. Then what?"

"Then we go home."

"Go home without any resolution?"

"That's not our job, but I wouldn't have any afterthoughts. Sounds to me like the guy got what he deserved."

***

Esper directed them out of town to State Highway 1; down S1 a few miles to a landmark billboard reading "Church on Sundays Saves Lives"; hang a right past the billboard onto a gravel and dirt road that would take them to the Moores.

Both sides of the rutted, narrow path were thick with growth that scratched along the side of the car. As they drove deeper into the shadows the vegetation encroached further and the brush graduated into a full-blown forest. What had been bright sunlight was now almost completely hidden.

"People bring their cars all the way out here to get fixed?" Prado asked, leaning forward to get a better view of where they were headed.

"Either that or he doesn't have much of a business."

"Ah," Prado said, sitting back and pointing at an opening ahead. "Civilization."

Fisher disagreed. "I'm not sure I'd go that far."

They drove into a large clearing. In the middle sat a large mobile home. The siding was glinting with moisture revealing that the aluminum had just been hosed down. A blue canvas awning shaded a concrete slab in front of the home on which sat a large barbeque and three Adirondack chairs. A picnic table fronted this area.

To the left of the home a dark dirt rectangle was marked off with string attached to four bamboo poles. Tomato vines were ripe with produce. Azalea bushes planted along the front side of the home were carefully manicured.

Two small dogs ran from the shade of the awning to greet Prado and Fisher as they stepped out of the car. Fisher bent down to pet the dogs as Prado inspected the sides of the car.

"This is going to cost the taxpayer," she said rubbing her hands along scratches etched into the doors.

The barking brought a call from inside the home. "Stop that noise you two." A tall, slim African-American woman appeared at the open door drying her hands on a kitchen towel. She stared at Prado and Fisher.

"Mrs. Moore?" Fisher said as he approached the woman.

"You must be the FBI agents I heard about."

"I wish I had the system of communication that exists in this town," Prado answered. "It's faster than some of the state-of-art hi-tech ones we use." She stood at the bottom of three concrete steps leading to the doorway. "I'm Special Agent Eileen Prado and this is Special Agent Ira Fisher," she said turning to Fisher who was still petting the dogs. "Is your husband home?"

"No, he's at work in town."

Prado let her head hang and said more to herself than the woman in front of her, "We weren't told he had a shop in town."

"He doesn't," the woman said. "He's working on a car at someone's home."

Fisher approached and asked, "Cute dogs. What kind?"

"Pomchis. A cross between Pomerians and long-haired Chihuahuas." The woman walked down the steps. "I'm guessing you've already talked to, John. To Sheriff Esper."

"We did," Prado said. "And I'm guessing you know why we're here."

"I do. About Ken, and I know you'll be getting the run around from everyone in town. No one's going to go out of their way to help you."

Prado smiled. "Yeah, that's what we're hearing. Alice, right," she said and reached out her hand, which the woman took. She answered the question with a nod which caused her head of silver-tipped curls to bob. Her large, expressive brown eyes shifted from Prado to Fisher, and held a wariness.

Prado continued. "As we explained to the sheriff, we're here because Mrs. Plough alleges her husband's civil rights have been violated and that the authorities and most of the people in Oletha are party to this violation. Our job is to determine if her allegation has any validity. We aren't here to find out who killed Mr. Plough. But when we conduct these sorts of investigations, we have to get as much information as possible, and that is very much like an investigation of the crime."

Alice Moore stared at Prado. Her thin face now placid, revealing no emotion.

"Would you be willing to talk to us about Mr. Plough?"

"I don't have anything to say that would interest you."

Prado could not stop the laugh that escaped. "So, you're part of the cover-up."

"No," she objected emphatically, "I really don't know anything about what happened."

"But you do know that Mrs. Plough has accused your husband of…."

"Of killing Ken. Yes, of course."

Prado hesitated before adding, "Maybe things just boiled over for your husband. The disappearance of your daughter, her having been seen with Mr. Plough, the rumors of her being Mr. Plough's daughter, and he reacted in the heat of the moment."

The woman remained placid, the only evidence that she heard Prado being a slight shake of her head.

"You know, we might be able to help find out what happened to your daughter."

Fisher gave his partner a "what the fuck" look.

The woman turned her head and stared across the yard. When her attention refocused on Prado her eyes were squinted, her lips curled over her teeth, a rictus of anger. She snarled, "That's really a nasty thing to do. Use my daughter as bait to try and get me to talk. And it's an insult to my intelligence that you'd think a cheap trick like that would work."

"You misunderstood me," Prado said. "What we're doing here has a lot of sidebars. And given what Mrs. Plough contends, the disappearance of your daughter is the major sidebar."

"A sidebar?" the woman said, her anger still close to the surface.

"My apologies. I could have said that better." Prado paused before continuing. "As we do what we came to do, we're going to be dealing with the disappearance of your daughter; and the more we know about her, about what happened, and about what you *think* happened, the better our chances of finding out what *did* happen to Alice. Make sense?"

The woman turned her shoulders toward the inside of the home and laid the dish cloth on a kitchen counter visible from where Prado stood. She started down the steps, Prado moved aside, and then followed her to the picnic table. Fisher joined the procession, dogs at his heels.

"Before you start," the woman said, sitting on one side of the table, Prado and Fisher on the other, "Alice is not Ken's daughter. I don't know how that despicable lie ever got started, but I think it might've been by Ken."

"Why would he do that?" Prado asked. "That would mean he was attempting to have a relationship with his own daughter."

"He didn't believe that. It was only to cause trouble. Pain. Haven't people already told you what he was like?"

Fisher nodded.

Moore's eyes went dark. "He was an evil person who liked to bully and control people."

"Your relationship with him," Prado started, "we heard....

"Yeah," she interrupted, "I know what you've heard." She sat very still a few seconds before continuing. "But here's what you should know. I was a stupid girl who was looking for attention. My mother and I never got along." She cocked her head and nodded at Prado. "Mixed?"

"Yes, black Cuban and white Puerto Rican."

Moore smiled shallowly. "Oletha is not exactly a diverse community and although everyone treated me very politely, it was an issue. Well, maybe I made it an issue. I had to prove myself. To separate myself and…," she hesitated, searching for the right words. "Not exactly separate so much as elevate." She waved her hands dismissively. "Never mind all that stuff. About Ken, truth is I did spend some time with him and it was awful. Awful," she added aggressively. "A little self-hatred on my part, no doubt. I accepted the man's racism and that makes my ever being with him even more humiliating and shameful. Fortunately, I got out fast unlike some of the others he caught in his web with his money and fancy cars." One of the dogs jumped up beside her and laid its head on her lap. "God, this makes me sound like such a fool."

"No," Prado said. "It doesn't. I was born and grew up in Miami. It's like a giant melting pot and I didn't know I was brown until I got to middle school."

Moore tilted her head and flashed a look of disbelief.

"True story. Until then no one said anything and I really had nothing to relate the color thing to. When it came up, at first I didn't give it much thought. Everyone was brown or black with a few other shades thrown in. I went from being me to being Hispanic, and then, one day, someone called me black. A short time later it was African American. I never considered myself anything but me." She shook her head. "How naïve is that? I resisted being labeled anything, but was willing to accept Hispanic. I *was* Hispanic, and most of my friends were Cuban or Puerto Rican. Then I got schooled about the one-drop rule and from there it was pick a side, and then I was faced with the workaday world and quotas." She shrugged. "It is what it is, but I fully understand what *it* is and what you're talking about."

"You know," Moore said, "whenever I hear these stories from people like you who grew up in large cities, I think maybe I'm really the lucky one. Yeah, I stood out, but no one paid much attention. Mostly, my problem was of my own making." She took a deep breath. "But enough of this. Is there anything else I can help you with?"

"Did he rape you?"

"Yes, he did. Once," she declared. "One time and I ran. Ran home and have not…did not talk to him ever again."

"You married Silas shortly afterward, right?" Prado asked.

"Yes, we had been seeing each other before I lost my mind for a few months. A hard way to learn to appreciate a good man." She looked intently at Prado. "Alice is his daughter in every way." She jabbed her finger on the tabletop. "In every way."

"Other than what you've told us, did Mr. Plough ever threaten you, or Silas, or your daughter?" Prado laid her hand across the table in a gesture of understanding. "I know he was seen with Alice before she went missing. We'll get back to that in a minute. What I'm asking is did he specifically threaten any of you in the years since your experience with him?"

"No more, no less than he did everyone. He would sometimes bring his trucks to Silas for repair and when the work was done, he'd withhold paying and string Silas along. He'd force Silas to ask him to pay so he could bully him. But he did the same with everyone. He'd go to breakfast at Jill's and leave without paying, then throw money at her when she brought it up the next time he came in. I saw that happen myself."

"Threw money at her?" Fisher asked. "Literally?"

"Yes," Moore confirmed. "Walked into the restaurant and threw money at her when she said something about his owing her money, then he laughed and told her to pick it up. He did things like that all the time to humiliate people. Same thing with Rusty Weiler at Dummy's. Or at the store in town where his kids stole things." She held up a finger. "Before you get high and mighty and ask why people didn't just refuse to do business with him…some people did try, including Silas, but it made things even worse. In Silas's case, Ken used to leave his truck here and if Silas wouldn't work on it because he hadn't paid his bill for the last time, he'd bring another one in, then another, then another, until they filled the yard. He was a monster."

Prado waited a moment before asking very gently, "About your daughter, the sheriff told us she was seen with Ken. Was that a regular thing?"

"Her friends and some of her teachers said they used to see her get into his car after school. I didn't know it was going on, not until she didn't come home, and I began asking questions."

"Did you ever say anything to Mr. Plough?" Fisher asked. "Confront him about this?"

She shook her head. "I told you, I haven't said a word to him since…." She didn't complete her thought. "Silas did and Ken did the same with him as he did with everyone. No, it was worse. He told him he'd never go for a half-breed. Called Alice all kinds of names and said she was a bad girl who probably ran off to sell herself for drugs."

"I've got to ask this…." Prado began.

"No, she didn't take drugs. I know all parents say that and, of course, I could be wrong, but Alice was not that type. She had friends. She did well in school. She was a happy child."

"Why do you think she took up with him?"

"Curiosity. Stupidity. I was a good girl, too. Like I said, I had some problems at home that Alice didn't have. I don't think she felt any of the things growing up that I did about who I was. How I fit in. If I fit in. And if I didn't, then what? These are different times. I'm not minimizing that part of who we are, but I didn't see any of it in her. I can see her being curious. Being impressed with Ken's money and fancy trucks. Plus, Ken was a smooth talker." She lowered her head and stroked the dog. "Saying this out loud sounds so bad, so obvious, but that's what I think got Alice."

"Why would he kidnap her?" Fisher asked. "Given the type of person he was, wouldn't it be more his style to do what he wanted with her and then let her come back home so he could taunt you about it. Embarrass you?"

"And given everything he did to you, to Alice," Prado added, "you're still convinced your husband had nothing to do with Mr. Plough's death?"

"Silas could never kill anyone," Moore answered. "He was…*is* convinced that Ken had something to do with her disappearance, but he doesn't even own a gun. He had a problem with that kind of thing once and would never, ever put himself in a position to do anything like it again." She buried her face in her hands and began heaving. Prado stood, walked around the table, sat down next to her, and rubbed her back.

Moore took a breath and sat up straight. "What sense would it make for Silas to kill the man he thinks knows what happened to our daughter?"

Prado looked at Fisher, arching her eyebrows in a sign of agreement, then asked Moore, "Has Silas ever mentioned what he saw the day Ken was killed, or said who he thinks might have shot him?"

"He hasn't said a word about it."

"Really?" Fisher blurted in surprise. "You two haven't talked about it at all?"

"He told me what happened, but we haven't discussed it since."

"Not a word?" Fisher asked in disbelief.

"No, not a word."

"I promise," Prado said, cradling the woman's hands, "that we will do what we can to find out what happened to your daughter as we work our way through this."

"Thank you," Moore said and stood, indicating the end of the conversation, adding one final thought. "But I'm afraid you're not going to be around very long. You're not going to find out anything."

***

As they pulled away from the clearing, Fisher said, "I take it you agree her husband didn't kill Plough."

"I think she has a point we should've given more thought to. If you think Plough took the girl, why kill the only man who can tell you where she is. But this isn't about *who* killed Plough. Well, I guess it is in a way. If we can identify *who*, we might be able to determine if the entire town is an accessory."

Fisher fought with the steering wheel jerking in his hands as they bounced along the rutted path. "What the hell was that about promising to find out what happened to her daughter? That's a little out there, isn't it?"

"It is," Prado agreed as they turned onto the highway. "It was a way to keep her talking, plus, frankly, I let myself get caught up in what she's going through." She looked at Fisher. "I know, I know, empathize but don't get emotionally involved. It just snuck up on me."

"Stop me if I'm crossing out of my lane, but are you talking about 'the black thing'?"

Prado smiled at Fisher's obvious discomfort. "Yeah, the *black thing*. No matter what she said about it being good that she grew up around here, she's really a stranger in a strange land. Hell, the people around here are damned near translucent. She's stood out like a sore thumb all her life." Prado shook her head. "Bad metaphor, but she has to have felt way out of place. And if she thinks her daughter had it any better, she's fooling herself. Probably fooling herself to keep from admitting that her daughter took the same path she did and for the same reasons. Enough of this. Back to what we're here to do."

"Let me guess. *Now* we go talk to Tricia Plough?"

Prado nodded. "Yes, let's pay her a friendly visit. After all, we are the cavalry responding to her call."

Fisher glanced at Prado. "Did I detect a note of sarcasm? Are we the cavalry?"

"We're doing what she asked us to do, but like I said, she might have an axe to grind. She *does* have an axe to grind or we wouldn't be here, but we might be able to get the hell out of Dodge if we figure out she's trying to use us to swing that axe."

"Or this could just be local law enforcement fucking things up."

"Or that," Prado agreed, "but let's stick to what we *do* know. I'd say we just knocked Silas Moore out of the picture, and if she can't help us see a bigger picture, we're outta here."

"Aren't you forgetting that the entire population of Oletha hated this guy? Isn't *that* the big picture?"

"There has to be a viable candidate for everyone to protect. Once we tell her that Silas Moore makes no sense, let's see where she goes next."

"Is it possible no one saw anything? That no one knows anything? And I'm not taking Moore out of the picture. Maybe he saw an opportunity and couldn't pass it up."

Prado moved her head from side-to-side in question. "As to whether it makes sense that no one saw anything, 'no', I don't think that's possible. Moore? Okay, maybe I'm being premature. It could be him. Like I said, I got a little too close, but I'm going to play my hunch that he and Alice were focused, *are* focused, on finding their daughter not on killing the man they think kidnapped her." She pointed at the GPS device on the dashboard. "Tricia Plough has an actual address, not a 'three trees down from the fork in the road' thing. I'm plugging it in."

Fisher studied the passing countryside. "Does anyone live in a single-family house? I mean a real house and not one up on blocks." He counted as they drove along: "One. Two. Three. Four double wides. Oh, wait a real house. Five. Six."

"There's Tricia Plough's," Prado said, directing Fisher onto a long gravel driveway leading to a large brick home. They parked behind a navy-blue pickup truck and sat a moment studying the ranch-style home, and weed-pocked, overgrown front yard. A riding mower sat in the middle of the shin-high grass, a testament to things not done.

"The husband gets killed and everything goes to hell," Fisher said as he and Prado stepped out of the car.

"I think that qualifies as 'mansplaining'. My guess is there's a lot going on inside" – she gestured toward the house – "that has her attention."

A stone walkway led from the driveway to a single concrete front step facing a blond oak door. As Fisher reached for a large, ornate brass knocker the door swung open. An attractive, somewhat stout young woman stood, her legs slightly apart and hands on her hips, a sentinel guarding the entrance. Long blond hair fell across her shoulders, one lock covered her right eye.

"You the FBI people"?" she asked, her tone flat and voice hoarse.

"We are," Fisher answered. "I'm Ira Fisher and this is Special Agent Eileen Prado." They held up their credentials.

Tricia Plough took her right index finger, hooked the errant lock covering her eye, and positioned it behind her ear. She allowed herself a moment to inspect the two, then stood aside. "Come on in," she said, moving away from the door.

They walked into a living room littered with children's toys. An empty pizza box was on a coffee table in front of a couch upholstered in a bright floral design dominated by reds, yellows and blues. Two high-backed chairs decorated in the same cloth pattern faced the couch.

Tricia pointed them to the couch. "Sorry for the mess."

"Just looks like you've been busy," Prado responded pleasantly and made certain Fisher caught her eye.

As they sat down, they could see past the chairs in front of them into a dining room where a table was piled high with laundry, some folded, some not. The smell of laundry soap filled the air. To the right the room opened into a kitchen.

Tricia sat on one of the chairs and folded her hands, placing them in her lap. She looked in Prado and Fisher's direction, but not directly at them. Her attention was on the yard beyond the picture window behind the couch. When she sat her figure settled erasing her waistline. She wasn't wearing a bra and large breasts pushed at the front of a white Tee-Shirt, hanging almost to the beltline of her jeans. She crossed her legs at the ankles and asked, "Would you like something to drink?"

Prado and Fisher demurred.

"Thank you very much for coming," Tricia said, straining for propriety. Her attention was now focused on them, her blue eyes shifting from one to the other. "You want me to tell you why I asked you all to come here, or you just wanna ask me questions?"

Prado answered, "It would probably be more comfortable for you to just go ahead and tell us everything you'd like us to know, but, first, you know you can have your lawyer present if you'd like."

"I know," she said, almost shyly, "but he's from Maryville and charges me for his trip here, all the while he's here, and then back, and all that other stuff. I really can't afford to have a lawyer sittin' with me for every little thing."

"Well, then, why don't you go ahead," Prado said invitingly. "We're all ears."

Tricia's attention went to the door. "Come on in."

Fisher and Prado stood as two women walked into the room bringing the smell of cigarette smoke with them. The taller and older of the two introduced herself as Crystal Truville. Thick, shoulder length, bleached blonde hair was beginning to darken creating a halo along her forehead. High cheekbones, a straight nose and full lips saved a face being aged by deep lines around the mouth, and a sagging jawline. Her eyes, rheumy and fading blue, retained a spark of life. Sliding toward the far side of middle age, Truville had managed to retain a shapely figure. She introduced Lurleen Ames, a younger version of herself; a luxurious head of bleached blond hair without the halo, largely unlined face, and still sparkling eyes set Ames apart from Truville. Standing side-by-side, Crystal, Tricia and Lurleen could have been sisters, or related at the very least. Interestingly, the eldest of the three had the most appealing figure, with Lurleen still retaining the outline of a waist, while Tricia was fast losing the battle of the bulge.

"Grab some chairs from the kitchen," Tricia directed the women, who disappeared into the back room. "Them's Ken's former wives," she said with a giggle. "I know this is strange, but we all love Ken and are friends. He insisted on it since we have his kids. Wanted'em to grow up close."

"He was a wonderful man," Crystal said, holding the back of a steel-framed chair which she set down next to Tricia. Lurleen followed, dragging a wooden stool, and took a place on the other side of Tricia.

"We hadn't begun yet," Tricia said somewhat defensively, her attention on Crystal. "I was about to tell'em what happened."

Crystal leaned to her right and pulled a pack of cigarettes from a large leather purse shaped like a saddle bag that she had dropped on the floor next to her. She lit her cigarette as Tricia and Lurleen watched her attentively. "It's real simple," Crystal said, taking the lead. "Someone shot Ken in cold blood and everyone's coverin' it up. No one will say nothin' to bring justice to Ken."

Prado nodded at Crystal and directed herself to Tricia. "You brought the allegation of the civil rights violation, correct?"

Tricia looked at Crystal, who nodded, and Tricia then acknowledged Prado.

"I want to fully explain to you why we're here. Okay?"

The three women nodded.

Prado proceeded. "It's a federal crime for anyone acting under the 'color of law' to willfully deprive or conspire to deprive a person of a right protected by the Constitution or U.S. law. Color of law means a person is abusing the authority given to him or her by a local, state, or federal government agency to deny those rights." She placed her forearms on her thighs and stared intently at Tricia. "That's why we're here. To investigate your allegations." She paused to allow the words to marinate before adding, "There is a penalty for anyone who makes these allegations falsely or for personal reasons. You understand all of that?"

"'Course we understand," Crystal responded irritably. "You think we're ignorant?"

"No, I don't, and if I gave that impression, my apologies. I just want to make certain we're all on the same page."

"We are," Crystal said sternly and nudged Tricia with her elbow.

"We are," Tricia agreed.

"Okay, then," Prado said cheerfully. "Go ahead and tell us what you think we should know."

"Crystal'll do that," Tricia said. "Me, her and Lurleen are all in this together."

"That's fine," Prado said, "and I'd like to hear from all of you, but you, Tricia, brought the complaint so it would be best if you spoke on the matter."

Tricia shook her head. "I'd like her" – she looked at Crystal – "to go ahead."

Prado was about to object but Fisher nudged her with his leg. She gestured at Crystal. "Go ahead."

Crystal smiled, took a deep drag on her cigarette, and tilted her head upward, exhaling as she spoke. "It's real simple. Ken was executed. There was lots of people around and no one will say nothin'." She leaned toward the couch. "You expect anyone to believe that no one saw nothin'? It's bullshit and everyone is in on it, includin' the sheriff."

"Why would someone want to kill your husband?" Prado asked, then corrected herself. "Your *former* husband. And why would all these people, including the sheriff, protect that person?"

"Simple," Crystal said, turning her head toward Tricia and Lurleen, "because they didn't like him."

"We're going to need a little more than that," Fisher said. Hearing condescension in his voice, he added quickly, "Please explain why you think they didn't like him."

Lurleen answered, "Ken came from a dirt-poor family. Just like us," she said tilting her head toward the other women. "He made something of himself, and no one liked it."

"They killed him because they resented him for being successful?" Fisher asked. "And who is *they*, exactly."

Crystal stood and went to the kitchen. Tricia and Lurleen sat silently. She walked back into the living room carrying a coffee cup into which she flicked her cigarette ash. "*They* is most everyone in town, and, yeah, *they* resented him and *they* hounded him. And us, too. If there was a pig stolen anywhere, it was Ken's fault. If somethin' was missin' from a barn or a house, it was Ken's fault."

"You probably gotta live here to understand," Tricia added. "Everyone is in everyone's business. They're all watchin' what each other does and if someone has more'n someone else, it gets talked about and not liked much. Ken had more'n anyone in town."

"And Ken always did have more'n everyone else," Crystal said. "No one would say he was smarter'n they were, which he was, and he found a way to get more'n they did. They was jealous so they said he stole it."

"If something was stole from the store," Tricia interjected, "it was our boy's fault."

Lurleen sat up straight. "Those fuckers accused us of everything and then when that wasn't good 'nough, they went after our kids. Ken wouldn't put up with it. He called'em on it and they didn't like that."

"Okay," Prado said, looking at each of the women. "I can understand how that would get annoying, but...."

"*Annoying?*" Crystal blurted.

Prado flashbacked to her exchange with the sheriff and wished she had the word back.

"*Annoying*? Is that some kinda FBI word for really fucked up? You try livin' with people talkin' shit about you every single day. Can't go into town without everybody lookin' like they want you dead. Havin' people always comin' to your house accusin' you of stealin' every time an animal goes missin'. It's way past Goddamn *annoying*."

"Havin' your kids bullied at school," Tricia added. "My little girl came home every day cryin'. Even the teachers pick on her 'cause they're married to men who own the farms or the stores 'round here and they all hated Ken."

"Really fuckin' *annoying*," Crystal scoffed.

"I apologize for appearing to play down your situation," Prado said. "Not my intent. Tricia, in the request for a civil rights investigation you pointed to Silas Moore as the person you believe shot your husband. Why him?"

"That's easy," Crystal interjected. "He accused Ken of kidnappin' his daughter. He dogged him something awful 'bout that. And it was his girl who was always pestering Ken, not the other way 'round. Ken didn't want to have nothin' to do with her."

"What?" Prado and Fisher spit out together.

"Yeah," Tricia said. "That little thing would show up at our house almost every day after school lookin' for Ken. He'd always have me shoo her away, sayin' he wasn't home."

Prado and Fisher swung their attention to Crystal when she added, "And after Tricia chased her off, she'd come knockin' on my door."

"And mine," Lurleen chipped in. "It was every single day and sometimes she'd wait outside on the steps 'til it was dark and then finally go home."

"You're saying Alice was the pursuer even though Silas and his wife say Ken used to pick her up at school and spend hours with her?" Prado asked, speaking slowly and precisely.

"Yes," the women answered together.

"Ken was a busy man," Crystal added. "He didn't have no time for that girl."

"We heard that Ken had a history with the girl's mother," Prado said and left her words hanging, waiting for one of the women to jump on them.

Crystal jumped. "I don't mean no offense here, but Ken didn't think much of colored people so that story makes no sense."

Prado poked the bear. "That's not what we've heard from Alice Moore or from others. We've been told she and Ken were a couple before she left him. That there's a history that might have prompted you" – she nodded her head toward Tricia – "to name Silas Moore as your suspect."

Tricia stiffened. "History?" she said angrily. "What history? That's something that bitch made up to get back at Ken and then everyone says it's true to make him look bad."

"If nothing happened between Alice Moore and your husband," Prado asked, "what would she have to get back at him for?"

Crystal answered, "She chased after him just like her daughter and he ignored her."

"Really?" Prado said unable to disguise her disdain. "Both Alice Moore and her daughter found Ken so irresistible that they couldn't stay away from him. Two women, a generation apart, and one the daughter of the other. You'll forgive me if I find that hard to believe."

"Sounds to me like you're takin' the side of people who talk against Ken," Crystal said. "You want the truth or you just wanna believe the lies? I'm wonderin' if maybe you have 'nother reason to believe the lies."

Fisher felt Prado begin to lift off the couch and pressed his hand on her arm. "Please, go ahead."

"I was around Ken when Alice, the mother, was botherin' him," Crystal said. "What the daughter did was 'xactly like what her mother did, and Ken didn't want to have nothin' to do with'em. He even thought the mother might've sent her daughter to do it and try to set him up for consortin' with a minor." She looked at Prado. "Truth be told, Ken hated black people. He thought they was like…like, well, like not as good as us. As white people. He wouldn't touch Alice or her daughter."

"Yes," Prado said calmly, "I got that from your earlier implication."

Crystal smirked, lit another cigarette, and blew the smoke across the coffee table.

"And all this talk 'bout that girl being missin' and it bein' Ken's fault is what we're talkin' 'bout," Lurleen said. "The first and only person Silas pointed at was Ken."

Fisher countered with, "That's because the girl's classmates and teachers all said they saw her with Ken. They said he used to pick her up after school." He allowed a pregnant pause before asking, "You never saw him with the girl, or anywhere near her or where she lived?"

The three women traded a quick glance. Tricia spoke up, "I did go out to Silas's house once with Ken." She hesitated a minute before continuing. "Ken's dead so this don't matter, but he went there 'cause Silas knew people in Maryville who cooked and sold meth, and Ken wanted to see 'bout gettin' in on that hisself. He asked Silas to give him some names. Silas said 'no.' Ken didn't much like and…."

"Wait," Prado stopped Tricia. "We heard that Moore had gotten out of all that. That he moved from Maryville to Oletha to get away from it. You're saying he was still involved?"

Tricia insisted that, "All I know is what I just said. We went out there. Silas wouldn't give him no names and it made Ken mad."

Prado and Fisher waited for more but Tricia sat with her hands folded in her lap and her eyes hooded.

"How mad did that make him?" Prado asked.

"What're you gettin' at?" Crystal asked.

"Did Ken threaten Silas?"

"Or Alice, the mother, or the daughter?" Fisher added.

"No," Tricia said. "We just left."

Prado stared at Tricia a moment before asking, "Do you think Silas killed Ken because he thought Ken kidnapped Alice as retaliation for him not agreeing to help with the meth connection?"

"Could be," Tricia said without commitment.

"But why would Silas kill your husband if he thought that? He needed Ken alive to find out what happened to Alice, didn't he?"

"You don't know how mad Silas was," Tricia countered. "He told everyone that Ken did bad things with Alice, and they believed it."

"Silas was *annoying*," Crystal said sarcastically.

"How do you know everyone believed Silas?"

"Like we been sayin', Crystal answered, "they always believed everything bad 'bout Ken. It even happened in church. In front of our kids. The preacher talked about how God will forgive your sins no matter how bad if you believe in him; and him being able to save you.

He talked about it 'specially bein' for people who sinned against young people. We" – she looked at Tricia and Lurleen – "know who he was preachin' 'bout."

"I definitely think it was Silas," Lurleen said. "I was sittin' in my truck in front of Dummy's waitin' for Ken and Tricia, and he walked right past my door. He came out ahead of the rest of the bunch and he walked 'cross the street to his truck."

"Did he have a weapon?"

"He had some kinda rifle on his truck rack."

"Did you see him with the gun in his hands?"

"I was looking at the men who was followin' Ken out of Dummy's."

Prado asked Tricia, "Where were you?"

"With Ken. I followed him out and we got in the truck. They just stood there lined up on the sidewalk in front of Dummy's starin' at us. I knew something bad was 'bout to happen. I knew it when I saw'em all go into Dummy's together, and I went in and I told Ken I thought somethin' bad was gonna happen. Then when we went outside it was like time stood still. Everything was happenin' in slow motion. I remember he lit a cigarette." Her eyes filled with tears and as she blinked, big drops rolled down her full cheeks, which were red with emotion. "And after that I don't remember nothin'."

"She was covered in blood," Lurleen managed to get out between her own sobs and coughs. "Blood all over her."

"And Ken's teeth and brains," Crystal added. "Can you imagine that? And everyone just disappears. No one tried to help or even check to see if he's still alive. They just walked off. We found out later that it took fifteen minutes for the sheriff to get there and turn off the truck, which was 'bout to blow up 'cause Ken's foot was pressing on the gas pedal. Got wedged between the gas and brake somehow."

"Everyone was standing in front of the truck when Ken was shot?" Prado asked.

"Kinda all along the front of Dummy's," Tricia said, waving her hand to indicate the line-up.

"Not to either side, but right in front of the truck?" Fisher asked.

Tricia nodded. "Like they was waitin' for it to happen."

Prado lifted her notebook out of her purse and turned a few pages before directing at Tricia, "And in the information you sent to us, you said all these men came into the bar at once, and they had been at a meeting where you think they planned how they were going to kill Ken."

"Yes, they came in a bunch from city hall where I heard they was meetin' 'bout Ken."

"About killing him," Fisher clarified.

Tricia nodded. "'Bout that."

"Who told you that?"

"No one needed to tell us anything," Crystal said, gesturing with the hand holding her cigarette, spewing ashes onto the coffee table. "They had that meeting. Then they all went into Dummy's, where they knew Ken would be like he always was." She leaned into her words, which were coming faster. "It was in the mornin' during the week for fuck's sake. Who has a town meeting in the morning when everyone should be out tendin' to their land? What do you think they was meetin' 'bout? Roundin' up stray dogs?"

"What about all the people in that diner place?" Prado asked.

"Jill's," Tricia said.

Fisher nodded. "Yeah, Jills."

"What about'em?" Crystal asked.

"Not everyone was at the meeting, then," Prado offered.

"For fuck's sake," Crystal shot back. "So there was some people at Jill's. The ones who planned the killing were at the town hall meeting."

"Just trying to set the scene," Prado responded. "We need to know who was where."

"Don't matter *who was where*, they all hated Ken," Lurleen said.

"Okay," Prado said, "back to the scene. "If you knew a person sitting in a truck right in front of you was about to be shot at, would you stand there? Right in front of that truck?"

Crystal blew a cloud of smoke across the table and dropped her cigarette into the coffee cup. Tricia shifted in her chair. The dripping of a faucet somewhere in the house was the only sound for an uncomfortable period.

"You ain't here to help us are you?" Crystal spit out angrily.

"We aren't here to hurt you," Prado answered tersely. "We're here to do a job and we can only do that by asking these questions."

"'Bout standing in front of the truck," Lurleen said, "everyone 'round here can shoot a gun real good. They hit what the aim at."

"You'd be confident enough to stand in front of a target that someone was firing at from a distance?" Prado asked. "And it had to be a pretty good distance so you" – she indicated Tricia – "and you" – pointing a Lurleen –"wouldn't see anything."

"One other thing," Fisher said. "Isn't it strange that everyone would stand around and watch if they knew this was going to happen and they'd be asked about it later? That makes them not only witnesses, but accessories. Wouldn't it have made more sense for everyone to stay in the bar and be able to say they didn't see anything, or leave as soon as they came out of the bar before the shots were fired? Why stand around knowing that something like that was about to happen?"

Crystal answered insistently, "They knew Ken was gonna get shot because they met on it. They agreed not to say who done it so it didn't matter that they was there. It's that simple no matter how much you try and make it seem like somethin' else."

"You've been very helpful," Prado said. "You've given us a lot to think about." She clasped her hands and dropped them to her lap. "Summing up. You think Silas Moore killed Ken because he kidnapped his daughter. But you say he got it wrong and young Alice was a nuisance to your husband....to, uh, Ken, and he had nothing to do with her going missing? But Silas Moore killed him anyway and the town is covering it up because everyone hated Ken. Is that about right?"

"And Sheriff Esper ain't tryin' to do nothin 'bout it," Lurleen added.

"There is one other thing," Tricia said with a look at Crystal. "Like we said, Ken, and us, too, tried to keep Alice away, but she kept comin' 'round, so one day Ken took her into Maryville with him."

Prado stiffened. "What," she croaked, shifting her gaze among the three women. "He took her to Maryville?"

"Which must be when her friends saw her in the car with Ken," Tricia said, "'cause there weren't no other time."

"Let's start this over," Prado said, annoyance in her voice.

"Fuck no," Crystal countered. "We don't have to start over. Everything's like we told you 'cept Ken took Alice to Maryville one time to get her off his back."

"How exactly does that get her off his back?"

"He made a deal with her," Tricia said. "He'd take her to Maryville, but she had to leave him alone after that."

Prado stared at Tricia a beat before asking. "You were there when he told her this?"

"Yeah, and I was with him when he took her."

"One of us," Crystal said with a nod toward Lurleen, "was always with him and Tricia. He never went nowhere 'less we was along in case anyone accused him of somethin'. That way we could say the way things really was."

"Built-in alibis," Prado said.

"It wasn't like that," Tricia objected. "At least not like you're sayin' it."

"You ain't been hearin' a thing we been sayin'," Crystal said.

"We've been getting a lot of that," Fisher answered.

"Then listen better," Crystal said forcefully. "It's real simple. Ken got blamed for every little thing that went wrong here and we was there to keep him from bein' blamed for stuff he didn't do."

Prado continued with Tricia. "Where did the three of you go in Maryville?"

"To Frankie's. We was talkin' 'bout goin' there when Alice was around and said she wanted to go along."

"Wait," Prado said and held up her hand. "I thought you said you chased Alice away whenever she showed up?"

A pause in the conversation was broken by Crystal. "She didn't always leave right away and one of these times Ken said he'd take her to Frankie's if she'd get off his back. All the kids wanted to go party with Frankie."

Prado rolled her shoulders. "Who's Frankie?"

"Jus' someone Ken wanted to talk to," Tricia answered. "Alice wanted to go 'cause of what Crystal said. The kids partied with Frankie and Ken took her to get her off his back."

"Does Frankie have a last name?" Fisher asked.

Tricia gave him a look. "Course he does. Hebert, Frankie Hebert."

"And why was Ken going to see Frankie?" Prado asked Tricia.

"He's the person Ken wanted Silas to tell him about. To go with him to meet."

Prado bobbed her head in understanding. "Okay, this is the guy who sells meth."

"Ken wanted to talk to him 'bout buying some to sell here."

"So Alice went with you?"

"Yeah, she said she knew Frankie because her and her friends bought meth from him."

Prado pulled her shoulders back and Fisher shifted to the edge of the couch. "Alice was using drugs?" Prado asked.

Tricia nodded. "That was one of the reasons she was always botherin' Ken."

"No," Crystal objected. "She was always trying to get it for free. This ain't good maybe, but if she wanted to buy it from him, he woulda sold it to her."

"No one has mentioned anything about Ken selling pot," Prado said. "We've heard a lot about other stuff he did." Adding "allegedly," quickly. "But nothing about selling pot. The sheriff didn't say anything about that."

Crystal laughed bringing up a cough that doubled her over. Tricia began patting her on the back and when Crystal had the fit under control, she said, "That's rich. The sheriff never said nothin' 'bout it. No shit, that's 'cause he's been protecting Ken."

"It keeps getting better," Fisher said under his breath.

"And Alice," Prado said, "she'd been buying meth from this Frankie person?"

"I guess," Tricia answered.

"For a long time?"

Tricia shrugged. "I don't know. All I do know is that Ken found out she knew Frankie and figured she could introduce him."

"Now you're saying Ken took her along so she could introduce him to this Frankie person," Fisher said. "Before you said it was because he wanted to get her off his back. Which is it?"

"Both," Crystal answered.

Tricia nodded. "But mostly it was 'bout getting her to leave him alone. He was plannin' on talkin' to Frankie anyway. Alice was a kind of a last-minute addition when he found out she knew him."

"Okay," Prado said firmly, signaling a restart of the conversation. "Ken is dealing pot here in Oletha. He wants to get into the meth business. He goes to Silas for an introduction to Frankie. Silas says he won't help." She leaned toward Tricia. "But he finds out Alice knows Frankie and agrees to give her a ride to Maryville so she can introduce him."

"And to get her off his back," Crystal interjected.

"Okay, Prado responded impatiently. "We got that." To Tricia: "So what happened in Maryville?"

"Frankie agreed to sell Ken meth so he could sell it here. They reached some kinda deal 'bout Ken paying Frankie part of what he made, and he agreed to only buy from Frankie."

Crystal added, "And Ken left Alice with Frankie so he had nothing to do with no kidnapping or nothin' like that."

"You just left her there?" Fisher asked.

"It wasn't like we ran off or nothin'. I mean we was plannin' on leaving her there, but we didn't sneak off. Frankie said she owed him some money and told Ken she could stay and work it off."

"Work it off?" Prado said, an edge taking her voice up an octave. "You must have known what that meant, and you just left her?"

"Seems to me your problem is with Frankie," Crystal said, lighting a cigarette, this time turning her head before exhaling the smoke, much of which still floated back across the coffee table.

Prado leaned away from the cloud and waited for the smoke to dissolve before asking, "When you heard that Silas thought Ken kidnapped Alice, why didn't you tell him about taking her to Maryville?"

"We don't talk to Silas," Crystal said contemptuously. "It woulda been a waste of time anyways. He wants to think Ken kidnapped her and that's all he cares about. That and tellin' everyone what he thinks."

"Did you say anything to the sheriff about this?" Prado asked, her frustration evident. "About Ken taking Alice to Maryville, and the visit with this Frankie person? It's a critical piece of information."

"First of all," Crystal answered, "we told everybody that Ken didn't have nothin' to do with Alice's goin' missing."

"But did you tell the sheriff that Ken took Alice to Maryville and left her there?" Prado asked.

Crystal nodded.

"This is the first time we're hearing about any of this," Prado said.

"Glad to help," Crystal said with a grin.

"So, if you left Alice in Maryville, and you told everybody that's what you did, and everything gets around this town the way you say it does, then Silas would've known and had no reason to come after Ken, right?"

Tricia shrugged. "Wrong, he jus' kept talkin shit 'bout him."

"But it is possible that it wasn't Silas, right" Prado pushed at Tricia.

"Could be."

"And if you take Silas out of the picture, you don't have a viable suspect for the town to cover up for." Prado stood and hovered over the women. "And that makes your case harder to justify. What you're left with is a standard whodunit."

"A who what it?" Tricia asked, her forehead a mass of wrinkles.

"I'm saying it looks to me like what you might have is an incomplete police investigation. Standard stuff."

"So, you're sayin' you ain't gonna help us?" Tricia asked

"No, I'm saying we have new information that has to be considered."

"I get the feeling you think we ain't bein' straight with you," Crystal said and stood so she was not looking up at Prado. "Like maybe we're holdin' out on you."

"You picked up on that, did you?" Fisher said, a smile sneaking at the corners of his lips.

"Why would we do that?" Crystal challenged.

"I'm not certain," Prado answered and pointed Fisher toward the door. As they started through, Prado turned and said, her eyes on Crystal, "We heard the girl Alice is Ken's daughter."

Crystal smirked. "Yeah, that's what some'll tell you. It's more shit from people who hated Ken. Just want to stir up trouble."

"We heard it was Ken who started the rumor," Fisher said.

"He wouldn't fuck no nigger," Crystal said, stood, and walked to the door, which she slammed shut.

***

"I think you hit a nerve," Fisher said.

Prado smiled. "I hope so."

As they drove away, Fisher started to laugh. "Where did you get all that stuff about" – he adopted a stilted tone — "'there's a penalty for anyone who makes allegations that result in a federal investigation that discovers they were made falsely or for personal reasons'? Is that even true?"

"Hell if I know, but I wanted to see how they'd react."

"And?"

"And nothing. That surprised me. I really believe there's something else going on here."

"Like?"

"I don't know. Yet."

***

A naked pole lamp sits in a corner furthest from seven wooden stairs descending into a basement. The cement floor is cold and damp. The smell of excrement and urine lays heavily, contained by a low, wood-beamed ceiling.

The door at the head of the stairs opens and light shines down the wooden planks painting a yellow rectangle on the dank floor. Light leaking from the pole lamp and the open door shows three mattresses on which three bodies are curled in various expressions of the fetal position.

Heavy steps cause the stairs to creak.

The figures stir. The chains around their ankles rattle. Little bodies push themselves to the walls against which the mattresses are positioned. They pull their legs tight to their chests as if trying to disappear.

A large, naked man – a pin light affixed to a headband – stands at the bottom of the stairs and looks from one figure to the other. "Hungry?" he asks. "Thirsty?"

The silence is disturbed by water dripping somewhere in the dark.

"Not hungry?" he asks and feints toward the stairs. "I don't want to waste this delicious food if no one wants it."

A tiny voice squeaks, "We're hungry."

The big man walks to the mattress closest to the stairs where he lays a paper plate on the floor; on it a small pile of corned beef hash, green peas, and a piece of bread. He stares down at the figure. "You don't eat, you're gonna starve." He continues staring until the nude figure of an emaciated, filthy young girl moves forward, grabs the plate, and scoots quickly back against the wall.

Enjoy," he says and moves to the second mattress directly across from the stairs.

The girl on this mattress is also nude though not as thin or dirty. Unlike the other, whose hair is greasy and matted, her hair hangs loosely across her shoulders. She uncurls and pushes herself onto all fours.

"Getting used to the place?" he asks and drops the plate in front of the mattress. The bread bounces onto the floor. "Whoops," he says playfully.

"Fuck you, you freak," the girl spits at him.

The man laughs and squats in front of the girl until his face is even with hers. "Fuck me? No, fuck you." He hits her with a closed fist snapping her head back violently and knocking her flat. He stands and grabs her by the hair, lifts her, spins her around, shoves her flat onto the mattress and places a foot on the middle of her back. As she fights, the man begins stroking himself into an erection. When engorged, he kneels behind her. "Fuck you," he says and shoves himself into her.

The other two quickly muffle their reactions. One buries her face in the mattress. The other turns and stares at the wall.

"Fuck you, fuck you," the man yells, his excitement fed by the chaos, the noise and the girl under him bucking, fighting and scratching at his legs.

His face contorts and his eyes close. "You can't see me," he yells at the top of his lungs. "You can't laugh at me if you can't see me." His growl is guttural and constant as he violates her brutally, first vaginally, then anally, yelling, "You can't see me."

Finished, the man stands over the girl who is bleeding profusely from her nose. A puddle of blood is wetting the mattress around her pubic and anal areas. She vomits on the mattress and begins choking. The man looks around him and locates a bucket which he slides toward her with his foot. "Water," he says.

He walks over to the mattress where the girl has her face turned toward the wall. He leans close to her ear. "You need to teach her some manners. You better teach her good or you'll never see her again."

He straightens and starts toward the girl who is pushing her face into the mattress, her hands pressing against her ears.

"Don't," the second girl screams, turning away from the wall. "Leave her alone."

"Don't worry. I'm not going to do anything. I just wanna make sure she's okay."

He walks onto the mattress and straddles the small figure, who shudders and begins shaking with sobs. He bounces on the mattress, once, twice.

"You okay," he asks. Silence. He turns and looks at the second girl who is staring intently at them. "She's fine." He turns back toward the girl beneath him. "Relax. You're no fun anyway."

He returns to the first girl who has scrambled to the back of the mattress. He smiles. "Big mistake, right?"

"I'm sorry" the girl squeaks.

The man holds his hand next to his ear and cocks his head in her direction. "What?"

"I said, I'm sorry." The words come haltingly between gulps of air.

The man laughs and urinates on her mattress.

He walks to a sink, turns on a faucet, and fills a bucket into which he places a long-handled brush. "Wash down that mess," he demands, waving at an open drain clogged with feces. "And try shittin' into the damn hole."

He drops the bucket in the middle of the room. "Eat up." His steps lay heavily on the stairs.

Waiting a few minutes until footsteps sound in a room away from the kitchen, where the door to the basement is located, the second girl crawls onto the freshly bloodied mattress. She places a hand on the prone girl's back and strokes lightly. "You have to stop makin' him mad."

"I'm not sorry," she gurgles through the blood flowing from her nose into her mouth. "I'm sorry I said I'm sorry. I'll die before I say it again."

"Make him mad again and you will die," the second girl answers. She points at a vacant mattress propped up against a far wall.

WEDNESDAY

When Prado and Fisher walked into Jill's they were again met with silence, but it did not linger quite as long this morning. The men – and it was all men except for Jill – returned quickly to their conversations about the likelihood of rain and the wisdom of holding off on planting a second crop until the earth was fully soaked. Talk of the makes and models of combines and the relative advantages of some and not others drifted from table to table. The quality of various fertilizers and GMOs were also popular topics.

Jill greeted the two as they walked toward the booth at the far end of the restaurant. "Rusty Weiler wants to talk to you." She raised her chin toward the booth where a man sat, a broad smile on his face. "He owns Dummy's."

Weiler stood as the two approached. He extended his hand. "Rusty Weiler." Prado and Fisher responded and the three slid into the booth, the agents flanking Weiler.

Weiler's smile held steady revealing yellowed teeth, victims of a three decade, two-pack a day cigarette habit only recently broken. His steel blue eyes were remnants of youth in a face aged by years in the sun that had dried his skin to a leathery brown. A straw hat, removed and placed next to him on the vinyl bench seat, left a ring in the thinning hair circling his head, and a red mark on his forehead. He lowered his eyes to the table where sat mugs and an urn. "Ordered some coffee."

"Thank you," Prado and Fisher responded simultaneously.

"I recommend the two-egg breakfast," Weiler offered. "And bacon. All comes from farms 'round here."

"Yes," Fisher said, "we had it yesterday. Very good."

Weiler raised his hand, got Jill's attention, and signaled with two fingers. "Done," she responded.

Prado noted the room full of eyes watching them as she asked, "What can we do for you, Mr. Weiler?"

Weiler's smile dropped into a purposeful expression. "I just thought I'd make your life easy and find you 'stead of you havin' to find me. I have to have breakfast anyway and assume you're gonna want to talk to me since it all happened right in front of my place."

"That's very thoughtful of you," Prado said. She spooned sugar into her coffee. "This is a pleasant surprise. We were told no one would be anxious to talk to us."

"That's 'bout right, and I'm not anxious either," he said, looking from Prado and Fisher. "I don't think I have anything useful for you, but I'm not one to sit around and wait for things to happen. First, you tell me 'xactly what you're doing here. There seems to be some confusion 'bout that. You tryin' to find out who killed Ken, or if we" – he gestured toward the room – "are coverin' up who did it?"

"We're trying to determine if there's a legitimate reason to pursue a civil rights case," Prado answered, her tone flat and benign. "More to the point, to see if there has been a violation of Mr. Plough's civil rights. To do that we have to gather as much information as we can and that includes asking about the details of the shooting. Who was there that day, who saw what?"

"And who saw who," Fisher interjected.

She stared at Weiler. "That answer your question?"

The man who had greeted Prado and Fisher with a warm smile had fallen cold. "Let's get on with it."

"Tell us exactly what you saw the morning Mr. Plough was killed."

Weiler cast his eyes down and stared at the tabletop. "I was standin' at the door and watched Ken and Tricia get into his truck. The sun was reflecting off the windshield which made it hard to see much, but I did see him light a cigarette." Weiler pushed himself against the back of the booth, his eyes squinted in concentration. "Then all hell broke loose. I heard some pops, two of 'em, which I recognized as shots from a rifle, and went flat on the ground. I felt something hit my back and get in my hair. It was glass from the windshield."

"Incoming," Jill warned as she approached carrying two plates. A tall, thin man, a bandanna wrapped around his head, followed with a third plate and another tumbler of coffee.

As Jill distributed the food around the table, Prado noticed that all eyes in the room remained focused in their direction. Jill leaned down and whispered in her ear, "You'll get used to it."

As soon as the plates were placed in front of each of them, the coffee mugs refilled, and Jill retreated, Prado motioned at Weiler. "Please, go on."

"When I was sure the shooting had stopped, I got up and ran around to where Tricia was sitting."

"You, didn't check on Mr. Plough?" Fisher asked.

"No, I knew he was likely dead and wanted to see if Tricia was hurt. I wanted to get her…."

Prado held up her hand. "Wait, you knew he was dead? So you knew he was the only target? That this wasn't a random shooting?"

Weiler raised an eyebrow. "Yes, I knew someone was shooting at him and considerin' the number of repeats, I figured he was either dead, or on his way to dyin'."

"How could you be so sure?" Fisher asked. "That this wasn't random."

Weiler took a bite of bacon which he chewed slowly and swallowed. "You talked to anyone else 'bout this yet?"

"A few people," Prado answered.

"You gotta know then that Ken was a first-class SOB. Hell, it's hard to believe he hadn't been killed a long time ago." Weiler looked at Prado and Fisher as if expecting a response. "You want me to go ahead?"

Prado nodded.

"I opened the door of Ken's truck." He made a face. "There was blood all over the cab, bits of Ken's…. Well, no need to go into all that. We're eating. He was deader than roadkill and Tricia was covered in his blood and whatnot. Lurleen – that's Ken's second wife – came 'round from her truck and I told her to take Tricia and get on home."

Fisher had been eyeing Prado throughout and nodding knowingly at her. "How many shots did you hear?" he asked.

"Two from the long gun."

"You're certain?"

Weiler answered through a mouthful of eggs, "I'm sure. One other thing. Two guns were used."

Prado glanced quickly at Fisher, then asked, "How do you know?"

Weiler set his fork on his plate and wiped his mouth. "You all are supposed to be big-shot FBI agents." He smiled knowingly. "Couldn't you tell the difference between a handgun and a rifle shot?"

"You heard shots from a rifle and a handgun?" Prado asked. "Is that what you're saying?"

"That's what I'm sayin'."

"Then what?"

"Then nothin'. I handed Tricia off to Lurleen and started lookin' around, the street was empty. Not a single soul around. And Ken's truck was roaring. Found out later that his foot got wedged between the gas and brake. I called 911, and then Marshal Staton in Maryville. I knew our town sheriff couldn't handle this." Weiler raised both hands. "Don't get me wrong. John is a great guy and does a real fine job for our little town, but this was way different than a broken taillight or a lost dog. This was going to be a big damn deal and Leo used to be a U.S. Marshal. He helped us before when we've needed it. Sometimes even stopped Ken when he was in Maryville just to let him know he was watchin' him. A non-nonsense kinda guy."

"How was a sheriff in Maryville going to be any help with this?" Prado asked.

"Like I said, he was a U.S. Marshal and....well, he's a man you want on this sort of thing. You're bound to meet him and you'll see."

"Okay," Prado said, resetting her thoughts. "You didn't find it strange that everyone...we understand close to 30 people were in the vicinity when the shooting began. You didn't find it strange that everyone just left? Disappeared?"

"Hell, no," Weiler said, laying his fork and knife across an empty plate. "If my place wasn't right there, I woulda left too."

"And then?" Fisher probed.

"And then I went back inside."

"No one thought it might be a good idea to stick around and answer some questions?" Prado asked. "Or to show a little respect for a dead man in the truck with his head blown off?"

Weiler slowly wiped his mouth with the large, white cloth napkin. He glanced around the room that had quieted, and then focused a hard look on Prado. "I did answer some questions John had. As to that respect thing, there isn't a man, or woman for that matter, in this town who had not been threatened or bullied, or likely had a gun pulled on them by Ken. So, *no*, no one stuck around to show their respect. There was none."

"What can you tell me about a meeting that was held and attended by most of the men who came to your bar directly from that meeting on the day of the...?"

Esper appeared at the table. "Excuse me," he interrupted Prado. "You two," he said, nodding at her, and pointing at Fisher, "need to get to Maryville right now. I've been asked to take you." He turned toward the door. "It's Leo. Marshal Staton. He wants to see you right now."

Prado looked at Weiler. "We're in the middle of...."

Esper shook his head. "I'm real sorry but Marshal Staton says it's important. He said to bring you 'right *fucking* now.' Those were his words."

"Hey," Weiler said, "if Leo says 'go', you gotta go."

"We appreciate your cooperation," Prado said to Weiler, "and we'll be following up. Sorry about this."

She and Fisher slid out of the booth, their breakfasts hardly touched. Fisher grabbed a few pieces of bacon and followed Esper and Prado.

***

As soon as the three settled into the cruiser, Prado said, "Weiler just told us he knows two guns were used to kill Plough."

Esper shot Prado a questioning look. "Did he say how he knew?"

"He could tell by the difference in the sound of the two weapons."

"Okay, a handgun sounds different than a long gun."

"You're going with that as a reasonable explanation?" Prado asked, doubt in her voice. "Even in what must have been a chaotic scene with people running in all directions, probably yelling, a truck being shot up? With all that going on, and Weiler probably being confused and scared, you're satisfied he had the presence of mind to make out the sounds of two different guns?"

Esper shrugged his answer.

"I'm asking because if we have doubts about that making sense, then we have a person of interest. You said it yourself. You held back about there being two different weapons because only someone involved would know."

"Rusty Weiler? He's the only person in town who had a half-way decent relationship with Ken."

"Decent enough not to want to see him dead like we're hearing everybody else in town did?"

"Ken gave him a hard time, too, but nothing like the rest of us 'cause he wanted to drink at Dummy's, and Rusty had a way of keepin' the peace when Ken was there. So, no, I don't think Rusty is a legitimate person of interest."

"Weiler also said he called Sheriff Staton when Plough was shot. Has he been involved in the investigation?"

"I've bounced some ideas off him. Nothin' official."

Fisher leaned from the back seat and asked, "What is the deal with calling the sheriff in Maryville 'Marshal'?

"He was a U.S. Marshal and it just stuck."

"From Marshal to Sheriff? Not the usual career path. There must be a story here, right?"

Esper nodded. "There is. Goes back 'bout ten years. Maybe a little more. He was transporting a prisoner. A real bad guy, Ned Tether. Takin' him from the county lockup to federal prison. He got loose somehow and killed Staton's partner and almost killed Staton before he killed Tether. Tether has a couple of brothers and they went after Staton's wife and kid. Killed'em. At least everybody thought it was them. Happened while Staton was in the hospital. He got out and Tether's brothers were found dead 'bout a week later. There was an investigation but they never found out who killed'em. Truth told, I don't think they tried real hard. Leo kinda disappeared after that. I mean, he was around, but no one saw much of him. About three years ago some folks in Maryville convinced him to run for Sheriff. More like they made sure he won. To go after the meth dealers that started croppin' up 'round here. That's pretty much it."

"Man," exclaimed Fisher, "that's some wild west shit."

"Speaking of meth," Prado said, "why didn't you tell us Plough was pushing it in Oletha?"

Esper opened his mouth to respond, shook his head, and glanced out the side window as if searching for an answer.

Fisher leaned further across the front seat wedging his head and shoulders between Esper and Prado. "Not even going to try and answer?"

"Okay," Esper conceded, "I heard the rumors 'bout Ken and meth."

"You heard rumors?" Fisher said, judgment in his voice. "Isn't it your job to investigate and find out if it was more than rumors? We're talking about a man who was a thief, liar, rapist, bully and…." He paused and stared at Esper a beat before adding, "Meth dealer fits right in, doesn't it?"

Esper answered, irritation in his voice, "There was talk, but that's all it was."

Fisher leaned until his face was almost touching Esper's. "It's your job to protect the people in your community. That includes investigating reports of meth dealing, don't you think?" He pushed himself away from Esper. "Jesus Christ, no wonder this Plough guy got away with everything. The sheriff was AWOL."

Esper's neck was flushing red. Prado waved Fisher off. "Did you know that the Moore's daughter was going to Maryville with her friends to get drugs?"

"All the kids go there to get drugs." Esper looked in the rear-view mirror at Fisher. "I called a town meeting a year ago to talk about that, about meth, and how we should keep our kids from going to Maryville. The parents who bothered to show up gave me a huge ration of shit. Said I was accusing their kids of being drug addicts, and making them out to be bad parents. The message I got was 'stay out of our business.'"

"How about weed?" Fisher asked. "Did you know he was pushing weed? Word is you did and didn't do anything about it." He shook his head and dropped against the back seat. "Never mind. I know. 'All rumors.'"

"'Course I knew, but like everything else Ken did; either there was no way to pin it on him, or no one was willing to come forward. Everyone knew what would happen if they did."

Prado asked, "Did you ever hear that Alice went to Maryville with Plough?"

Esper shook his head.

"Well, she did," Fisher said sharply.

"From pieces of the story we've been able to put together about Alice, the last time she was seen was just before she went to Maryville with Plough. Tricia told us he left her there with a man named Frankie."

Esper's foot eased off the gas. "Tricia told you that? I talked to her about Alice and she never said anything about that. I talked to her, Crystal and Lurleen, and none of them did."

"Did you press them?" Fisher asked. "Did you ever bring them into your office and press them about why they insisted Silas killed Plough?" Fisher came back toward the front seat. "They were accusing a man of committing a murder for fuck's sake. Didn't you feel the need to press them about that? Maybe the information about Alice would have come out if you had."

Esper sped up. The two-lane blacktop widened into a four-lane highway and Maryville materialized on the horizon. Without any significant landmarks interrupting the bare, open, flat land, the miles fell away quickly. Plugs of sprouting crops that painted the land with a green patina gave way to low-rise buildings. Warehouses and industrial parks introduced Maryville, then came neighborhoods dotted with clapboard houses sitting on postage stamp-sized lots. Most of the yards were dirt-filled. Those without dogs chained to clothes lines, not strewn with old cars and trucks, or littered with the bones of furniture and other household castoffs, had patches of grass.

"That was the South side," Esper said as they bounced over a railroad track, where the surroundings changed suddenly and dramatically.

"Really?" Prado said as she looked across manicured lawns that ran up to small but well-kept houses. "So there are places that have a right and wrong side of the tracks."

Esper nodded. "North and South sides are divided by the railroad. There's a West side too, but no East side."

"How can there be no East side?" Fisher asked.

"There's an East," Esper answered, "but no *East side*. Nothing out that way to speak of. North and South just kinda run out the string over that way."

"Run out the string?" Fisher asked, then added, "Never mind."

"What's the population of Maryville?" Prado asked.

"'Bout fifteen thousand. It's the county seat."

The neighborhood graduated from solidly middle class to distinctively upper middle class with homes set back on large lots; many were sheltered behind low rock walls, others were clustered in compounds surrounded by high concrete ramparts and protected by security gates. Parks and lakes punctuated the neighborhoods; and schools with campuses marked with large green fields competed with churches for the most impressive architecture.

"Is it the railroad that feeds all this?" Prado asked, gesturing at the office buildings they were now passing that established a sizable downtown.

Esper craned his neck and looked up at the taller buildings. "No, the railroad doesn't even run through here anymore. It's the dairy farms on the West side that bring in most of the money. Some of the largest ones in the country. That brought in the trucks to transport the milk, and when the highways were widened for the trucks, and the truck stops and garages came in, it made sense for the farmers from all around to use Maryville as a place to ship their crops from. Warehouses and silos got built to store corn and soy beans."

"What about the warehouses on the other side?" Prado asked. "Where we came in to town. What are those for?"

"Nothing much now. Used to be for the railroad, I think," Esper said, and braked to a stop in front of a large, cream-colored stucco building shaded by large oak trees growing on either side of a path leading to the front entrance. Large letters painted on one side of the double glass front door identified the Office of the Sheriff; on the other, Leo Staton, Sheriff.

A tall, broad-shouldered man sauntered out the front door, putting on sunglasses as he walked toward the car. A Stetson hat, a sidearm in an embroidered leather holster hanging from a thick-belt that also held a pair of handcuffs anointed the man with an aura of authority. His square-jawed, thin-lipped, no-nonsense demeanor reinforced this impression. He held up his hand indicating the three should stay in the car.

Fisher said, "Well, he looks like the real deal."

Esper lowered his window as the man approached the car. "Afternoon, Leo."

"Don't wish your life away, John," the man said as he leaned on the door. "It's only 11:00." He lowered his gaze and looked past Esper. "Leo Staton," he said to Prado and Fisher. "I appreciate your taking the time to drive over here. I heard you were in Oletha looking into the whole Plough situation and want to get your opinion on a matter I'm dealing with."

"Not a problem," Prado said with a nod, adding, "Eileen Prado and Ira Fisher. What matter?"

Staton grimaced and pushed away from the car. He took off his Stetson and ran his fingers through a thick head of dark, close-cropped hair. "Better if I show you." He turned his shoulders toward a cruiser parked two spots away. "Follow me," he directed to Esper. "We're going to the woods."

As Esper pulled out of the lot following Staton, Fisher asked, "Woods? Around here?"

"Yeah, about twenty acres."

"I've haven't seen anything but flat lands and crops. Haven't seen a stand of trees here or in Oletha, or anywhere in between. Some kind of park or protected area? Man-made?"

Esper shook his head. "Been there forever as far as I know."

A short drive back through the downtown area, and a few turns took them to a single lane road following the railroad tracks before jumping a railroad crossing. The land off a dirt road on the opposite side of the tracks was not planted or in any way cultivated. It was untamed brush that overwhelmed what had been log and barbed wire fences. A line of naked telephone poles ran along both sides of the narrow road. The hungry brush slowly morphed into a thick, completely untamed forest of trees and ground shrubs. A small, hard-dirt packed parking area at the end of the road provided just enough room for the cruisers.

Staton, Esper, Prado and Fisher met between the cars where Fisher nodded at the thicket. "This is not anything I'd expect to see around here."

"Before it all became farmland, there were large patches of forest," Staton said, directing the group toward the trees. "There's a hidden path just ahead."

As they approached the thicket, Prado asked, "What is this all about?"

"Like I said" Staton responded, "best if you see it. I couldn't possibly explain."

Staton kicked his way through a hedgerow that gave way reluctantly.

"Hidden path is right," Prado said, struggling across the hedgerow, slowing to wait for Fisher and Esper.

"It opens up a little just ahead," Staton assured her as he pushed aside low hanging tree branches and held them for Prado, who did the same for Fisher and Esper. "Good thing you're wearing slacks and those," he said pointing at her mesh Skecher walking shoes.

"I learned a long time ago that it makes better sense to be comfortable than stylish."

As they walked further into the woods, where the tops of the trees grew closer together, the shade deepened into darkness. With the sunlight and rain blocked, the bushes and live outcroppings disappeared, but the detritus from the trees increased and the four were soon wading through a thick ground cover of leaves and branches.

"The next time I don't wear a suit," Fisher said.

"The next time?" Prado said as she jumped over a large branch. "I'm getting the feeling we don't want there to be a 'next time.'"

"No, you don't," Staton said, stopped, and stared ahead. "There."

Prado walked around Staton and stood next to him. "Is that a human being?"

"Used to be."

Fisher walked up next to Prado. "Holy shit."

Staton took two steps forward. "Some kids found it late last night."

"How?" Prado asked. "It's dark here in the middle of the day."

"According to what I was told by the parents, the kids had flashlights and were playing some kind of 'hide and seek' game last night – or so they told their parents – and almost ran right into it. They're always out here, the kids, drinking and smoking dope, and whatnot. And there's a pond a little ways beyond they swim in. I got the call this morning, came out earlier to verify what I was told, and called you as soon as I got back to the office. I didn't disturb the scene. This is as close as I came."

The nude body of a woman was suspended from ropes tied around her wrists and looped over the branches of two trees standing side-by-side. She had been cut open from the top of her chest, down between her breasts, to her vaginal area. Her throat had also been cut through to her spine, causing her head to hang back between her shoulder blades.

Esper turned around and began walking away.

Staton said, "This is something like the way hunters hang deer to clean them." He took a few steps closer to the body. "She hasn't been gutted." He turned around toward Prado and Fisher. "She wasn't killed here. Not a lot of blood. This is why I said you had to see it."

Fisher swallowed hard. "A little warning wouldn't have hurt." He squinted and craned his head toward the body. "Is that plastic wrap around her middle?"

Staton nodded. "Like I said, she hasn't been gutted. That's the only thing holding everything from spilling out. We need your help with this."

"Not our help" Prado answered quickly. "This is way out of our depth, but I can put you in touch with someone who can help."

"Good because this is the second one."

"The second?" Prado blurted and pointed at the body. "Just like that?"

"By the time the first one was found, all that was left was a pair of forearms hanging from the ropes, with a pile of bones underneath. There was a sheet of plastic too." Staton nodded at the body. "Didn't make sense then. Does now."

"Jesus Christ," came from Fisher as he turned away from the carnage.

***

"We have a situation," Prado said, as she paced between the cars. "Two girls have been hung up like animals and butchered. They...." She stopped talking and listened. "Sorry, I'm a little rattled. Make that a lot rattled." She took a deep breath. "Okay, from the beginning. We're in Oletha." She listened and nodded. "Yes, the civil rights case. Well, we're not in Oletha right now; we're in a neighboring town. Maryville. We got a call from the Sheriff's office asking for help with this...this thing. Not my wheelhouse, so I'm calling you. From the very little I know about what is going on here...." Prado paused, listened, then continued. "Yes, it happened in Maryville about 30 miles from Oletha. Anyway, this is something you really need to get on as soon as possible. I remember that lecture you gave to us when we were going through training about how these things usually get worse." Prado leaned back against Staton's cruiser and massaged the bridge of her nose with her thumb and forefinger. "Bob, this looks like one of those. You have to get out here."

Staton approached and raised a finger to get Prado's attention.

"Bob, hold a sec," she said and lifted the mouthpiece of cell away from her chin.

"Four girls are also missing," Staton said. "Might be related."

"You hear that," Prado asked, grimacing at Staton. "We're headed back to the Sheriff's office. Leo Staton will be calling you."

***

Staton ushered Prado, Fisher and Esper into the bright, marble-floored building, leading them down a wide corridor. Columns of light funneling through a series of skylights were absorbed by stucco walls that matched the color and texture of the exterior of the building. Staton opened a glass door leading into a conference room. He gestured at a long, oval-shaped Cherrywood conference table surrounded by black mesh-covered, ergonomically-designed, high-backed chairs with hard-wheel casters to accommodate a thickly carpeted floor.

As they settled, Prado said to Staton, "I've been meaning to ask how you knew we were in Oletha."

Staton placed his Stetson on a neighboring chair, stroked his hand across the top of the conference table and smiled. "We have what we call around here the 'tin can express'. You're way too young to remember, but when I was growing up we'd take two tin cans, poke a hole in the bottoms and join them together with a wire. You could talk into the can at one end and hear through the can on the other end. Of course, we were usually so close we could have heard without the cans, but no matter, it made us feel like we were on walkie-talkies." He held out his arms. "Word travels quickly from mouth-to-ear around here, especially when there's something special going on like the FBI visiting one of our towns. Our own kind of 'tin can express'. I've been hearing about what you all are up to in Oletha." He waited a beat and added, "And I still have friends in the Marshal's Service in Washington. They got a courtesy call from the folks at the Bureau telling'em about the case, and I got a call from them saying you'd be coming."

"I'm sorry we had to meet like this," Prado said, "but we were going to talk to you at some point anyway about our case." She shrugged. "And here we are. The timing could be better, but since we are here, could we talk to you for a few minutes about what we're up to?"

Prado passed her phone to Staton. "First, that's Bob McCay's cell number. He's with the Bureau's Behavioral Analysis Unit."

Esper stirred. "The serial killer people?"

Prado nodded quickly and focused back on Staton. She briefed him on their investigation concluding with, "According to Plough's wife, well, his wife and ex-wives, they left the girl here with a Frankie Hebert and that's the last time anyone saw her. What can you tell us about Hebert?"

Staton drummed his fingers on the table. He nodded his head slowly as if arranging his thoughts. "The girl was left here with Frankie? I'm curious about that because Frankie is a real scumbag and uses girls to pedal his drugs, among other things, but I don't see him killing anyone. He's a low-life, yes. A murdering low-life, no.

"I knew Ken Plough. A real shitbag, and that's going easy on him." Staton dropped his head back and closed his eyes. "About Silas Moore killing Ken, makes no sense. He'd be killing the only person who could tell him what happened to his daughter if you believe Ken had something to do with the disappearance, and apparently Silas does." Staton straightened and looked at Prado. "No, doesn't make a whole lotta sense."

"Yes, we've considered that. Right now I'm just chasing down all the details. Someone had a reason to kill Plough and…"

"A lotta people had a reason to kill him," Esper interjected.

Prado ignored the remark. "Alice's friends and teachers all say they saw her with Plough a few times. He used to pick her up after she got out of school. Plough's wife" – Prado waved her hand – "wives, say it was the girl who pursued him and to get her off his back, he brought her here. And it so happened the girl knew Frankie Hebert and…."

"Probably from her father's association with him a few years ago," Staton said. "Silas cooked meth for Frankie."

Prado nodded her agreement and continued. "Plough wanted to talk to him about getting into the meth business in Oletha. So, things fell into place, and she came with Plough."

"Ken used the girl as an introduction to Frankie?" Staton asked.

"Looks like, and he wanted to unload her."

"And Frankie was good with that?"

"He said she owed him some money and he wanted her to *work it off*, if you can believe that."

"Frankie Hebert," Staton said with a note of disgust, "feeds young girls meth, gets them hooked, and then pimps them out. Those four missing girls I told you about are some of those girls. We could put him away on some minor drug charges, but why cut off our noses? We need to know what happened to those girls. We think he knows, so we need him out and about doing what he does. That might give us something that leads us to those girls." He hit the table hard with his fist causing the others to start. "Pretty fucked up, isn't it. We're waiting for more girls to go missing."

Staton waved his hand dismissively. "You don't need to know about my problems." He squared his shoulders. "About Frankie Hebert. He runs the south side and he's smart, slick and, when he has to be, real scary, but killing someone," Staton said with a shake of his head. "Like I said, I don't see it."

"Where do we find him?" Prado asked.

***

The houses along the few blocks closest to the railroad tracks when entering the South side from the North were not as ramshackle as those they passed when arriving in Maryville. Pride of ownership showed on the small clapboard homes. The yards were well-kept and the neighborhoods clean.

"Gentrification is crossing the tracks," Fisher said as they circled a block searching for the address Staton had given them. A difficult task since gentrification had not advanced as far as erecting street signs on most blocks; only a few houses were numbered, and what numbers there were had been painted on the curbs "in the last century," Fisher guessed, and most were faded beyond identification.

On the second pass around a block that had the most promise, a man appeared on the porch of a corner house; on the third pass, he was joined by another who had a gun tucked into his beltline.

"Bingo," Prado said, gesturing for Esper to pull over.

As she stepped onto the sidewalk, the man with the gun ducked back into the house, emerging with two others who were not armed. These three stood in a line behind the man who had remained on the porch.

"FBI," Prado announced as she approached the walkway leading to a wood porch circling the home.

"You're shittin' me," the man in the middle of the pack said and began to laugh. The laughing evolved into a hacking cough which doubled him over.

"Frankie Hebert?" Prado asked.

After recovering from the coughing fit, the man answered hoarsely, "The one and only." He smiled showing a gap where his front teeth should be. He was shirtless and his jeans hung low on his hips. Tattoos ran up both arms and circled his neck. He cheeks were hollow and his pallor unhealthy. What might have been a handsome face was tired, worn. "Ma'am, I'm honored to have you here and if I'd knowed the F-fucking-BI was comin', I'd a been better dressed. Woulda worn a shirt and washed up some," he said combing his fingers through a wild shock of graying hair. He raised his hand and the three men standing around him retreated into the house.

"We need to talk to you."

"I'm right here in front of you."

"Inside?"

"Course. Never had the feds come visit me. Visited with them a few times. Well, it was only the Sheriff way back when he was Marshal. Not high level like you people." He turned toward the open doorway and signaled them to follow.

Prado, Fisher and Esper stopped a few steps into a dark room that smelled of cigarettes and body odor. As their eyes adjusted to the dark, a voice invited them to: "Please, come on in and take a load off."

Hebert reclined in a faux-leather lounge chair. He had put on a wife-beater decorated with an American eagle, the Confederate flag in its beak. A beer can sat in a cup holder on the arm of the chair. He lit a cigarette and blew a cloud of smoke at the ceiling. A cloth couch to the left of the front door was covered with newspapers, empty drink containers and fast-food bags. The coffee table fronting the couch was littered with crushed beer cans and three ashtrays gorging butts.

"Just brush that stuff off the couch," Hebert instructed. "Sorry, I'm not much of a housekeeper."

"I'm Special Agent Eileen Prado." She held up her credentials and introduced, "Special Agent Ira Fisher and Sheriff...."

"Yeah, I know John," Hebert said dismissively. He squinted and looked at Fisher, a smile animated his face. "Ira, that's like a Jew name, ain't it?"

Fisher leaned in toward Prado and said "My turn" as they picked up the newspapers and food containers and placed them on the coffee table. "My people killed Christ," he whispered.

Prado brushed cigarette ashes off the arms of the couch before sitting down.

"This here's a real honor," Hebert said. "Never had Special Agents right in my house before." He raised his chin toward Fisher. "Didn't mean nothin' bad by that Jew thing." He pointed at a large flat screen television. "Just saw somethin' 'bout Israel and the soldiers there. Mean sons-of-bitches." He leaned forward. "And they have women soldiers. And not just sitting behind desks. Those ladies fight along-side the men. Now, that's some serious shit." He laughed, again causing a coughing fit. "Bet none of those girls get hit on 'less they want to," he croaked through his coughing.

"No, I'm sure they don't," Prado said, not even trying to hide the disgust in her voice.

Hebert let himself fall against the back of the cushioned chair and took a long sip of beer. He lifted the can. "Want one?"

Prado, Fisher and Esper shook their heads.

"I get it. On the clock and all. What can I do for you fine folks?"

"We're trying to locate a girl named Alice Moore," Prado said. "From Oletha. I understand a lot of the young kids come here to party and you're the one they come to see."

Hebert took a drag on his cigarette and stared at Prado before shaking his head. "Yeah, I entertain, but that name don't ring a bell." He turned toward a door to the left of his chair and called out, "Princess." A girl appeared in the doorway and stared vacantly at

Prado, Fisher and Esper. A too large Tee-Shirt with a Guns and Roses logo hung down to her knees. Her expressionless eyes were rimmed red with dark circles underneath. This discoloration was pronounced enough to have been caused by a beating, but there was no swelling. Her legs looked too skinny to support her weight. "This is Princess. She might know about, uh…give me that name again. Probably the same age or near-abouts."

"Alice Moore," Prado said and watched the man who had the gun tucked into his waistband appear behind the girl and put his hand on her shoulder.

"Would you mind stepping away from the girl," Prado asked, "and turn around slowly?"

The man smiled, lifted his arms away from his side, and turned. "Clean," he said adding, "left it in the kitchen. I got the registration if you want to see it."

Prado shook her head. "Not necessary, but I would like the other two gentleman to step out here."

"Can't," Hebert said. "They left. Thought you might appreciate a smaller group." He laughed. "To keep it friendly."

Hebert jabbed a thumb in the direction of the couple. "That's Butch. Princess's husband."

"Husband?" fell out of Fisher's mouth.

Butch pointed at Fisher. "I know what you're thinkin'." He leaned into the girl and squeezed her shoulder. It was not an affectionate gesture and the girl pulled away. "She's older'n she looks and I'm younger."

This caused both men to laugh and high five. Hebert asked, "Princess, you know someone named Alice Moore?"

She shook her head and stepped around Butch disappearing into the dark. Hebert pointed Butch to an armchair against the wall to the left of the couch.

"Why you askin' 'bout this Alice person?" Butch said as he sat down heavily in the chair sending up a cloud of dust motes that added a mustiness to the odors permeating the small living room.

"This was the last place she was seen," Prado answered. "She came here with Ken Plough."

"Ken," Hebert said animatedly. "Man that was a long time ago. 'Fore he was killed. Guess I didn't have to say that." This set off another round of hilarity and high fives.

After a session of coughing that followed the laughter, Hebert declared that, "Yeah, I remember he brought some little girl here a while back. A pretty little colored thing." He looked at Butch. "Big tits and an ass that wouldn't quit like all of them people." Hebert adopted a serious look and held out a beseeching hand toward Prado. "No offense meant Miss FBI lady."

"Did Plough leave her with you?" Prado asked.

"Shit, no," he said with a laugh. "We teased Ken that he wouldn't be able to keep up with her and, truth told, neither could I. She'd a killed me."

"You don't remember saying he could leave her with you because she owed you money and you would have her work it off?" Fisher asked.

"Nope."

"Plough left with the girl?" Prado asked, leaning forward, resting her forearms on her thighs.

"What the fuck do you really want?" Hebert asked, his tone now flat and suspicious.

"I want to know about the girl." Prado straightened. "I don't give a rat's ass about what you have going on. About how or who you *entertain.* I'm here about Alice and only Alice. I know Plough was talking to you about buying your product and selling it in Oletha." Prado gestured with open palms. "I don't care. All I want to know is what happened to that girl."

"Why?" Butch asked.

"Why?" Fisher responded sarcastically. "Because she's missing and her parents are concerned."

"And because it might have something to do with who killed Plough," Prado added. "Now, why don't you tell us what we need to know?"

Hebert took a final drag on his cigarette, burning it down to his fingertips, and crushed it on the top of the beer can. "Ken was a dipshit. The world is better off without him."

"Not what I asked about."

"He came here and wanted to do business with me. I wasn't crazy 'bout the idea 'cause Ken was such a God-awful dipshit, but money's money. I knew he was selling lots of weed in Oletha and could probably do the same with what we got. Butch took him to one of our labs to show off our product. He came back here to talk some more and left. That's the last we seen of ole Ken."

"We're asking about the girl, not Ken," Prado reminded Hebert.

Hebert stood, pulled his pants to his waist, and walked slowly to the couch. He squinted and stared down at Prado and Fisher. "I'm being real with you. I got nothin' to hide about this Alice girl. I wouldn't be telling you nothin' 'bout nothin' 'cept I want you to know 'xactly what happened that day. Staton has got it in his head that I have something to do with all those other girls that's missin'. You be sure and tell him I leveled with you so maybe he'll stop harassing me 'bout them." Hebert tugged at his slowly sliding pants. "You tell him that."

"One other thing," Prado said and stood. "Was Plough's wife Tricia with him when he came here?"

"Yeah," Butch answered. "She was waitin' in the truck and went with us to the lab. There was another one too," he said and looked at his shoes searching for the rest of what he had to say. "I think I heard him call her Crystal." Butch nodded. "Yeah, Crystal. She was with him too. In another truck and followed us. That Alice girl rode with her."

***

"You believe him?" Fisher asked as he, Prado and Esper returned to the car.

She nodded. "He wants to get out from under this. Staton's looking over his shoulder and it's disrupting his business. I'd believe him before I'd believe Tricia, Crystal or that other one."

"Lurleen," Esper interjected.

"The middle child always gets ignored," Fisher gibed.

Prado continued, "They have reason to lie and deflect attention from Plough to Hebert. The alibi ladies did what they do."

"You're saying you think Plough did have something to do with Alice goin' missing?" Esper asked.

"No, I'm not ready to make that leap," Prado answered. "Plough was scum for sure, but kidnapping?" She shook her head. "Why would he bother? He didn't need to do that."

Fisher said, "Every time we turn over a rock something new crawls out."

"We're in the rock turning business," Prado said.

***

Esper, Prado and Fisher sat in Staton's bare office. A government-issued steel desk and accompanying chair. Both institutional green. No In or Out boxes, and no computer. A rotary phone which Fisher toyed with. A bookcase with a few volumes. All law manuals. No framed credentials or commendations on the wall. No family photos on the desk.

Prado relayed the details of their conversation with Hebert concluding, "I believe him about Alice. He had no reason to tell us why Plough came to him other than to show he has nothing to hide. It was his attempt to gain some trust."

"Trust?" Staton said sardonically. "That's not happening, but I'm willing to look beyond Frankie for what happened to those missing girls. You think what we saw today is related?"

Prado shook her head. "I have no idea. Bob McCay can help answer those questions."

Staton took a full breath and blew it out. "Well, I talked to McCay after you left. Described what we found today, and what I could about the first one, but that wasn't much since we didn't find much other than what I told you. The bones, rope and plastic."

Fisher asked, "What were his thoughts?"

"He said we have a serious problem."

"Just what you wanted to hear, I'm sure," Prado responded.

"About the first one," Fisher continued, "did you find the remains in the same place?"

"Near there. Again, it was some kids fooling around in the 'shadows'; that's what people around here call it. And 'the Woods'. They were doing what they do and, like with the ones today, stumbled onto it."

"Jesus," Fisher said. "Can you imagine *stumbling* onto something like that? That'll stick with them for a while."

Staton fell back in the chair and pointed at Fisher and Prado. "I probably should've called your folks earlier, but...well, I didn't know what the hell I had. I was focused on trying to find out who was hanging out there. And, honestly, I was trying to figure things out on my own. An ego-thing. Bad move. If I had gotten McCay involved then, maybe the second one wouldn't have happened."

"You can't take that on," Prado said. "You did what you've been trained to do. Speaking of that, who was the first victim?"

"Never found out. Not much we could do forensically with the bones. The coroner was able to say it was a young girl. He found some nicks on the ribs and pubic bone that were likely caused by some kind of blade. Got everything photographed. You can see it if you'd like."

"No," Prado said forcefully, "that's what McCay does."

Esper raised his hand. "I think I might know who the girl you found today is," he offered timidly. All heads jerked in his direction causing him to respond defensively. "I didn't get a good look because of how…." He stopped and cleared his throat. "Because of how her head was hanging back like it was, but I could see enough to think it's Rochelle Lee. She's from Oletha and her parents reported her missing a while back."

Staton pulled his cell from his shirt pocket and scrolled. "I have a few pictures here," he said and handed the phone to Esper. "Didn't get real close, but these are from behind and might give you a better look at the face. Can you tell from those if it's that person?"

Esper turned the screen away from his face and took a moment before looking. He grimaced as he scrolled. "Fuck," he said and laid the phone on Staton's desk. "Yeah, I'm almost certain that's her."

"Her parents reported her missing a while back?" Fisher directed at Esper. "What'd you do about it then?"

"You know, asked around and tried to find out who saw her last. Talked to her friends. Kids at school."

"And," Fisher challenged, "what did you find out?"

"Same thing as with Alice. Just that she spent some time in Maryville and the last time anyone talked to her she was coming here."

Fisher looked at Staton. "Did he tell you any of this?"

"First I've heard of it."

"What the hell?" Fisher said to Esper.

"Her folks said she went missing all the time. I told'em what I found out and they didn't seem to much care."

Fisher looked at Prado and Staton, before refocusing on Esper. "Are you shitting me? That's it? You asked a few questions and her parents didn't seem to care? What the fuck is wrong with you?"

"This was when the whole mess with Ken happened," Esper answered. "That kinda took over my life."

Fisher started to push himself out of his chair. Prado put a restraining hand on his arm. She said, "We're going to need everyone pulling in the same direction, to coin a phrase." She waited a beat keeping an eye on Fisher who slumped low in his chair, pulling agitatedly at his lower lip.

Staton said to Fisher, "John handled things the way I would have." He raised a hand when Fisher made an attempt to interrupt him. "It's a lot different when someone goes missing around here than when it happens in…." He shrugged. "I don't know, say Chicago. The reasons are different. The kids are different. There aren't a lot of places to get lost. They usually turn up."

"Except this time," Fisher retorted. "It looks like things are very different. Two of those missing girls aren't ever going to *turn up*."

Staton considered his response. "You're right. This is different, but I don't think we're doing much good going back and forth with the 'woulda, coulda, shouldas'."

"Speaking of which," Prado said, "what about dental records for the first victim? Were you able to find anything out that way?"

"Got nothing, but now I'm thinking we didn't go wide enough." Staton pushed away from his desk allowing him to open the top drawer. He placed a sheaf of papers in front of him and shuffled through them. "We went to a bunch of local dentists but maybe we should have gone wider, like to Oletha, especially now that we know this Rochelle Lee was from there. Looks like the missing girls from around here are on top of what you got with this Rochelle Lee," he directed himself to Esper. "There was something else. The first one had a condition that made one of her legs just a little shorter than the other."

"Oh, shit," Esper said and buried his face in his hands. "That's Alice Moore."

"This 'tin-can express'?" Prado said, "didn't it get the word out about the missing girls here and" – she looked at Esper – "in Oletha?"

"Yeah," Esper responded. "But like Leo just said, 'cept for maybe the parents of the girls, and even they didn't freak out or anything, it wasn't news. Another youngster took off and would be back. Maybe in a while, maybe longer."

Prado asked, "What kind of response did you get from the media?"

Staton huffed. "The media? We have a local paper. If we hadn't issued a press release each time one of the girls went missing, even the small item that did show up wouldn't have been there. It was basically a reprint of our press notice, which didn't say much because we didn't know much."

"Television?" Fisher asked.

Staton shook his head. "Nothing local, or even regional. Missing girls, like we said, aren't big news."

THURSDAY

Jill was standing in front of the booth a broad smile on her face. She made a show of pulling a dish rag from the waistline of her apron and wiping the table clean. She welcomed Prado and Fisher with "A very good morning to you" as they slid across the bench seats.

Prado glanced around the silent room as they settled. "The frowns have turned upside down," she said to Jill. "What's this all about?"

The large woman leaned on the table, her full, round face was splotchy from hours in and out of the kitchen, and strands of hair, having pulled free from the tight black netting covering her head, fell across her face. Her violet eyes shined. "John was in here earlier and told us 'bout you all finding Rochelle and Alice. That's a nice thing for those girls' parents." She let her head drop. "Not what I'd call good news, but it beats not knowing."

Eyes wide, Fisher said, "I sure as hell hope the sheriff told the parents before he used the 'tin-can express' to get the news out."

Jill's face screwed up in question. "Tin what?"

Prado talked past the question. "Sheriff Staton told us...."

"We call him *Marshal* Staton," Jill said pointedly.

Prado nodded her acknowledgement. "Marshal Staton told us there hasn't been much of anything in the news about the girls or, from what we can tell, about Plough. How do you get...?"

Jill's shaking head stopped Prado. She looked around the diner. "This is how we get the word around." She folded the dish rag in half and tucked it into the waist of her apron. "We don't have a newspaper anymore. Lost it three years ago, I think it was. If I remember right there was something in the Maryville paper 'bout the girls. Not much, but I wouldn't expect there to be. They run off all the time. Not much keeping'em here. Some TV people did come 'round 'bout Ken." She smiled and pointed at Fisher. "Hey, I just got the tin can thing. Two soup cans and a wire, right?"

Fisher nodded. "When you did have a newspaper, did it cover much about the allegations against Plough? Or anything at all about him?"

Jill stood looking down at Fisher, a blank expression on her face. He held up his hands. "I know, I know. We haven't been listening."

"That's right," Jill agreed. "I do recall one-time years ago, the paper ran an editorial that didn't use Ken's name, but said that livestock was bein' stolen and Sheriff Lawrence, the guy before John, should maybe hire some more people to control that sort of thing. Everyone knew who he was talkin' 'bout and Ken was in a pretty bad mood for a time. Made a bigger ass of himself than usual. Came in here for a week and ate without paying, always sayin' he'd get me the next day. Did the same at the store and Dummy's. It got so bad people were going to Gene, that was the name of the editor, Gene Autry, if you can believe that, and telling him to not do that again."

"Un-freakin' believable," Fisher said. "The guy controlled the press too."

"But enough 'bout that," the woman said as she ambled toward the kitchen. "Breakfast's on the house."

"Best thing I've heard since we got here," Fisher said, making a show of grabbing his knife and fork and holding them upright in anticipation.

"Speaking of 'best things,' what the hell is it with you and Esper? You just don't like the guy, or what?"

As if deflating, Fisher blew out a breath and slumped in the booth. "I think the guy's in way over his head. You said something about Tricia, Crystal and" – he waved his hand – "the other one, maybe using us to get back at everyone who had it in for Ken. I think you're right and I don't think we'd be here if Esper had done his job. I think it's more his fuck up than a case of people not talking, and if he'd just done his job, there'd be no grounds for even claiming a civil rights violation."

Prado nodded thoughtfully. "Yeah, Tricia, Crystal and Lurleen might be using us, and Esper is definitely on the Barney Fife scale of law enforcement, but there could be a lot more going on. Everyone is obviously hiding something. They've made it a point to tell us they're not going to cooperate. That's suspicious, don't you think?"

"I'm saying if Esper had been more competent, maybe more forceful about doing what needed doing right from the start, someone would've said something." Fisher turned toward Prado. "Thirty people were there and no one saw anything? No one felt a twinge of guilt that could have been massaged to find out what really happened? And then we find out about those girls." He was now speaking through gritted teeth. "We saw a girl strung up and split in half and Esper never pushed to find out what happened to her after she was reported missing? The guy is a fuck up."

"I'm not disagreeing with you, but if you let it get into your head, it's going to keep you from focusing on what we need to do. I need you clear-headed."

Jill called out, "Hope you're hungry," as she approached with two plates. "Double helping of everything. Four eggs. Eight strips of bacon for you," she said to Fisher, "and three sausages for the pretty FBI agent."

"This should improve your attitude" Prado said to Fisher as they looked down at way too much food. "Consider this a new start."

***

"We're going to assume Esper has notified them," Fisher said as they stood in front of the mobile home,

"Yes," Prado replied. "We're going to assume that. We need to get a few things straight about their daughter before we circle back and talk to Tricia."

She mounted the three concrete steps leading to the glass storm door and knocked. A man appeared and stared at them without making any move to open the door. "I'm FBI Special Agent Eileen Prado." She turned her shoulders slightly bringing Fisher into the man's line of sight. "This is Special Agent Ira Fisher. We'd like to talk to you, please."

The man continued staring at Prado, still without any indication that he was going to open the door, prompting her to repeat, "Special Agent Eileen Prado." She placed her badge against the door at his eye level. "We'd like to talk to you, please."

The man disappeared and there was nothing for a long moment before Alice Moore opened the door. "I've already told you everything I know." Her eyes were badly bloodshot and her cheeks and nose were raw.

"We're very sorry about your daughter. I know this timing isn't ideal, but we have a few questions we'd like to ask now about...."

"Now that you know she's dead," a man's voice called from the back of the narrow home. "Now that you know she was strung up like an animal and left like so much garbage."

"We're following up on what happened to Alice and Rochelle Lee so we can...."

"Waste more time?" The voice came from a tall, thin man who had been at the door. He walked from the shadows of a hall leading from a back room. His hair was slicked back, wet, as if he had just emerged from a shower. A damp cotton Tee-shirt clung to his body. His shorts hung loosely on his hips. His eyes were so deep set as to be black holes. He waved a long arm as if dismissing them. "Go do your damn job and leave us alone."

"That's what we're trying to do," Prado said. She reached across the entrance, offering her hand, which the man ignored. "Five minutes, please."

Alice waved them into the home. "Five minutes."

"Thank you," Prado said.

Silas Moore leaned against the jamb of the door dividing the front room from the back of the trailer and folded his arms across his chest. "I gotta get to work. Some of us have to make an honest living."

Alice stood across from a couch lining the wall of the room facing a small kitchen area. "Please." When they were seated, she slowly lowered herself into a facing armchair. Her arms shook against her weight as she did, and she gripped the arms of the chair tightly when she settled.

A small side table was dwarfed by a large, framed photo of a pretty girl who looked like a younger version of her mother. She was smiling broadly, holding a handful of flowers.

Seeing Prado glance at the photo, Moore said, "Rather than sitting here, why don't you get out there" – he pointed at the door – "and find out who took all those years away from her?"

"We're hoping you can provide us with some information that will help us do that," Fisher said.

"You mean *help* like the sheriff has," Moore replied bitterly and took a step toward the couch. "You're here 'cause of Tricia and her saying I killed Ken and everyone else is…." He shook his head in frustration. "You don't give two shits about what happened to Alice."

Alice Moore turned toward her husband. "I told you she promised to find out what she could while doing the other thing." She pivoted back to Prado and Fisher. "That's right, isn't it? You're still going to do that?"

"I promised you we would," Prado answered. "And we will, which is one reason we're here right now."

"Okay, then," Alice said. "What do you want to know?"

"Tricia Plough told us that your daughter spent a lot of time with her husband and other members of his family. That she pursued him, not the other way around."

"And you're buying that shit?" Moore exploded. "He kidnapped my daughter. He's always been mad all these years 'bout Alice leavin' him. He wanted to get back at her and he did."

Prado let a moment pass before continuing. "According to what they've told us, Alice went to Maryville with them, willingly, and was a regular there, spending a lot of time with a man named Frankie Hebert."

Moore came toward her so quickly, Prado had no time to react. Fisher shot out off the couch, his arm extended, and stepped in front of Prado. "Please, stand back, sir."

Moore was shaking with anger, his fists clenched. He looked at Fisher, then down at Prado. "I know Hebert. He's a low-life. Worse, he's evil. My daughter would never have anything to do with him."

Fisher repeated. "Please, stand back." He placed his hand in the center of the man's chest and pushed gently.

Alice Moore pulled on her husband's arm and he retreated. Fisher waited until the man settled against the door jamb before sitting down.

"My Alice and Frankie Hebert," Moore hissed. "What a load of shit."

"This is new information to us," Prado said, "and we're trying to track as much of it as we can."

"Yeah, well, Alice's having anything to do with that man is bullshit."

"According to Mrs. Plough," Prado directed herself to Silas Moore, "on the day Alice went missing, she asked to go with them to Mr. Hebert's, and she asked them to leave her there."

"No, no, no," Moore said emphatically, but without anger, almost pleadingly. He walked over to his wife, placed a hand on her shoulder and caressed it gently. "Ken asked me to put him in touch with Frankie. He wanted to start doin' business with him so them two could start pushin' meth here in Oletha. Ken knew I used to work with Frankie. I said 'no' and that pissed him off. No one says 'no' to Ken. It really sent him over the edge. First Alice and then me tellin' him 'no.'" Moore jabbed a finger as he spoke. "He threatened to get back at me. That's what this is all 'bout. Tricia's tryin' to get back at me, and at Alice, even with Ken in a grave."

"We talked to Mr. Hebert and he told us some of that," Prado said. "Your corroboration it is very helpful. There are a few other things you can help us with." She nodded at an armchair next to his wife's. "This might take longer than five minutes."

Moore looked from his wife to Prado and back at his wife, who patted the seat of the armchair.

When he was seated, Prado continued. "I honestly don't think Mr. Plough had anything to do with what happened to your daughter, but I do think it's possible he took her to see Frankie Hebert, who said Mr. Plough visited him with a young girl called Alice who meets the description of your daughter."

Moore shook his head slowly and worked his jaw as his wife stroked his arm.

"Please, just hear me out," Prado said and scooted forward on the couch. "The way your daughter was found tells me there is something else going on here. I mean beyond what Mr. Plough might have had to do with any of this. The similarities between what happened to Alice and Rochelle Lee…." She paused and looked from Alice to her husband. "Did you hear about her?" They both nodded. "What happened to both of them; the ugliness…that tells me it wasn't Plough. He was a bad person. A despicable one, but there's no indication that he had ever done anything like that before, and you don't go from being a thief, a bully, and well, basically a real asshole, to that kind of crime. We have people coming from the Bureau who can tell us more, and I'll keep you posted on everything. Okay?"

Alice shrugged. "Anything else?"

"Did your daughter know Rochelle Lee?"

"Yes, they were good friends."

"Did you know they spent a lot of time in Maryville?"

Silas Moore began to uncoil, but Alice placed a restraining hand on his arm. "Yes, I did. For about the six or eight months before she disappeared I suspected she was doing that, and I confronted her. She admitted she and Rochelle were going there."

"What the hell?" Moore blurted, turning his body to face his wife. "You never...."

Alice gave her husband a look and tightened her grip on his forearm. "She promised me she and Rochelle were going to the mall there to hang out with friends, and go to the movies. I believed her."

"Do you think it's possible she got a ride to Maryville with Tricia and Mr. Plough?"

Alice nodded. "I think that could've happened."

During this exchange Moore was staring at his wife, tears running down his cheeks.

"I have a question," Alice said. "How is what happened to Alice related to Ken getting killed?"

Prado shrugged. "Frankly, Mrs. Moore, I'm not sure. I think Mrs. Plough has lied to us about some things and I'm trying to get to the bottom of whatever is going on. But one thing is absolutely true. Ken Plough was killed and someone knows something. Mrs. Plough is wrong about your husband being responsible." She looked at Moore. "That just doesn't make sense. But, like I said, I don't think Plough had anything to do with what happened to your daughter. Our responsibility" – she gestured at Fisher –"is to find out if there's been a civil rights violation, and I can see that we're going to have to cut through all this other stuff to find that out."

***

As the car bounced down the pitted road leading from the Moore's, Fisher said, "Okay, so now we know for sure the daughter went to Maryville. She admitted that to her mother."

Prado nodded. "Right, and I'm glad I'm not around for the hell that's breaking loose between Alice and Silas, who obviously didn't know any of it."

Fisher nodded, "Tricia was telling us the truth about taking Alice with them, but she lied about leaving her with Hebert." He gave Prado a sidelong glance. "If you believe Hebert, which you do. Right?"

She shrugged. "I just don't see what he has to gain by lying. In his mind, he has bigger fish to fry but can't with people all over him about Alice and those other girls. So, yeah, about that one thing, I believe what he's telling us."

***

A man was bent over, his head under the hood of one of three trucks parked in Tricia Plough's driveway. He glanced up as Prado and Fisher pulled in behind the truck he was working on, then dove back into the engine.

Fisher offered a "Hello," as they walked past the man and up the walkway to the house. A grunt followed them.

"Friendly sort," Fisher said as he knocked on the door.

Tricia appeared, drying her hands with a dish towel. "Heard what you found in Maryville," she said as she pushed open the screen door. "I told you Alice stayed behind."

Momentarily startled by this matter-of-fact delivery, Prado and Fisher hesitated at the doorway until Tricia followed with, "I'm guessing that's why you're here."

As they walked past her, Prado said, "Yes, but the primary reason is that you lied to us."

Tricia froze in the entryway to the living room. She watched Prado and Fisher sidestep their way between the coffee table and couch, where they remained standing. Fisher considered the toys littering the couch.

"I didn't lie 'bout nothin'," the woman insisted. She remained in the entryway, standing stiffly, her hands on her hips.

"Let's see if we can't get this straightened out, then," Prado said. She nodded at the chairs on the other side of the coffee table while Fisher pushed the toys to one side providing sitting room for him and Prado.

"What's going on?" Crystal Truville's voice came from another room. A cloud of smoke preceded her into the living room. A pained expression crossed her face when she saw Prado and Fisher. "What now?"

"We went to Maryville and talked to Frankie Hebert," Prado answered.

"And?" Crystal said sitting alongside Tricia.

"Tricia, you told us Alice stayed behind with Frankie," Prado said. "But he says"—she turned her attention to Crystal – "she left with you."

"Well, then, he's damn liar."

"He said she drove in the truck with you when you all went to visit one of his meth labs and that was the last time he saw her."

This declaration caused Crystal to pull back her head in surprise. "He just came out and told two FBI agents that we went to one of his labs? You expect us to believe that?"

"The point is we have two very different stories about what happened to Alice and we need to find out who's telling the truth."

Crystal admitted, "She went with me when we visited the labs."

"Let's back up a step," Fisher said. "No one told us about a caravan of people going to see Hebert. All you said was that Ken took Alice to Maryville."

"We always go everywhere together," Crystal said. "That ain't nothin' we'd even think to mention."

"Next time," Fisher said, "think to mention everything to us."

"Like the fact that Alice was with you when you left Maryville," Prado said. "You didn't leave her at Frankie's."

Crystal stood and walked to the front door where she called out, "Orin, get in here."

The sound of heavy footfalls filled the foyer, and a moment of mumbling, preceded the appearance of a huge man. The kind of huge that blocks out the sun when in a doorway or in front of a window. He stopped a few steps into the living room and wiped his hands on the front of his green Tee-shirt leaving swipes of grease. He held his head in a bow. Long hair hid most of his face, but prominent brows were visible and served as a shelf over his dark eyes. The right side of his face was covered with what looked like burn scars that pulled that side of his mouth into a frown. The scars also swirled down his right arm to the top of his hand, the fingers of which appeared to be frozen into the shape of a claw.

"This here is my brother Orin," Crystal said to Prado and Fisher, both of whom rose and offered their hands.

"No," came a rumbling response to their gestures. The word, which sounded as if it came from deep in the man's chest, hung in the air until Crystal explained that, "His hands are greasy from working on the truck." She looked at Prado and Fisher and instructed the man to, "Tell these people about the time we took Alice to Maryville to visit Frankie."

He stared blankly at Crystal and answered. "Yeah, you took her to Maryville."

"Did we come home with her?" she asked him.

"No, she stayed at the red house," he replied, his attention remaining intently on Crystal.

"Thanks, Orin. How's it coming with the truck?"

The man raised his large hand giving a thumbs up as he left the room.

"That doesn't answer my question," Prado objected. "Even if I take your brother at his word that Alice stayed behind, my question was why did you" – she raised her chin at Tricia – "lie and say you left Alice with Hebert?"

"It wasn't a lie," she answered insistently. "That red house is where Frankie's girls hang out. Some of 'em even live there."

"You left her at this 'red house?'"

"Yeah 'cause she said she wanted to stay."

Prado pursed her lips before taking a deep breath and exhaling. "You know, Tricia, we're getting a lot of half-truths and partial stories from you that aren't helping us do our job."

"Which we're doing for *you*," Fisher said pointedly.

Prado sat up and squared her shoulders. "As I've told you, I don't think it makes any sense for Silas Moore to have killed your husband."

"He was mad enough to do it," Tricia said emphatically.

"Maybe, but let's put that aside," Prado said. "Your husband was murdered. Someone knows something. Give me some names of people, other than Silas, who you think might have killed Ken and why they would have done it."

"Get a phone directory for Oletha," Crystal said with a snorted laugh.

"Not helpful," Prado answered, her annoyance obvious. "Let me put it this way, and listen very carefully." She took a breath and pointed at Tricia. "You" – then pointed at Crystal – "have no damn idea who killed Ken. You picked who you thought was the most likely candidate based on what was going on at the time, which was the disappearance of Moore's daughter, and rumors about her and Ken, and pinned the tail on the most likely donkey." She stared hard at the women. "Right?"

"What difference does it make?" Crystal answered, exhaling a cloud of cigarette smoke with her answer. "Ken was killed like a dog in the street and the whole town watched and no one's sayin' nothin'."

Fisher leaned forward. "You want to know what difference it makes?" he responded angrily. "You got us here with an accusation that is beginning to smell like…."

Prado put her hand up, stopping Fisher. "You two lied. You have us chasing our tails and looking foolish, and I don't like looking foolish," she said, leaning into her words. "Yes, someone killed Ken and it doesn't seem likely a street full of people didn't see anything. We're going to do the best we can to find out if your claim makes any sense, but I'm telling you right this damn minute that you're lucky we don't walk away. But any more bullshit and we're outta here. Understand?"

"I'm not lying 'bout Alice stayed behind in Maryville," Tricia said. "It might not a happened 'xactly like I said the first time we talked. I might've forgotten some details."

"Like you didn't leave her with Frankie Hebert," Fisher said.

Crystal answered, "Orin told you she went to the place where Frankie keeps his girls. She did stay behind."

"No more of this kind of shit," Prado said and stood. "When I ask you something, you give me an honest answer. Got it?"

***

"Feel better?" Fisher asked as the two walked toward their car.

"Something just occurred to me," Prado said and doubled back to the truck in the driveway. "Excuse me," she said, approaching the large man, half-hidden under the hood. He peeked at her without pulling away from the engine. "I apologize for interrupting you, but can I ask you a few questions about Alice Moore?"

"Yeah," the man said, remaining half-hidden under the hood.

"When we talked to Hebert about Tricia, your sister and Alice visiting him, Butch, I think his name is...."

"Yeah, his name is Butch," the man confirmed.

"He didn't say you were with them."

"I wasn't."

"Then how do you know Alice stayed behind?"

"I was at Frankie's when my sister and them came. Left when they was talking."

"Why were you there?"

"To hang out."

"But you left before your sister and the others started talking?"

"Yeah."

Prado stood back and waved him forward. "Would you mind coming out from under there? It's hard to hear you."

He slid from under the hood and stood with the right side of his face turned away from Prado. "Thanks, she said. "So, if you left before they did, how do you know Alice stayed behind?"

"'Cause I was at the red house when she got there."

"Red house? What exactly is that?"

"Where everyone parties."

"How did Crystal know you were there?"

"I was standing outside when she, Ken and Tricia dropped Alice off."

Prado smiled at the man and said, "Thanks. I appreciate your talking with me."

***

Staton watched McCay slowly circle the body after which he stopped in front of the figure, widened his stance, and raised his chin. "The skin at the wound margins is white and void of blood. Tells me that whoever did this probably kept her someplace they consider safe, tortured her, sexually molested her, killed her and brought her here to display her."

"I don't know much about this stuff, but you're talking about an 'organized' killer, right?"

McCay nodded. "Yes, that's a descriptor we use when we're talking about some serial offenders. I don't know for certain if that's what we have, but based on what you told me about the other body, or the remains of the other one you found, I'd say we might be on that track. He transported the victim from the crime scene so we wouldn't have one to investigate."

McCay studied the ground around the body. "It doesn't look like he left anything behind we can use to track him. All the attributes of an organized offender, including wrapping the body in plastic to keep it whole and show off his work."

"I thought maybe he wrapped it so he wouldn't have a mess to deal with."

"No," McCay said and lifted the tails of his light brown raincoat off the ground as he squatted. "He wants us to see the art of his kill." He pointed at the body. "The clean lines and precision of what he did to her." He cocked his head slightly and stared at the body. His green eyes held steady, probing. A head of thinning red hair was flecked with gray at the temples. A round, boyish face was made younger by a line of freckles running across the bridge of his nose. He let his focus drop to the ground in front of him and ran his fingers through the leaves, an act less of detection than one of contemplation. "And there are other girls missing in the area, right?"

"Four."

"Not good," McCay said and stood. "We'd better find out who did this fast because he's not going to stop."

"So you *do* think we're dealing with a serial killer."

"I think that's as likely as not, and this guy is a bad one." McCay ran his fingers through his hair. "That was stupid. There aren't any 'good' ones, but this first look says to me he's an angry guy who does what he does because he hates women." He tilted his head toward Staton. "Probably stating the obvious, but it's part of how we classify these offenders. He planned both the rape and murder. Killing them is the final act in his ritual." He pointed at the body. "And he took her right index finger."

Staton stepped past McCay and confirmed this fact. "Didn't notice that what with all the…." He left his thought hanging and turned away.

"Maybe a trophy," McCay said. "A keepsake he can revisit and think about what he's done. Takes him right back to the murder and the pleasure he derived from it."

"You said 'planned'. He picked her for a reason? This wasn't random?"

"No, not random. He has a routine he follows to satisfy his needs. And he has a type that satisfies those needs."

"Young," Staton said. "According to the coroner, the other one was about fifteen."

"He's a sadistic killer or what we call an 'anger-excitation' killer who gets off on torturing his victims. He identifies them. Lures them somehow. Keeps them a while, tortures them, kills them, and then does this." He lowered his head toward the body.

"Jesus Christ. Here in Maryville? That's stuff that happens in Los Angeles, Chicago, New York, not" — he gestured around him — "here."

"This can happen anywhere. And it's likely he lives in the area. They kill in a comfort zone."

"We're not maybe dealing with a long-haul trucker? Jesperson, was that his name? The guy who drove trucks and dumped the bodies all over the country."

McCay nodded. "Keith Jesperson did dump bodies all over the place. Florida, California, Wyoming, Nebraska, Oregon, Washington. He even wrote letters to the press and police departments confessing to his murders and signed them with a smiley face."

"The 'Happy Face Killer'," Staton said. "That's why I remember him. Bizarre name."

"It's not likely that we're dealing with a transient. Whoever put her here," McCay said, nodding at the body, "and the other one, knows the area." He turned and walked away a few steps. "The other one was left around here too if I remember the information you sent."

"About three hundred yards from this spot."

"Okay, then," McCay continued. "We are likely dealing with someone who knows the area. A person driving through wouldn't be familiar with these woods and sure as hell wouldn't be trekking through all of this" – he kicked at the ground cover – "unless he has a specific reason to display the bodies here. He's attracted to this area for some reason."

"Didn't Bundy drag bodies into the mountains in Washington and Colorado, miles away from where he lived?"

"You really don't want this guy to be from around here, do you?

"Hell, no."

McCay smiled dourly. "There's always a possibility that whoever's doing this is not from around here, but that's not the way these people usually operate. Granted, I just got here and there's a lot I still don't know. There's no fool-proof template for this" – he gestured at the surroundings – "but my experience tells me we're dealing with someone who lives and works around here. At least within a 25-mile radius."

Staton cocked his head toward his shoulder microphone and responded to a call from a dispatcher. "Who wants to see me?"

***

Staton walked briskly down the hallway, McCay in tow. As he passed the receptionist's desk she stood and called after him apologetically, "I told him he couldn't smoke in the conference room."

Staton pushed through the door in the wall of glass and demanded, "Put out that cigarette or I'll kick your ass out of here."

Frankie Hebert, slouched in a chair, his feet on the table, took a long drag on the cigarette burning it down to the filter, and held the butt toward Staton. "Where?" A wave of smoke came with the question.

Staton filled small cup with water from a cooler and set it down in front of Hebert, who made a show of dropping the butt into the water.

Staton slapped Hebert's feet off the table and walked to the opposite side, gesturing for McCay to join him. He sat and stared at Hebert a moment before asking, "What the hell are you doing here, Frankie?"

Hebert nodded at McCay. "Who's your friend?"

"Special Agent Robert McCay meet our local scumbag, Frankie Hebert."

Hebert sat up in the chair and pulled it closer to the table. "Another Feeb? We're crawlin' with'em." He brushed ashes off the front his long-sleeved black shirt. "Sure glad I got dressed up to come down here." He patted his thighs. "Even put on my good Levis, and tie-up shoes." He raised one foot. "Socks too."

"What do you want?" Staton asked impatiently.

"I want to help you find those missing girls."

Staton turned his head slightly, eyes remaining on Hebert. "You want to help me find the missing girls?" he asked incredulously.

"I had a nice conversation with those other FBI people and it got me thinkin'. You and them think I have somethin' to do with them girls, but I don't." Hebert's face tightened, his habitual smirk disappearing. "I'm telling you, Leo, I don't know nothin' 'bout them. I swear on my mother's grave."

Staton blew out a laugh and directed himself to McCay. "He testified against his mother as part of a plea deal to stay out of jail when they were both arrested for manufacturing and selling meth."

"Yeah, I did, 'cause she told me to. Said there was no reason for both of us to go to jail. That's how much she loved me, and after she got out, I took real good care of her 'til the day she died."

"Guilt," Staton shot at Hebert.

"Just the love of a son for his mother."

"Such bullshit, but, for the sake of argument, let's say I believe you about the girls, which I don't, how can you help?"

Hebert put his forearms on the table and looked at McCay. "This must be real serious shit. Bringin' in the feds. Why is it I think there's more goin' on here? More than just some missin' girls." He raised his arms. "Not that that's not a big deal, which it is," he said without conviction, "but it ain't all of it, right?"

"You don't get to ask questions. Only answer them. Now, how can you help us, other than admitting you had something to do with the girls going missing?"

"What're the chances you and all your FBI people can walk into the South side and get any answers? And that's where you'll be goin' 'cause it's where the girls hung out." Hebert raised his eyebrows. "I'll tell you what your chances are." He touched his index finger to his thumb and held it in front of Staton. "Zero. And if you tried, I'd be the first one to hear 'bout it. My people would come to me and ask what I wanted'em to say to you." He smiled. "So, whaddya say you cut out the middle men, and that sweet thing Ellen, or whatever her name is, who ain't gonna find out shit, and you just deal with me directly? Let me see what I can find out. Tell me what you want to ask. Tell me what you got and what else you're lookin' for." Hebert reached toward a cigarette pack on the table, pulled one out and twirled it between his fingers. "You know, make me like a deputy or somethin'. When I ask, my people give me answers. Answers you're gonna need." He raised his chin toward Staton. "Be realistic, Leo, they ain't gonna say nothin' to you."

"Where were the girls from?" McCay asked Hebert.

"From?"

"Were they runaways? Were they locals? How old were they?"

"Yeah, some were all of those things and mostly young." Hebert smirked. "We get a lot of rich kids from the North side, too, and they all come to me so, like I said, you gotta go through me to find out what you need to know. We good?"

Staton drummed his fingers on the table a moment before responding. "You should already have an idea what happened to the girls since they hung around with you. Why not just tell me what you know if you're sincere about this."

"I don't know shit right now. I ain't tried to find out 'cause until those other feds came knocking" – he raised his right hand interrupting himself – "truth be told, I didn't much care. But, and I'm being square with you, Leo, if we have you pullin' out all the stops, and the FBI nosin' around, it interferes with my business. Scares folks, my customers, and I can see this ain't goin' away anytime soon." He pointed at McCay. "And now you got even more of'em running around" – Hebert sat up straight and mimed adjusting a tie – "with their suits and ties and lookin' all official. Let's just say I recognize it's in my best interests to work with you. It'll keep you outta my business."

Staton forced out a laugh. "You think you can keep me out of your business by getting into mine? Are you out of your mind?"

"I know you've gotta stay on me about some of my stuff, Leo. I ain't thinkin' you're gonna stop the regular cops 'n robbers shit. That's what makes it so much fun." Hebert gestured at Staton. "You 'gainst me. I like that part of the game."

Staton came out of his chair. "Game?"

"Oh, for fuck's sake, Leo. Relax. This thing with the girls is a whole different thing than our usual dealings. It'll bring you and your buddies here 'round early and stayin' late. You'll be on me like stink on shit.

You ain't gonna find nothin', but you'll be a fucking nuisance." Hebert laughed. "Yeah, you'll be nothin' but a bigger nuisance than you are now, Leo, and you'll get nothin'. Believe me, I can help."

"In exchange for what?"

"Nothin'. Well, that ain't entirely true. I won't have to worry 'bout seein' you and your idiot cops, and" – he pointed at McCay – "the Feebs in my neighborhood, which is something. You all won't be scarin' people off the streets." Hebert put the cigarette in his mouth. "One other thing I'll need if we're gonna be cooperatin' on this."

"I didn't say we're going to be cooperating."

"But if we was, I'd need to be given immunity for smokin' in here."

***

The man stood in the middle of the darkened room. It smelled of cigarettes and urine. Yellow from sodium street lights filtered through broken blinds. He walked over to a couch – the single piece of furniture in an area strewn with fast food wrappers, soft drink bottles and beer cans – and poked the person lying face down. No reaction. He kicked at a figure on the floor sprawled across the cushions that had been removed from the couch getting a "Fuck you, leave me alone."

A boy was propped up in one corner of the room, his legs stretched out in front of him. He was singing softly and picking at bleeding scabs on his face.

The man walked into the kitchen directly behind the front room. The cabinet doors were open, some only the remnants of doors that had been ripped off their hinges. The cupboards were bare. Pots and pans, utensils and broken plates were scattered on the floor. Piping and wires poked out of the walls where the refrigerator and stove had been. A dishwasher had been pulled away from the wall but was still attached to rubber hoses.

A soft light that changed colors and danced along the walls of an adjoining hallway attracted his attention. He walked into the hallway and saw that the light was coming from a door facing him. He could hear conversation as he approached. As he neared the opening, kicking debris out of his way, the light and sound shut off. He stopped at the door, which had been forced open, the top was hanging at an angle, and peeked inside. A girl sat on a mattress in front of a window. The light from the street allowed him to see her silhouette in the dark room. He pulled his hoodie over his head and tightened it around his neck.

"Hey," he said, almost in a whisper.

The girl stared at him.

"Whatcha got?" he pointed at an object in her hand.

The girl raised her hand from her lap displaying a phone.

"Been listening to music?"

She nodded.

"What kind?"

"All kinds," she said. "Been waiting for my boyfriend, but I don't think he's coming."

"This is a nasty place to wait for someone."

The girl poked at her phone and it lit up showing her plump face, which would be pretty when the high cheek bones and straight nose defeated the baby fat. She used the sleeve of a stained hoodie to wipe away tears that were rolling down her cheeks. "It's better'n sleepin' in the street." She looked at him, her face pinched in question. "What're you doin' here?"

He shrugged. "Nothin'."

The girl returned her attention to the screen, the light from which played colors across her face.

"I got some meth."

The girl jerked her head up. A smile animated her face. "Really?"

"Not with me. I got some at my place. Be happy to share. More fun than bein' alone."

The smile faded. "You're not gonna make me suck your dick or anything like that are you?"

"No," the man said, shaking his head. "I just don't like bein' alone."

The girl surprised the man with her energy as she leapt off the mattress and skipped toward him. He raised his shoulder as if preparing to deflect a punch.

"How far?"

"Oletha," he said and backed into the hallway.

The girl hesitated. "Oletha? That's where I live." She laughed. "I come all the way here to wait for someone who's supposed to be bringing me some meth and wind up going back home to get it."

"I can take you home after."

"Probably stay with you a few days. Make my Mom worry so when I come home she's too busy thankin' God to be mad at me."

"Whatever you want. My truck's up the street."

The girl passed him as they walked into the kitchen and she started toward the front room. "No," the man said redirecting her to a door leading out of the kitchen into the back yard. "Truck's out back."

They walked through the overgrown yard. He cautioned her to avoid an engine block hidden in the high grass, and ushered her through an opening in the fence, where the planks had been pushed to the ground. They emerged in an alley that ran behind the block and followed it to a side street, where they got into a Ford pickup.

"Ford F-100," the girl said as she bounced playfully on the bench seat. "My Dad had one. This sucker's old." She ran her hand along the dashboard. "You take real good care of it."

"Got it as a present and feel like I should keep it nice. Your Dad shoulda kept his and given it to you."

"He ran off in it," she said matter-of-factly. "I'm gonna get one just like it when I have 'nough money."

"You work?"

"Still in school, but this is my last year and then I'm gonna get a job."

"What kinda job?"

"One that will pay me enough to get an F-100," she said with a laugh.

The girl sang along with the music on the radio, stopping only to remark on the neighborhoods they passed. "I like it here in Maryville. Better'n Oletha, right?"

The question hung in the air for a beat before the man said, "I never seen you there before."

"At the red house?"

"No, Oletha."

"That's 'cause I'm in Maryville most of the time. Nothin' to do in Oletha, but I seen you." She poked him in the arm playfully. "You're easy to remember."

The man felt himself stiffen and a white-hot poker of anger stabbed him in the chest, almost doubling him over. He gripped the steering wheel tightly and took in a deep breath cooling the anger enough that he could speak. "Oh, yeah? You remember me?"

"'Course 'cause you're so big. Like a bear."

The man felt himself relax. He forced a laugh. "Yeah, I guess so." The girl started singing again and he waited a few minutes before saying, "Your boyfriend ain't a good person for leavin' you alone."

"He probably went home. All his parents wanted was for him to get me outta the house. I was there for a coupla days. He's an asshole and it serves him right that I'm gonna get some and he ain't." The girl stared blankly out the windshield a beat before adding, "I kinda liked his parents." She laughed loudly. "That's funny, but I didn't mean it to be. Sometimes the funniest things are stuff you don't mean to be funny."

"Yeah, well, you don't need him or his parents," the man said as he pulled in front of a small house centered on a large, well-kept lot.

The girl pushed out of the truck and stood on the edge of a swale. "You got a real nice house, mister." She looked up and down the street. "You ain't got no neighbors. Way away from anything. Nice and quiet, I imagine."

"Yeah, real quiet."

She ran down into and up out of a dip in the swale and up toward his house, which was set on a rise. The yard was dark, escaping illumination from the single light mounted high on a telephone pole halfway down the block. She pointed at a screened in porch. "Can we sit out there and smoke?"

"Sure," the man said as he pulled a chain from his pocket and played with a handful of keys. "Whatever you want."

The girl ran up the stairs to a wooden porch, then down to the far end and peeked around the corner of the house. "Is that a pond back there?"

"Yeah and it is," he answered, pushing open the front door.

She rushed into the house and made a beeline for a kitchen to the right of the entrance, where she brushed her hand along the inside wall looking for a light switch. The man hurried behind and grabbed her arm. "No," he blurted, startling her. He pulled his hand away quickly and pointed overhead. "I'm sorry but those are too bright." He walked across the kitchen to a set of polished cedar pantry doors, which he opened, and a dull yellow illuminated a number of shelves. "Better, right?" he said standing away from the rectangle of light that painted the floor in front of the doors.

"Mind if I eat something?" she asked, walking to a refrigerator that sat between the pantry and a stove; her hand poised to open it. "I'm starving. Been like two days since I ate anything."

"Why don't you let me grab some cookies and chips?"

"Got any ice cream?" she asked.

"I do." He pointed to a door on the back wall of the kitchen. "Go on down into the TV room and make yourself comfortable. Got a 52-inch flat screen and we can get music through the speakers, if you want."

She peeked into the pantry at empty shelves. "There's nothing in there."

He nodded toward the refrigerator. "I'll get us some stuff to eat. You go ahead and I'll bring it along."

She scrunched her brow in question. "You keep chips and cookies in your refrigerator? That's weird."

The man took in a long breath and stared at the floor. Breathing out, he said, "Just go on down and I'll bring lots of stuff to eat."

"I thought we was gonna smoke on the patio? Can we eat out there before we smoke?"

He stood still a moment before moving abruptly toward the girl, grabbed her by the arm, and yanked her toward the door. Momentarily confused, she did not resist until she was looking down a dimly lit wooden staircase with cold air rushing up toward her. She stiffened. "You promised me...."

Before she could complete her thought he threw her down the stairs. She tumbled head first and hit the cement floor hard. He walked down and stood over the girl, who was bleeding from her forehead. Her right arm was bent awkwardly beneath her body.

"Get up," he demanded and kicked her violently in the side. She whimpered but remained still.

The light coming from the single pole lamp extended across the ceiling falling on two of the other three girls in the room. One sat on her soiled mattress facing the wall; the other lay on her side tucked tightly into a fetal position. The third girl was barely visible, only her shackled ankle and calf showing from the shadows under the stairs.

The man grabbed the unconscious girl by the hair and dragged her to a mattress propped up against the wall. He pulled it down, yanked her up onto the stained padding, and reached for the cuff on a chain that extended from an iron plate screwed into the wall. He secured it around her ankle, locked it, stood, and shook his head. "What'd you have to go and make me do that for?" He gestured at her misshapen arm. "You broke your damn arm. That's gonna hurt like shit."

He stepped away from the mattress, stood in the middle of the cold, dank room, and looked at the other three figures. "Okay," he said proudly. "A new friend for you." He walked over to the girl who was facing the wall and grabbed her shoulder, turning her toward the open room. "You know her? I found her at the red house."

She shook her head, eyes glazed, not focusing on the man or her surroundings.

"Dina Rounds," came a nasal response. "We went to school together." The third girl propped herself up on one elbow and scooted from the shadows. Her eyes almost swollen shut, the bridge of her nose pushed under her right eye, she spit out, "You motherfucker. She's even younger and smaller than the rest of us. She's not right in the head. Gonna fuck her, you ugly piece of shit."

"Shut up," came from the girl who popped up out of her fetal position. "Please shut up," she pleaded. "Don't make him mad."

The man stood, hands on his hips and stared at the badly beaten girl. "I'm ugly?" He walked to her and pulled the mattress from under the stairs causing her leg to be yanked hard as the chain lost its slack. She screamed and reached toward her ankle where the cuff had cut a deep gash.

"Please," the fetal position girl yelped. "She's not thinking right. We'll teach her better."

"I'm ugly?" the man spit, oblivious to the begging. He was animated with anger which seemed to add to his size. He stood straight, his head almost touching the ceiling, held his arms out from his sides and repeated, "I'm ugly?"

"No," the girl screamed. "No more." She curled back into a fetal position, burying her face in the mattress.

"You should see what you look like." He fumbled through his keys, separated one from the rest, unlocked the cuff, grabbed her by the neck, and threw her off the mattress onto the cement floor. "You're too ugly to fuck. So ugly I wouldn't even let you suck my dick. Say goodbye to your friends. It was getting' too crowded down here anyway. I ain't made of money. Can't keep feedin' all of you."

MONDAY

Prado, Fisher and Esper walked into the conference room where Staton and McCay stood over the table littered with open files and single pages.

"I think you all know each other," Staton said to Prado, Fisher and McCay. "Sheriff John Esper, this is Special Agent Bob McCay."

Prado approached the table. "What are we looking at?"

"These are the files on the murdered and missing girls," McCay answered. "We spent the weekend going over them."

"We spent the weekend trying to sort through what we've come up with, which, unfortunately, isn't much," Prado said and stared down at the files. "Anything of particular interest for us?" She added, "I mean does it help with what Ira and I are doing here?"

"I think it might," McCay said, "but first things first." He gestured toward the chairs surrounding the table. "Let's sit." He remained standing. "From what I can tell based on the coroner's reports, the second girl died from a loss of blood. Incidentally, Marshal Staton, please thank the coroner for his swift work."

"He's a she. Our local undertaker, but I'll pass that along. And call me Leo."

McCay started pacing. "Rochelle Lee was tortured severely; punctured a number of times with a knife, or something like a knife, could've been a screwdriver; she had some broken bones in her face and a few broken ribs." He stopped pacing and tapped his index finger on a page with large block letters spelling out "Rochelle Lee" and containing the outline of a figure. "Those lines" — he pointed at some etchings in the abdominal area – "are sewing needles he inserted into her anus and vagina."

Prado, Fisher and Esper deflated, shoulders and heads dropping. "Sewing needles?" asked Fisher.

McCay nodded.

Esper asked, with a quick glance at the drawing, "While she was alive?"

Another nod from McCay. "We're dealing with a sexual sadist."

Staton held up his hand. "Wait a minute. Yesterday you described him as an anger-'something' killer."

"Yes, anger-retaliatory killer. And he is. He's also a sexual sadist. What we call a "mixed offender, meaning he has multiple motivations." McCay tapped his finger on the coroner's report. "This tells me he needs the stimulation of sexual torture to satisfy his compulsion. These offenders get sexually aroused by inflicting pain. The more pain the greater the arousal. Sometimes torture is the only way they can get off. These" – he turned the rendering of the figure toward the others and pointed at the markings indicating where Rochelle Lee had been violated with the needles – "is what really gets him off. Then he kills them and that allows him to fully vent his anger. He's likely acting out revenge on a symbolic target."

McCay sat down, located a briefcase at his feet, which he placed on the table, opened, and lifted out a sheaf of papers. He shuffled through them, picked some out and created a pile. "Information on what we're dealing with." He asked Staton, "Would it be possible to get copies made for everyone?"

Prado asked for "A time out, please." She placed her hand flat on top of the coroner's report and directed herself to McCay. "I have a question. And I even know the answer to what I'm about to ask, but I need to hear it out loud from your mouth. We have two dead girls. It takes three for an investigation to be identified as involving a serial murderer. Are you *saying* there are more victims? Are you *assuming* there are more? Hell, are you saying the first and second victims were killed by the same person?"

"Whoever did that" – McCay nodded at the report in front of Prado – "is a sick puppy, and he will do it again. Yes, I believe the two were killed by the same person. Like Rochelle Lee, the first victim was missing her right index finger, which is very significant. She also had broken ribs and her skull showed indications of a beating. The same injuries were inflicted on the second girl. And I'm almost certain we'll find there are more victims."

"You said this guy is venting his anger," Esper said. "What the hell is he so angry about?"

"When we figure out who he is, I'll answer that for you," McCay responded. "As to what we do know, we've found that the most significant forces driving these killers are power and control. Ted Bundy said something I'll never forget. It's burned into my memory. He said, 'You feel the last bit of breath leaving their body. You're looking into their eyes. A person in that situation is God!' It's about control for a lot of them and that's because most of these offenders have little to no control over their own lives. Our guy was probably bullied as a child, likely sexually abused, had no mooring, no stable home life, and as an adult he has failed in his relationships, especially with women. He has also failed professionally, or at the very least not accomplished what he wants in life; what he expected to accomplish. This causes him to act out in ways that give him a feeling of control."

"'Acts out,'" Fisher said. "Now there's a euphemism if I ever heard one."

"Based on what I saw," Prado said, "we're dealing with an organized killer, not someone like Mullin or Ramirez, right?"

"You already know a little about this," McCay said. "You'll learn more from that material." He nodded at the stack he had pulled from his briefcase.

"Hold on," Esper said. "Organized? And who are" – he nodded at Prado – "Ramirez and the other person?"

"Mullin and Ramirez were serial killers," McCay said and shifted his attention to Esper. "An organized offender plans his murders and is under control when he kills. He is well organized to the point of being meticulous. Every detail of the crime is planned out well in advance, and the offender is careful to leave no incriminating evidence. It's likely he holds down a job, could be married and have kids. He probably has a car to transport his victims."

"Has a job and is married?" Esper questioned. "I thought you said they failed professionally and in relationships."

"I did. Gary Ridgway, the Green River Killer, was married but felt unfulfilled. He also had other problems, but failure at home was a key. He also was bullied at work and not satisfied with his job. He didn't feel like a success. He didn't feel like he was in control of his life. He took out his frustrations on the prostitutes he frequented, killing them, and leaving nothing that authorities could trace back to him. Until they did."

Prado offered, "What we see on the outside is a family man with a good job. Ridgway killed 44 women."

McCay corrected her. "Forty-eight. The definition of the banality of evil. Then there's the not so banal. The disorganized offender. Loners. No relationships at all, not even bad ones. No one wants to have anything to do with these people. They can't hold down a job. They kill spontaneously and perform sex acts on the dead body. They don't make any effort to cover up what they do and sometimes don't even recall any details of the crime."

"Christ," Esper said, "I thought *all* these loonies were disorganized and out of their damn minds."

"'Out of their minds'," McCay said, "is relative. I've seen some who were truly out of their minds. Eileen mentioned Herbert Mullin. He killed 13 people in a five-month period to, as he put it, prevent earthquakes from ravaging California. No planning. No attempts to cover up what he did. He killed a priest during his confession because he claimed the man wanted to be sacrificed. Killed another man who he said was Jonah from the Bible and wanted to be thrown off his boat. He was later diagnosed as a paranoid schizophrenic. In other words, he *was* out of his mind.

"But that's not our guy. What we have going on here is more along the lines of Ridgway. Maybe even more calculating. Rochelle Lee had marks on her ankle like she had been chained up somewhere. And our Unsub must have a safe place; a place he can spend time with his victims to do what he needs to do."

Esper stared at the tabletop, slowing tapping it with his index finger. "You're saying he's going to be hard to find and he's gonna keep doing this stuff unless we find him."

"Yeah," McCay answered. "That's what I'm saying. These guys don't stop because they can't stop."

"Jesus Christ," Esper said through his hands, now cradling his face. "Have you ever dealt with anything like this? I'm talking personally not something you studied about."

"Unfortunately," McCay said, "I have. David Parker Ray soundproofed a truck trailer he called his 'toy box,' where he tortured women using sex toys, restraints, masks, syringes." McCay waved his hand. "The comparison isn't perfect, but I'd say it's similar. Unlike Parker, who was so controlled he had an audio-tape of his voice that played when he wasn't physically in the trailer that explained what he was going to do to his victims, I think our guy is more driven by anger. He is a sexual sadist for sure, but leaning toward the anger-retaliatory killer on the spectrum. He intends to kill his victims. It's no accident, or mistake. With Parker the killing often came as a result of torture. Almost a by-product."

"You're basing all your conclusions on what you found in" – Prado pointed at the coroner's report – "that?"

"No, not entirely. When we reconstructed the skeletal remains of the first victim, we found... Well, it's more what we didn't find. The area where she was found showed no signs of blood. What I see is a scene pretty much like we found with the second victim, which is what tells me she was likely tortured and killed somewhere else and brought to where she was displayed. And, not incidentally, both were displayed in the same way."

"This just keeps getting better," Fisher said, stood and walked to the window looking out across the front of the building.

The room fell into a silence. Fisher turned away from the window and said, "I attended a few lectures at Quantico when I was in training and I understand the difference between a signature and the MO in these types of cases. If this guy's signature is splitting open his victims and hanging them up like animals. What's his MO?"

"Wait," Esper demanded, his hands falling away from his face. "Signature? That's different from his MO?"

"Completely" McCay answered with a nod. "MO is what the offender has to do to subdue his victim before committing the crime.

Bundy knocked his unconscious with a tire iron. Randy Kraft used drugs and alcohol to incapacitate them. Jack the Ripper blitz attacked his victims to gain control.

"The signature, on the other hand, is the murderer's personal touch, his stamp that makes the act uniquely his. Positioning bodies in a humiliating way, biting victims on the breast, covering their faces, washing their hair. A case I worked, Charles Albright, removed the eyes of each of his victims. That was his signature. I heard later he spent all of his time in prison drawing women's eyes. Jack the Ripper's was hacking and mutilating the bodies. With our guy, posing the bodies and splitting them open appears to be the signature we're currently working with."

"So," Fisher said, "any ideas on how our guy works? His MO?"

"No," McCay said. "That's not clear yet."

"But the two girls we found in the Woods and the four missing ones do have a common denominator," Staton said. "Ken Plough."

"We haven't found any of that," Fisher blurted.

Prado nodded at Fisher. "No, we haven't. We know the Moore girl and Plough were linked, but you're telling us you've found evidence that *all of them* have some connection to him?"

"Yes," Staton said. "Once we ID'ed Lee, I remembered I'd seen her before. She'd been arrested for dealing drugs, and on a hunch I brought up the files of the other missing girls, and all of them had a jacket for dealing. And they all admitted they sold to Ken Plough."

McCay jumped in. "This Plough connection creates common ground for *your*" – he gestured in the direction of Prado and Fisher – "and *our* investigations. We trade information as we go."

"Hello all," caught everyone in the room by surprise. Frankie Hebert leapt through the door, arms spread. "As requested, here I am."

"As who requested?" Prado asked.

"Me," Staton answered.

Hebert took a seat at the head of the table and, with a flourish, slapped down a pack of cigarettes. "Damn right. Leo asked me to join you wonderful people. Class up the joint a little."

"Why?" Prado, Fisher and Esper asked simultaneously, looking at Staton, who opened his mouth to respond.

"'Cause I knew all of'em," Hebert shoehorned in the answer. "Ken, the girls. All of'em. Business and pleasure brought'em to me."

Staton acknowledged that, "Frankie made a suggestion in an earlier discussion and as much as it pains me deeply to admit it, it has some merit, so I thought you'd like to hear what he has to say."

Hebert beamed. "That might be the nicest thing you ever said to me, Leo."

"Just say what you have to say," Staton responded flatly.

"You all sure as hell can't come into my neighborhood looking all FBI- and Sheriff-like and get any answers you'll need to find out what happened to those girls."

Fisher studied Herbert's blue-jeaned, tie-dyed ensemble. "Fashion makes that much of a difference?"

"Really?" Prado said, her voice high-pitched. "We're going to use him?"

"I'm willing to use whatever we can to make some headway," Staton said. "We have four girls missing. Leslie Rainey, 16, hasn't been seen in almost two years. Wanda Reed, 15, not for a year. Brenda Yellin, 16, six months, and Susan Alvarez about a month."

"And we have three in Oletha," Esper said. "Gone three years. Ida and Wilhelmina Geist, and Lydia Slocum."

"We have absolutely nothing of substance on any of them, other than who they are, including the two we found strung up in the Woods."

"Strung up?" Hebert said. "Whaddya talkin' 'bout."

"I'll explain later," Staton said. "Right now, tell us what you have in mind."

Hebert lit a cigarette. He pointed at Staton. "I got immunity, right?

Staton waved away a cloud of smoke Hebert blew in his direction. "You're killing yourself, asshole."

"I know all the girls Leo mentioned," Hebert said proudly.

"That should put you high on the suspect list, then," Fisher responded.

"Why would I want to harm any of'em? They were friends of mine," Hebert said insistently. "And – if we're being honest – good customers. Bought a lot of weed and meth, and brought me people.

Makin'em disappear would be like Walmart chasin' people outta their stores."

Fisher looked around the table. "Seriously, we're working with this guy?"

Staton held up a hand, stopping Hebert, who was shaking his head and about to respond to Fisher. "The girls dealt for Frankie and bought meth from him with the proceeds of their sales. Somewhere along the line they figured out they could make a few extra bucks by selling some of it to Plough, who, according to what John discovered, was reselling it in Oletha."

"Didn't know nothin' 'bout that shit," Hebert said.

"The girls were working around you, Frankie," Fisher said with a healthy note of self-satisfaction. "Had their own businesses on the side."

Hebert smiled. "Actually proud of 'em. They was using their heads. Made some money for themselves. Wouldn't have to spread their legs that way."

"Charming," Prado said.

"My girls did me a favor," Hebert said directly to Fisher. "Got Plough into the business and then he needed more product and came to me. Woulda worked out real good if he hadn't got killed."

"Where the hell were you during all this?" Fisher asked Esper.

"Already told you, I did what I could. I never could catch Ken dealing or holding, and I got no help from the parents, and, of course, nothing from the kids."

"And the missing girls?" Fisher directed at Staton. "Didn't you let him know that the four from here had this connection to Plough?"

"The first girl went missing two years ago. The second a year ago. Then six months. These were individual cases. We didn't put two and two together until we started looking at all the information and the bigger picture emerged within the past few months."

McCay raised his arms. "Revisiting what 'we could have done' maybe 'should have done' isn't getting us anywhere."

"So," Fisher said, "how are we going to go about this?" He cocked his head in the direction of Hebert. "How are we going to work with him?"

The way we would with any CI," Staton answered.

Fisher pulled his head back in surprise. "Let him go on his own?"

"You want to babysit me?" Hebert asked Fisher.

"We go ahead and work the case and take a look at whatever Frankie brings us," Staton said. "If he brings us anything worthwhile, and we need to move on it, we'll figure out how when it comes up."

"Meaning?" Prado asked.

"Meaning," Staton replied, "if we need to corroborate what he tells us, or move on it, and we still need his involvement, we'll find a way to handle it."

"Fancy way of sayin' he thinks I might lie to you all," Hebert offered, "and you'll need to – what is the fancy word for makin' sure I ain't lying? 'Corroborate' what I tell you."

"Him aside," Prado said, with a wave in Hebert's direction, "is this now a single investigation?"

"We'll be operating around the same axis," McCay said. "Ken Plough. We'll likely go in different directions from there, but I'm sure we'll be sharing information."

Staton walked to the door of the conference room where an officer was waving to get his attention. He stepped into the hallway, listened and then bent over, putting his hands on his knees. The officer looked into the room, his face a combination of question and alarm.

***

Prado pushed herself away from the wall directly opposite a door that read "County Detention." Fisher and McCay walked into the hall dressed in blue jumpsuits at least two sizes too big. They had rolled the sleeves up to their wrists and hiked the pant legs around their ankles, but as soon as they started walking the cloth fell down around their shoes.

"Very fashionable," she said as they walked toward the building exit.

"I'm not about to ruin another suit," Fisher said.

Prado suggested, "We need to get a picture of this. FBI agents in prison jumpsuits."

An officer waved them over to a cruiser. "You're the FBI agents, right?" he asked, staring hard at Fisher and McCay.

"We are," Prado said, "as difficult as that might be to believe."

After a moment's hesitation, calculating his response, the officer put his hand on the top of the cruiser. "I'll drive you to the scene."

In the passenger seat, Prado leaned forward to see the officer's nameplate. "Deputy Laydon, I'm Special Agent Eileen Prado and" — she turned her shoulders toward the backseat — "these well-dressed men are Special Agents Robert McCay and Ira Fisher. We didn't get a lot of detail about what's going on other than there's another body in the Woods. Is that right?"

"Yes, ma'am" he answered stiffly.

"What else can you tell us?"

"LeeAnne Womack and her boyfriend Lem Barney skipped school and went to the Woods." He glanced quickly at Prado. "You want to know everything?"

"Everything."

"They were…uh, making out when LeeAnne saw what she thought was a mannequin hanging from a tree."

"That'll ruin the mood," Fisher interjected.

"They went to check it out and it was a body that had been split open. She called 911 and then she and Lem came to the station."

"Thank you," Prado said. She turned to Fisher and McCay. "That explains why Staton grabbed John and pushed us out the door. He wanted us out here quickly. They must be talking to the kids."

As the car pulled into the small parking area, McCay pointed to a blanket lying on the ground at the head of the path leading into the thicket. He asked Laydon, "Did the kids say anything about seeing or dropping a blanket out here?"

"No, sir."

The four got out of the car and walked to the blanket. McCay squatted, pulled a pen from his suit coat pocket, and straightened a folded corner. "Dried blood." He nodded at a large stain.

"Blanket's not the kids', then," Fisher said. "Think the victim was carried out here in that?"

McCay stood. "Could be." He instructed Laydon to "Cordon off this entire area" and pointed at the narrow entrance to the parking area. "Starting there."

Her eyes on the blanket, Prado said, "That's really sloppy. Our monster has made his first mistake."

"Maybe," McCay said and started toward the shrub line. "And don't think of these people as monsters. If you do, you're going to be looking in the wrong direction."

"An emotional response," Prado said. "My bad. I'm still trying to wrap my head around what we're dealing with. It's one thing to sit in a classroom and read about this sort of thing. It's different out here in the real world."

"It's messier," McCay said. "As far as leaving the blanket behind, he could be getting careless. Ted Bundy once said that, 'The first time you're careful. By the thirtieth time, you can't remember where you left the lug wrench.'"

"Perfect metaphor from the man who clubbed his victims over the head with a tire iron," Fisher remarked and almost ran into McCay who had stopped.

McCay held out his arms, making sure no one walked past him, and yelled, "Officer, we need you."

Prado and Fisher stood on either side of McCay. A small figure was tied spread eagle, her arms and legs secured to two trees.

"Officer, where are you?" McCay yelled without taking his eyes off the body.

"Coming," a voice replied.

As the man came up on them, McCay said, "Tape it off. Maintain a twenty-yard radius."

McCay approached the body. "Same offender for sure," he said, and squatted, studying the ground underneath. "The cutting was done somewhere else and she bled out there." He pointed at the victim's right hand. "Index finger is missing."

McCay stood and circled around behind the body with Fisher and Prado facing him. He walked closer and examined the bindings, then looked up at the trees. "He's very comfortable here. That's going to help us."

"How?" Prado asked.

"If he's compelled to bring his victims here, and I think he is, we have the body dump site and he'll return."

"Really?" Fisher said. "That would be stupid."

"I don't mean he'll come back to this exact spot. There's a lot of acreage for him to work with. But we have narrowed it down some."

"And there's something else," McCay continued, backing away from the body, keeping his focus on the figure. "These used to be called 'stranger killings' because the offender and the victim don't know each other. Most homicides are committed by someone known to the victim, police focus on family, friends, business partners, lovers. The majority of serial murderers, however, don't know their victims. There is no visible relationship between the offender and the victim. But I'm thinking that might not be the case here."

"Why?" Fisher asked.

"We have a relatively small demographic, and a circumscribed physical area. The missing girls operated in a world that revolved around Hebert, and they all knew Plough. They were also selected from that circle, so I'd say the chances are good the offender was, at the very least, familiar with the people in that circle."

McCay walked around the body and stood with Prado and Fisher. "I apologize if I sound clinical and detached."

"No apology necessary," Prado said. "It's the nature of what we do. You need some distance."

"Make sure it always remains what you do," McCay said.

"Don't take your work home with you," Fisher translated.

"Or let it seep into who you are. I've seen this sort of thing take a bite out of people's souls. It almost killed John Douglas."

"The profiler John Douglas?" Fisher asked.

"The same," McCay answered. "He nearly died from viral encephalitis. He worked himself to the brink of exhaustion, which was piled on top of the psychic damage from constant exposure to this depth of violence. It wrecked his body. He was diagnosed with PTSD. He was a mess. This" – he raised his eyes to the body – "can blacken your soul."

"How do you handle it?"

"I lie to myself. I tell myself that every case is going to be my last one. That I'll retire.'" McCay chopped at the air, gesturing a change of subject. "But before I do, we have this to deal with this."

Prado held onto a dozen questions prompted by McCay's warning and went with, "Where do we go from here?"

"'Why' plus 'how' is going to tell us 'who'," McCay answered and began another circle around the body.

"What the hell does that mean?" Fisher asked, following McCay.

"Read the stuff Bob gave us," Prado answered, moving around the opposite side of the body. "Educate yourself."

"Yeah," Fisher answered. "I'll do that, but in the meantime...." He let his thought hang in the air as he stopped next to McCay.

"If we can figure out *why* the offender does what he does," McCay said, "and I mean *why* in the sense of *why* it satisfies his needs; then couple that with *how* he does what he does, I'm talking about the methods and tools, then we can begin to look for a personality that fits the crime. The *who*."

McCay walked closer to the figure. "A lot of anger and need for control here."

"Yeah," Fisher agreed, leaning in with McCay. "She's pretty beaten up. Her nose is broken. Badly broken, and it looks like her jaw might be too."

McCay nodded. "And the coroner is going to tell us that there is a sexual component. I'm certain of that."

"Why did he beat up this one so badly?" Prado asked.

"He might have been provoked. The beating came before the ritual, which he has rehearsed in his mind many times, and he perfects it with every victim. The plastic wrap for instance. I'm guessing that came after stringing up the first one and having the innards spill out. It ruined the picture he had in his mind. The fantasy."

"He's learning as he goes?" Prado asked.

"Perfecting his ritual," McCay answered. "Practice makes perfect. He fantasized endlessly about how he was going to kill this one, and the others, and display them for us to find. He spent a lot of time thinking about it. All the offenders I've talked to, well, more than half, said they began fantasizing about raping and violating someone when they were young. Pre-teens in some cases. That fantasy grows more intricate in their imagination, and when they finally act out, the violence might escalate from one victim to the next, but the routine is honed so less and less evidence is left behind."

McCay pointed at the torso. "This one was brutally beaten in the face. The others weren't. She must have angered him, but the signature wound is the same as the others. No worse. If he was escalating his violence as part of his ritual, he'd remove the organs, which are still intact, or cause more damage to her pubic area. That isn't the case here. He spent a lot of time doing what he always does and enjoyed every second of it."

"Enjoyed?" came from Laydon standing a few feet away.

"Yes, *enjoyed*," McCay said. "But that," he pointed at the pulpy face, "is not part of his fantasy."

"Fuuuck," Laydon said and knelt on one knee.

"But," McCay said, "this is the kind of thing that's going to confirm 'why' he does what he does. Why this particular ritual satisfies whatever urges he has, and when we get that down, we move on to the 'how' and the 'who.' And we're pretty close on the 'how.' There are probably some things we can't see with the naked eye. Like the sewing needles."

Fisher stepped away from the body. "I'm just not seeing how we get to the 'who' after we work out the 'why' and 'how'." He gave Prado a quick glance before saying to McCay, "I promise to read the material you gave us."

"We're on track to pinpointing that we're dealing with a serial sexual rapist who acts on anger. That's the 'why' and you're looking right now at the 'how.' Here's where you two" – he looked at Prado and Fisher — "come into this. You help me find the 'who' using that world class training you got. He'll be someone who likely has a record of sexual assaults, maybe even kidnapping, violence, perhaps with a knife, given what we see here. None of these offenders go from 0 to sixty. They work themselves up to this." He tapped Fisher on the shoulder. "Do your stuff."

Prado looked at McCay. "Bob, this just isn't what we do. This is your thing. That's why I told Staton to call you when we found the first girl. Well, the second one, really."

"Think of this like a criminal investigation," McCay answered, "only with a twist."

"A twist?" Fisher said, his eyes on the body.

"Yes," McCay said, "a twist. Start at the inner circle. In this case where the girls were known to congregate. Where they spent time with each other. Ask their friends if they.... Hell, I don't have to tell you how to do your job."

"But," Prado started to protest.

"This one is actually going to be more traditional than the others we get." McCay cocked his head toward the victim. "As I've said, she and the others, and I'm including the ones who were kidnapped, probably knew the offender. We usually don't get that kind of break in these cases. You'll be starting ahead of the game."

"Why are we even in this part of the game?" Prado asked. "This isn't why we're here. We're here on a civil rights case and…."

"And I think this is all related. This Ken Plough person was connected to all the girls who have been killed, and to the others who have disappeared. We aren't working on different tracks anymore. We're basically working the same case. Whatever you find will tell us something about" – he cocked his head toward the body – "that."

***

Staton and Esper followed McCay, Prado and Fisher into the conference room. As the others settled around the table, Staton went to a bureau against the far wall, opened a door revealing a small refrigerator and grabbed five bottles of water.

As he returned to the table he said, "The girl and her boyfriend were pretty shook up." He looked at files spread across the table. "I guess that's stating the obvious, but I think they held it together enough to confirm some of what we already know."

"They didn't see anything, other than the bodies?" Fisher asked. "Didn't hear anything?"

Staton acknowledged Fisher. "Nothing else."

McCay asked, "Did you get my message to ask them about the blanket?"

"Yeah, I got it. After a lot of crying and handwringing the girl said it was hers. She was a virgin and, well, you can take it from there."

Prado said, "If it had been our guy's, and he saw those two kids, we'd probably be looking at two more bodies."

"Nope, I don't think so," McCay said with a shake of his head. "Our guy had taken care of his urges, and unless they literally ran right into him in the act of posing the body, or saw enough to identify him, I think he would have slipped away without doing a thing."

"So, we don't have a thing except another body," Fisher said.

"No," McCay objected. "We pick something up with every event." He stood and began pacing. "This offender is likely responsible for the missing girls who he keeps, tortures, sexually violates and then kills. He's local. He's compelled to return to the same dump site. It's likely he has a history of sexual assault and violence."

McCay walked back to his seat and retrieved his briefcase, which he laid on the table and opened. "Here," he said, sliding monographs to Staton, Esper, Prado and Fisher. "Should've included this with the other stuff. Different from what I've already given you." He gestured at papers spread around the table. "Those are primers on the subject; definitions, typologies, pathology, causality, forensics and so on. These provide the specifics on investigating and finding the offenders."

Prado read, "*Serial Murder: Pathways for Investigation*, and *Serial Murder: Multi-Disciplinary Perspectives for Investigators*."

"We mainly use them when we come into situations like this and need to provide a quick and dirty education for investigatory purposes."

"More light reading," quipped Fisher.

"They're a little more exciting than" – McCay eyed the larger pile – "those."

Prado raised her eyebrows. "Exciting?"

"Includes information on offenders like Ed Kemper, Jerry Brudos, David Berkowitz, Herbert Mullin and a few others, and their first-hand responses to the 'whys and wherefores' of what they did. Some chilling stuff, but coming straight from their mouths, it can be fascinating reading."

"Fascinating?" Fisher said, with a shake of his head, and sorted through the other material. "*The Development of Serial Killers: A Grounded Theory Study*. The title alone makes me want to dig in."

"That one is a little more academic," McCay said. "But it's important you understand what we're dealing with. I need you to appreciate the sickness, the depravity and the dangers. Read those and absorb as much as you can."

McCay sat and stared down at his hands, which he had brought together and rested on the table in front of him. "The Sheriff asked me earlier if I'd ever been involved in a case like this and I mentioned David Parker Ray. You'll pick up other cases from that." He nodded at the monograph Fisher held in his hand. "I've thought of a couple of others that I want you to pay special attention to.

"Maury Travis, from St. Louis, kidnapped his victims, shackled them with ropes and handcuffs and covered their eyes with duct tape. He held them in his basement where he tortured them, videotaping the tortures and rapes, before killing them He tried to hide the blood splatter on the walls by repainting them several times, blood, paint, blood, paint and so on. We figured that he killed as many as 17 women.

"Todd Kohlhepp is another offender who has, I think, things in common with the person we're looking for. Kohlhepp kidnapped a couple of women after killing their boyfriends. He stored the women in a shipping container. He sexually assaulted them, killing the first one. Police freed the second one. He also murdered four people in a motorcycle shop because they wouldn't return his money when he was dissatisfied with a motorcycle they sold him; that went unsolved for years until we caught up with him for the other murders.

"Both Travis and Kohlhepp had criminal histories. Travis, however, gave absolutely no outward signs of being troubled. A good employee. Nice guy. Soft spoken. The cliché fits him: 'Not that guy. I'd never have guessed it.' Kohlhepp the same thing, to a lesser degree. He was a very successful real estate broker and owned a good-sized company. His employees and clients spoke very highly of him, however, his criminal history included sexual assaults and he spent time in a psychiatric hospital when he was young. Some of those we interviewed about him said he had an unpleasant edge to his personality that surfaced when he was under some kind of pressure or thought he had been disrespected, which manifested itself with the murders in the motorcycle shop."

McCay sat silently for a beat before continuing. "Travis and Kohlhepp aren't perfect examples for what we're facing here, but I think our guy has a lot in common with these men. He's a shell of a human being. No empathy. Immune to pleas for mercy. Absolutely no compunction about causing pain. Quite the opposite, he enjoys inflicting it."

Fisher glanced at Prado before asking McCay, "You're saying we should be looking for someone like that while we're trying to figure out if we have a civil rights case?"

"I'm saying that given the connections we're discovering between Plough and the murdered and missing girls, there's something else in this mix. There's something connecting all of this. Just stay alert to the possibilities."

McCay turned his attention to Staton and Esper. "I think he's replacing each girl he kills with another one. He just killed one so it's likely you'll be getting another missing person's report. Another young girl."

Prado said to McCay, "There hasn't been much, if anything, in the local or regional press about the missing girls." She raised her chin toward Staton. "Runaways aren't a big story around here. And almost nothing at all about what happened to Plough."

"We," Fisher said with a nod at Prado, "have a whole different thing going now."

Prado looked at Staton. "Maybe we should do more to let people know what's going on. Like having a press conference."

"That would definitely be a step up from what *hasn't* been done so far," Fisher said contemptuously. He cocked his head toward Esper. "It might've helped find those two girls before they ended up spread eagle in a forest."

Staton leaned toward Fisher, his eyes slits and mouth pursed. His anger was on the surface. He blew out a sigh and relaxed a moment before answering. "You have to keep in mind where you are. We followed the protocol for informing the public. And, anticipating your next question, yes, we also asked the public for help finding the missing girls. We did get some responses, but, again, keep in mind where you are. This is rural America. Kids are running off all the time for what they hope will be a better life. It's almost a rite of passage. And in this case the kids were doing pretty risky things." He looked at McCay. "Leading risky lifestyles is probably how you'd describe it and putting themselves in harm's way."

"And the parents?" Prado asked. "How are you dealing with them? They must be at your door every day."

Staton and Esper both shook their heads. "Some are, some aren't," Staton answered.

"And when they were kids, most of'em ran off at one time or another," Esper added.

"But they returned," Fisher said.

"Obviously," Staton responded, "but in most of the current cases, we're dealing with parents who were having trouble with these girls and weren't surprised when they took off, and haven't followed up with us. Not like you'd think they should. I don't know why. It's not the way I'd deal with things if were in their shoes."

Prado thought she detected a hesitation in Staton's cadence. A reluctance to put himself "in their shoes."

"And it's obviously not the way you'd handle it, but it's the way of the world around here more often than not."

"Good to know," McCay remarked quickly noticing Fisher ready to pounce. "Coming in from the outside, we often don't have a full understanding of what goes on where we visit. Frankly, it's something we should do a better job with; we should be more aware of the circumstances you" – he glanced from Staton to Esper – "are dealing with. The background briefings and materials we're provided don't go beyond the cold, hard facts. They don't give us what we need to put a human face on what we're walking into."

After waiting a beat for a rejoinder that did not come from Staton or Esper, Prado asked, "So, how are you going to handle this latest development? Marshal, you mentioned issuing press releases in the past, but what we're dealing with is, well…." She struggled for words. "Shit, there's someone running around kidnapping and slicing up young girls. Don't we have a responsibility to turn up the volume? To make sure a warning reaches everyone around here?"

McCay said, "Usually at this point I would recommend getting on a bullhorn and making as much noise with the media as possible. All the regular things. A toll-free number. An appeal for everyone who might know anything at all to come forward, but, in this instance, I'm going to advise against that."

Prado and Fisher shifted forward in their chairs, primed to object, but were stopped by McCay's raised hand.

"Let me finish. Most of these offenders are egomaniacal. They love attention and even court it. From Jack the Ripper right on down the line through Berkowitz and Rader, they wrote letters to the media, even called the cops to report their killings. Not this guy. He does what he does strictly for himself, his own gratification, and doesn't look for attention. He probably shuns attention and lives a very solitary life. If we start putting on a full court press, it's going to frighten him. He's not going to see it as some sort of paean to his prowess and intellect the way a lot of these people do. He might leave or, worse still, it might trigger him to escalate. And" – McCay nodded at Staton – "if you're really considering involving Hebert, any media attention on this is going to scare that guy right out of the picture. He's not going to help us if there's a media spotlight shining brightly on what we're doing.

"And, in your case" – McCay said to Prado and Fisher – "a media horde descending on Oletha is about the worst thing I can imagine. The folks there are already reluctant to talk to you. What do you think will happen if cable news trucks with their nests of satellite dishes begin rolling into town?"

Prado nodded, "Okay, got your point."

"One other thing," McCay said. "On this Hebert business. I think we ought to go ahead with it. And I think you" – he pointed at Prado – "should work directly with him. Where he goes you go."

Staton looked from McCay to Prado. "With Hebert? You want her working directly with him? I don't think he'd go for that, and he'd be right; in his neighborhood, she'd stand out like a sore thumb. He'd get nothing with her around."

McCay smiled at Prado. "What do you think? You have some background in this sort of thing, right?"

"You've been digging into my file," she responded. "That was a long time ago, when I was a beat cop in New Orleans."

"Not so long ago from my perspective," McCay answered, smiling. "Of course, I'm a lot older than you are. And you were successful. You helped put away some bad people. Biggest dealers in the South."

Prado took a moment before asking. "What do you have in mind?"

TUESDAY

Prado waved at Jill as she and Fisher walked toward their table. "Got a minute?" she asked.

"Give me five," the woman said, responding to her husband's call to pick up a raft of dishes sitting on the "order out" counter.

Prado and Fisher settled into the booth and acknowledged a number of now familiar faces. There were even a few smiles scattered among the deadpan looks directed their way.

Jill approached with a tumbler, put two mugs on the table and filled them. "What can I do for you this morning? The usual?"

"Did the word get to you about...?"

"It did," Jill replied. "Do you know who it is?"

"Can I buy you a cup of coffee?" Prado asked the woman. "Or would you prefer breakfast?"

"Coffee," the woman replied. "The breakfasts here will kill you with the amount of grease we use. Speaking of that" – she ran her finger across her forehead – "let me clean up a bit." She disappeared through the swinging door leading into the kitchen, re-emerging before Prado and Fisher had downed their first cup. Her hair net was gone, hair brushed away from her face, which was clean, bright and still damp from being scrubbed. She sat down, cup in hand, poured herself some coffee, and looked from Prado to Fisher. "What can I do for you?"

"You can start by agreeing that what we'll tell you remains with the three of us."

"'Course, if that's what you want."

"Really," Fisher said, letting his eyes go to the open room, "not a word."

Jill replied flatly, "Okay, I understand."

"The three girls we've found," Prado continued, "and all the missing girls, have a connection to Ken Plough."

Jill's eyebrows shot up. "No, shit."

"We're also pretty certain the three girls were killed by the same person."

"Couldn't be Ken," Jill said, more to herself than to Prado or Fisher, staring ahead sightlessly doing mental calculations in her head. "He was dead before...." She stopped and asked, "How're they connected to Ken?"

Prado explained and, again, asked Jill to keep the details to herself.

"You must not know very many honest people," she responded to this repeated request.

"We tend to meet a lot of dishonest ones in our profession," Fisher said.

The woman looked away and slumped against the back of the bench seat. "It's like we're snake-bit. And this used to be such a quiet, peaceful little town."

"Our investigation has been rolled into the one in Maryville about the missing and murdered girls. An FBI profiler is working with Marshal Staton and Sheriff Esper."

"Wait." Jill pushed herself away from the back of the booth. "What're you sayin'? I got the part 'bout them girls knowin' Ken but how does that...?" She sucked in her breath and stared ahead. "You're sayin' him being killed has something to do with what happened to all those girls?"

"That's what we're trying to figure out, but we're thinking that as we peel back the layers on what happened to Plough, and since he is tied to the girls, we'll hit on someone who might lead us to what happened to them."

"'Cause Ken knew'em all," Jill said, confirming what she had heard.

"That's the road we're going down."

Jill shook her head. "Ken was a lone wolf. Sure, he used those girls, but he kept his distance from everyone else 'cept his three shadows." Her mouth open to add to her thoughts, she stopped abruptly and rolled through her reasoning before adding, "Could *they* have somethin' to do with all that stuff in Maryville?"

"That's exactly the kind of thing we're looking at," Prado said. She poked Jill's forearm to call back her attention still focused on the middle distance. "Don't let your imagination run away with you."

The woman took a sip of coffee and slowly placed the cup on the table. "You're telling me we have a serial killer out here in the middle of fucking nowhere?"

Prado nodded. "It looks that way."

To which Fisher added, "And what he's doing is as bad as anything you can imagine."

Prado put a hand on Jill's arm. "We need your help."

"Me?" Jill said loud enough to turn heads at nearby tables. She smiled and nodded at the faces turning her way. "How?"

"I'd appreciate it if you'd pick three or four people you trust who I can talk to about Plough. People who will tell me what they know."

Jill jerked her head back. "No one's going to…."

"Wait," Prado stopped her. "Hear me out."

"Go ahead."

"I am going to ask about Plough. About what they think happened, but I'm going to explain exactly what we're dealing with. That this thing is way bigger, and worse, than anything we thought we were getting involved in. Or anything they could imagine would ever happen around here. I'm going to ask for their help to try and stop it, because it will continue unless we *do* stop it."

"You want me to stand up for you is what you're saying."

"Yes, I'd like you to tell them you trust me, and they should too. I know I'm putting you in a difficult position. These are your friends."

"And my livelihood."

"I'm asking you to trust that I won't be putting any of that at risk." She leaned close to Jill. "If you'd seen the things we've seen these past few days, you'd know what kind of horror we're dealing with. Whoever is killing these poor girls…."

"….and kidnapping and torturing them," Fisher added.

"…has to be stopped. You can help us."

"You're asking me to convince" – Jill raised her chin toward the room – "them that you want to know 'bout Ken only because of what's going on in Maryville? You won't be pressing'em to find out what happened here in Oletha?"

Prado shook her head. "Like I said, my questions will have to deal with what happened here so I can work my way through everything. But I'll promise them that anything they share with me won't come back to them. I won't use their names or ask them to talk to anyone else. Ever."

"I have your word on that?"

"You don't know many honest people, do you?" Fisher jabbed.

"Okay," Jill agreed. "I'll ask a few people if they'll talk to you. You gotta know they might talk 'bout this. I mean afterwards to other folks." She looked ahead. "Over breakfast. I can't promise they won't."

"That's up to them. I can only promise I won't say anything."

Jill sat perfectly still before confirming, "If they want to answer your questions, they can. If they don't, you won't hold it against'em. Right?"

"All I want is an opportunity to see what I can find out," Prado said. "We'd like to meet with them here at the end of their workday today and talk for no more than an hour."

Jill slid out of the booth and stood over Prado and Fisher. "You only got one chance like this with me. You fuck me over and you find breakfast someplace else, and there ain't no place else."

"Understood. I'll call later today." Prado handed Jill her phone. "Put your cell number in there." As the woman tapped at the screen, Prado asked. "Another favor. Can I borrow some clothes?"

***

"That was a weekend well spent," Fisher said to Prado as they walked up the stone path toward Tricia Plough's door. "One item down on the agenda we worked out now that we have Jill doing her thing." He stepped up to the door and knocked. "And I got through most of my homework reading. Now this."

"I ain't talking to you no more," Tricia said through the screen door.

Prado suggested, "Why don't you call Crystal and Lurleen and tell them we're here and we have some new ideas on who might have killed Ken. We have a better suspect than Silas Moore and want to talk to all of you about that."

Tricia stood, arms crossed, and stared at her feet. "You all wait in your car," she said and turned away from the door.

"Okay," Fisher said as they leaned against the hood of the car, "you said on the way over here you had some ideas on how to get Tricia to open up about Plough's connection to the girls. This 'other' suspect is what you're going to use? You really have someone in mind?"

"No, but I had to think of something to get her to talk to us."

"I'm still not seeing how this gets us further down the road with *our* case."

"Neither do I, but let's work the big picture like Bob suggests. We've hit a wall. Broadening the discussion might lead somewhere for us. It can't hurt."

"Thanks for sharing," Fisher said, a hint of annoyance in his voice. "Were you planning on running any of by me before we sat down with" – he gestured toward the house – "her?"

"I needed some time to distill it." Prado turned toward Fisher. "If you've got a better idea, or any refinements to what I'm thinking, I'm all ears."

"No, no bright ideas, but next time, don't catch me by surprise." After a beat of silence, he asked, "How're you going to handle this?"

"Here's what we know. Plough was buying meth from the girls and selling in Oletha. That had to piss some people off. He was working around the conventional dealers."

"You mean he was pissing Hebert off."

"Him, yeah, but there are probably others, too. Plough dipped his toe into a whole new world. He was using the girls for their drugs, and who knows what else. He could've pissed off some other people besides Hebert. Maybe the boyfriends of the girls, or maybe the girls had people who pimped them out and Plough was getting to be a nuisance."

"That still brings us back to Hebert. According to him, no one does anything like that in Maryville without him knowing about it."

A shadow fell across the car and briefly crossed Fisher's peripheral vision. He turned and watched a red pickup truck slow to a stop. Crystal and Lurleen got out and started toward them. A figure in the truck asked, "When do you want me back here?" Crystal answered over her shoulder. "This won't take long. I'll call you."

Prado and Fisher pushed away from the car. "Thanks for agreeing to talk to us," Prado said as the two women walked past without acknowledging them. She whispered to Fisher, "I have no idea how this is going to go. Probably have to make up a lot of stuff as I go. Try not to look surprised."

Tricia held the screen door open as the troop walked into the house. Lurleen and Crystal went into the kitchen and retrieved chairs, everyone took their now accustomed places in the living room and waited while Crystal lit a cigarette. "Whaddya want?" she asked, blowing a cloud of smoke directly at Prado and Fisher.

"I'm guessing you know that a number of bodies of young girls have been found in Maryville and there are also four girls missing," Prado said.

"Yeah, and?"

"And all of the girls had a connection to your ex-husband." She added, "Your husband," looking at Tricia.

"Oh, for fuck's sake," Crystal exploded. "This is why you wanted to talk to us?" She stood, widened her stance, locked her knees and demanded that Prado and Fisher, "Get the hell outta here."

"We don't think Ken had anything to do with the dead or missing girls," Prado said. "He couldn't. The chronology doesn't fit."

Crystal relaxed her stance and dropped her shoulders. She sat back down. "Why're you here then?"

"Ken might have ruffled some feathers when he got involved with those girls."

"He wasn't" — Tricia curled her fingers around the word – "'involved'."

"He bought drugs from all of them."

"And?"

"Let's go with that," Prado said, "and let's say it was nothing but business."

"It was," Tricia responded indignantly. "That's all it was."

"What if he upset some people in Maryville who were involved with the girls or with drugs? They might've had reason to go after Ken." Prado let her suggestion marinate before asking, "Can you think of anyone he might've irritated?"

"*Irritated*?" Crystal said sarcastically. "You got a way with words, lady. What happened to *annoyed*? Maybe he *annoyed'em*."

Prado allowed herself a quick smile. "Can you think of anyone he might have annoyed? Anyone Ken might have angered with what he was doing? I'm referring to what he was doing in Maryville," she clarified.

The women looked at each other. "We don't have any names," Crystal answered. "You got some folks in mind?"

"Maybe some friends of the girls, their boyfriends, family?"

Crystal reached into her purse sitting on the floor next to her chair and lifted out a cell phone. "Wait a minute," she said as she tapped at the screen. She listened. "Where are you?" She listened. "'Round back here? Come on in." Dropping the phone into her purse she said, "My brother. He usually went to Maryville with Ken. He might know something."

Tricia gave Crystal a quick glance before saying to Prado and Fisher, "You seen her brother before, right?"

"The last time we were here," Prado answered.

"Okay," Tricia said. "Don't stare. He'll get upset-like and won't be able to say nothin'."

The screen door squeaked open and slammed shut. Tricia's caution still hung in the air when the large man filled the arched entryway leading into the living room. He turned slightly to his right, raising his shoulder and dropping his head, shielding his face. "What?" he asked quietly, his voice soft.

Crystal asked, "When you went to Maryville with Ken to buy from those girls, you ever see anyone with'em, like boyfriends, or any other people?"

The man stared at Crystal, who reassured him, "It's okay, tell'em what you know."

He shook his head. "Never saw no boyfriends."

"How about other people hanging around?" Prado asked. "Men who were with the girls regularly?"

"We always only went to the red house and the same people was always there."

"Like who?" Crystal probed, a bit impatiently. "Tell us what you saw."

"I don't know their names, but it was the same people. Just a bunch of'em, sleeping mostly. Waitin' to get high."

Prado asked, "The red house, you said?"

The man nodded. "Can I go now?"

"Yeah," Crystal answered, waving a dismissal.

"Thanks very much," Prado said, her words following the hulk out of the house.

"What else?" Crystal asked. There was a finality in the question.

Prado stood, grabbing Fisher's sleeve and pulling him up with her. "Nothing for now. Thanks for talking to us."

She walked quickly out of the house, Fisher in tow. "Excuse me," she called to the big man after she was certain she was at a distance from the house where the women wouldn't hear her.

The man got into the truck and stared straight ahead. Prado stood at the driver's side door. "Were you always with Ken when he went into Maryville?"

"How would I know that?"

A wry smile pulled at the corners of Prado's mouth. "Fair enough. You said you spent time at this red house and knew some of the people there, right?"

The man's eyes rolled toward Prado without him moving his head. "No, I said I saw the same people. I didn't know any of'em."

"Did you know any of the girls who have gone missing or were killed?"

"Some of'em."

"How well did you know them," Prado asked, not hearing Crystal and Lurleen approaching the truck.

"We ain't got nothin' else to say to you," Crystal pronounced harshly as she slid into the cab.

"Let me guess," Fisher said as they watched the truck drive away. "The red house is next on the list."

"Maybe not next, but soon."

***

Hebert looked at McCay, his face pinched in question. "No fuckin' way," he said forcefully, and turned his attention to Prado. "Take her with me? Are you kiddin' me with this?"

"Look, hard guy," Prado spit back at him, her eyes flashing, "I've dealt with people who make you look like a Goddamn Boy Scout. Don't give me any of your shit."

Hebert threw back his head and coughed out a laugh, then continued coughing. He managed to wheeze out, "A Boy Scout? I *was* a Boy Scout."

"No, you were not," Staton said, facing Hebert across the conference table. "You were a Cub Scout for about two seconds." He turned his attention to Prado, Fisher, McCay and Esper. "He tried to kick the Scout Master, or whatever they're called, in the balls because Frankie here thought he should get a merit badge for starting a fire with a lighter." He looked back at Hebert who was still coughing violently. "Boy Scout, my ass."

"This isn't negotiable," McCay continued. "We're only interested in getting information on the girls. This isn't related to your 'business' and anything we find out is off-limits, as in we let it ride."

"I said I'd help, not that I'd set myself up for Leo to swoop in and arrest my ass. He's been lookin' for ways to string me up for years and I ain't gonna walk into his noose by having a fed followin' me around and knowin' all my stuff." Hebert gulped air trying to control his coughing and squeaked out, "Not that I have anything to hide."

"I give you my word that we'll ignore anything that isn't directly related to this case," McCay said.

Hebert grunted. "I don't need her to do what I gotta do."

McCay glanced at Prado who was coiled, preparing to spring at Hebert, and stepped on whatever she was about to spit out, saying, "Keep in mind you need an end to this as badly as we do. You can either work with us or we do what we have to do and that will make things very uncomfortable for you. You said yourself a bunch of cops nosing around is not a good thing."

Hebert lit a cigarette and pushed back in his chair, his face still reddened from the coughing fit. "You're calling me stupid, then. You don't think I can handle this myself."

"You're being ridiculous," McCay responded. "We're saying we know how to get what we need." He leaned toward Hebert. "You understand the world you live and work in. You provide the entrée and we do the rest. Let's pool our expertise and put things right. It just makes good sense for you to cooperate with us."

Staton added, "You don't work with us now and I promise we will have a battalion of narcs all over you and anyone else who comes within ten feet of your door."

Hebert blew out a gray cloud of smoke and watched it travel across the table and flatten against a window. He settled his attention on Prado. "Look at her for Christ's Sake. She looks like a 'Help Wanted' ad for the fuckin' FBI. She walks into a room with me and I'm immediately pegged as a CI."

"I spent eighteen months working undercover in the gutters in New Orleans," Prado said. "I don't think I'll have a problem here in Maryville."

Staton got up and stood over Hebert. "Here's the deal, Frankie. You have two choices. Either she joins you or we send in an army. I still have contacts at the U.S. Marshals Service." He gestured toward McCay, Prado and Fisher. "They can call for reinforcements from Washington. And we go to the media. Not the locals, but the big boys. We tell them about a serial killer. You don't think that'll get attention? We'll make sure we tell the ones with microphones and cameras where to find you and what they should talk to you about." He leaned close to Hebert. "They'll want to know all about those girls and how they're connected to you. Before you know it, they'll be calling you 'a person of interest.'"

Hebert smiled at Prado. "Workin' with the FBI. What a fuckin' hoot. And I get to be seen with this little piece of brown sugar. Might up my cred since your kind is runnin' things most everywhere else but our little piece of heaven right here in Maryville."

Prado stared at Hebert. "*My kind* would eat you alive. You couldn't run with them. They're smarter and a whole lot meaner than you are."

***

Staton, McCay, Prado, Fisher and Esper watched Hebert walk out of the conference room and down the hall where he stopped and leaned across the reception desk. The woman he was flirting with was clearly charmed.

"He's a piece of work," Staton said. "You'd never know it but back in high school he was one hell of an athlete. A real physical specimen. All State football and track. Passable student too. He could have gone to any university in the state, but stayed here. What a waste."

Esper reacted, saying, "He's put together a pretty good living for himself." He raised his hands defensively. "I know it's the wrong kind of living, but it's a living, and in these parts, right now, that's mostly what counts."

"And that's what I'm talking about," Staton answered. "If he'd applied his talents to something productive, his story could be entirely different. He's a smart guy with an entrepreneurial streak." He shook his head and laughed. "Listen to me. I sound like a damn sociology professor."

"Okay," Prado said, slapping the table. "So what does everyone think? Can we pull this off? I've been pouring through the stuff you gave me," she said to McCay. "Fortunately, some of it I already knew from a few conferences I attended where Douglas and Dietz lead symposiums, but there is a lot of Greek mixed in with your material."

"John Douglas *and* Park Dietz," McCay said. "Impressive. I had the opportunity to work with Douglas a little while before his retirement from the Bureau. A legend. He essentially created the field of profiling and set up our first unit at the Bureau. I think he's probably interviewed every violent offender of the past thirty years.

And you took a class with Dietz, too? He wrote the definitive book on forensic psychology."

"Yeah, well, I hope it helps me through whatever it is you've gotten me into." Prado said. "I can't believe I have to work with that scumbag."

"You'll be fine. All we need you to do is listen, ask a few pertinent questions, and bring it all back to us."

"And," Staton said, "if Frankie causes any problems at all, remind him I have a phone and will have no problem using it to call in reinforcements and the press."

***

As they walked away from the conference room, Fisher said, "I thought you were going to take Hebert's head off? What was that all about? He's a moron. Ignore the guy."

"It wasn't about him," Prado responded.

"Then what's it about?"

***

She could hear water dripping into a sink. The sound had become hypnotic. Almost soothing.

She tried to open her eyes but the best she could do was permit a sliver of light to work through the swelling. She knew her nose was broken and that caused a lot of the swelling under her eyes; she also suspected her cheekbones were shattered. The pain, so excruciating when they began on her, was almost non-existent. Her face was numb. She bit down on her lip and the metallic taste of blood ran down the back of her tongue into her throat, but she felt no pain.

She stopped counting the number of times they raped her, but she did remember at least five times when they shoved something inside her and, she guessed, ruptured her bladder causing urine and blood to leak down her

legs in a continuing stream.

Before her eyes swelled shut she counted at least seven open gashes on her right arm, four on her left, and three to each of her thighs. The large knife they used was heated with a blowtorch before they started in on her. She did not know what a Bowie knife looked like but imagined it looked something like what they sliced her up with.

She was certain that a vertical slice down her lower right leg went through to the bone. Whoever cut her clearly admired his work and told one of his partners, "That's bad. Straight through the muscle. She'll likely bleed out, but Stupid B said he wanted this slow so he could do a video or something to send to Houston. Show'em how we handle the pigs here in New Orleans. Prove we can handle business there."

She ran her tongue along what remained of her teeth. Funny, she thought, the only ones that had not been broken or knocked out were her wisdom teeth. She had been planning to have them removed. She started to laugh.

"This funny?" echoed in what she assumed was a large warehouse. The Dooney Boys handled most of their business out of Kenner so she figured that is where they took her. She did not bother to respond.

She felt a presence behind her. "You should be praying not laughing. You saw what we did to your boy Shawn. That's not stuff to be laughing at."

She tried to concentrate on the dripping water but the increased buzzing in her ears was making it hard. It felt like her brain had been rattled so hard it was splintered. The synapses must be misfiring, she figured. She could not hold a thought, but she could picture Shawn sitting across from her. If possible, he had been beaten worse than she was. So bad, one of his eyes had been knocked out of its socket. She couldn't believe she was thinking

about this without a pique of anger or revulsion. After a week there was no feeling left, either physical or mental.

She lifted her head and again tried to open her eyes. A sliver of light allowed her to see an empty chair.

She had never felt so relaxed in her life. She guessed that was because she was fully aware she was going to die and there was absolutely nothing she could do about it. She leaned in to the inevitable and it felt liberating.

***

"And the next thing I remember was being in the hospital. The Tulane University Hospital to be exact. Kind of interesting," she said almost wistfully, "because I never went there the whole time I was at Tulane. I don't even think I was aware of where it was because it wasn't near our campus."

Fisher stared out the windshield, gripping the steering wheel tight enough to begin cramping his hands. The landscape looked the same from the edge of Maryville to the horizon. Flat. There was no change in scenery to give away their movement. The humming of the tires did that.

"I had a locator in one of my earrings," Prado said and leaned forward to engage the wide-eyed Fisher. "Hello?"

Fisher blinked as if coming out of a reverie. "Sorry. I didn't know anything about any of that. I mean…," he stuttered out, "I mean I knew you had done some undercover work in New Orleans, but not the details."

"The devil's in the details." She looked at Fisher. "And how'd you know anything about what I did in New Orleans?"

"Google."

Prado laughed. "When did you Google me?"

"When I found out we were going to be working together."

"I got your bio when I found out. You didn't get one on me?"

"Yeah, but there wasn't much on what you did in New Orleans, just that you were undercover, helped put the Dooney Boys away, and got all kinds of commendations. I wanted to know more about that."

"No, shit. I've never Googled myself. Maybe I should check myself out."

"Would you mind if I asked you a few questions?"

"Shoot."

"You were undercover for about a year and a half. How far under? I mean did you have to live with them." Fisher glanced at Prado. "Did you have to....?"

"I lived with them. Ate with them. And all the other things you can imagine. It was a good time," she said coldly.

"How did they figure out you were a cop?"

"Not sure. None of the Dooney Boys talked after they were popped, but I figure it was around the time they started to creep into Houston. After Katrina hit New Orleans their market shrank and they had to look elsewhere. They decided on Houston without giving much thought to the people already there. Most of the gangs were Mexican or MS-13. Vicious, bloody, bad news on a level the Boys hadn't anticipated. Long story short, the Boys got caught up in a war when they tried to shoulder into the market in Houston, and they called everyone on deck. I became a commodity since I could speak Spanish and I was supposed to gather intelligence on how the Mexicans and MS-13 operated, who the leaders were, how turf was divided. That kind of thing. We managed not to get caught up in any of the strong-arm stuff in New Orleans, but once things got really bad with the gangs in Houston, our reluctance to back them gave us away. They expected us to go to war with them and we couldn't. That would've put us permanently on the wrong side of the law. Killing people. A no-no."

"Your partner?"

Prado shook her head. "Didn't make it."

Fisher let her response sit before asking, "What happened? I mean what was the outcome of it all?"

"Stupid B is...."

"Who?"

"The guy who ran things in New Orleans, Ivory Harris. Stupid B was his street name. I don't know why, although trying to muscle into

Houston might offer a clue. Anyway, he's in jail. He was the main person we were after. A real piece of work."

"What about you?"

"What about me?"

"The hospital. How badly…?" Fisher stopped mid-sentence. "None of my business."

"It's okay. I spent almost eight months getting put back together; surgery and rehab." Prado tapped her forefinger against her front teeth. "All new, and most of this" – she gestured at her face – "plastic surgery. A lot of other work on other parts. And rehab wasn't just for the body parts. I got hooked on cocaine. Wasn't supposed to sample the merchandise, but you can't do what we were doing and keep pretending. I'm not that good an actor. Anyway, there was a silver lining."

"Silver lining? If it wasn't a solid gold lining, and a lot of it, I'd have a real hard time finding a positive."

"I worked with the local Feebs and it got me to Quantico and into the Bureau."

"How'd you end up in the NOPD to begin with?"

"I was at loose ends after I graduated from Tulane and on a whim I took an exam for the PD. Long story short, I ended up there."

"How'd you even end up at Tulane?"

"Scholarship. Swimming."

"So, you got an offer you couldn't refuse and packed up and left New Orleans? No regrets?"

"Hell, no. A chance to work at the Bureau? What do you think?"

"No ties holding you down?"

"No, no ties. Not married. No relationships."

Fisher waited a beat before offering, "I got bored working for a K Street law firm in D.C. basically being a lobbyist for the one percent. My marriage was breaking up and I needed to wipe the slate clean. I knew someone at the Bureau and had an in."

"Don't take this the wrong way, but I don't care."

"How could I possibly take that the wrong way?" Fisher replied, wound in his voice.

She took a deep breath and blew it out. "It's not you, Ira, it's about staying focused, and learning from experience. I don't want to care." She looked at him. "Understand?"

Fisher nodded. "I do," he said with a smile. "I do."

"Okay, then, about this meeting we're going to have with Jill's handpicked group; she sent me a text with a few names and said she had to work hard to get them to agree to talk to us. Said she doubts they're going to give us anything at all." Prado beat a tune on her thighs. "So, here's what we're going to do to convince them otherwise."

She lifted her purse onto her lap and pulled out a manila envelope. "Got these from Staton. Some photos of the bodies."

Fisher glanced at the envelope. "Taken where?"

"At the location."

"Jesus."

It took five minutes from the outskirts of Oletha until they parked in the front of Jill's.

"You'll follow my lead, then?" Prado asked Fisher, who nodded his consent.

***

Jill was standing inside the door, which she unlocked for Prado and Fisher. She pointed them to the counter at which sat three men and a woman.

"Here," Jill said and ushered Prado and Fisher behind the counter where they stood facing the group. She started the introductions from her left. "Ben Rhoades. Lincoln Williams. Betty Rheam. Larry Lawrence and" – she circled around and joined the others sitting at the counter – "me."

Prado and Fisher met the looks of suspicion and discomfort with forced smiles.

Rhoades was the youngest of the line-up at what appeared to be fortyish. His face was beginning to melt into jowls and his prominent veined nose was taking on a red and blue tinge. Lincoln Williams, a very distinguished older man, his gray hair slicked back from a clean-shaven face, was wearing a sport coat. Betty Rheam, spilling around the stool, was barely contained in a floral sun dress straining at the seams; she held her purse tightly against her chest. Larry Lawrence was drumming his long fingers on the countertop. His narrow, hatchet-shaped face mixed suspicion and discomfort with severity.

"You asked me to find some folks I trust," Jill said. "I've known Ben, Lincoln, Betty and Larry my entire life. Ben's a former mayor. Lincoln manages the bank. Betty runs the beauty store."

"I own the hair salon," the woman interjected sharply.

"Yes, owns it," Jill agreed. "And Larry was our sheriff before he retired." Jill spread her arms. "And there's me."

Prado smiled and let her eyes run down the line. "Thanks, Jill, and thank you all for agreeing to meet. I'm Special Agent Eileen Prado and this is Special Agent Ira Fisher."

"We know," Rheam said and clutched her purse tighter to her voluminous chest that began shoulder high and was contained at her beltline.

"I've seen you all in here every morning…," Prado began.

"Not me," Rheam interjected.

"No, not you," Prado agreed, "but I'm guessing all of you know what brought us here to Oletha."

"To find out who killed Ken," Rhoades said.

"Not exactly." Prado said. "We're here to find out if Mr. Plough's civil rights were violated under the color of law. That's different."

"That means you're working for Tricia to find out who killed Ken and if we're covering up for whoever did it," Rheam said, letting loose of her purse with one hand long enough to gesture at her seat mates.

"No," Prado said with a shake of her head. "Not exactly, and I haven't asked to speak to you with anything like that in mind."

Heads turned toward Jill as if she might better explain what was going on and why they had been asked to meet with these FBI agents.

"A little background," Prado said. "Yes, we're here in Oletha because Tricia Plough alleges that her husband's civil rights are being violated." She leaned stiff-armed on the counter. "We are also well aware of Plough's relationship with this community."

Lawrence huffed. "Relationship. There was no relationship."

Jill put a hand on the man's arm. "Let'er finish."

Prado placed the manila envelope on the counter. "In the course of our investigation we found out that Mr. Plough was connected to a number of missing and murdered girls."

"You talking about Alice Moore?" Rheam asked.

"Her and Rochelle Lee and all of the other missing girls," Prado said. She pulled a sheaf of photos from the envelope. "I have some photos here of what happened to the girls who were killed. They are very graphic so you should think twice before looking." She placed them face down on the counter.

"What the hell is going on?" Lincoln Williams asked.

"We think there is a very strong possibility a serial killer is active in the area, including Oletha."

"Holy shit," shot out of Betty Rheam's mouth and her face went crimson. "I'm so sorry. Just slipped out."

"No," Prado said, "'holy shit' is right. And the connection between Mr. Plough and the girls means that the case we're investigating is tied to the one being investigated in Maryville, where the murdered girls were found. We have a much larger canvas we're working on beyond the civil rights case."

Rhoades shook his head. "All it says to me that is someone saved the state a lot of time, aggravation and money by getting rid of that SOB."

"Not really," countered Prado. "If you're implying Mr. Plough was involved in the murders and kidnappings, the chronology doesn't work for the killings and for only a couple of the kidnappings."

"Just tell us why we're here," Lawrence demanded.

"Mr. Plough was using the girls to supply him with meth, which he was selling here in Oletha," Prado said. "As you can imagine, that complicates things for us. It widens our field of inquiry from Oletha to Maryville. It's possible he got caught up with some nasty people there, or, even, beyond. So, we need to adjust how we go about our investigation. We're hoping you or someone you know saw something that could help us not only with what we're doing here, but with the awful things going on in Maryville. What's going on there could spill over into Oletha."

"Actually," Fisher said, "it already has. Moore and the Lee girl, both victims of what we believe now is a serial killer, were from Oletha."

"Let's be clear," Lawrence said, "if we give you information that helps with what you're doing here, we're putting ourselves in your crosshairs. We can be accused of having withheld information earlier on, or, at the very least, we put ourselves in the position of being called as witnesses if what we say leads you to identifying whoever killed Ken. And I think I speak for everyone" – he received nods from the others – "when I say we're all law-abiding folks and want to help, especially with these murders, but we don't have any information that can help you with your investigation of Ken Plough."

Prado slowly turned over the photographs. "I promise you we have absolutely no interest in identifying any individual for the murder of Ken Plough. Our task is only to report back what we find as far as the civil rights case. We haven't been asked to find out *who* killed Mr. Plough."

"That still doesn't address what Larry said," Williams responded, "about the position we might find ourselves in."

"I will deny ever saying this, and I have a witness who will agree I never did," Prado said with a nod at Fisher, "but if you give us information, we can use that assists us with this" – she glanced down at the photos – "there will never be a report from us that there was a violation of Ken Plough's civil rights."

"There wasn't a violation," Rheam said insistently.

"Not that we've found so far," Prado answered, "and there definitely will never be one if you help us with this," she said, holding up a photo in front of the group. Rheam let out a groan and turned her head away. The others also averted their eyes.

No," Lawrence said. "Not good enough. You said *if* you get information that helps with your other case, you can make the civil rights thing go away. What if we all cooperate as best we can, but what we give you doesn't help with what's going on in Maryville?"

Prado let her eyes scan the group. "I'm not trying to be evasive or clever. We don't give a good Goddamn if Plough was killed by someone and you're covering it up." She put her hands on her hips. "How's that?"

"You're thinking that maybe all of this is related," Williams said. "So whatever we give you about what happened here might help with what's going on in Maryville? That about it?"

"We'll take whatever you have," Prado confirmed.

"I've got something for you." Rhoades said. "I saw one of the shots that killed Ken. It came from the roof of the old post office."

"You *saw* one of the shots?" Fisher asked.

"I saw a flash from a gun," Rhoades said. "I was down the street away from Dummy's looking up toward town.

Lincoln Williams volunteered, "I was getting into my car parked in front of the bank near the post office and heard something. It wasn't loud like most gunshots, and for a long time I've wondered if what I heard was a shot, but given that Ken was killed when I heard something, well, that's gotta be it, right? Especially with what Ben just said."

"I also heard a second round of shots," Rhoades said. "After the one, or maybe it was two, from the roof. A different sound. Closer."

Twenty minutes later Prado stood at the door with Jill thanking everyone for coming. She and Fisher stepped onto the sidewalk and waited while Jill locked the door.

"That's the most I heard out of anyone since Ken was killed," Jill said. "I hope it helps because that's the best you're gonna get."

WEDNESDAY

Staton, McCay and Esper stared at Prado as she walked into the conference room. Fisher enjoyed their reactions.

"What? You've never seen a woman dress down before?" She pulled at her Levi cutoffs, short and made even shorter because she had to fold them under at the waist to fit her. A too large plaid shirt covered a bright purple tube top.

Fisher noticed that she spent a moment studying her thighs and rubbing at faint scars. He caught her eye and shook his head.

"Those are Jill's, right?" Esper asked brightly. "I've seen her in that shirt and top. Works better on you." Surprised by his own comment, he added, "Sorry if that was out of line."

"I'm guessing you're meeting Frankie this morning," Staton said, directing everyone to take a seat at the table.

"He's taking me to the red house." She waved them onto another subject. "First, we have some interesting news to share. Jill," she nodded at McCay, "the woman who owns the diner in Oletha, organized a meeting for us with some people in town. We learned the initial shots that killed Plough were fired from the roof of the old post office."

"Who told you that?" Esper asked. "And how the hell did you get them to tell you anything?"

"I promised to keep it between us" – she tilted her head toward Fisher – "and them."

Esper looked nonplussed. "I can't believe they'd talk to you and not me."

"Let me finish," Prado suggested, "and it should make better sense." She waited for Esper's nod in response before continuing. "The first shots were fired from the post office roof according to this person. He was standing down the street, south of Plough's truck, looking back toward the post office. Everyone else was nearer to the truck and had their eyes on Plough. He saw a flash from the roof and went to the ground, then heard a few other shots. He said the sound of the second volley was different. From a different gun. Which matches what we heard from Rusty Weiler, and tracks with the coroner and forensics reports. Different bullets. Different weapons."

"He's certain the first shooter was on top of the post office?" Esper asked.

Fisher jumped on the question. "It never occurred to you to take a good look at the surroundings and consider all the possibilities?"

Staton answered, "The idea that someone could take a shot from the roof of a building at least two hundred yards away with a crowd of people in the line of fire, and hit their target dead-on, without any collateral damage, never entered our thinking."

"Why don't you boys let me finish before getting into a food fight?" Prado suggested.

"Sorry," Fisher volunteered. "My bad." He kept his head turned away from Prado who was bombing him with a withering look.

She continued, "No one remembers anything distinctive about the second volley of shots except they happened. No one saw anything else. All we could get was that after everyone got up off the ground, they noticed the driver's side window was shattered. That has to be the direction from which the second group of shots was fired."

"Okay," Staton said, "The post office thing is new." He nodded at Fisher. "We'll look into it."

"We already did," Fisher he said. "This morning before coming here." He tossed a small cloth beanbag onto the table. "We found that on the ledge of the roof about where a rifle would be placed to get a good angle on the truck. We called some people at the Bureau who know about these things…distance shooting, weapons, that kind of stuff, and they told us" – he pointed at the bag – "snipers use those."

"Specifically," Prado explained, "to steady the weapon."

McCay looked from Prado to Fisher. "The distance of the shot, the bean bag, and the follow up with a second weapon, the coup de grace?" He stared expectantly. "A professional, right?"

"Oh, come on," Esper whined.

"I think it's worth considering," Prado said directly to Esper. "We've heard a lot about how everyone around here knows how to use a gun, but the person who shot Plough was a marksman. Not just someone who knows how to use a gun. And the people we talked to at the Bureau said the follow up with a second gun is often the hallmark of a professional hit. SOP."

"Look," Esper said, "Ken was a bad guy. Worse, he was what many would call evil, but he was a small-town asshole. A professional hit? Really?"

Staton looked intently at Prado. "Are you suggesting someone in Oletha hired a pro to kill Plough? Actually, it would take everyone in town to afford it."

"This is ridiculous," Esper said. "We're talking about a bunch of farmers hiring a hitman? C'mon, let's get real. It doesn't make any sense."

"Hear me out," Prado asked. "After talking to the group Jill pulled together for us, one thing we're pretty confident about is that no one is hiding anything." She raised both hands in a sign of surrender. "Let me rephrase that. We don't think anyone knows who killed Ken Plough, or had anything to do with it. Initially, when we heard about the town meeting just before Plough was killed, we suspected it was planned and executed – no pun intended – locally. But everyone we've talked to, and that includes our discussions yesterday, has been very consistent in saying the group left the meeting and went directly to the bar. They have been consistent in saying no one lagged behind or left the group, other than Silas Moore, and we've accounted for him. Everyone was within sight of everyone else when Plough was shot."

"Not *everyone* from Oletha was at that meeting," Esper said. "I was there and we were missing some folks."

"And were any of them capable of shooting the eyes out of Ken Plough from two hundred yards?" Fisher asked.

Esper did not answer.

"Any of them likely to be hiding and then pop up to shoot him at close range?" Fisher pressed. "And then just disappear without being noticed?"

Again, nothing from Esper.

"Okay," Prado said with finality. "We got the post office thing and another confirmation of a series of shots coming at close range."

"You're willing to accept the word of these people?" McCay asked. "You have no doubts whatsoever that they might be lying to cover up for someone?"

"We were able to offer them something that worked as a truth serum. We gave Oletha immunity on the civil rights violation. We traded it for the information we got."

McCay shook his head. "I didn't hear that."

"It was a good trade," Prado said. "Granted it doesn't look like it opened any doors to what's going on with the girls, but we brought that up and showed those photos, which is what got them to move off the dime."

"And it was a fair trade," Fisher said, "since we don't think anyone is covering up anything. What they know, they're telling us, which, as it turns out, really isn't much at all."

"Where does it leave us? Esper Asked.

Prado said, "I'm thinking Plough got sideways with some very bad people and they got rid of the problem."

"Frankie Hebert?" Esper asked.

Prado laughed. "He's a big fish in a very small pond. I wasn't kidding when I called him a Boy Scout. I'm sure he's hurt some people; he's also a low life of the first order; trades women for drugs and all the rest of it; but that guy hiring a hit man to get rid of a nuisance?" Prado shook her head. "No."

"But it makes sense that someone here in Oletha would do that?" Esper asked incredulously.

"I didn't say that," Prado answered.

"Okay, then what are we left with?" Staton asked Prado.

"A lot of new stuff to follow up on," Prado answered. To McCay. "And I have an appointment with Hebert to talk to some people and see if we can find a serial killer."

Her attention back on Staton. "Do you have an impound lot where I can find an old piece of shit car to drive to this meeting? I don't think it makes much sense to be dressed like Daisy Duke"—she stood and raised her hands away from her sides – "and then give everything away by driving up in a cruiser."

***

"I like what you've done with the place since my last visit," Prado said looking around Hebert's living room. "The newspaper and trash theme has been replaced by beer bottles and dirty clothes."

"Take a load off," Hebert said as he pushed his lounger into an almost prone position.

Prado curled her lips in disgust as she considered a pile of clothes on the couch. "Not a chance. Let's do what we have to do." She started toward the door.

"Your ass really looks good in those shorts," Hebert said, a smile in his voice. "Why don't you lose that ugly shirt so we can get a look at the rest of you?"

Prado stopped in the doorway a beat before stepping onto the short porch. She took a deep breath and announced, "I'll wait in the car."

"It's just up the block," Hebert called after her. "Easier to walk."

Prado stood on the sidewalk feeling self-conscious. She started to button the shirt but thought better of it. The point of the outfit was to alter her appearance completely.

"Been askin' around 'bout you," Hebert said as he walked up to her. "You're one tough broad."

Prado did not respond. She took a quick look back toward the house.

"It's just you and me."

"What? No armed guard? Don't you feel naked without Butch and his big gun?"

"Nah," Hebert said, pointed them down the block, and lit a cigarette. He exhaled, leaving a trail of smoke in his wake, and asked, "What caused a pretty little girl like you to become a fed?"

"I wanted to get assholes like you off the street. Speaking of which, since you said you knew these girls, they must have been snatched right out from under your nose. Someone obviously isn't afraid you'll come after them."

"Ain't that what we're doin'? Goin' after'em?" Hebert said as they walked past a row of houses. "Let's get something straight between us," he said, hesitated a moment, and let out an explosive laugh, followed by the habitual fit of coughing. He had to stop and catch his breath. "Now, that was funny."

"I didn't get the funny part."

"Yeah," he said, "a tough broad." He took in a deep breath. "Anyway, like I was sayin'" – he gestured ahead and they continued walking. "Snatchin' these girls up isn't what this is all about for me. They come and go. Mosta the time the cops don't give a shit about whoever" – he snapped his fingers – "'poof,' disappears. But with them now gettin' cut up and all, it's a big deal, and like we talked 'bout, could bring down a hail of cops, and more of you guys, 'less I do somethin' 'bout it. So, for me, this ain't 'bout anyone snatchin' people from under my nose. I don't give a rat's ass 'bout that."

"Aren't you sweet?"

"No, I'm not. All I want to do is protect what I got." He stopped and turned in a slow circle, his arms raised. "This is upscale. I like livin' upscale. I know it don't look like much to you. You probably grew up in a nice house, and went to a nice school, were a cheerleader, went to prom and all that shit. For me, this beats the hell out of a shack and a hole in the yard to shit in. I plan on keepin' what I've worked hard to get and I'm gonna get a lot more. I can't do that with some maniac runnin' around grabbin' girls, killing'em and scarin' others off."

"Spare me the poor boy act, struggling through life. You had opportunities and made your choices, and they were bad ones."

"Leo's been fillin' your head with stuff, ain't he?" Hebert smiled broadly. "Me and him was once kinda like friends. Not good ones, but we knew each other. That's how he knew 'bout the Boy Scout stuff. We grew up in the same places, did the same things. He just took what he learned and went in another direction."

"I don't care. Let's just concentrate on what we have to do."

Hebert stopped and dropped his cigarette butt on the sidewalk. He started up a cracked and uneven cement walkway leading to a ramshackle house with a bright red door. Gutters along the front of the house hung loose. The roof was moss-ridden and most of the windows were broken. Patches of grass dotting a dirt front yard had grown thigh-high. The remains of a tricycle and a rusted swing set, monuments to another life, were contained within the border of a chain link fence missing most of the "link."

"Ain't had time to do much with this place. Did put on a nice door though, right?"

"You own this house?"

"Free and clear," he said proudly. "A fixer-upper, when I get 'round to it. Thinkin' of buyin' up a lot of places and maybe becomin' a real estate guy. Go legit."

"More like a slumlord," Prado said and pushed past Hebert. "Shall we?"

The two stood a few steps inside the door of the house as their eyes adjusted to the dark. The living room was still. No movement. No sound. Prado went left, Hebert right. She stood over a couch where two bodies were entangled. Both nude. Both female.

"Psst," Prado noised and Hebert walked to her side. "You know them?"

Hebert reached down and poked one on the shoulder. "Norma." The figure stirred then fell still. "Dolly," Hebert said loudly and the second girl squinted up at him.

"Frankie," she said, smiling easily.

"Sit up," he demanded. "Where the hell're your clothes?"

The girl seemed confused by the question and looked down at her naked body. "I don't know." She sat up and looked down at the figure next to her. "Who's that?"

Hebert shook his head and looked around the room. He pointed at a pile of clothing next to a threadbare cloth chair. "Get dressed." As the girl left the couch, he sat down and pushed the second girl causing her to yell "Go away." He squeezed her shoulder, digging his thumb into the soft spot near her neck. "Hey, that hurts," she squealed and sat up quickly.

Dolly walked back to the couch and threw a pullover and shorts on top of the girl on the couch. "Must be hers," she said to Hebert. She was still nude. "Can't find mine."

Prado took off her shirt and covered the girl with it.

Hebert got up from the couch and instructed the girls to "Wait right here with this lady." He walked toward the back of the living room and disappeared through an arched opening.

The girls sat hunched forward staring at the floor.

"You two don't know each other?" Prado asked.

The girl in Prado's shirt leapt up and walked to a corner of the room where she threw up.

"We know each other," the one still on the couch said. "Well, we don't *know* know each other, but we seen each other here before."

Hebert returned followed by a boy and a woman who looked to be in her early twenties. He directed them to "Go to the kitchen and get a coupla chairs." The boy walked away. The woman stood glassy-eyed. Hebert pushed her. "Go get a damn chair."

The plaid-shirted girl returned to the couch and plopped down hard causing the other to bounce. "Stop," she whined without taking her eyes off the floor.

"Here," Hebert said to the boy and woman, instructing them to put the chairs in front of the couch. He directed them to join the girls. He sat on one of the chairs and pointed Prado to the other.

"Dolly and Norma," Hebert said sharply. "I need you two to answer some questions." He reached out and rapped them both on the tops of their heads with his knuckles, causing the girls to sit up straight. "Okay?"

The plaid-shirted girl asked, "If we do, you got anything for us?"

Hebert reached into his shirt pocket and produced a small aluminum packet. "For all of you, if you behave."

The girls, along with the boy and the woman, squared their shoulders, eyes brightened, and they appeared to have magically joined the living.

"Okay," Hebert continued. "You all are my favorites, you know that don't you?" He smiled and lit a cigarette, offering the pack. The boy slid out a cigarette and leaned toward Hebert's lighter. Hebert turned away from Prado to exhale a burst of smoke, saying to her as he did, "Dolly and Norma been with me since they was barely out of diapers."

"Not since diapers, Frankie," Dolly objected playfully, "but a long time."

Prado couldn't help herself and asked the girls, "What about their parents?"

Hebert and the two girls laughed.

"Ann," Hebert said to the woman who responded to her name with a grin that revealed a mouth full of rot. "She's like their mother." He nodded at the boy. "To Billy, too." Hebert straightened and raised his arms. "My big, happy family."

"You all live here?" Prado asked, disbelief in her voice.

"Pretty much," the woman replied.

"She keeps our shit together," Dolly said. Now alert, the girl was aware of her nakedness and wrapped the shirt tightly around her shoulders. Golden hair spiked from her head and the sharp blue of her eyes sparkled. She would never be a pretty woman but she had an open countenance that could have been appealing.

Hebert leaned close to Prado. "I bring'em food and clothes sometimes. Ann hooks to bring in a few extra bucks."

"I do, too," Norma said. She had wiggled into her Tee-Shirt and shorts. "Ann sends some of 'em to me when they don't wanna wait on her."

Ann reached across the boy and squeezed Norma's arm. "They're startin' to ask for you, honey. Must be those big tits," she said teasingly to the overweight girl, who made a "thank you" face.

Prado leaned against the back of the chair. "The new American nuclear family."

"Nuclear what?" the boy asked, his acne-laden brow furrowed in question.

"Never mind," Hebert said. "What we need to know is 'bout some of the other girls that used to hang out here. One's you maybe ain't seen in a while."

"Like Dina?" Norma volunteered. "Ain't seen her for a while."

Hebert sat forward. "I saw her here like 'bout a week ago. Maybe sooner." He said to Prado, "Nice girl but simple-minded." He pointed at his head. "Not all there."

"Don't remember when was the last time 'xactly," Norma said. "But it's been at least a few days."

"Yeah," the boy agreed. "Last time I saw her she was in one of the rooms doin' her usual thing. Talkin' and singin' to herself." He snorted a laugh. "She was always sayin' things that pissed people off. Never meant to I don't think, but never seemed to know that she was doin' it."

"It's called Asperger's, you asshole," Dolly said angrily.

"Dina has Asperger's?" Prado asked.

"Think so," Dolly answered. "My aunt's got it. She and Dina do the same kinds of things. Talk a lot 'bout shit no one else cares 'bout. Don't understand when someone wants you to shut the fuck up. My Dad's always on her 'bout that kinda stuff."

Prado said to Hebert, "The perfect victim. She can't pick up on social cues and has no idea what someone's intentions are."

"Did you see her with anyone?" Hebert asked, eyeing the four. "Did she bring someone with her? Maybe leave with someone?"

The boy nodded. "Yeah, she did."

Prado moved to the edge of the chair. "And that was last time you saw her?"

The boy took a deep drag on his cigarette and lifted his head toward the ceiling as he exhaled. He stared at the rising cloud and nodded. "Think so." He stared at Prado as if seeing her for the first time. "Who're you?"

Hebert reached across the table and gave the boy hard tap on his chin with an open hand. "She's a friend of mine. Just answer her questions."

"Can you describe this man?" she asked.

"All's I remember is someone coming in and leaving with Dina. It was late. Dark."

"He was a big guy," Norma said. "He walked 'round in here a little then went in the back where Dina was. She walked out the side door with him."

"You ever see him in here before?" Hebert asked.

Dolly shook her head and Norma gave her a look. "Yes, we have," she objected. "I seen him a few times, I think." She knit her brow bringing an amusing seriousness to her plump little girl face. "Yeah, I'm sure I seen him here before."

"What did he look like?" Prado asked.

Norma lifted her hand over his head. "Tall and" – she spread her arms – "just really big."

"Dark hair?" Prado prodded.

"Hard to say. He always had on a hoodie, but I think his hair was dark."

"Shit," Dolly teased. "Probably wouldn't know him if he fell over you."

"Fuck you," Norma responded sharply and looked at Hebert. "I'm telling you what I saw."

"Anything else you can remember about this man? Anything at all?"

"He didn't say much when he was here. Most of the time he just kinda looked around and left. Sometimes I thought he was trying to find someone, then other times it was more like he was just lookin'."

"That all? Nothing else," Prado asked. Norma shook her head and Prado shifted her focus to the others on the couch. "What about the rest of you?" Silence.

Ann held out her hand toward Hebert. "We answered your questions."

"I have a few more. Alice Moore," Prado said at the group. "Rochelle Lee. They both hung out here, right?"

All heads nodded.

"Did you see either of them with this large man? Or any man?"

"Yeah," Ann replied. "I saw Rochelle with him at Stacy's."

Prado turned to Hebert. "Stacy's?"

"A bar," he answered. "Really more like a…."

Before he could complete his thought, Prado asked the woman, "Was it the only time you ever saw her with him?"

"Yeah, 'cause I was surprised to see her with him; with anyone. She wasn't very friendly."

"Rochelle didn't like nobody," the boy said. "She was a bitch and just came 'round here to try and get people to give her meth. Never had no money but would blow you if you'd share. Did what she did, then left. Didn't hang out."

"Rochelle *was* a bitch," Norma agreed. "I never seen her with anyone anywhere 'cept where she could beg for drugs."

"Did you ever see anyone else with this man?" Prado asked. "Anyone from here?"

"Just Dina," Willie answered.

Ann held out her hand again. "Now?"

***

Staton, Esper and Fisher walked through the clouds of dust they stirred up pushing open the front door of the abandoned building. Shafts of sunlight stabbed between boards nailed across a line of windows on either side of the door.

Esper stood in the middle of the room. "I remember coming here as a kid. It was a busy place back then."

"Why was it closed?" Fisher asked.

"Didn't need a post office here anymore. When it was built, Oletha had close to ten thousand people. When it was closed, we had less than five hundred."

Fisher surveyed the counter area that cut the room in half. Three service docks were marked by old cash registers and wooden stools. He leaned across the counter and studied the space behind. "It made sense to shut the place up, leave this stuff behind, and abandon the building?" He wiped at a line of dust imprinted across his chest, smearing it onto the lower half of his shirt. "That's a decision that could only be made by the government. A perfectly good building just sitting, useless."

"In case you haven't noticed," Esper replied, "there isn't much use for a building this size in town. Who'd want to open anything here?"

"In back." Staton's voice came from behind a wall that separated the counter area from where he was calling to them.

Fisher and Esper walked into a large room where the sun tunneled through transoms spaced along the top of the back wall creating spotlights in which dust motes danced. Esper pointed at a stack of wooden cubbyholes marked with address labels. "I recognize some of those addresses," he said, leaning toward the stack. "Most of the people who lived there are gone. The houses aren't even there anymore. Hey," his voice raised an octave in excitement. "Here's my old address."

"Exciting stuff," Fisher said and walked toward Staton, who was pointing at a stairwell. "Yeah, leads to the roof."

The three trudged up cement stairs and pushed open a steel door. They squinted and blinked in the bright sunlight, standing together a moment before following Fisher across a flat, tarred surface to a corner of the building. "Here's where we found the bean bag," he said and put his hand on the thick wall surrounding the roof.

Staton eyed the distance between where they stood and where he had come upon Ken Plough slumped over the steering wheel of his truck. He kneeled and sighted the target area. "That was one hell of a shot. Definitely a few hundred yards. Right square into Plough's head." He stood and repeated, "That was one hell of a shot. Two, actually. Two incredible shots."

"And someone told you they saw a flash?" Esper asked Fisher. "They're sure they saw it coming from up here?"

Fisher pointed down the street past Dummy's. "He was standing there somewhere."

"And the person who heard the shot was right below us?"

Fisher gave Esper a look. "Yes, and let's not forget we found that bean bag right there." He pointed at the wall. "Where are you going with this?"

"I can maybe understand no one 'cept this one person seeing anything. They were looking in the right direction at just the right time, but only one person heard anything? Does that make any sense?"

Fisher walked to the wall and leaned against it so he was facing Esper and Staton. "The people we talked to at the Bureau said most professionals use sniper rifles designed to mask noise and muzzle flash. The best ones are built in, of all places, Canada."

"A Canadian sniper rifle," Staton said thoughtfully. "Seems like an oxymoron. Canadians are way too nice to be producing sniper rifles. Seems like Russia would be the place for that."

"Nope, Canada," Fisher confirmed, "and the Canadian sniper forces are the best in the world. Plus, according to what we learned, the flash and sound, though muted and muzzled, can be seen and heard under the right circumstances." He turned and faced the street. "Seen from down the street and heard from right below here."

"If we go with the theory Eileen proposed," Staton said, "we're supposed to believe he was killed by a contract killer who might be from Canada. I'm with John. That's pretty 'out there' speculation."

Fisher mimed holding a rifle to his shoulder. "The shooter doesn't have to be from Canada, but we're sure as hell not talking about someone from around here getting lucky with a hunting rifle."

"What about the two other shots?" Esper asked. "Or whatever the final number was. They came from a handgun down there somewhere." He pointed at Dummy's. "Explain that to me."

"It remains a mystery," Fisher said dramatically.

"And that's what we do," Staton said. "We solve mysteries."

***

Prado eyed the line of pickups and motorcycles in front of Stacy's Bar and Grill. She slid across the front seat console to let herself out the passenger side. The driver's side door was caved in and held together with duct tape. As she stepped onto the gravel of the parking lot, the aroma of urine, vomit, tobacco and stale beer drew a wince.

Hebert skidded into the space next to her, just missing Prado. "Sorry," he said, barely visible through a cloud of smoke billowing from the window. "You coulda ridden with me," he said, hopping down from the cab of his 350 Ford pickup, which was jacked up to accommodate oversize tires.

"The conversation would have been unpleasant and the second-hand smoke might've killed me."

Stacy's had a false front that mimicked an Old West saloon with a wood plank porch decorated with a pair of rough-hewn rocking chairs, a spittoon, and fronted by a hitching post, complete with a large plastic horse tied to the rail.

"I guess if someone said fuck you and the horse you rode in on, it would make sense here," Prado said as they approached the swinging half doors.

Hebert eyed Prado from head to toe. "You certainly look the part sweet cheeks, but let me do the talkin'. I'm guessin' even those brain-dead kids at the house made you."

"Paradise City" wailed from the juke box in the crowded, smoke-filled room. An ebony bar took up the wall to the right of the entrance and was backed by a large neon sign that flashed "Stacy's." To the immediate left a staircase rose to a walkway leading to a line of doors decorated with posters of men and women engaged in various sex acts.

"Don't tell me," Prado said. "Your favorite place to relax and share tales with the boys."

"No, more like where I come to do business. Find business, really."

Hebert walked to the far end of the crowded bar and gestured to a stool. "My spot." He smiled and high-signed the bartender, who nodded.

Prado stood a moment and eyed the noisy space. Arrow back chairs circled round tables with an occasional pub table for anyone who wanted to stand and drink. She noticed that most of these were surrounded by men with motorcycle club patches stitched across the backs of leather jackets. Prado turned toward the bar just in time to be greeted by the bartender. "And what will this lovely lady have today?"

"Anything on tap," Prado answered. She looked at the amber liquid in a glass in front of Hebert. "Starting early?"

Hebert made a show of looking at his naked wrist. "Maybe a little, but if we want Stacy to stick around and answer a few questions, it never hurts to spend a few bucks."

"Thanks," Hebert said to the bartender who put a thick mug down in front of Prado and wiped up the foam spilling over the top onto the bar. "And this here," he said, announcing the arrival of a man who approached along the back of the bar, "is the owner of this fine establishment, Ned Stacy." Hebert held up his empty shot glass. "Another."

Stacy set a bottle of bourbon down in front of Hebert. The man looked like a former fullback gone to seed. Middle-aged, thinning hair cut almost to the scalp, his broad shoulders aligned almost evenly with his paunchy lower body creating a square package. His dull brown eyes sat below a prominent brow shading a nose that looked like it had been broken many times and was never properly set. Deep scars across the bridge of his nose testified to the severity of the damage.

Stacy eyed Hebert warily before shifting his attention to Prado.

"This is Lynette," Hebert said.

"Good to know you, Lynette," Stacy said in a soft, gentle voice belying his appearance. "What's a lovely thing like you doing with a jerk like Frankie?"

"Slumming," she replied, trying to disguise her honesty with laugh.

"Got a question for you," Hebert said before knocking down his shot of bourbon.

"No," Stacy answered, "I don't need anything, but I have your number on speed dial."

Hebert shook his head. "No, something else. You heard 'bout them missin' girls?"

Stacy nodded. "And about the ones hangin' in the woods. Pretty grim shit. Your girls, right?"

"Some."

"When I stopped seein'em 'round here, I thought you was finally doin' what I been askin' you and tellin'em to stay away. They was all underage." He wiped a spot on the bar. "Sorry to hear 'bout what really happened."

"Who brought them in here?" Prado asked, surprising Hebert, who was teeing up a question of his own. "I'm guessing they didn't try and come in alone."

"They knew better than to even try and come in. Usually just asked someone comin' in to buy a bottle and take it out to them." He nodded toward the door. "They'd wait outside and I'd have to chase'em off."

"Lynette is cousins to one of them missin' girls," Hebert said. "We just want to know if you seen anyone in particular with any of'em.

Might give us somethin' to work with to see 'bout her cousin."

"No one in particular," he said as he rinsed his bar cloth in a nearby sink. He started to walk away, pivoted, and returned. "You heard they was hangin' 'round with someone who comes in here?"

Hebert nodded. "Some people told me they saw one of the girls in here with a man." He looked at Prado. "A guy with her cousin."

"Rochelle Lee," Prado added. She was surprised at how smoothly she and Hebert were working together, occurring to her that it would have been smarter for them to have worked out this routine before ad-libbing it. Still, so far, so good.

Stacy grimaced. "Yeah, I remember a girl called Rochelle, but I don't remember seein' her with anyone in particular. Like I said, the girls used to hang 'round outside." To Hebert: "If you're nosin' around, it's likely the cops will be in my face 'fore long. Where you go, trouble follows."

"Don't recall you havin' a problem with me comin' 'round when you need some of what I got so you can turn around and mark it up double."

"I know how to reach you. I don't need you bein' in here."

Hebert nodded thoughtfully and pulled a cigarette from behind his ear. "Light?"

"You know there's no smoking in here."

This audacity caused Prado to check the surroundings. A haze of smoke sat a few feet above the bar and tables. Most in the room were sucking on cigarettes, a few were sporting huge cigars.

Hebert put the cigarette behind his ear. "Look, man, she came to me" – he cocked his head toward Prado – "'cause she knew her cousin hung with some of the people I know. We didn't go to the cops. I don't want'em in my business any more'n you want'em in yours. Truth of it is my business ain't bein' helped by all this shit goin' down, and it's probably gonna slide right into here," he said, turning and gesturing toward the room, "unless we do something 'bout it. I heard some of those girls was chopped up pretty bad and Leo is thinkin' 'bout bringin' in the Feds." He motioned Stacy toward him and leaned across the bar. "You know they're already over in Oletha investigatin' what happened to Ken."

"Yeah, I heard."

"Well, maybe we can head that off. Whaddya think?"

Prado stoked the flames. "I don't want the cops anywhere near me or my family. That's why I went to Frankie. But I want to know what happened to my girl and…"

"Thought you said she was your cousin? Stacy asked.

"She is. I just call her that. She's like my own." She narrowed her eyes and lowered her voice. "Me and her parents don't have real good relations with the cops so we don't want to have to deal with them any more than we have to."

Hebert jumped in. "Lynette here is one my best producers. Her and the girl's parents. So we need to do this without any cops getting' anywhere near us."

"Whatever you got," Prado said insistently, trying to work up some tears, "that can help find my girl would be good." She put her hand on Stacy's forearm. "Please."

Stacy looked at Hebert, then at Prado. "You all are really worried the cops are gonna get in our business over this?"

"I guarantee it," Hebert answered. "They already been 'round my place." He pretended to shudder from a chill. "Some of these girls were cut up pretty bad. Serial killer kinda shit. Leo and the sheriff from Oletha are getting' real worked up and that ain't good. They'll be up in our shit if we can't work this out ourselves."

Stacy stepped back and folded his arms across his chest. "I'm thinkin' this is more your problem, Frankie, than it is anyone else's. What goes 'round comes 'round. Fuckin' with underage girls is bad stuff and you been courtin' disaster."

"It's anyone's problem who had anything to do with them girls."

"I didn't have anything to do with'em," Stacy objected.

"They was seen 'round here," Hebert said. "I don't know all that much about cop shit, but I'd say that's enough to get their attention. They'll likely be at your front door as soon as they find out the girls used to hang here."

"And how would they know?"

"'Cause they ain't stupid," Hebert answered intently.

Stacy returned to cleaning the surface of the bar in front of Prado and Hebert, scrubbing in circles. He shuffled to the sink and rinsed the cloth before returning. "The girls upstairs," he said with a glance at the upper floor, "asked me to keep an eye out for the big guy who used to come 'round with Plough. The guy with burns on his face. He creeped'em out."

Prado felt her shoulders jump. *Orin?* "Has he been in lately?"

"No, not since Ken was killed. He only came in with him. Never on his own."

"You ever see him with any of the girls?" Hebert asked.

Stacy shook his head.

Prado hopped off the stool and tugged on Hebert's sleeve as she thanked Stacy. "I appreciate your talking to us."

"I ain't gonna be happy if the cops show up here, Frankie," Stacy called as Prado and Hebert walked away from the bar.

"He's talkin' 'bout Orin," Hebert said as they pushed through the half doors. "He hangs around my place and the red house."

Prado nodded and put her hand on top of Hebert's as he went to light a cigarette. "Lynette?"

"We didn't work out a name for you and I was tryin' to think of some country singer's name, but all I could come up with was Tammy Wynette. You don't look like a Tammy and I just fell onto Lynette."

Prado nodded. "I'm definitely not a Tammy."

***

Crystal and Lurleen sat opposite each other at a square kitchen table. The only sound the click of a clothes washer in an alcove just beyond the kitchen. Their conversation had stalled.

The silence was broken by a declaration from Crystal, "We gotta make sure he stays away for a while. They're gonna want to talk to him 'bout Ken. He get's talkin', and they use their ways of keepin' him talkin', and Lord knows what'll come outta his mouth. He's gotta stay away. Everyone thinks he's still livin' here so this is where they'll come lookin'. We just gotta say we ain't seen him. That he's gone."

"How's that gonna do any good? It's not like they're gonna just stop and go away if they can't find him."

"No one's been sayin' nothin'. We keep Orin away from'em and the well runs completely dry. Then, they'll leave." The words trailed behind Crystal as she walked to the refrigerator, opened it, and held up a can of beer. "Want one?"

Lurleen shook her head. "We still need someone they can blame, don't we? Wasn't that the point of doin' all this? They don't believe it was Silas."

Crystal sat, took a long swig of beer, lit her cigarette, and, eyes narrowed, stared across the table. "We *thought* we needed someone to blame. We thought wrong. No one's lookin'. No one cares. No one's sayin' a word. Now, we need'em to go just away. No. Matter. What." She punctuated each word with a jab of her finger on the green-and-white checkered linoleum table top. "We need'em gone to make sure they don't find nothin'."

"Maybe they'll believe their own bullshit 'bout Ken pissin' off some people by tryin' to horn in on their drug business." Lurleen laughed. "Can't believe they told you that. Boy, what a crocka shit."

"We hired that damn lawyer to raise hell 'round here. To bug John and keep him chasin' his tail. Keep everyone lookin' the other way. He got nuts and filed that whatever the hell it's called with the government. He musta thought he was gonna get some money or somethin', and now we got the Goddamn FBI up our asses. What a fuckin' mess."

"Yeah, turns out we coulda just sat back and let it ride," Lurleen said. "We didn't wait long enough." She stood. "I think I'll have a beer after all." Returning to the table, she added, "Who knew no one was gonna give a shit that Ken was killed right in front of'em."

"It still don't make no sense to me that a man could get killed in the middle of town and everyone acts like nothin' happened." Crystal chugged down the rest of the beer. "I mean we know everyone hated him, but no one woulda guessed that was gonna happen. Thinkin' they're protectin' someone. It just made sense for us to hire a lawyer and have him try and get John to go after Silas. Shine the light somewheres else, but that don't mean bring in the fuckin' FBI."

"They hated him worse than we thought." Lurleen looked across the table, her brow furrowed in concentration. "Did you think they hated him *that* much?"

"We got better reason to hate that fucker," Crystal said, anger raising her voice. "All the shit we put up with. Plus, we gotta live off his drippings. He threw around nickels like they was manhole covers." She lit another cigarette. "We was the ones who kept him outta jail," she said, talking the smoke out of her mouth. "'Tween his stealin' and his sellin' drugs he put together a small fortune, and we got shit."

"I still think we coulda included Tricia. She put up with the same shit and…"

"No," Crystal bellowed. "Absofuckinglutely not. We did it the right way. She ain't had to do half the shit we did when Ken was full of hisself. 'Fore his dick got soft. She still thinks his shit don't stink half as bad as it does. Half as bad as it *did*." She sucked hard on the stick burning it down to the filter and blew out the smoke aggressively. "Plus, she did like I said she'd do and is givin' us way more'n Ken ever did. We ain't scrappin' along like we used to. Fact is, we're doin' real good. She's easy to work with," Crystal said with a broad smile.

Lurleen shrugged. "But we still got those FBI people to deal with. Never shoulda hired that dumbass lawyer."

"We was wrong 'bout that one thing." Crystal pushed away from the table and looked out a window at the back yard. "Hindsight is perfect."

"20/20."

"What?"

"Hindsight is 20/20. That's the sayin'."

"Ain't 20/20 perfect sight?"

"Yeah."

"Then what the fuck're you talkin' 'bout?"

THURSDAY

"I only know her as Rochelle," Hebert said to McCay as he pushed the crime scene photo away. "Man that's some awful shit."

"No one's filed a missing person's report," Staton added. He looked at Fisher. "This is what we've been telling you about. These kids go missing and their parents figure they've run off, or they've been having trouble with them and, well, some simply don't care. Most of the time the only way we find out they're missing is through their school. Their teachers or friends get hold of us."

Fisher said, "I don't understand that at all. Kids falling off the edge of the earth and it's no big deal."

"You're missing the point," Staton answered. "It's not a 'deal' at all. It's a sad reality of life in many rural communities."

"Not only in rural communities," McCay said, "and something I had no handle on until this." His eyes dropped to the photo Hebert was pushing further away. "It goes beyond what we have here." He produced his I-Pad and tapped it. "According to the National Runaway Safeline as many as 3 million young people run away each year." He swiped across the I-Pad. "The NIH reports that 41 percent of runaways said they had a 'poor relationship dynamic with their parents.' In English that means they were either sexually or physically abused. Or both. Not surprising, I suppose, that some of these children aren't reported missing, and when parents are questioned many claim their child was 'acting out,' or was 'incorrigible'."

"Please don't think I'm insensitive to the problem," Prado said with a nod at McCay's I-Pad, "or to what happens to these kids, but how does this help us?"

"It means our Unsub has a ripe killing ground. He has an open field in front of him and he can pick his victims, kill them, and be on to the next one without breaking stride. He's an organized killing machine who is relishing this bounty." To Prado. "I don't know if that's the kind of 'help' you're looking for, but it offers a perspective, a full color perspective, on what we're dealing with."

Esper leaned into the conversation. "I hear a lot of numbers and fancy language sayin' what I've been sayin' all along."

"Okay," McCay followed, signaling a shift in focus. "That bar owner you mentioned," he said to Prado and Hebert, "do you know the man he was referring to?"

"Yeah," Hebert said, "he used to come into town with Ken. He spent some time at my place. Not a lot. But some. I didn't know he went to the red house 'til yesterday."

"We met him when we went to talk to Tricia Plough," Prado said.

McCay dug into his briefcase and pulled out a laptop. "Name?" he asked Prado.

"All I know is his first name, and that's Orin, but he's Crystal Truville's brother, so I assume his last name is Truville."

Esper nodded his confirmation. "It's Orin Truville."

McCay typed in the name. He felt Esper leaning over his shoulder. "National Crime Information Center," he said, nodding at the screen. He stabbed at the keyboard, taking him deeper into the database bouncing from a fugitive database to a sex offender registry and into the National Instant Criminal Background Check System. He scrolled. "Nothing there."

"This is not a guy I'd expect to be clean," Prado said. "If he spent time with Plough, somewhere along the line he had to get jacked up for something."

Esper said, "I never had any reason to hassle him, but he did run with Ken. Even heard he was a driver for Ken when he used to steal hogs. The closest I ever came to runnin' him in was when I found his jeep and trailer stuck in a ditch, and a bunch of hogs runnin' in a nearby field."

"Here's a thought," Fisher said. "Did you ask anyone if they were missing their hogs?"

"'Course I did, and they were," Esper answered defensively, "but that doesn't mean shit. I could suspect all I wanted but there was no evidence that those hogs were stolen by Ken, or Orin."

"Moving on from hogs," McCay said. He pressed Esper. "There's nothing more you can tell me about him?"

"He's a weird dude, but he stays pretty much to himself. Hardly saw him 'round much. I'm really surprised to hear he was in Maryville."

"Weird," McCay said. "How so?"

"Weird like he hardly says two words at a time. Weird like he looks weird. He got burnt pretty bad when Ken set fire to the house. He turns away from you like this"— Esper demonstrated, turning his left shoulder in toward his body and hanging his head – "so when he talks you can't see the side of his face that's scarred."

"Wait, back up," McCay said. "Ken Plough burned down a house?"

"Yes," Esper said with a 'can you believe it' look. "The Truville's house. To get back at Crystal's parents for not letting her be with him. Orin got caught in the fire."

McCay looked around the table. "Plough burned down the house because he was mad, and Orin, the little brother, got caught in the fire?"

Esper nodded. "And the family moved away right after. Crystal stayed behind with Ken."

"Willingly?" McCay asked, clearly perplexed. "She let her family leave and stayed with Ken?"

Esper shrugged. "That's the way it happened. She was married to him for about twelve years and has a couple of his kids. When he switched her out for Lurleen, Crystal stayed close to Ken."

Prado said, "Every time we meet with Tricia, Crystal is there."

"So's Lurleen," Fisher said. "One big happy family, and not a dysfunctional one as far as I can see."

"And the brother?" McCay asked. "He moved with the rest of the family after the house burned down?"

"Yes," Staton and Esper answered simultaneously.

"Anyone know when he returned to Oletha?"

"'Little more'n three years ago," Esper answered. "He's been living with Crystal and, like I said, he did stuff for Ken."

"He worked with the man who burned down his house and almost killed him?" McCay said as if trying to make sense of what he was saying.

"Well," Esper answered, "it was never proved that Ken did it."

"Okay," McCay said as he massaged the bridge of his nose with his thumb and forefinger. "Let's say we take the leap and suspect Orin of having something to do with the disappeared and murdered girls." He pointed at his computer. "Most of these types of offenders have an arrest record. Like about 80 percent. They don't suddenly jump from say, stealing hogs, or whatever else it's alleged he did, to kidnapping and killing people. Most have been arrested for assault or a sex offense. Almost half have been diagnosed with personality disorders. Development problems. Something."

"Look, the guy's weird, like I said, but he doesn't come across as violent or strange to the point you think he might be a whack-o," Esper said.

"I think I've made the point that these offenders don't come across as *whack-o's*. Most don't anyway, especially the organized offenders, which our guy appears to be. But they usually have a criminal record." McCay sat back and stared at the computer screen. "I can't find anything like that about him."

"What about VICAP," Prado suggested. "Maybe you can find something there."

"Great minds," McCay said, pecking at the keyboard.

"VICAP?" Hebert asked. "I heard of the other one, the NCIC." He laughed. "Bet I'm on it, but I never heard of VICAP. What's that?"

"A data information center that collects, collates and analyzes violent crime," McCay responded as he leaned close to his computer screen.

Fisher explained to a blank-faced Hebert, "Where we keep information on bad people and their crimes."

Continuing without acknowledging Fisher's shorthand, McCay said, "Analysts examine crime data and patterns to identify potential similarities among violent crimes, create investigative matrices, develop time-lines, and identify homicide and sexual assault trends and patterns."

Hebert looked at Fisher who translated. "It's where cops go to find out if what's going on where they are matches anything happening anywhere else. They can compare the crimes they're working on with those reported from around the country and maybe get some leads to help them solve their own cases."

McCay held up his hand. "This is going to take a while." He gathered the files spread across the conference room table and stacked them in a neat pile next to his computer. "I have to enter all of this and…."

"All that stuff is about what's going on here?" Hebert asked.

"Yes, it is," McCay answered. "I'd appreciate it if you would leave me alone and let me enter it into the system." He lifted some loose pages from his briefcase and added them to the pile. "One thing, Marshal, do you know where the Truville's went after they left Oletha?"

Esper answered, "Toronto."

"Canada?" Staton and Fisher exploded.

Esper's face clouded in question. "Is there one in the States?"

Fisher jumped on Esper. "The other day, when we were on the roof of the post office and I said the weapon used to kill Plough was made in Canada and used by their sniper force, it didn't occur to you then to mention that the Truville's moved to Canada?"

"Didn't think of it," Esper responded and studied those around him as if searching for someone to help him understand what he was missing. A moment and his eyes widened. "You think Orin shot Ken?"

"Orin lived in Canada," Fisher replied intensely. "The weapon identified by experts at the FBI as a likely tool is Canadian. What the hell, man, it's something that deserves serious attention, don't you think?

"Orin lives with Ken's ex-wife, who's his sister," Esper countered. "Ken was his brother-in-law. He was friends with the guy, and even likely helped him do all that stuff he did."

"All true," McCay said, having turned away from his computer. "But the man was almost killed by Plough. The crosscurrents here are confounding, which makes *everything* worth looking in to."

"Okay," Esper's said softly. "Got it."

McCay was on his phone asking for "Deputy Commissioner Rankin, please. This is Special Agent Robert McCay of the FBI."

McCay tapped the conference icon on his cell, laid the phone on the table, and said to those around him, "David Rankin heads up the Emergency Task Force within the Toronto Police Services. I've worked with him on a couple of cases."

"Bob," came a high-pitched voice. "Good to hear from you."

"Back at you, David. Unfortunately, it seems the only time we talk it's about something unpleasant."

"That's the business we're in," the voice said with a soft laugh. "What can I do for you?"

"Forgive what will be a rather muddled request since I'm not sure what we have here."

"Try me. I've heard almost everything in my 30 years doing this."

"I'm here with Special Agents Eileen Prado and Ira Fisher, and Sheriffs John Esper and Leo Staton. We're in the middle of a serial kidnapping and murder investigation in Iowa covering the city of Maryville and neighboring Oletha." He nodded at Prado and Fisher. "And various other things."

"Wait while I bring the area up on Google maps," Rankin said. The sound of tapping on a keyboard was followed by, "Got it."

"Eileen and Ira are in Oletha investigating an alleged civil rights violation and Sheriff Staton brought them into a case of missing and murdered girls. They called me, and here I am."

"How many victims?"

"Three dead so far. We're not certain about how many…or even if the missing girls are related to this."

"How can I help?"

"We've developed some evidence in the civils rights case, in which a man was assassinated…."

"Assassinated?"

McCay looked at Prado and she jumped into the conversation. "This is Eileen Prado. Special Agent Fisher and I are working on the alleged civil rights violation. It's a long story I don't think I need to waste your time with, so I'll stick to how you can help us. Whoever killed the person in Oletha might have used a weapon manufactured in Canada, one we're told by our people is preferred by snipers. In other words, what a professional might use."

"Probably the C14 Timberwolf MRSWS. It's the sniper rifle used by the Canadian Armed Forces arsenal."

Had that on the tip of your tongue, did you?" McCay said teasingly.

Just happen to know because my son is a member of the Canadian Forces, the sniper unit."

We came to the right man on a number of levels," McCay said.

"And you want to know who might have been hired from here to do such a job?"

McCay answered, "Yes and no."

"Give me the 'yes' part."

"The person of interest in the kidnappings and the serial murders lived in Toronto and…"

"Wait," Rankin interrupted. "The same person is at the top of your list for the serial murders and the…., uh, I think you called it an assassination?"

"It's a bit of a stretch, maybe," Prado said, "but something we need to look at."

McCay stepped in. "He lived for a time in Toronto and I'd appreciate it if we could get some information on this person."

"If we have it, it's yours."

"His name is Orin Truville." McCay looked at Esper. "I'm introducing Sheriff John Esper of Oletha, the town where this person lives, and where he lived prior to moving to Toronto."

"Sheriff John Esper here. Orin Truville left for Toronto with his family about twenty years ago. He returned here a little more than three years ago." Esper glanced at McCay. "That's about all I know."

"No," McCay objected, "you know about the family and the circumstances that took them to Toronto."

"Right," Esper agreed and provided the relevant background concluding with, "We were actually surprised when Orin showed up back here. He was still in bad shape when he and his parents left and some of us heard he didn't make it."

"Okay," Rankin said. "What you need, then, is as much information as I can find on Orin Truville."

"Yes," McCay replied, "and while you're at it, we'd like to know if you've had any problems there that look like what we're dealing with."

"You'll be sending along some background I can work with?"

"Yes, I'll email the coroner's reports, photos, forensics results and my preliminary considerations. Orin Truville has no record I could find during a preliminary search, but as you heard he's only been back here a few years. Maybe you have something more on him. You should know we're dealing with a man who survived a traumatic event as a very young child. He was badly burned in that fire and likely has endured a very unpleasant life since, given his deformities. Things to keep in mind as you conduct your search."

"Will do. You certainly have your work cut out for you, Bob. Kidnapping, serial killing, and a murder for hire. Better you than me."

"On the sniper thing" Prado chimed in. "Send us whatever you can find on anyone who is known to handle this type of business. Maybe even forensics on any cases you suspect were contract killings, and the coroners' reports."

"I can do all that for you," Rankin said. "Bob, you never got back to us about a time when we can properly thank you for your help with Bernardo and McArthur. There are a number of politicians and muckety-mucks with the RCMP, the NPR, and my outfit waiting to get their pictures taken with you. Word is there's even a chance the PM might want to shake your hand."

"One of these days I'll be up your way, but right now, as you can see, I'm up to my ass in alligators."

"I'll get what you need soonest. Always good to be able to return favors."

"Bernardo?" Fisher said as soon as McCay hit the "end call" button. "Wasn't that like 20 years ago? Rape and murder."

"Multiple rapes and murders," McCay corrected. "And, yes, it was a while ago. Not unlike what we're dealing with here, without the more gruesome aspects."

"Depends on how you define 'gruesome,'" Prado countered. "We studied Bernardo in that symposium with Deitz I told you about. More than thirteen rapes. Dismembering one of the victims."

"And the other guy? McArthur?" Fisher asked.

"Bruce McArthur," McCay said. "A Dahmer-like serial offender who killed at least eight men. We used our experience with Dahmer to help Rankin with his investigation. But let's not get sidetracked," he demurred and turned toward his keyboard.

"Where do we go from here?" Fisher asked. "I'm guessing we're not going to wait around for whatever is coming from Canada."

"No," Staton said. "We're not going to wait around. We need to find Orin."

***

Crystal Truville's house was an exact replica of Tricia's. The only difference being the toys that littered Tricia's yard were absent in Crystal's.

The similarity was not lost on Fisher who stopped halfway up the walk, stared at the house, and remarked to Esper, "Same as Tricia's, right?"

"Yeah, Ken built both of'em. And Lurleen's too."

Esper, Prado and Fisher continued single file toward the front door, their concentration so intent on their task they failed to notice Crystal sitting on her haunches planting bulbs in a small flower garden about ten yards to the left of the entrance.

She watched as Esper knocked on the screen door and peered into the house. "Y'all lookin' for me?" she asked, stood, dropped a trowel from her hand, and wiped dirt and grass from the back side of her shorts.

"Got a minute? Esper asked.

Crystal eyed the three before settling on Esper. "This must be really, really serious," she said teasingly. ".A three-on-one deal this time." She walked past them, opened the screen door, and gestured for them to follow.

"Looked familiar outside and…." Fisher bent forward allowing him to see into the dining room. "The same layout in here. Never really have to leave your comfort zone as long as you keep your social circle small enough."

Crystal removed her gardening gloves and put them in the front pocket of the apron she wore with the words "God's little helper" stitched across the front. "Yup. Ken liked things to be a certain way. Made him comfortable that he could walk into any of his homes and sit down on the couch in the same place. Had the TV in the same place. Could find the frig in the same spot and grab a beer. But that ain't why you're here. To talk about our houses." She sat in an armchair facing the coffee table, prompting the three to settle on the couch opposite her.

Prado ran her hand along the cushion noting the same floral pattern found at Tricia's. The armchairs were also a match.

Crystal directed herself to Esper. "What can I do for you?"

"We'd like to talk to Orin. Is he home?"

"You know," Crystal said with an amused look on her face, "I was gonna come 'round and ask you if you'd seen him."

"Meaning?" Prado asked, the suspicion in her tone was pronounced.

"Meanin', I ain't seen him for a few days and it's worryin' me."

"Do you have any idea where he is?"

"If I did would I be askin' John if he's seen him?"

"Do you know why he'd leave?"

"Hell, I don't even know why he came back in the first place."

Prado sat forward on the couch. "That's an interesting response. Do you think he's left the area?"

"Have no idea." Crystal stood. "Why don't we end this so you can go find him?"

"We have a few more questions," Prado said and lowered her head indicating that Crystal should retake her seat.

"Excuse me," Crystal said and walked into the kitchen returning with a beer, an ashtray and a pack of cigarettes. "I'd offer you one," she said, holding up the can, 'cept I know you all can't drink while on duty. Got water in there if you want. Go on in. The glasses are in a cupboard."

"You said you don't know why your brother came back," Prado said.

Crystal lit a cigarette, exhaled at the three in front of her, picked a piece of tobacco from her tongue, wiped it on her apron, and took a sip of the beer. "That's right. I don't."

"He just showed up one day and that was it? No explanation?"

"That was it. He ain't a big talker."

"You never asked?

"Nope."

"You didn't have any contact with him or your parents after they left Oletha and moved to Toronto?" Prado scooted further forward on the couch. "You did know that's where they went when they left here, right"

Crystal smiled broadly and looked at Esper. "You never told these people 'bout Ken and my parents."

"We know," Prado answered. "It just seems unusual that your brother would end up back here after years of not being in touch. And on top of that, he never said anything about why he came back, especially considering why he and your parents left."

"Like I said, he ain't much of a talker, and I'm not real fond of talkin' 'bout all this. I don't know where Orin is. We done?"

Prado sat a moment and pulled the next subject out of the air. "Tell us more about Ken's trying to get into the meth business here in Oletha." She felt Fisher stir and hoped he would settle and play along.

"I didn't get into his business."

"Actually, you did. You already told us about going with him to talk to Hebert. But before he decided to hook up with Hebert, we're wondering if Orin tried to connect him with dealers in Toronto."

Crystal gave her a look. "What the hell're you talkin' 'bout?"

Prado bargained for time, asking, "You really don't know?"

"No."

Prado could feel Fisher's eyes on her. "It'd be best if you leveled with us."

"'Bout what?"

"One of the reasons I was assigned to this case is because we knew Ken was angling to get into the drug market in a big way in this region," Prado said, finding her stride. "You saw that yourself when he talked to Hebert about going into business together. And we think he was also looking for other sources."

"Come on," Crystal said with a laugh. "You're fulla shit."

"I worked with Canadian authorities in Toronto to break up an Asian narcotics syndicate there that imported drugs from the Golden Triangle into the U.S. through Toronto."

"Golden what?" Crystal asked.

"The Golden Triangle in Southeast Asia where a lot of drugs come from. It's where Laos, Myanmar and Thailand come together. One of the largest opium-producing regions in the world. A lot of heroin comes from there."

"And?" Crystal said, taking a long pull of beer.

"A cartel called 'Brother Number Three'," Prado continued, digging into her memory for the facts she remembered hearing from a colleague who had worked with the Canadians on drug interdiction, "is looking to expand into the Midwest. I'm thinking maybe Orin put Ken in touch with some of these people."

Crystal stared at Prado. "My brother can barely follow directions to drive to the store and pick up milk. Give me a break."

"But he did come here from Toronto, right?"

"As far as I know."

Esper broke into the conversation. "What'd he do in Toronto?"

"I don't know. I already told you he never said much 'bout livin' there."

Prado asked, "Do you think he might've gone back?"

"Could've," Crystal said with a shrug. "All I know is he ain't here and I haven't seen him for days."

"Does he have friends in Toronto?" Prado asked, but didn't wait for an answer. "Who would he live with? How would he make a living? If he can barely follow directions to get milk, does it make sense to you that he'd go back without any support system?"

Crystal shrugged, took a final drag on her cigarette and exhaled the smoke across the coffee table where the cloud hugged Esper, Prado and Fisher, and then crawled up the wall behind the couch. She took a long gulp of beer, and dropped the butt into the empty beer can. "Your guess is as good as mine."

"You don't have to guess," Prado challenged. "I think you know exactly where he is."

"I don't know where he is. I have no reason to lie 'bout that." She stood and headed toward the kitchen, asking as she went, "He ain't done nothing bad has he?"

"Yes, we suspect he's done something bad," Prado called to Crystal, "and we're going to find him. When we do, you'd better hope he's smart enough not to implicate you. Thanks you for your time."

***

Esper waited until they were halfway down the walk before saying, "You just called her a liar in her own home. I don't know 'bout how this works where you're from, but that's a reason for her to never talk to you again."

"First of all," Prado said, stopping dead and facing Esper. "She's lying. Second, I just let her know we know she's lying. It might cause her to do something stupid, like lead us to Orin. That's how we do things where I come from."

"Where'd you get all that about Canada, and the Asian gang stuff?" Fisher asked as they pulled the doors of the car shut.

"I wanted to keep her talking. She was about to throw us out. When Toronto came up it reminded me of a conversation I had with someone in D.C. just before we came here. Some of it was actually true."

"Like?"

"Like the Asian drug syndicate using Toronto as a jumping off point for funneling drugs into the States."

"That's really a thing?"

Prado nodded. "And it occurred to me that since Ken wanted to up his drug game, it's not a stretch to think he might've talked to Orin about what's going on in Toronto."

"You really believe that's possible?"

"It doesn't matter what I believe, only what we can get Crystal to believe. She and her crew of harpies have a very inflated view of who Plough was, what he was capable of, especially Crystal. Remember, he wanted to use Silas as an entrée with Hebert. He established a precedent in their minds of using a connection to spread his wings." She raised a hand in caution. "I know the comparison between a local meth dealer and an established criminal enterprise in Canada is a stretch, but, hell, it's a shot, and not one entirely in the dark. But the point is we need to make Crystal nervous. Keep her unsettled and she might do something stupid."

"Like?"

"Like say something or do something that leads us to Orin, or brings him out of whatever hole he's crawled into."

"You just made all that up?" Esper said incredulously.

"It kind of took shape while I was talking," Prado answered.

Esper asked, "Why go through all that story-telling and not just tell her we think Orin might've killed those girls? I can't believe she'd be okay with that. If she knows where he is, she'd tell us."

"I'm with John," Fisher said.

"Really?" Esper spit out in surprise.

"Yes, really. Canada. Drug connections. Golden Triangle. That's a very circular route to get at Orin."

"You two really need to read the material Bob gave us," Prado said with a note of impatience. "No one *ever* believes someone close to them is killing people, especially family members." She looked at Esper and turned toward Fisher in the back seat of the cruiser. "*They never believe it*," she said emphatically to bring home her point.

"I got it," Fisher said, "but we have some pretty convincing bread crumbs leading to Orin, and if we tell Crystal what we…."

"Bread crumbs?" Prado interjected, leaning further across the front seat to look squarely at Fisher. "She'd buy Canada and drugs before she'd ever accept that her brother is a serial killer. If we tried to sell her that, she'd relax thinking we are out of our minds. We definitely don't want her relaxed. We want her nervous as a cat. Orin is mixed up in this stew of the girls being missing and torn up; and he's a key, somehow, to our business with Plough."

Fisher held up his hands in surrender. "Okay. Got it."

Prado jerked herself around to face front. "And if you two want a lesson on how hard it is for people to accept the reality of the deviancy we're dealing with read the damn stuff McCay gave us. And pay real close attention to a guy named David Williams who is, it just so happens, Canadian. He commanded Canada's largest military airbase and was a decorated pilot. Meanwhile, he was breaking into homes and stealing women's underwear, which he dressed up in. He graduated from that to serial rape and murder. Imagine trying to convince anyone that this guy was a really bad dude."

"Devil's advocate," Fisher said cautiously. "You say she wouldn't believe Orin's capable of killing anyone. Why'd he take off then? I mean why does *she* think he took off?"

"I have no idea," Prado said and tapped Esper on his arm. "You keep an eye on Crystal and Lurleen and Tricia. They might lead us to Orin."

"How can I watch three women? I'm a one-man operation."

"Here's a thought," Fisher offered. "Crystal is the brains of the outfit. None of them is going to do anything without her." He patted Esper on the shoulder. "Watch her and you'll be okay."

"What he said," Prado said with a wink at Esper.

***

The plates were lined up along one arm, glasses in the opposite hand. He advanced slowly, both feet on each stair before stepping down to the next. The girls pushed themselves against the wall, into the shadows.

"Now that I gotta stay here with you, I got time to make better food," he said proudly, laying a plate on the cement floor in front of each mattress. He pointed at the plastic plates. "Bought'em at the Dollar General. They almost look like real ones."

A moment of silence passed before one the girls responded, "Thank you."

"Corned beef hash and green peas," he said and walked to the farmers' sink, where he filled a green plastic garden watering can. He held it up as if a displaying a prized possession. "Fresh water for everyone." He placed it in front of the mattress closest to the stairwell.

The girl on this mattress, which was partially hidden under the steps, moved forward into the dim light. "You're that guy who almost got killt in the fire," she said, both astonishment and surprise in her voice.

"Shut up," pleaded a small, terrified voice.

The man looked at the figure emerging from the shadows. "What?"

She raised her hand and pointed at his arms. "That."

The other two girls, who had been inching toward the plates of food, retreated. Reaching the wall, one leaned her back against the cold cement and raised her knees as if trying to hide behind herself. The other turned her face toward the wall.

He looked down at his naked arms, studying the mottled skin. The raised scars swirled up his arm from the top part of his hand to where his skin disappeared under the sleeve of his Tee-shirt. Ribbons of light purple, green and red threaded through the welts.

"My brother went to school with you," the girl continued. "He told me what happened." She crawled forward on her hands and knees. "The fire and all 'cause of your sister." Wonder in her voice.

The man stepped forward and grabbed the girl by her hair, lifted her straight up off the mattress, as high as the chain allowed, and tossed her on the floor in front of him. "You think you know what happened?" he hissed and removed his shirt. The scars covered his chest and stomach. He lowered his pants. The welts continued down his groin and onto both legs. On his legs, the wounds took a thicker and more complicated pattern, almost appearing to shine.

"I didn't mean nothing by it," the girl wailed, whipping her legs to propel herself onto the mattress.

"I didn't mean nothing by it,*" he said, mocking her. "Didn't your mother teach you no manners?" He lowered his face until his nose almost touched the girl's. "It ain't nice to make fun of people."*

"I wasn't making fun, honest. I wasn't doin' that," she said, tears streaming down her cheeks. "I sometimes say things without thinkin'. People say that 'bout me. I don't know why." She touched her mouth. "The words jus' come out."

"Yes, you was makin' fun of me. I know what people think. 'That ugly man. He better not come near me.' Like they'll catch some kinda disease or maybe these" – he slapped his chest – "will crawl onto their skin."

"No, please, I'm sorry. I'm sorry, really." The girl was on her knees, prayer-style, her hands clasped in front of her face.

"You ain't sorry," the man said and kicked her in the side of the head knocking her off the mattress. He flew on top of her and began slamming her head on the concrete. "You ain't sorry." He was screaming at the top of his lungs

and smashing her head again and again and again. Blood splashed across his face and chest.

When what was left of the girl's face came apart in his hands, he stood and threw her scalp on the floor. He started stroking his erection and walked over to the girl facing the wall, her shoulders shaking, and ejaculated on her.

He backed up slowly, bent over, hands on his knees, and stayed this way, breathing heavily. "You two wanna help me dump her in the pond?" he asked calmly. "She liked ponds."

He straightened and flexed his back, pulled on his pants and shirt, and went to the sink, where he washed the blood off his hands and face. He attached a hose to the faucet and hosed down the area around the body, then walked to a darkened area of the basement and returned with a plastic shower curtain. He laid it on the floor, rolled the body onto it, and secured the bundle with duct tape.

He walked over to the girl still huddled in a fetal position and unlocked her ankle chain, then to the other, releasing her from the cuff.

"There's a bar of soap in the sink. Go get it." When neither girl moved, he stood, arms on his hips and asked calmly, "Whatsa matter? You don't wanna go for a little swim in the pond and wash up some? You both smell like shit."

The girl closest to the sink crawled over and pulled herself up to the bowl. She stood unsteadily, gained her balance, and held up a small bar of soap.

"Good," he said.

He lifted the plastic-wrapped body and hoisted it over his shoulder. The two girls remained frozen in place, one gripping the sink, legs shaking, the other on the mattress.

"C'mon. Stand," he said to the one. When she struggled to push herself up, he held out a hand which she looked at warily. "Let's go. It ain't gonna be dark forever." He held her hand until she took a few steady steps.

The girls leaned on each other and followed him up the steps, using the handrails to pull themselves along. Once in the kitchen, they collapsed onto the chairs around a small table. They both squinted and turned their heads away from the overhead light. One of the girls ran her hand along the top of the table and looked around the room, her face impassive, but eyes darting. The second leaned to better see into the living room where the sound from a television set announced the "Late News."

The man tossed the body onto the floor of the kitchen and approached the girls, who got small and considered him warily. "I have to get a wheelbarrow." He jerked his head toward the bloody shower curtain. "You move from these chairs, that's you."

***

"Your hair," he called out to the girls. "Make sure you wash your hair. It smells really bad." He sat on the bank, which inclined toward the small pond and watched. "Wash each other's back," he instructed.

Sitting next to the wheelbarrow, he put his hand on top of the shower curtain feeling the warmth of the body. "Can't do it," he muttered to himself. "It just wouldn't be right."

MONDAY

McCay took up his position, kneeling in front of the body. Staton stood close behind. Prado and Fisher circled the inside of the cordoned area, careful not to disturb the scene.

"That's different," Staton said. "Why'd he do that?" He breathed out a deep sigh. "A ridiculous question." A beat of silence. "Because he's out of his fucking mind."

"I assume you're referring to what's left of her face," McCay answered. "And, no, it's not a ridiculous question." He pushed himself upright. "This is different from the others. Not consistent with his signature. It's more violent and it could be telling."

"How?"

"In a couple of ways," McCay said, stepping closer to the body. He studied the bindings and the wounds. "The MO looks to be the same." He turned and gestured to the surroundings. "This is the same. It's his comfort zone."

"Which we've staked out," Staton said. "But we're talking about 20 acres."

"Most of this," McCay said, pointing at the body, "is done somewhere else. He only has to get in here to display the body. The final step in his ritual. He can do it relatively quickly and without being seen, obviously."

"Almost useless to surveil the parking area," Staton said, "but we have people in and out of there."

McCay eyed the surroundings. "He could've come in from anywhere."

"And did," Staton agreed. "So, we're dealing with the same guy who ain't stupid."

"No, he isn't," McCay agreed and stepped nearer to the body. "The wounds are the same, other than those to the face. There are signs she was shackled. The right index finger is missing. This is definitely the same perpetrator." McCay took a pen out of his pocket and brushed back what was left of the victim's hair on what remained of her scalp. "Could be he needs this increased level of violence to get himself off, or he's in a frenzy."

"A frenzy?" Prado, standing across from McCay, asked, her pitch strained. "All of them have looked pretty frenzied to me."

McCay backed away from the bloodied figure and stood, legs spread, arms folded across his chest. "This is worse than any of the others." He continued in a monotone. "He couldn't control himself. This killing is disorganized. His urges might be driving him to extremes."

"The others weren't extreme?" Fisher asked.

McCay, circling the body, did not hear the question. "He could have entered the frenzy stage," he said nodding as he spoke. "At this stage, Ed Kemper bludgeoned his own mother to death with a claw hammer, decapitated her and raped her severed head. Ted Bundy roamed around a sorority house in the middle of the night and bludgeoned four women with a log. Some of those victims were sexually assaulted and bitten. Mary Anne Kelly, Jack the Ripper's final victim, was torn up so badly the corpse was barely recognizable as human. Her breasts and legs were cut off and her major organs were removed."

"I take it there isn't another stage after frenzy," Prado said.

"No, and it's the one that usually results in them getting caught. It did with both Bundy and Kemper. They were so out of control they left evidence behind. Bundy left his DNA all over the bodies. Kemper reached the end of his tether and just gave himself up."

Fisher walked up beside McCay, turning his shoulder and head away from the corpse. "I'm guessing this means Orin is still around."

"A possibility," McCay agreed, "or he isn't the person doing this and *that* person is still around."

"Where does that leave us?"

"In deep shit," Staton answered.

***

"He's called a few times," the receptionist said, handing Staton a phone message, which he passed to McCay.

"Rankin," McCay read from the small piece of paper.

Staton handed her back the message and instructed, "Call that number and put it through to the conference room."

As Staton, McCay, Esper, Fisher and Prado hurried away, the woman's fading "I tried to call you" followed them down the hallway.

"Sorry, David," McCay said and pushed the conference button on a phone unit. "We were out at the site of another one." He glanced around the room. "I had my phone muted and I guess the rest of us did too, or we just didn't hear…"

Rankin interrupted, "No need to apologize. I've been where you are too many times. Everything else just kind of fades into the background."

"Only you and a handful of others would fully understand that," McCay answered. "Same group's here you talked to last time."

"Hello all," Rankin said. "It took us a little while to get a bead on your guy. We found out someone by the name of Orin Truville was living in Toronto for a few years and then it's like he disappeared from the face of the earth. We had him up until the age of ten. Found him through information from the Children's Aid Society, which will make sense in a minute. Anyway, when he was still Orin Truville…"

"*Still* Orin Truville?" McCay asked.

"Let me run through everything I have and it will fall together," Rankin answered. "His name initially surfaced in some CAS reports that came about after his teachers reported the child was unkempt, overly thin, shy, unresponsive and a long list of other problems, including physical injuries like bruises, a split lip that required stitches, and a black eye." The sound of shuffling papers preceded his adding, "We found other CAS records saying the boy's parents weren't taking him for treatments for his burns. Child Services case workers also reported the parents were abusive to each other."

"Abusive to each other?" McCay questioned. "Any details?"

"The parents called the police on each other all the time. So did the neighbors. Fighting. Screaming. The usual. Cut to the bottom line, the mother killed her husband, and the boy went into the foster care system. After a few years of getting shuttled around, we lost Orin Truville."

"Lost him?" McCay asked. "That's all you have?"

"Patience," Rankin cautioned. "Patience."

"Sorry," McCay apologized. "Go ahead."

"Orin ended up with a couple, Edith and Max Schneiderman. But it wasn't an official handoff, or it doesn't look like it was because there is no adoption record."

"What does that mean? How did he end up with them?"

"Not sure, but I've seen similar things before. The kid gets handed off and the entire transaction is under the table so the foster parents can continue collecting the support money."

"I'm sorry to interrupt," Prado said. "Are you saying he wasn't officially adopted?"

"Yes, I mean 'no', he wasn't, which is why I said he *ended up* with the Schneidermans. There is no record of an adoption, but that's not an entirely unusual happenstance. If it went the way the others I know of did, the Schneidermans wanted a child and somehow connected with Orin's foster parents. The kid ends up in a new home but nothing is legalized so the foster parents continue to collect the child care allowance. There's a sophisticated underground network here that organizes this sort of thing. Puts foster parents together with people who want a child. We're constantly breaking up these connections and they're constantly re-emerging. Children are also sold this way for sex and child porn."

"Jesus Christ," Fisher said, slumping forward, sliding his elbows onto the top of the table as he covered his face with his hands.

"So, Orin Truville became Orin Schneiderman?" McCay asked.

"Yeah," Rankin acknowledged. "Not officially, like I said, but from everything we can find, he was well-treated and cared for."

Prado asked, "How did his foster parents explain that he wasn't living with them? I assume there were regular visits from whoever runs the foster care system."

"As happens in so many of these cases, the house he was assigned to had a lot of kids running around, and the case worker just checked off the required boxes. Until you asked us to find him, there was never any reason to suspect foul play."

McCay asked, "How did you find out that he ended up with the Schneidermans?"

"When we first talked you mentioned he was burned pretty badly, so after we lost the trail for Orin Truville, we started looking for hospitals and rehab centers specializing in burn therapy. Once we hit on one that treated an 'Orin', we were able to connect the dots."

"Did you speak to the Schneidermans?"

"They died."

"When?" McCay, Prado and Fisher asked simultaneously.

"A little more than three years ago."

"Orin ended up here about that time," Esper said, confirming what the others were thinking.

"I've got a lot more," Rankin said, "and it's not good."

"Why doesn't that surprise me?" Fisher said.

"When he was in high school, he grabbed a couple of neighborhood girls, took them to an abandoned house and molested them. We're talking about two ten-year olds. He told them if they said anything, he'd kill their families. They didn't say anything."

"How'd you find out about it?" McCay asked.

"He was charged with raping a classmate about a year later. She did tell her parents and they pressed charges. The earlier incident came out then. I'm guessing the girls told their parents when they heard about the rape charges. The prosecutor tried to include the first incident with the rape charge, but it was ruled inadmissible. Hearsay. No evidence. You know the drill. And it ended up being his word against hers about the rape. His defense was that it was consensual. This was a bench trial and the judge basically cut the baby in half. He gave Orin a choice. Enlist in the army or go to jail. He chose the service and was trained as a sniper."

Prado lifted out of her chair and braced herself, arms on the table. "A sniper?"

"I thought that might get your attention," Rankin said, a smile evident in his voice. "Yes, indeed, and apparently he was a pretty good. In fact, and please excuse the xenophobia, but Canada has the best snipers of any military in the world. Our boys have been credited with shooting a top Islamic State fighter in Iraq from more than two miles away. A record for distance."

"Orin did that?" Esper asked.

"No, no," Rankin clarified, "that wasn't him, but he did get all kinds of recognition from the Canadian Special Operations unit where he was assigned."

"Jesus," Prado exclaimed and shot a sidelong glance at McCay. "You said something about 'crosscurrents' blowing through both of these cases."

McCay nodded. "This is terrific, David. I really appreciate…."

"Oh, there's more," Rankin said. "Schneiderman came back to Toronto after his enlistment ended. He was living in a boarding house here, in a sketchy area known as Jane and Finch. One of the boarders was a woman working as a prostitute, and according to other boarders she was real tough on Orin. She ridiculed him all the time. Long story short, she was found in her room cut open from her neck to her pubic area. He had hung her up in her closet, displayed like the carcass of an animal that had been killed by a hunter."

Everyone in the conference room edged closer to the conference call console as McCay described the crime scenes in Maryville. "Does that sound like what you found?"

"Exactly, except for the plastic wrap part. Our victim's insides were spilled all over the closet. If your Orin Truville is our Orin Schneiderman, and I'd bet a year's pay he is, we'd be very interested in talking to him when you bring him in, which, I'm guessing is the next step."

"Indeed it is," McCay agreed, "but first we have to find him. He's disappeared."

Rankin grunted. "I wouldn't presume to tell you your business, Bob, and you know that. You've always been the person I've gone to for help and advice when we have a problem. But from what I learned about Schneiderman on this end, I don't think he'll go far. He doesn't seem to do well on his own. He's around there somewhere."

"Agreed."

"One other thing," Rankin said. "Snipers in the Special Operations units can buy their weapons and take them when they leave the service. Of course, they're expected to register the weapons. Schneiderman bought his but never registered it."

Once off the phone, Prado said, "Ira and I spent the weekend game-playing where Orin might have gone. Toronto was one possibility, but I agree with Rankin that it's not likely. We even hiked around the Woods to see if he had erected a shelter out there for himself. He wasn't at the red house. That takes us back to one place."

***

"Now's the time to lay it all out," Prado said to Fisher and Esper as they pulled to a stop in front of Crystal Truville's home.

"Really?" Fisher said. "Just like that? In her face today, but not a hint yesterday."

"Timing's everything, especially given what we just learned. And since she's not one to hide her 'charm' under a bustle, her reaction should be telling."

"For sure, she's not going to be glad to see us after calling her a liar," Esper said. "Wouldn't be surprised if she didn't let us in."

"She'll let us in," Prado said confidently.

As they got out of the cruiser Crystal appeared at the screen door and called out to them. "You all are visiting more'n my kids."

"We have some information on your brother," Prado said as they walked toward the house. "I was wrong about him. I think you'll appreciate knowing what we've found."

Crystal stared through the door, took a drag on her cigarette and blew the smoke in their direction. "I already know he's not some kinda big time drug dealer."

Prado waved away the smoky assault. "Can we come in?"

Crystal pushed open the door and walked away. She disappeared into the kitchen where the sound of a popping can was followed by "No beers, right?"

"No, thank you," Prado responded as she walked to a side table on the opposite end of the room and studied a cluster of framed photographs. She picked out two and returned to the couch, joining Fisher and Esper as Crystal sat opposite them.

Fisher leaned toward the photo Prado held in her lap. "Your father, mother, and brother?"

Esper added, "I remember your mother and father."

Crystal looked at the photo. "Make yourself at home," she said sarcastically.

Fisher pointed. "And there's you. How old?"

Crystal didn't answer.

Prado made an exercise out of reaching down, picking up the photo, and handing it to Crystal. "Before all the trouble?"

Crystal laid the frame face down on the coffee table.

"Now this one's impressive," Prado said, tapping the glass on the second photo.

Crystal's eyes went to the photo.

"You told us you had no idea what Orin was doing in Canada," Prado said as she handed Crystal the frame.

Crystal laid this one atop the other without looking at it. "Never asked him 'bout it."

Prado lifted the photo from the table and held it toward Crystal. "Orin in his uniform. He was in the Special Forces. A sniper. He was decorated for his service." She continued holding the photo across the coffee table until Crystal took it from her.

"Never talked 'bout it."

"Really? Your brother spends most of his life in Canada. Joins the service there, which is another story altogether, and it never occurs to you to ask him about any of it? His life. Your parents. He never told you your mother killed your father…."

Crystal squirmed in her chair.

"…and he ended up in the foster care system, then with a couple that brought him up? You really expect us to believe that?"

Crystal laughed. "I don't give a shit what you believe."

"That's an interesting way to motivate us to continue our investigation into what happened with your ex-husband's murder," Fisher offered.

"You ain't here 'bout that or you wouldn't be asking these stupid questions."

"You're wrong," Prado said. "This has everything to do with it."

"The last time you came in here," Crystal said, irritation in her voice, "you was sayin' Orin was helpin' Ken become some kind of big-time drug dealer." She waved her hand. "That he was puttin' Ken together with some people in Toronto. Now, you're askin' 'bout him bein' a soldier. I'd say you don't know what the fuck you're doin'."

"Your brother was a decorated sniper," Prado said and stared at the woman who averted her eyes and shielded her face in a cloud of smoke exhaled from her mouth and nose.

"So what?"

"He was forced into the service by a judge who, rather than sentence him to jail for sexual assault, gave him the choice to enlist." Prado pointed at the photograph. "But he never discussed any of this with you?"

"Nope, and I don't believe any of that shit 'bout sexual assault. He can't talk to a woman without practically faintin'."

"Which would explain why he assaults them," Fisher said forcefully. "Then he doesn't have to talk to them."

"He never told you that your mother killed your father?" Prado asked sharply.

Crystal stood. "Get out."

"He never told you that the reason he came back to Oletha was because he was about to be arrested for murdering a woman."

"Oh, give me a fuckin' break," Crystal said aggressively. She pointed at the door. "Get outta my house."

Esper began to push himself off the couch. Prado grabbed him by the arm, pulling him back. "We can do this here in the comfort of your home, or we'll come back with a subpoena, cuff and arrest you," Prado said harshly. "We'll also get a search warrant and go through your house with a fine-toothed comb. It's entirely up to you."

"Arrest me for what?" Crystal barked. "Get a search warrant on what grounds?"

"Sounds like you've been through this before," Prado said. "You must know then that I'll think of a good reason for getting the warrants."

Crystal put her hands on her hips and stared at Prado. "You got five minutes."

"I'll take all the time I need," Prado said, and ordered the woman to "Sit."

Crystal remained standing and pulled a pack of cigarettes from the pocket of her sweat pants. She made a show of selecting a stick, packing the tobacco against the face of her wristwatch, and lighting up. After a full inhale, she sat.

"In addition to the murder in Toronto, your brother is a person of interest in the murder of at least three girls in Maryville and the kidnapping of…what?" She looked at Esper and Fisher. "Four?"

"At least four," Esper answered.

Crystal sank back into the chair and, hands now shaking, looked around the room before snarling, "This is bullshit. What's a 'person of interest'?"

"In the old days we'd have called him a suspect," Fisher said. "This is just a gentler way of saying we have very good reason to believe your brother is a serial killer and kidnapper."

Prado pushed herself forward on the couch. "What does it tell you that the woman he's suspected of murdering in Canada was killed in the same way as the ones in Maryville? You know about the girls, right?"

"I know some girls ran off. They're always runnin' away. I ran away with Ken, for fuck's sake. Youngsters get bored and run away."

"But you haven't heard a thing about the ones found in Maryville, strung up and cut open like animals?" Prado asked, challenging Crystal. "You don't know that one of those girls was Alice Moore?"

"Now, you're tryin' to say Ken had something to do with all those things? You all are really chasin' your tails."

Prado shook her head slowly. "You missed what I'm saying altogether. There is a relationship in all of this, and to Ken getting shot in what now looks like a professional hit."

"Oh, for fuck's sake?" Crystal exclaimed. "A professional hit?"

Prado raised a hand. "We'll get to that. Girls go missing and some have been discovered killed, gruesomely so. And your brother appears to have some sort of relationship to all of it."

Prado took a breath and stared at Crystal. "Bottom line. The murders around here started about the same time Orin came back. And we've talked to people who saw him with some of the girls. What does that tell you?"

Crystal stood abruptly and pointed at the door. "It tells me you oughta get outta here right the fuck now. You wanna talk to me ever again, go ahead and arrest me for whatever, and get a subpoena or you're never getting' in here again."

Crystal followed them to the door where Prado stopped and faced the woman, invading her personal space. "Don't you want to know why we think Ken was killed by a pro?"

"Fuck you, bitch," Crystal said and slammed the door.

"She's definitely not hiding her charm under a bustle," Fisher said as they walked away from the house. "But I can't tell if we pissed her off or scared her."

"You said something the other day about Crystal being the lead dog," Prado said as they got into the cruiser. "I have a bad feeling about that."

"About her being the lead dog?"

"About what kind of control she might have over *all* of this."

Esper asked, "You think she has something to do with Orin's killing those girls?"

Prado stared out of the windshield. "I don't really know what I mean. I just have a bad feeling about how she might be involved with everything, and that's what she's hiding under her bustle."

***

"The owner of that bar?" Prado questioned Hebert as they stood outside the conference room, huddled with Staton, Esper and Fisher.

"Yeah, Stacy talked to his girls about what we told him. You know, a warning kind of talk. Afterwards he said Gretchen" – Hebert nodded at the figure sitting at the conference table – "told him some stuff and convinced her she should talk to me. Man, she told me some really fucked up shit. You gotta hear it yourself, and I think that guy McCay too."

"Why didn't you tell me about this?" Prado said.

"I am!"

"No, I mean tell me and take me with you when you went to talk to her."

"Stacy made you for a cop right off," Hebert said. "And he's really pissed at me for bringing you around. Also, he had to force her to even talk to me. She's scared as hell and is convinced if she tells the cops, or anyone, her name'll get out and the guy'll come after her."

"What guy is that exactly?" Staton asked.

"Best if you hear all of it from her," Hebert said, glancing at the girl who had pulled her hoodie over her head and, legs up on the chair in front of her, was a tiny figure who was trying to disappear. "I told her she really needed to tell you what she told me 'cause other girls are gettin' killed. I practically had to drag her in here."

McCay ran toward them from the building entrance. "Sorry," he said breathlessly and bent forward, hands on knees. "I was with the coroner. You have someone who survived an attack? Is that right?"

"Kinda," Hebert answered. "I was just sayin' you all need to hear everything she told me, but I don't think she's gonna talk 'less I'm with her. Hell, I don't know for sure if she'll talk to you anyway. She sure as shit didn't want to come here."

Staton said, "Bob, I think it'd be best if you do this. A crowd is going to be intimidating." He nodded toward the girl who remained statue still, hugging herself tightly. "Talk to her in there. If she's that skittish, an interrogation room would freak her out."

"Shit, yes, it would," Hebert said. "Even tryin' to move her in there would likely freak her out."

McCay pointed at a phone console. "If I hit the conference button, is there somewhere the rest of you can listen in."

"My office," Staton said.

McCay let Hebert precede him into the conference room. The girl's eyes followed the men as they came into the room. Her shoulders shook and she tightened her grip around her legs.

McCay walked to the opposite side of the table letting Hebert sit down next to the girl who he introduced as Gretchen Donovan. She lowered her legs to the floor and pulled back her hoodie. Her pallor was almost gray. McCay recognized it as fear.

Hebert spoke slowly and softly. "No one is gonna know you talked to us. This man is from the FBI and…."

"No," Gretchen said, shaking her head, spraying the top of the conference table with huge teardrops. "You didn't say nothin' 'bout no FBI." She pulled her legs back onto the chair, wrapped her arms around her shins, and buried her face between her knees.

"He needs to hear what you tol' me." Hebert gently pulled her hands apart and she let her feet drop to the floor. "He can find this man and make sure he's put in prison for a long time, and a long ways from here. That's what he does. Finds'em and puts'em away."

The woman slumped forward, staring into her lap.

"You're being very brave, Gretchen," McCay began. "My name is Bob McCay. As Frankie said, it's safe to tell us what you know. I'm not going to take any notes. Nothing is going to be written down or recorded, but what I'd like to do is press this button here" – he pointed at the phone console – "so those other people who were with us outside can hear what you have to say. They won't write anything down either, and what you say stays with us. I just need them to hear you and then they can help me find this person you're going to tell us about. Okay?"

Gretchen raised her eyes and looked at Hebert. "You really think I should be doing this?" she asked, her voice trembling. She sniffed and wiped her nose with the sleeve of a pink hoodie matching her sweat pants, which were adorned with Hello Kitty characters. "I don't know if I should be doin' this."

McCay walked to the bureau and picked up a pile of napkins from a small wicker basket, brought them back to the table, and handed a few to the girl. He could see she had once been beautiful. High cheekbones, full lips, and a classic profile had given way to a haggard, hollow-cheeked shell. He knew her dull green eyes and physical gauntness were the result of the fear that ate away at her. She was not a victim of drugs or alcohol. He had seen this sort of physical deterioration in victims of the horrible crimes he had made a career trying to prevent. And it was the continual parade of victims that often caused him to question his work. How much did it matter? How successful was he? Did he ever bring any solace to the victims? To their families? The burden was soul-crushing and he too often found himself absolutely spent after walking away from encounters with prey like Gretchen Donovan. As he had done so many times before, McCay comforted himself as much as he did the person across the table by saying, "We have no choice. We can stop this evil."

Hebert put his hand on the woman's shoulder. "Please tell him what you told me."

Gretchen lowered her head, closed her eyes and took a deep breath. Only the buzzing of fluorescent lights disturbed the quiet. She exhaled and sat up straight. Her eyes brightened and she took command of her emotions. In a flat but steady voice she said, "Me and three friends was gonna go skinny-dipping like we did every Friday night after it got dark." Her voice was quiet but steady. "Only when it was warm, of course.

"Ida, Lydia and me was friends from like first grade. Willie was there too. She was Ida's sister. She was two grades behind us."

McCay saw that Hebert was about to interrupt, no doubt, he thought, to ask the same questions he was considering. Where? When? He shook his head and mouthed, "later."

"I was never real big on swimming with nothin' on. You wouldn't know it to look at me now but back then I had kinda nice boobs and the boys was always lookin' at'em and used to say the most ugly things. Anyway," she said with a swipe of her hand, "I was in the bushes, kinda scared to come out. I always was like that. Always the last one to run into the water. Ida, Willie and Lydia was already in the water. I was headin' toward the water but still not out of the shadows when this huge man"—she raised her arms to indicate his height – "comes runnin' down the bank and tells'em to get out. That it's his property and they can't swim there. I'd never seen him before and we'd been goin' there for the whole summer."

Gretchen closed her eyes and fell silent. Hebert looked across the table at McCay and shrugged his shoulders. McCay gestured 'patience' with an open hand.

"He grabs'em" – Gretchen made a sweep with her arms – "and 'cause he was so big he could hold'em all at once. Like corral'em. I was afraid to move and laid down flat as I could. I was thinkin' of goin' back to get my phone, which was with my clothes, but I was afraid to move. I don't think I coulda moved. He took them to what looked like a burnt house and I could see that he pushed Lydia and she musta' fallen into a hole there. He had Willie and Ida by the hair and it looked like he lifted them up" – she held her arms away from her side– "and carried'em down into the hole."

Gretchen stopped and stared at the top of the table. "Give me a minute," she said. "I ain't let myself think 'bout this in a long time. Spent most of my time tryin' to forget." She shook her head and repeated, "Always tryin' to forget the details." She reached for the napkins and blew her nose.

"Take as much time as you need," McCay said. "I'm going to get a bottle of water. Would you like one?"

She nodded her answer and surprised McCay by getting up and pacing along one side of the table. He opened the small refrigerator, looked at Hebert for a signal that he wanted water. Hebert waved him off. He brought two bottles back with him, offering one to Gretchen. She took a long swig, blew her nose, and sat down.

She continued, her voice strong. "I waited a while and then snuck up to the house. What there was left of it anyways. Everything was pretty burnt down. There wasn't really nothin' but a staircase that went down into a basement lookin' place."

Gretchen took another long sip of water, closed her eyes, and lowered her head. The clicking of the fluorescent lights created a background chorus.

"So," she said suddenly, causing McCay and Hebert to flinch. "I could hear'em screamin', but I couldn't see nothin'. The only light was flickerin' like it came from a candle. The screamin' was bad. I never heard nothin' like it before, or since. Not like screamin' at a movie or when something scares you, but like screamin' 'cause you're gonna die. Then…" Gretchen stopped and sat a moment. "Then, I see Ida's head bouncin' around at the bottom of the stairs. I shit." She looked at the men. "I really shit. All over myself and I couldn't move. This man grabs the head and sees me lookin' down. He throws it at me and starts to run up the stairs."

Gretchen laid her head on the table.

"Do you want to take a moment," McCay asked. "Take a break for a few minutes?"

"No," Gretchen said sharply, raising her head. "If I stop, I might not be able to start again."

"Okay," McCay said.

"I don't remember a whole lot after that. I never went back for my clothes or anything. I ran home and got in the shower before my Mom could see me. I remember thinkin' he was gonna come after me and take my head off. I never said nothin' to nobody. I don't think I slept at all for a year. I ain't never slept more'n a few hours a night since."

McCay waited to be certain she was finished before asking, "I have a few questions, if that's okay."

Gretchen nodded. "But like I said, other than what I jus' told you, I don't remember much else."

"When was this?"

"Four years ago."

"Four?" McCay asked. "Are you certain?"

"It'll be four this summer." Gretchen poked her temple with her index finger. "It's stuck in there and I ain't never gonna be able to forget it."

"You never said anything to your parents or anyone else?"

Gretchen shook her head. "Nothin' to nobody." She buried her head in her hands. "That was bad, I know, but I was scared if I did, he'd find out who I was and come get me. I kept thinkin' it would come out without me sayin' anything. Someone would say they was missing and they'd go lookin'."

"Did the other girl's parents report them missing?"

Gretchen nodded.

"Didn't anyone ever ask you about them since you all were out together?"

"No, we never told no one what we did. That we went to the pond to skinny dip. We all just left our houses and met up and went there together."

"The pond here in Maryville?" McCay asked. "In the Woods?"

"No, the pond outside Oletha. There ain't nothing 'round there. No one ever goes to that one. Everyone goes to the one here 'cause it's bigger and you can row boats on it. The one in Oletha is small and kinda dirty. I never even noticed that burned down house before that night. It was burnt to the ground, and you couldn't see nothin' 'less you was right up on it. Never even heard no one talk 'bout it."

"Can you remember what the man looked like?"

"He was big, and he was really ugly. There was somethin' wrong with his face, but I didn't get a good look. And now I'm done," she said, stood, and turned toward Hebert. "Get me the fuck outta here."

"One more question, please," McCay said. "We heard a man who looks like that has been to Stacy's." He waited for a reaction, getting none, he continued. "Have you ever seen him there?"

Gretchen stared at the top of the table. "I know someone like that comes in." She shook her head. "But I ain't never seen him. Told the others to tell me if they see anyone like him and I stay in my room."

"He has been there, you were told, and you stayed in your room," McCay clarified.

She nodded and started toward the door. "I'm done and I ain't never gonna talk 'bout this again."

Hebert trailed her out of the room and down the corridor.

"She's barely out of high school," Prado was saying as she walked into the conference room. "She's working at a whore house and looks like she's in her thirties. Like she's been worn out."

"Seeing your friends swept up by a maniac and one of them decapitated will do that to you," Fisher responded.

"So will guilt," Staton added. "Imagine living with what she saw and not saying a word to anyone. That will eat at your soul."

As Staton, Prado, Fisher and Esper settled around the conference room, McCay was placing a stack of folders on the table. "I have one for each of you and you need to read it carefully and do so now. Please excuse any typos, and the grammar and sentence structure might be rough. I put it together quickly after our latest conversation with David Rankin. I think you'll find it confirms what we just heard."

Prado objected. "No, we have to get out to that house she described. He might be there."

"She was talkin' 'bout the old Truville place," Esper said.

"Where he's probably hiding," Prado said insistently.

Fisher asked Esper, "It didn't occur to you Orin might be there? That we should've looked there for him already?"

"The only thing left is the basement," Esper said. "And the ruins of the house have caved in. I was surprised she and her friends went anywhere near there. It's a ways out of town, and the pond she described is nothing more'n a mud hole. People go to the lake near the Woods if they want to swim, never that pond. Like she said, no one ever gets out there."

Prado insisted that, "It's exactly the kind of place he'd go."

"Not likely," McCay said. "He wouldn't go back there. He doesn't know Gretchen didn't say anything about what happened."

"Yes, he does," Prado shot back. "He knows because he hasn't been arrested, or even questioned."

"It's a lot more likely he's convinced no one believes her, not necessarily that she hasn't said anything," McCay countered. "He won't go near the place. He's doing his killing and acting out someplace clean and hidden. That's where he is now, not in a dirty basement where he was seen.

"Now, please read these," McCay said, distributing the folders around the table. "It helps explain why he wouldn't go back to that house. You need to know everything about Orin Truville if you're going to find him."

Fisher fanned through the thick document. "You want us to read all of this right now?"

McCay leaned toward Fisher and started to jab a finger in his direction when Prado intervened. "This is a bit much to absord right now, Bob."

McCay relaxed and paged through the document. "Read point six." He paused, reviewed the document, and added, "The addendum too. The rest later, but read it all. It could save your lives."

***

6) The subject was in the Canadian Armed Forces and served in Afghanistan as a member of a six-man sniper team with the Sniper System Project (SSP). The Canadian team received praise for its extreme long range shots and for killing a significant number of and combatants.

Identification of Psychosocial Factors in the Development of Serial Killers in the United States by Tiffany Brennan: Castle and Hensely (2002) suggest that the military may be a location that serial killers could gain exposure to killing. The exposure to brutalization and desensitization to violence that begins in boot camp could aid in the classical conditioning used by the military to assist budding serial killers to begin to "associate violence with pleasurable 28 consequences."

And…

Serial murderers that are later classified as organized are more likely to have been in the military than disorganized serial murderers. Having military experience was split in the 15 case histories determined to be lust-oriented (53% not present; 47% present) and the seven categorized as power-oriented (43% not present; 57% present)

Sociological and Psychological Predispositions to Serial Murder by Katie Marie Krueger: It should also be noted that while the majority of the serial killers did not serve in the military, the percentage of those that did was statistically significant when compared to the military service of the general population. Therefore, military experience might also be considered a pre-dispositional factor to serial murder.

MY NOTE: The subject's team commander Master Corporal Leonard Duggan described the subject as "an excellent marksman but a lousy soldier" who received a number of commendations for his success as a marksman, but was discouraged from re-enlisting. Duggan said it was his evaluation of the subject as "not being a team player" and "a loner who often disappeared for days at a time to the point of being reported as AWOL on more than one occasion" that influenced the SSP not to encourage the soldier to re-enlist, and to actively discourage him from doing so when he requested the paperwork to re-enlist. Duggan also said that no spotter wanted to work with the subject who was "belligerent," "disrespectful," and "just plain unlikable." When he was asked if he thought the subject might have been operating on his own and even against those not deemed the "enemy," Duggan did not hesitate to say "that was always my concern."

Referencing the studies above pointing to the likelihood that "military experience might also be considered a pre-dispositional factor to serial murder," it is clear that the offender in the events under investigation is an organized killer. He exhibits five of the seven phases associated with organized serial murder (phases 6 and 7 have yet to be confirmed for this particular subject) as developed by psychologist Joel Norris:

1. Aura Phase

The first phase serial killers experience is withdrawal from reality. It may go unnoticed by those closest to them, but life has lost all meaning for the killer. Their senses are heightened. Violent fantasies begin to form and they feel the urge to act on them.

2. Trolling Phase

This is the phase in which the killer starts to search for their victim as well as looking for a place to commit the crime or dump the body. This phase can last for months or just days, until the would-be serial killer has found the perfect victim.

3. Wooing Phase

This is when the killer sets out to gain the victim's trust to put them at ease before attacking them. They may present themselves as charming, wanting to help – or harmless and in need to help themselves. This phase is experienced by only the most organized serial killers.

4. Capture Phase

In this phase, the killer reveals his true sadistic self. The victim becomes incapacitated, whether knocked unconscious or restrained or trapped somewhere.

5. Murder Phase

This is the phase where the murder takes place. Organized killers often chose to kill their victims slowly, causing them much suffering and torture before they die. Disorganized killers are more likely to kill their victims instantly and commit further acts, such as necrophilia or mutilation, on their corpses.

6. Totem Phase

In the totem phase, the thrill of the kill begins to dissipate for serial killers. To keep some of the excitement, they will often take a souvenir from their victims, such as the clothes they were wearing or newspaper stories about the crime. These serve to remind the killer of the moment they made their warped fantasy real.

7. Depression Phase

The final phase in the cycle. The anticlimax causes a depression in the serial killer who comes to feel that his fantasy was not properly fulfilled. Some may even kill themselves in this phase. Those who don't, will soon begin to experience the violent fantasies of the aura phase and the cycle begins again.

ADDENDUM

The MO, signature and forensics indicate a single organized offender is responsible for the Maryville/Oletha murders. The victims are all young girls who were sexually assaulted and disposed of at a similar location.

Identification of Psychosocial Factors in the Development of Serial Killers in the United States by Tiffany Brennan: The serial killers examined killed for a variety of reasons including revenge, hatred, pleasure, money, etc. but overall the motive for killing was to gain something. They all had a type of victim and the motives remained the same. Serial killers may pick their victims based on something symbolic to them such as killing someone that looks like the person that abused them (Ioana, 2013).

by JE Douglas, AW Burgess, AG Burgess, RK Ressler - 1992 - ncjrs.gov: Crime scene characteristics for organized killers are noted to show planning and control prior to and during the criminal act, targeting of a stranger for the victim, personalization of the victim, use of restraints, and ability to transport and hide the body after the murder is complete.

Serial Murder—Pathways for Investigation, U.S. Department of Justice, Federal Bureau of Investigation: In this study, 329 of the 480 victims were killed by an offender who was sexually motivated. Female victims comprised 85.4% of these victims, male victims were 14.6% of this category.

We are pursuing a dangerously impaired individual who is a power-control oriented, serial sexual sadist. He lacks empathy of any kind and will continue kidnapping, torturing, and killing young women and girls until he is caught or killed.

Serial Killer: The Mechanism from Imagination to the Murder Phases by Nicola Malizia: The serial killer does not stop of his own accord. Unless prevented, the serial killer will kill again and again (Holmes & De Burger, 1988). Each successful murder exhilarates the killer, both confirming and reinforcing the act. Simply put: serial killers tend to increase their killings; it appears they have to kill often to maintain their equilibrium. The fantasy and psychic high that they obtain induces bold and more frequent attacks, sometimes with a complete disregard of risk (Geberth, 1990).

And…

This is, in certain respects, no different from the alcoholic using their drink of choice as a coping mechanism. Just as addicts tend to fall into a downward spiral, until all else in their lives centers around the addictive substance, the serial killer's life begins to revolve around fantasy. The revolution becomes so dominating that eventually fantasy becomes the center of the serial killer's life. And just as the heroin addict's need for a fix may drive him to steal, the serial killer's obligation to the fantasy drives him to murder. In short, the cycle of the serial killer is no different from the cycle of any other addict, the end result of murder being functionally the same as the heroin addict's theft.

The UNSUB is most likely local and not a transient given the number of killings happening in a relatively short period of time in and around a single point.

Geographic Profiling of Serial Murderer, Gary Ridgway, to Assist Law Enforcement in the Apprehension of Future Serial Murderers by Rachel Neldner: Rossmo (2000) found American serial murderers generally encountered targets at an average distance of approximately 22 km (13.662 miles) and left their victims' bodies on average of approximately 34 km (21.114 miles) from their home location. A breakdown of Rossmo's (2000) results indicated residence-to-crime distances were shorter than 20 km (12.42miles) for 46% of his sample. The results show the residence-to-crime distance distribution follows a decay pattern, whereby the likelihood of disposing of a body decreases as the distance from the murderer's residence increases, and furthermore the median and average distance from the murderer's residence to the body recovery locations are roughly 8 km (4.968 miles) and 30 km (18.63miles) (Snook et al., 2005).

Geographic Profiling by D. Kim Rossmo: Offenders "consistently in neighbourhoods they personally know well or are very similar in physical, social and economic characteristics to their home (Brantingham & Brantingham, 1995, P. 13). Familiarity with, access to, and departure from a scene affect an offender's target choices (Beavon, Brantingham & Brantingham, 1994).

A nod to Leo Staton and John Esper.

The Development of Serial Killers: A Grounded Theory Study Meher Sharma: Bundy said (speaking in the third person): "In his readings and in his observations and what have you - in his fantasy world - he'd imagined for some reason people disappearing all the time. He was aware of how people dropped out and became runaways and whatnot. In devising his scheme, he'd taken the somewhat unrealistic conclusion that under the correct circumstances he could select any person as a victim and that there'd be virtually no attention paid to that person's disappearance. People disappear every day. It happens all the time." (Michaud and Aynesworth, 1999, p. 326)

***

One by one, first Prado followed by Fisher, Esper and Staton, closed their file folders. Prado got up and walked to the refrigerator, opened it and signaled to the others, asking "Water?" All nodded and she returned to the conference table with a handful of bottles.

"Well," she said as she passed the water around, "that was sobering."

"And depressing," added Fisher.

Staton said, "I have a couple of questions. First, did you put this together to convince us Orin is the guy?" He looked around the table. "I thought we were already there."

"Certainly what Gretchen just told us took us all the way there," McCay said. He nodded at his study. "I put this on paper to be certain I was thinking clearly and making the correct assumptions."

"So," Staton said, his hand on the report, "this is the bible. This is the 'word' on what we're dealing with."

McCay nodded thoughtfully. "Bible? That's probably a stretch. The truth is that what I do is less a science and more an art."

"What we have is a serial sexual sadist?" Staton asked.

"We're dealing with a human being, a very disturbed human being, and there are no absolutes. Sexual sadism is among his traits, but as I've mentioned somewhere along the line, he's what we call a 'mixed' offender. He has more than one motivation. After considering everything, and lining it up to look at in a comprehensive way, I think we're dealing with someone who has little to no control over his own life and finds satisfaction in abducting, torturing and killing his victims. It's the only thing he can do that gives him a sense of control. Of *being*.

"Plus, it's likely he can only find sexual gratification when he tortures his victims. My guess is he has an elaborate fantasy life and has since he was very young. These fantasies drive him, and they are the source, or determinant, of his MO, his ritual and his signature."

Fisher nodded. "This is part of that 'how, why, who' equation isn't it? *How* he does what he does tells us *why* he does it, and that leads us to *who* does it."

McCay rummaged through the contents of his briefcase and pulled out another folder, which he opened. "Dennis Rader, the BTK serial killer, wrote this and sent it to a newspaper. He tried to disguise it with typos and misspellings to throw the authorities off but…." McCay waved his hand. "More than you need to know." He read: "'I can't stop it so the monster goes on, and hurt me as well as society. Society can be thankful that there are ways for people like me to relieve myself at time by daydreams of some victims being torture and being mine.' It describes pretty well what I think Orin goes through with his fantasies."

"Rader, Bundy, Gacy," Fisher listed, raising a finger with the mention of each name. "Randy Kraft, even Dahmer, none of them *looked* like serial killers. This guy looks the part. Acts the part. A real strange dude."

"Looks the way most of the world sees these people, maybe," McCay said. "Acts the part, no. Herbert Mullin, who killed because he thought it would stop earthquakes in California, or Richard Chase, the Vampire of Sacramento, who said he needed the blood of others to keep himself alive, they *looked* the part. They were slovenly and ill-kempt. They were also disorganized killers who murdered wantonly and left behind traces of themselves. This sets them apart from the more put-together people you mentioned. Orin, like Bundy and Dahmer, plans his killings, utilizes restraints, commits sexual acts on live victims, and controls them through manipulation and threats. He's careful not to leave behind any trace of himself on those he kills and, so far, there really is no evidence to connect him to the victims."

"I'm not about to let this sniper and Canada business sneak by me a second time," Esper said, his attention on Fisher. He shifted his focus to McCay. "I get the part about how being in the military can play into the other stuff, but does it really point at him being the shooter in Ken's case?"

McCay nodded. "He certainly has the skill set and from what we've been told, he has the weapon."

"What's the motive?" Staton asked. "Orin was Ken's running buddy. I saw them together all the time. We know about him being an accomplice of Ken's, his strongarm, even though we couldn't nail them on anything they did together."

"Frustrating as hell," Esper contributed.

"And Ken is Orin's former brother-in-law," Staton continued. "Big family connection. Sure, there's the sniper thing in his background, but isn't it a helluva leap to say that Orin could be the shooter?"

"A leap," McCay admitted as he shuffled through the pages in his report. He found his spot. "As I wrote in another section: 'Although I have no hard evidence of precisely what his relationship is with his sister…." He stopped and looked around the table. "Apart from their kinship." He found his place and continued. "Or his relationship with

Mr. Plough, I have gained some insight into these relationships from my interactions with people who knew all the parties and saw them interact. I think it's safe to say that both his sister and Mr. Plough dominated the subject and controlled him thereby creating another level of anxiety in his life.'" He closed the file. "The anxiety that *might* have been created by his sister and Plough, and those other stressors he carried around with him, are a deadly combination." He raised a finger. "But whether those conditions could have caused him to kill Plough in a single and separate act of violence, other than what it looks like he did to the girls, is another thing altogether. Frankly, I think there's something else going on here that might have compelled him to target Plough."

"You're saying it is a possibility?" Staton said.

"Yes, a possibility," McCay answered.

"You said there's something else going on," Esper said. "Like what?"

"Find him and we'll ask him."

"So," Staton asked, "now that you've put your finger on Orin, can you massage any of what we have and figure out where he's gone? Back to Toronto, maybe?"

McCay shook his head. "He's somewhere he feels safe. And that's not Toronto."

"Then you think he's still around here somewhere," Fisher said.

"I don't think he's left the area. Here he has family and a support system. Fitting in will always be a problem for him, but he's largely ignored here, which is the best he can hope for."

"Ignored until now," Prado said. "Fading into the shadows is not going to be possible with us looking for him. He's got to know that. Why would he stick around?"

"As I said, he has family and a support system. He'll cling to that."

"You've told us these people can't stop doing what they do, which is kill people," Esper said. "Fucking terrific."

***

Butch leaned forward so he could get an unobstructed view of the house. "We're all the way on the other side of the pond."

"Well, it's the only one anywhere 'round here," Hebert answered, staring at the house through the side window of his truck. He leaned across the console separating him from Butch and looked at Gretchen who had tucked herself into the space behind the passenger seat. "You sure that burnt up house we saw 'round the other side was the right one?"

"How many burnt up houses you think there are 'round here?" Butch mumbled.

"I'll never forget it," Gretchen said, the words muffled as they snuck out between her hands, which were pressed against her face.

Hebert returned his attention to the darkened house. "Well, if I was lookin' to hide somewheres, way out here where there ain't no one else is a good spot. Lucky we just kept on 'round the pond or we'd've never happened on this place."

"Yeah, well Orin told me he lived near a pond outside Oletha," Butch said. "Far as I know this is the only pond outside Oletha."

Hebert nodded toward the back seat. "As soon as she talked 'bout that burnt out old house, I figured it was worth a look-see."

After a moment of silence, Hebert turned toward Gretchen. "Okay, here's what's gonna happen. Butch is gonna go see if this is where he's livin'. If it is, he's gonna think of a reason to bring him out to the porch and you'll take a quick look. If he's the guy, I'm gonna' kill him. End this shit."

Gretchen whimpered. "I don't wanna look at him. Please don't make me look at him," she pleaded.

"Jus' one quick peek is all. He can't see you. It's dark in here, and Butch'll be right there 'side him so he can't do nothin'."

"You gotta give me a few minutes," Butch said. "It ain't like I can just ask him politely to please step out onto the porch so someone can ID him. It might take a while to think of a way to get him out there."

"After you bring him out, step to the side."

Butch stared at the front of the house. "I can't believe we got the right guy. Orin's like a kid. He's scared of his own shadow and gettin' any girls to come way out here with him, well, that's just not happenin'." Butch leaned his shoulder against the passenger door and started to push. "I never even seen him ever talk to a woman."

***

He saw the headlights punching two holes through the dark at least a half-mile out. Except for the girls he brought, no one had been to the house other than Ken when he helped build it. Crystal refused to come anywhere near the pond.

He walked into the kitchen and made certain the door to the basement was closed. Back into the living room, he stood in the dark looking out the picture window at the front yard, a source of pride. He cut and trimmed the grass a few days earlier and the lights lined up along the front walk showed a clean, well-kept plot of ground that extended 20 yards to the swale. The car stopped on the hard-packed dirt road in front of the house and he thought it strange the driver did not pull into the driveway to the left of the porch. He recognized the man who got out of the car. He could not see who was driving.

He watched him walk toward the house and backed further into the dark. He could ignore the man. Not answer the door. But maybe it was better to find out what he was doing there.

Did I have some business with Butch? No, I'm all paid up with Frankie. Haven't even bought meth for weeks. Had enough to draw the girls here. Why else would Butch be here? How did he even find me?

He stepped from the dark, switched on the living room and porch lights, and opened the door.

"Orin," Butch said as he approached. "How're you doing'?

"Pretty good. What're you doin' here?"

Butch stood at the screen door a moment before asking, "Mind if I come in?"

"'Course not," Orin said and stood aside.

Butch walked into a bare but pristine living room. A brown cow hide rug took up most of the floor space in front of a scarred but serviceable Barcalounger, the only piece of furniture in the room.

"Hey," Butch said, pointing at the chair. "Looks like Frankie's."

"What're you doin' here?" Orin repeated, standing in front of Butch.

"You got another chair?" Butch asked, looking around the room.

Orin disappeared and returned with a bright blue plastic Adirondack chair.

"Thanks," Butch said and sat. He nodded at the Barcalounger. "That looks comfortable. Relax, dude."

Orin sat down stiffly and leaned forward, staring at Butch.

"We had cops comin' 'round askin' 'bout you and I thought you'd wanna know."

Orin didn't take his eyes off of Butch.

"Heard also they been askin' about you at Stacy's. What's the deal, man? Havin' the cops askin' 'round ain't good. What'd you do?"

***

Hebert watched closely as the men sat down. He reached over the seat and grabbed Gretchen by the shoulder, pulling her up. "That the guy?"

"I can't tell for sure," she forced out of a closing throat. "It was dark," she squeaked, "and I only saw him for a second."

Hebert kept a tight grip on her shoulder. "That look like him?" As he completed his question, the men stood and walked out of view. "Shit," he said and released the girl, who quickly curled into a tiny bundle. "But you're sure the guy who you saw that night had a burnt-up face." Hebert illustrated, running his fingers along the side of face and down his neck. "Ugly scars."

Gretchen nodded.

Hebert reached across the passenger seat and opened the glove box. He removed a handgun and checked the clip and the chamber. "I'm gonna go with that's him," he said and opened the door. He stood and shoved the gun into his beltline along the small of his back and pulled his Tee-shirt over the weapon.

Hebert stooped low and hurried around the side of the garage to the back of the house. He climbed the porch steps very slowly and peered through the door into a lighted kitchen. A small table and three chairs sat in the middle of the room. Appliances lined the outside wall. On this side, next to a large sink were a refrigerator, stove and dishwasher. The facing wall held cabinets and a two-door pantry. A door was open through which he could see steps descending into the dark. A light went on below the porch line alarming him. He waited a beat and squatted, spying a small window at the base of the house.

Hebert opened the kitchen door wide enough to let himself in. He stepped lightly toward the open door where the light showed wooden steps leading to a basement. That explained the light underneath the porch. For a moment he considered retreating and simply going around to the front door and knocking. After all, it was two old friends visiting. Why was he sneaking around?

No, this is a guy who kidnapped girls, cut'em open, and strung'em up like animals.

He stood, barely breathing, and listened. Nothing. No voices. That couldn't be good. He pressed himself against the counter from where he could see the living room. Empty. He spied a dark hallway showing a wing of the house he assumed held the bedrooms. Dark and quiet. He considered his options. They had to be in the basement but he hesitated to walk to the door knowing his footsteps would likely be heard below if they hadn't been detected already. He got down on his hands and knees and crawled toward the door. As he leaned forward to see down the stairs, he felt a large hand grab him by the back of his collar, and another grip his beltline, lift him off the ground, and throw him down the stairs. As he hit the concrete floor head first, his vision blurred. It took him a moment to realize blood was pouring into his eyes from his forehead. A large foot pressed into the middle of his back, pinning him to the floor.

"Hey, Frankie," penetrated his pained and only partly conscious headspace. "Welcome to my humble home. Next time, try the front door."

He recognized Orin's voice but, unlike other times, rather than the words being squeezed out and the sentences coming humbly, almost always as questions, this voice was strong and confident.

"If you're wonderin' why you don't feel your gun under my foot, it's because I'm aiming it at your head."

"What the hell're you doing? We just came to warn you about the cops and…."

"Yeah, I know," Orin interrupted. "They been askin' 'bout me. You gonna be a hero and turn me in?" He placed the barrel of the gun at the base of Hebert's skull. "Kill me more like it."

"What're you talkin' 'bout?" Hebert said, trying to sell his innocence.

Orin snorted out a laugh. "Butch gave you away. Come to save my girls? They'd never leave me."

Hebert struggled to push himself up but Orin stomped him down hard. "Whaddya talking 'bout, man," he said pleadingly. "You got it all wrong."

As the words were spoken, Hebert caught a glimpse of Butch lying next to a mattress, the side of his head caved in from his temple to his cheekbone. He was gurgling as blood seeped out of the wound, his ears and nose. Hebert lifted his head as far as he could and saw a small girl beyond Butch, on the mattress. She was facing the wall.

That was the last thing Frankie Hebert ever saw.

TUESDAY

Prado and Fisher climbed into the cruiser. "When did you get the call?" she asked Esper.

"Right before I called you."

Prado looked at the digital figures on the dashboard. "So, about 2:30."

Esper nodded. "Staton said he'd just gotten off the phone with Ned Stacy. Gretchen practically crashed Frankie's car into the bar and ran in all hysterical. Stacy got enough outta her to call Staton, and here we are."

"Shit," Prado spit out violently, getting a look from Esper and Fisher. "Fucking Frankie." A pall of silence fell heavily until she demanded, "Go ahead. What'd she say?"

"She said that Frankie took her out to Orin's to see if he was the guy she saw at the pond."

"Took her to Orin's? What does that mean? I thought he lived with Crystal?"

Esper shook his head. "All I know is he took her to see if Orin was the guy she saw at the pond. After she told Stacy that, he called Staton."

Fisher yawned broadly and leaned across the front seat. "I only caught part of that. Frankie took Gretchen to see Orin?"

"No," Esper said with a quick shake of his head. "Well, sorta. Frankie took her to see if she could ID Orin as the guy who grabbed her friends when they all went skinny-dipping."

"He must have forced her to do that," Fisher said. "She never would have gone otherwise."

"Ya think?" Prado exclaimed, anger still in her voice.

"So," Fisher asked Esper, "where are we going?"

"Where Gretchen said Frankie took her. Near where the girls were last seen."

"A wild guess," Prado said, her attitude adjusted down a notch or two. "The Truville house. The place Plough burned down, right?"

"No, around the other side of the pond to a house I didn't even know was there."

"We should've gone straight out to the other place right after what we heard from Gretchen," Prado said. "I knew it was a mistake not to do that, especially after Bob's profile nailed Orin."

"Not sure that was a profile," Fisher forced through another extended yawn. "Profiles don't name the person." He sat forward and, in a stilted voice, said, "They give us the personality and of an individual based on analysis of the crime. See, I have been reading all that stuff Bob gave us."

"Okay, smart ass. My point is we should've gone right out to the house and nosed around ourselves. We might've found this other place ourselves. Now, who knows what the fuck we're going to be dealing with?"

"All that's out there is a burned-out husk of a house, right?" Fisher said, falling back, his eyes closed. "There was nothing compelling us out there at that point."

"Wrong," Prado said adamantly, "there's a lesson here. Once we know who our subject is, follow up immediately on anything that might point you to where they are."

"Don't beat yourself up," Fisher said. "Or McCay. What he said made sense."

"If we had gone," Prado insisted, "we would've seen there was another house out there. A knock on that door might've short circuited this fuck-up."

"Not likely," Esper said. "The burned up Truville house is surrounded by trees. Can't even see the pond. Not likely we'd've seen anything else 'round there."

"Those trees must've been where Gretchen hid," Fisher said.

Esper pointed ahead. "There's the place Gretchen said Frankie took her to. It's all the way on the other side of the pond from the Truville house. I didn't know there was anything out this way"

As they slowed to a stop in front of the darkened house, Fisher said, "One thing before we walk into God knows what. You said Gretchen got back to the bar in Frankie's car, right"

"Right," Esper answered.

"Without Frankie? I didn't miss the part that Frankie was with her, did I?"

"Nope," Esper responded. "She was alone."

"Which means Frankie is probably in there," Prado said, nodding at the house.

Fisher pointed at an open garage door. "Empty."

"Honk," Prado said to Esper, who leaned on the horn. The sound laid across the land, flattening and fading as it crossed the pond and died in the stand of trees on the opposite side.

Prado got out of the cruiser, lifted her sidearm from its holster, checked to see that a bullet was chambered, and said, "Let's go see what's going on."

Fisher went around the left side of the house, Esper to the right, while Prado, crouched and holding her weapon straight out in front of her, made her way slowly toward the house, avoiding the lighted walkway. She climbed the steps to the porch, walked to the front door and leaned against the house. She slowly opened the screen and tapped the butt of her gun on the polished oak door. "Special Agent Eileen Prado," she said loudly enough for Esper and Fisher to hear, alerting them to where she was. "Open the door."

Keeping her back against the side of the house, she slid along the wall and peeked into the large picture window. Other than a silhouette of a large chair, nothing was visible. She side-stepped her way back to the door and again knocked and announced herself. Nothing. She tried the doorknob, which turned, and announced herself again before walking into the house very slowly. She cleared the living room and made her way into the kitchen as Fisher was coming in the back door. Neither spoke. Fisher followed her back into the living room. He went to his left toward a hallway and she walked into a dining area on the right. A hexagon-shaped, faux wood picnic table filled the room.

"Nothing back there," Fisher called. "A couple of bedrooms. One has a bed. Well, a mattress. The other is empty. Bathroom has some soap, a toothbrush and one towel."

Esper appeared from the kitchen, having come in the garage door. "A door is open to a basement that looks empty."

They stood in the middle of the living room. Prado holstered her gun. Fisher found a light switch. The three stood surveying the empty space.

"Looks familiar," Fisher said.

"Just like Tricia's," Esper said.

"And Crystal's" Fisher added.

Fisher walked into the dining room. "This place is immaculate. Spartan, but what there is looks like it's just been deep cleaned." He studied the wood floor. "It looks like it was just polished."

"This makes sense," Prado said. "Assuming we're right about Orin; that he's an organized killer. This reflects that mentality. Everything has its place."

Fisher leaned over a small table next to the Barcalounger, put on some surgical gloves he pulled from his pocket, and began leafing through a small book. "Look at this." Prado and Esper stared at the photos in the book as Fisher turned the pages.

"That's Crystal," Esper said and leaned closer to the page. "Same photo we saw at her house."

"That's Orin, I'm betting," Fisher said, nodding at the image of a small boy between two adults.

"Yeah," Esper agreed. "That's Mr. and Mrs. Truville."

Prado straightened and went into the kitchen where she stood at the open door leading into the basement. She returned to the living room and asked Esper. "Did you go down into the basement?"

He shook his head. "We just cleared the first floor."

"Fuck," Prado whispered, put a finger to her lips, slid her gun from its holster, and signaled for Fisher and Esper to follow her.

Prado stood at the door and listened for a moment as she peered down the stairs. The light was on. She could see to the bottom of the staircase and about three feet of empty concrete floor. She took a step and waited, then another, and leaned forward. She could see a pair of feet in the shadows and straightened. She took a deep breath and swung her gun toward the open space. "FBI," she yelled. "Come into the light."

She heard Fisher and Esper's footsteps behind her and held up her hand, stopping them. She repeated, "Come into the light," and slowly lowered herself to her haunches and swung her gun around in a semicircle, covering the room from wall-to-wall.

She turned, motioning Fisher and Esper to follow. A pole light in the corner of the room shone brightly and blindingly forcing Prado to turn away as she stepped onto the concrete. Her line of sight went directly to two bodies lying next to each other, blood pooled around the heads and ran together into a coagulated crimson stream leading to a drain in the middle of the room.

"Frankie," Esper said, nodding at the body closest to him.

"The other one?" Fisher asked.

"The guy we saw at Hebert's," Prado said. "I think his name is Buster."

"Butch," Esper said. "His name is Butch."

"I'm sure his child bride is going to be very upset when she finds out he's out of her life," Prado mumbled, then shook her head slightly as if surprised by her reaction.

"Holy shit," Esper said as he scanned the basement. "Holy motherfucking shit."

"Yeah," Fisher said, walking toward one of the mattresses. He kicked at the chain and shackle. "Guess what we found."

Prado felt her legs buckle, turned away, and found a sink, over which she lowered her head.

"This is where he kept'em," Esper said as he scanned the room. He pointed at a bucket. "That's…." He didn't complete his thought.

Prado lifted her head and stood a moment, supporting herself on the ledge of the sink. She tried to say something but the words caught in her throat. She coughed, pulled her shoulders back, turned and looked around the dark, damp space. "Just like McCay said." She pointed at stains on the line of mattresses. "I'm betting some of those are recent."

Esper neared one of the mattresses and was cautioned by Fisher, "Don't touch anything."

"I wasn't going to." He gestured at a cup in front of one of the mattresses. "This has water in it." He turned sharply toward Fisher and Prado. "I'm thinkin' Orin took someone with him."

"I'm betting more than one," Prado said and ushered them toward the stairs. "Let's get out of here before we contaminate the scene."

***

Gretchen had bolted into the bar screaming incoherently; she fell trying to take the stairs two-at-a-time, and refused to leave the landing onto which she collapsed. Twenty minutes and two shots of Scotch later, Stacy managed to calm her and get the sketchiest of details about what happened. He tried to coax her off the landing, at one point physically lifting her, but she collapsed limply. She fought two bouncers, a scene that emptied the bar, before pulling herself the rest of the way up the stairs and into her room.

McCay sat on a folding chair Stacy brought into Gretchen's room. She was on her bed, huddled in a corner against the wall, legs pulled up to her chest, eyes so tightly shut her eyelids were hidden. She did not acknowledge that anyone else was in the room with her.

They sat in the dark. The only illumination came from a Hello Kitty nightlight plugged into an outlet facing the bed.

Only when Gretchen moved, lying down, her arms tucked between legs, eyes still shut, did McCay speak. "I hope you don't mind me being here with you." He let a moment pass. "Do you remember speaking to me at the sheriff's office?"

Gretchen did not respond.

"I'm going to ask you a few questions. You can answer any of them, or none. If you need anything let me know, okay?"

Gretchen tucked herself tighter.

"Ned told me what you said about Frankie taking you to identify Orin. Is that what he did?" He repeated the question a few times. No response. He forged ahead with of a number of other questions, all went unanswered, including those trying to determine whether she went into the house; what she saw; and what she heard.

"How long were you there?"

Gretchen opened her eyes, looking past McCay.

"Can I get you anything? Maybe some water?"

Gretchen eyes shifted from the middle distance to McCay's face, and a spark of life flickered. "Yeah, some water."

McCay looked around the room for the first time since entering and spied an open door leading to a bathroom. "Glass?" he asked as he stood. She motioned toward the bathroom. He went in and flipped on the light. Gretchen made a small sound and turned her face away from the glare. McCay closed the door slightly. The floor was covered with a Hello Kitty bathmat and shower curtain with the same design. A plastic cosmetic organizer on the counter included a drawer filled with condoms. He found a glass holding a tube of toothpaste and a toothbrush. He dumped both on the counter, rinsed the glass, and filled it.

He walked slowy to the side of the bed, handed Gretchen the water, and sat down. "Gretchen, you gave me a lot of useful information yesterday and…."

"And all it did was practically get me killed," she said forcefully. "He used me like bait. If I hadn't of gotten outta there, I'd be dead."

"We didn't know Frankie was going to do that." He watched Gretchen gulp down the water. "More?"

She shook her head and handed him the glass.

"He did that on his own. It was wrong."

"It don't matter," she said resignedly. "It's my fault for even talkin' 'bout any of it."

"No," McCay said softly. "You did the right thing. We should have been more, uh…," he struggled for the word. "Been more aware, more protective, because what you told us confirmed Orin is someone we have to find and put away. You helped us and we should have been much more careful about protecting you until we find him." He scooted forward on the chair. "We need one last thing from you. Orin has…."

"I saw Lydia," came out of Gretchen in a burst of emotion. "I saw Lydia," she repeated, her eyes flashing. "She was in the house." She began to shiver uncontrollably.

McCay, alarmed she might be going into shock, grabbed a blanket wadded up at the end of the bed and wrapped it around her shoulders. She tugged it tightly around her, cocooning. "Thank you," she whispered.

He waited a moment before asking, "Who did you see?"

"Lydia, one of my friends that he took when we went skinny-dipping."

"Lydia," McCay repeated to give himself time to absorb what she was telling him. "You were in the house?"

"I was in the back seat of Frankie's car and peeked out. Saw her through the front window. She was with another girl. I think the other one was Willie. They both looked right at me," she said through chattering teeth. "That's when I took the car and drove away."

"Willie was the other girl who was with you that night?"

Gretchen nodded.

"You didn't see Orin?"

"Don't know. I saw someone." She peeked out from the folds of the blanket. "Where's Frankie and that other guy?"

McCay debated with himself on how to answer. He had an idea what happened to them and decided not to share that with Gretchen. "Let's get you to the station where we can protect…."

"No," Gretchen objected sternly. "I want to stay here." She pulled the blanket up around her face. "I don't want to go back outside."

McCay hesitated a moment before agreeing. "Okay, I'm going to make sure we have someone watching you, Gretchen." He handed her his phone. "My contacts include the Marshal, Sheriff Esper and two FBI agents." He showed her how to access the numbers. "Call me if you need anything or just want to talk. Okay?"

"Okay," she said and pulled the blanket over her head.

***

"Get her the fuck outta here," Stacy screamed at McCay as he left the room and came down the stairs. "I want her gone. She's chasing people outta here with all that screamin' and cryin'."

McCay stood one step above Stacy and called to Staton, who was sitting at a nearby table. "Marshal, I want a man posted at" – he turned and pointed at Gretchen's door – "right outside her room." He stepped down level with Stacy and stared at him intently. "She stays here until I say otherwise. You're going to make sure she has food and whatever else she wants." He poked Stacy hard in the chest with his index finger. "She's a material witness in my case and I expect you to be a good citizen and take very good care of her. If you don't, I'll have you arrested."

"For what?" Stacy said defiantly. "You can't do that."

McCay stuck his face close to Stacy's. "I can and I will. Don't fuck with me, asshole."

***

"She said she saw two girls and one of them was definitely one of her friends?" Prado asked McCay as she followed him around the house. "That can't be right."

McCay stopped abruptly in the middle of the living room and stared out the front window. "She saw her standing right about here with another girl she thinks is the other one."

Prado shifted her body so she was looking straight into McCay's face. "What do you mean 'the other one'?

"The other one she was with that night," McCay answered in a monotone staring into the darkness. "He kept them in the basement," he said, now speaking to himself. "But that's not where he killed them. Not where he tortured and killed them. He needed somewhere safe and private to do that. He couldn't have gotten what he needed without being alone with them." He started to pace around the living room.

"We need to talk to Crystal," Prado said. "Maybe we can get more out of her now that we know" – she gestured at the surroundings –

"all of this. She might not know what he's doing here, but she's got to know more than she's told us."

McCay walked away from Prado without acknowledging he heard what she said. He went into the kitchen, stood a moment, and peered out a window looking toward the pond. He walked closer to the window, through which the early morning sun sent a bright shock of light. He shielded his eyes. "Have you been out there?" He turned and looked at Prado, Fisher and Esper.

"No," they answered.

McCay threw open the back door and charged onto the well-manicured yard sloping toward the pond fifty yards away. He stood and surveyed the area. "He's going to kill those other two girls if we don't find him fast. We have to find out where he's been killing the others. It wasn't the basement. He'd need a table or something to lay them on. And he'd need, uh, stuff. Knives. Saws. We have to find that place. That might tell us something."

"Like what?" Staton asked.

"I'll know it when I see it. It has to be near the house. He wouldn't take them too far away. This is where he felt comfortable enough to keep the girls, and it's probably where he felt safe and secure enough to do what he did to them."

Prado looked around the yard. "Around here?"

"Yes," McCay answered. "Has anyone been over to the old house? It's across the pond, right?"

"Yeah," Esper answered. "If you're thinkin' he might've used that place, he didn't. I checked it out. There isn't even a basement left. The house caved in on it."

McCay walked to the edge of the pond and stood staring into the brackish water before turning back toward the house. "This ground is soft," he said excitedly and pointed up the slope. "All of this is fill." He began running around the yard. "Look for a pipe coming out of the ground. It might have some sort of screen over it. And it's likely closer to the house than the pond. Near the pond, you probably can't go down too far without hitting water."

Prado gave Fisher a look. He asked, "What the hell is going on?"

McCay was dashing around pointing at the grass. "It's here somewhere."

Esper, Staton, Prado and Fisher stared at him.

"It's under the ground," McCay screamed. "He's got a killing room under the Goddamn ground."

"Holy shit, Fisher exclaimed, suddenly animated.

Everyone fanned out across the yard and Esper called from the top of the slope, "No pipe but there's a big square of fake grass right here."

"Can't see it from anywhere in the yard," McCay said as he ran toward Esper, who was lifting the turf as the others surrounded him. A panel of plywood sat underneath. McCay grabbed one corner, Staton the other, and they lifted it revealing a black hole and a wooden ladder.

McCay and Staton straightened and, along with the others, stared into the abyss. Echoing what all were thinking, Fisher whispered, "Fuck, this is bad."

McCay stepped onto the first rung of the ladder and asked Staton, "Do you have a flashlight in your car?" Before he could get an answer, he called up from a few rungs further down, "Never mind. I found a…." Before he could complete his thought, he moaned and laid his head on the ladder.

The others stared down at McCay, who was now bathed in light coming from the opening, but no one moved until he descended to the floor. Prado followed and stopped Fisher who started to come behind her. "Wait, let's see what we have first and how much room there is."

McCay had not moved from the base of the ladder and Prado stepped on his shoulder as she descended. "Sorry," McCay said in a hollow voice, but remained frozen in place. Prado managed to hop off the ladder to his side. He was holding an electric cord with a switch at its end that connected to overhead panels with track lights. They stood on a rough cement floor.

Drywall panels lined a large, cold room. A fan hummed. To the right side of the ladder was a pegboard that covered the wall. Neatly arranged on the board were chains with collars; whips, some with razored tips; cattle prods; sheathed knives of all shapes and sizes; and a shelf with an assortment of dildoes, butt plugs and ball gags.

In the center of the room was a gynecological chair with a mirror overhead. Prado walked over to the chair. "How the hell did he get this down here?"

"In sections," McCay answered in a whisper.

Next to the chair was a long stainless-steel table with a drain and hose, and an assortment of drawers built into the side. On a smaller steel table, arranged neatly on a clean white towel, were various medical instruments, including scissors, forceps, clamps, needle holders, electrodes, knives, blades and retractors.

"Looks like an operating room," Prado said.

"Except there's no anesthesia set-up," McCay replied as he walked over to a leather swing hanging from a large wooden beam, one of three that supported the roof of the dugout. "A sex swing."

Prado bent over and rested her hands on her knees.

"You okay?"

"Fuck no, I'm not okay. How the hell could anyone be okay with any of this?"

"Yeah," was all McCay could think to say.

"Sorry, but this is.... Shit, I don't know what it is."

"That's exactly right. You wouldn't know what it is, and thank God you don't."

Prado straightened and stared down at the table holding an assortment of surgical instruments. "How did he know what any of this is? How'd he know what to do with these things?" She looked at McCay. "He didn't have any medical training."

McCay walked over to the table. "He didn't have to know much. It's not like he was operating to save anyone's life. These were used to torture and kill. He probably learned which ones fit whatever it was he needed to do to satisfy himself. Like most of these people, he got better with time."

"Better?" Prado asked, disgust in her voice.

McCay let the moment sit before answering. "Better as in he learned how to do what he wanted to do without killing them immediately. Without hitting a vital artery or piercing an organ that would cause them to bleed out."

Prado studied the surroundings. "This is surreal. How did he manage to build this?"

"It was part of his compulsion. He willed himself to do it so he could take care of his urges. These kinds of chambers, bunkers, whatever we want to call them, have a sordid history." McCay continued in a steady monotone as he walked slowly around the space. "H.H. Holmes, one of the first American serial killers, built an entire house dedicated to killing, torturing and disposing of victims. It had soundproofed rooms and mazes of hallways. Most of the rooms had chutes that dropped down to the basement where he had acid vats, quicklime, and a crematorium to dispose of his victims' bodies. Charles Ng and Leonard Lake built a bunker where they tortured and killed their victims. I've already told you about the 'Toy Box Killer.'"

McCay let his head drop, closed his eyes and stood stiffly. "God, I'm so sorry for that recitation." He opened his eyes. "It helps me steady my nerves in the midst of all this inhumanity."

Prado started to lean on the large stainless-steel table, realized this would compromise the scene, and fell straight down onto her backside, where she sat cross-legged. McCay started toward her, his body language shifting from mechanical to animated. "I'm okay," she said. "Just need a moment."

"This is what I thought we'd find in the house. I'm guessing he wanted this completely separate from where he lived. Where he led a somewhat conventional life."

"Except for the girls in the basement."

"Orin is a master at compartmentalization. He disassociates as soon as he leaves here and returns to his day-to-day affairs."

"Nope, not understanding any of that." Prado let her eyes scan the space. "Disassociate from this?" She shook her head. "Not getting how he could do that."

"Of course not. You're not a psychopath. Devoid of empathy. You feel guilt and remorse when you do something wrong. Orin, Bundy, Rader and all the rest of them have no such barriers to overcome.

They kill, then put that aside, and return to their lives without a second thought."

"When he left here," Prado said with a look around the chamber, "he really put it all out of his mind?"

McCay nodded. "He needed them in the house to take care of, to feed, and, I imagine, to brutalize whenever the urge struck. I'm surprised he didn't bring those girls Gretchen saw down here after he killed Hebert and his friend. He knew he'd have to leave, but I'd of thought he'd want one final use of this sacred space."

Prado got to her feet. "Maybe he didn't bring them here because he saw Frankie's car leave and didn't think he'd have enough time with them."

McCay stood in front of a small refrigerator. He popped on a pair of surgical gloves and rested his hand on the door, let his head drop, took a deep breath, and pulled the door open. He stared at a two levels lined with canning jars, a finger in each one. Prado started toward him and stopped abruptly. "Fuck."

"His trophies," McCay said and slowly pushed the door closed. "Remember I talked about there being a frenzy stage for some serial killers?"

Prado nodded.

"The anxiety he must be feeling right now; the anger; are creating a storm in him. Even the most organized and controlled killer," McCay said, looking at the immaculate horror surrounding him, "will go off at some point. We've got to find him."

Prado was on the second rung of the ladder before McCay completed his thought. "We've got to go talk with Crystal," she said, climbing fast.

As they reached ground level, McCay called to Esper, who was setting up a perimeter around the area. As Esper walked toward him, McCay pointed across the pond, asking, "Did you say the house that was burned down is over there, behind those trees?"

"Yeah, that's where the old Truville place was."

"That might explain why he strung up the bodies where he did."

Prado and Fisher, overhearing McCay, approached and, along with Esper, stood side-by-side staring across the pond. "I'm betting,"

McCay continued, "Orin played in those woods when he was kid, before everything happened, and those are good memories for him. He wanted to put the bodies somewhere that made him feel good, feel safe, but he knew he couldn't do that around here. Next best spot... probably the only one around here with a lot of trees, was where he put them."

***

Orin stood over Crystal's bed and poked her in the shoulder with the barrel of a rifle. She stirred, rolled over, and fell back into the rhythmic breathing of sleep. He poked her again, this time jabbing at her face.

Crystal reacted by throwing her hands up knocking the rifle barrel away from her face. She sat up, rubbing her hand, blinked rapidly, and coughed violently before recognizing Orin and dropping back onto the pillow.

"What the hell're you doin' here?" Her voice was hoarse and she reached for a cigarette lying ready next to a pack. "I told you to stay at the house." She raised her chin, indicating the rifle. "What's with that? You was supposed to get rid of it. I don't want it here, if that's why you brought it."

"Frankie came to see me."

"Frankie Hebert?"

"Yeah."

Crystal held down the trigger on her lighter as she processed what Orin had said. She released the trigger and the flame extinguished. A cloud of smoke pushed toward Orin when she asked, "What the fuck are you sayin'? No one knows 'bout the house. That's why I said to stay there."

"Frankie found it."

"How?"

"I don't know. Well, I might've said something 'bout havin' a house but I never said nothin' 'bout where."

"What'd he want?" she asked, but before Orin could respond, she realized the rifle was pointed at her chest. "Careful with that thing," she said, pushed it aside, swung her feet onto the floor, and stood. A pair of too large sweatpants started to slide off her hips. She swam in a tie-dyed Tee-Shirt. "Kitchen," she said hiking up her pants, took a few steps toward the door before stopping abruptly. "Wait a minute." She turned back toward her bed and focused on her clock radio. "It's fuckin' 4:30 in the morning." She stared at him, a question in her eyes.

"He showed up a few hours ago."

"In the middle of the Goddamn night?"

Orin nodded.

"This better be good," she said. "Once I'm awake, I can't never get back to sleep. I don't like bein' woke up like this."

A trail of smoke followed behind her as she walked into the kitchen. "Coffee?" she asked absently, spooning grounds into a squat machine which she filled with water.

Orin shook his head.

"Sit," Crystal said, turning away from the counter, pointing at the kitchen table. She sat down and stabbed her half-smoked cigarette into a piece of stale pizza laying in an open box. Realizing what she had done, she pushed the box away. "What'd Frankie want?"

"I had a good thing goin' 'til you fucked it all up," Orin spit out angrily. "Ken helped me build a nice house. I had a job doin' things for him."

"What're you talkin' 'bout?"

"Things was real peaceful until you really fucked it up."

"Peaceful? He used you like an old dishcloth to clean up after him." She made a face. "It was like, 'Orin tote those hogs to market.' "Oh," she said, raising a finger, "'but first steal'em. Wash my truck. Mow my lawn. Take out the garbage. Pick up the dog shit."' She looked hard at her brother. "He had you carryin' those hogs, and whatever else he stole, so if you was caught with'em, he'd skate free. Same when he'd make you smash open the doors of those houses so he could go in and steal stuff. You ever notice how he'd wait aways off down the road 'fore going in hisself?" She lit another cigarette and tilted her head up and to the side, exhaling. "That was so if anyone came, he could leave real quick. Also why he had me and Lurleen and Tricia follow him 'round so's we could say he was with us. He never said nothin 'bout us sayin' we was with you if you got caught doin' anything.

"And that house you say he helped you build? He was building it for me, but he got mad at me for askin' him for more money. I said I'd tell the Sheriff about some shit he had goin' on at the time, and after beatin' the shit outta me, he decided to give you the house instead. To punish me. And speakin' of beatings, he knocked Lurleen around, and Tricia, too. Sometimes the kids. Oh, yeah," she said mockingly and lit a cigarette. "Things was fuckin' wonderful.

"And you? You was nothin' but an afterthought, Orin. He never shared any of what he stole with you." Crystal turned her chair to face him squarely. "All those runs you took 'tween Maryville and here carryin' his drugs? Ever wonder why he never went along, or why he had you do all of'em?" She waited a beat before continuing. "'Cause he didn't want to get caught with a car full of meth and whatever else you was carryin'. Did he ever pay you much more'n what you needed to live off of?" she asked, lifting slightly out of the chair as she spoke. "Well, did he?" her voice raised. "Did he ever think 'bout you needin' more money to buy food and pay for" – she waved her hand dismissively – "your 'lectric bill and cable?"

"He always gave me what I needed and….

"What you *needed* not what you deserved, dumbass."

"…and if Tricia had it so bad, how come you didn't say nothin' to her 'bout what we was doin'? She shoulda wanted out bad as you. How come it was just you, me and Lurleen?"

"Cause she was still under his thumb, and I know how that is. He'd make it so you couldn't leave. Told you he'd beat you if you tried. Throw you outta your house. Take away the kids. Never give you no more money. What was she gonna do? She had babies and no one to take care of her. Me and Lurleen, we could see what things was really like. We had some, uh…some distance. The clouds had parted for us."

"But he gave you and Lurleen money. He made it so you could live real nice."

Crystal shook her head. "You're not listenin'. It was never fair. We got what we needed not what we deserved. And we was still performin' for our keep. He called, we went. Do you know he sometimes came 'round to me, and Lurleen too, and made us do things with him?" She stared at Orin. “Sometimes together, sometimes with Tricia. You know what I’m talkin’ ‘bout?”

Orin stared ahead.

She exhaled through her mouth and nose sending a fog of smoke up in front of her face. ”Sometimes he’d make us, me and Lurleen, do things to each other while he watched, and then he’d join in. Yeah, boy, things sure was sure fuckin’ great.”

Orin stood unmoving, dead-eyed.

“With him gone, all that went away. Tricia got what he had and she’s been helping us out real nice. We finally got more’n just enough to survive.” Crystal carved the ash of her cigarette along the inside of a half-filled glass of water. “Why all this now? Shit, Orin, he burnt our house down and did that” – she jabbed the cigarette at him –“to you.”

Orin raised the rifle and walked toward Crystal who pulled her head back in surprise. “What the hell’re you doin’?”

“You think I’m some kind of idiot?” he spit at her. “I know it was you. I smelled the gasoline. The smell woke me up. You was the one who poured it ‘round the house. I saw Ken waitin’ out in the driveway. You set the house on fire.” He thrust the weapon at her. “You did this to me.”

“You got it all wrong,” Crystal said. “Let me explain the way things really happened, okay?”

“Nothin’ to explain.”

“Yeah, there is,” she insisted. “And it’s gonna take a while.” She pointed at the counter. “It’s gonna take a lotta coffee.”

Crystal stood slowly. “Sure you don’t want none?” she asked as she walked to the counter. She opened a cupboard door, took out a cup, and asked again, “Coffee?” Not getting a response, she filled her cup, and returned to the table, keeping her hand on the .38 she had lifted from the utility drawer and slipped into the pocket of her sweatpants. “I woke Mom and Dad before I left the house and told’em what I done ‘cause they wouldn’t let me be with Ken.” She made a face. “I was one stupid ass girl.” She refocused on Orin. “They was supposed to wake you and get out. I don’t know what happened.”

"What happened was you washed everything with so much gas that by the time they figured out what was goin' on, they was almost caught in the fire." Orin pointed at his face. "I was."

"Things is better with him gone," she said insistently. "You gotta see that. We're all livin' good. He ain't around to give us shit every single damned day."

"He ain't around no more 'cause I listened to you. You made me do it."

"I didn't make you do shit. You was happy to do it. Maybe you got guilt or somethin' goin' on inside you now, but I didn't have to twist your arm." Crystal smiled without any joy reaching her eyes. "Sides Mr. Marksman, you didn't do the job. If I hadn't been right there to finish him off, he mighta lived. He was still breathin' after you shot him."

"He was gone. I never missed a shot. You just wanted to put a bullet in him."

She took a long sip of coffee. "Now, what did Frankie want?"

"Don't matter. He's dead, and Butch too."

Crystal dropped her cup on the table and coffee splashed onto the front of her Tee-Shirt. "You killed Frankie? Who's Butch?" She wiped at the coffee stain. "You gonna tell me what this is all about?"

"I'm in a shitload of trouble. Frankie knew and came looking for me."

"You do something to him?"

"No."

Crystal was corralling the spilled coffee with a cloth napkin and pushing the puddle to the middle of the table. "You gonna tell me what the fuck this is all about?"

"All you need to know is Frankie knew I was in some shit. He found me. He was gonna kill me. I'm sure 'bout that, so I got him first, and I had to leave the house."

Crystal laid a pile of napkins across the now single puddle of coffee, wiped up the spill, and wadded up the soiled cloth. She scooted close to the table, slipped the weapon from the pocket of her sweatpants and held it in her lap. "Those FBI people came by a few times. Told me lots of stories. One 'bout you and Ken workin' with some drug people from Toronto. 'Nother time they asked me 'bout those missing girls and more or less said you was responsible. They also said somethin' 'bout you killin' someone in Toronto. Any of that have anything to do with why Frankie came to see you?"

Orin looked away long enough for Crystal to stand, raise the gun and shoot Orin in the forehead, taking the back of his head off. He stumbled a few steps, his eyes rolled up into his head, he fell to his knees, and then straight down onto his face. Crystal waited a beat before approaching Orin. She kicked the rifle away from his hand and then nudged him with her foot. "Sorry," she said.

Crystal went into her bedroom, picked her cell up from a night table and jabbed at the numbered face. "Lurleen, get your ass over here. We have to clean up a mess."

A confused "What the hell?" came back at Crystal, followed by "It's the middle of the night."

"I know what time it is. Just get here, *now*."

She returned to the kitchen, opened a cabinet door under the sink and removed an industrial-sized black garbage bag, which she placed on the table. She walked over to Orin's body, picked up the rifle, returned to the table and sat down. She took a sip of coffee, lit a cigarette, and took the rifle apart. She deposited the pieces into the garbage bag, took a final pull on the cigarette, and dropped the butt into the remains of the coffee. She carried the bag to the kitchen door leading to the garage and stepped down into the room. She grabbed a step ladder and took it to the front of the garage where a line of shelves was built into the side wall, just out of her reach. She climbed the step ladder, laid the bag on the uppermost shelf and brought a small box down with her, opened it and lifted out a .22 handgun. Returning to the kitchen, she positioned the .22 into Orin's hand, raised it to line up where she had been sitting at the table and pulled the trigger.

"What the hell was that?" a voice called from the living room.

"In here."

Lurleen stopped short and froze in the doorway. She retreated a few steps. Her mouth moved shaping words without sound. She struggled to breathe.

"Deep breaths," Crystal said. "Nice easy breaths and a cup of coffee should get you straightened out real quick."

Lurleen's legs buckled. Crystal walked her to the living room and lowered her onto the couch. She went back into the kitchen and returned with a glass of water. "Drink this slowly." She sat down and rubbed Lurleen's back until the woman's breathing normalized. "Ready for that cup of coffee?"

"What the hell?" Lurleen asked. "And who are those awful looking girls in Orin's truck? They're chained together like animals."

Crystal bolted off the couch, ran out the door to the truck. Two cowering, emaciated, dirty, foul-smelling girls held onto each other tightly and leaned away from Crystal.

***

Prado, Fisher, Esper and Staton walked into the living room their eyes going immediately to the couch where a lump of withered humanity shivered. The girls hid their faces in the crook of the other's shoulder.

"You told the 911 operator there was a shooting," Esper directed at Crystal who was sitting across from the girls, Lurleen next to her.

"It's Orin," Crystal said. "He's in the kitchen."

"He's who was shot?" Esper asked as he darted toward the kitchen.

"He's dead."

Esper stopped abruptly. "What?"

"Orin's dead. I killed him."

Esper looked at Prado, Fisher and Staton as if expecting one of them to jump in.

Crystal continued, "He told me 'bout all he's been doin'." She raised her hands to her face and whimpered out, "I tried to talk him into giving me his gun but he told me he was gonna leave with the girls. When I tried to stop him, he…." She raised her hand gesturing that Orin had tried to shoot her, turned away, and hid behind her hands.

"What exactly did he tell you?" Prado asked.

"That he'd took those girls and been doin' awful things to'em."

"He came here to tell you that?" Prado asked, disbelief in her voice.

Face hidden in her hands, Crystal answered, "He said he was leavin' and wanted to say goodbye, and it all just came out."

"And she tried to stop him," Lurleen added.

"Did a pretty good job of that," Fisher said under his breath.

"When did you get here?" Prado asked Lurleen.

"Right after I shot Orin," Crystal answered. "She comes over for coffee every morning."

Prado made a show of looking at her watch. "This early?"

Lurleen nodded. "I'm up early 'cause of the kids."

"So, Orin came over to talk about this?" Prado asked, her eyes on the girls.

"No, he didn't come over 'specially for that. Like I said, he was leavin'. He was scared you was onto him. It all came out when we was talkin'."

"How does something like that just *come out*?" Fisher asked.

"I pressed him 'bout some of the stuff you tol' me. I thought 'bout it when he was talkin' and asked him."

Staton took a step toward the couch and the girls cowered. He stepped back. "Did Orin do this to you?" he asked, not knowing where else to start. "Did he keep you at his house?"

Crystal said, 'We've been tryin' to get'em to talk to us but they won't say a word. This is what you was tryin' to tell me about, wasn't it?" she asked Prado. "I'm sorry for not believin' you."

Prado asked Crystal and Lurleen to come into the kitchen with her and Fisher. Seated around the table, she asked, "Did Orin tell you about the other girls?"

Crystal's eyes widened. "Others?" she asked, and hurried into, "There really are others?"

"We think he kidnapped, tortured and killed a number of girls."

"Could I get some water?" Crystal asked, visibly shaken.

Lurleen stood. "I'll get a glass for you. You all want anything?"

Prado and Fisher shook their heads, their attention riveted on Crystal.

"Others?" Crystal said. "You talkin' 'bout all those other missing girls." She took a long sip from the glass Lurleen handed to her. "I thought it was just those two." Her eyes filled and tears spilled down her cheeks. "I never paid much attention to the talk 'bout all that." She stared down at the tabletop. "Orin's been doin' that?" She bolted for the sink where she threw up.

Lurleen began mumbling "Oh, my God," which she repeated over and over.

"I'm not certain I understand what you're telling us," Prado said. "Orin comes over to tell you he's leaving and it comes out he's been abusing those two girls? Is that what you're telling us?"

"I'm sayin' he said he did bad stuff to those girls he had with him."

"And he brought them into the house?"

"No, he just said stuff 'bout'em," Crystal answered, frustration in her voice. "I don't remember every little thing. Shit, my brother tol' me about some awful shit and I didn't think of what all to ask. I don't even remember much after he said what he did."

"What he did," Fisher said harshly, "was torture and kill and cut up a lot of girls."

Crystal turned her face away from Prado and Fisher, laid her arms on the table, and lowered her head.

"Why would he bring a gun with him?" Prado asked.

"Probably 'cause he was plannin' on killin' her," Lurleen said intensely. "He was fuckin' nuts or are you not gettin' that?"

"Then he didn't come over just to tell you he was leaving? He came over to kill you?"

Crystal shook her head slowly. "I don't know. He said he came over to say goodbye. He had a gun. I don't really know why."

Lurleen repeated, "He was crazy. Why's this so hard for you to get through your heads?"

"So you shot him in self-defense? Right?"

Crystal nodded.

"You had a gun with you?

Crystal stared at the table. She looked briefly at Lurleen before answering, "When Orin was tellin' me 'bout the girls, I got scared and I got it from where I keep it in a drawer." Her eyes went to the counter.

"And then he shot at you?"

"He got mad 'bout some things I was sayin'. I was callin' him out 'bout what he was sayin' and it made him mad."

"Were you two sitting at the kitchen table?"

"I was. He was standin' near the door. He got really, really mad and shot at me."

"He shot at you and missed?"

"Yeah, and then I shot him."

"You two sit tight," Prado said, tapped Fisher on the arm and motioned toward the living room.

Staton walked over to them as they entered the room. "I don't think they know anything about what Orin was involved in," Prado said, "but a lot of what she's telling us just doesn't make sense. Actually, it makes sense as far as it goes, but there's a lot missing."

"It makes sense to you that an expert marksman would miss a shot ten feet in front of him?" Fisher asked. "She can't remember what he told her because she was so upset, but she was under control enough to shoot and kill her brother after he had taken a shot at her?"

"Okay," Prado conceded, "there are a few things that don't make sense." To Staton. "Let's take them to the station and continue there."

Fisher looked past Staton at the girls. "Anything?"

Staton shook his head. "Did Orin tell her anything about Frankie? Butch?"

Prado eyes went vacant.

"You didn't ask?"

"Totally blanked on that. I was so focused on the other stuff."

"Okay," Staton said, moving toward the door. "Let's get everyone to the station, pump us full of coffee and do this."

***

Prado looked through the one-way window into the narrow, sterile interrogation room. The walls were scarred white wallboard. The flooring gray linoleum. "So, do we believe Orin tried to kill her?" she said to McCay and Fisher, nodding at Crystal Truville, her head cradled in her hands.

"It's possible," McCay answered. "He had just killed two people and was likely in a manic mode. It could have brought up anger he was harboring toward her."

"What happened to him being calmed by killing people?" Fisher asked. "Not just killing them, but beating them to death."

"Altogether different thing," McCay answered. "What probably drove him to go see Crystal was, well… A parallel anger. It was always there but he kept it buried, controlled; sometimes calmed by what he did to the girls. Hebert coming after him flipped the switch. Made him face the fact that his miserable life began when he got caught in the fire. He blamed his sister for that and for everything that followed. And his anger exploded to the surface, likely aggravated by his being at the pond, in the environment he had been in when he was disfigured. His sister was at the center of him becoming the wretched creature he did."

"Okay, then," Prado said, "we're going with he came to kill her and she acted in self-defense."

"I'm only offering a likely scenario," McCay said.

"Then it is possible there's something else going on here," Prado said, frustration in her voice. "I can't help thinking we're missing something."

"McCay nodded. "Probably. Nothing is ever as simple as the obvious."

A silence hovered until Prado broke it asking, "What was he going to do with the girls?"

"Kill them, I imagine. I'm sure he felt he had no choice, but I'm thinking he really wanted to find a way to keep them for a while; to find some place he could store them, for lack of a better way to put it. Otherwise he would have gotten rid of them at the house."

"I just can't buy her explanation about how things went down with Orin," Prado said. "Until I mentioned the other girls, the missing ones, it seemed she was going through the motions. Like she had prepared a script and was reading from it. Very controlled. Not a lot of emotion considering she'd just killed her own brother."

"People react differently to tragedy. I've seen parents not react to the death of a child; husbands and wives not blink twice when one or the other was killed. They appear to accept it, almost shrug it off and go on like nothing has happened. No grief evident at all. I've also seen others go into immediate shock. Go comatose. And a lot of variations between."

They walked away from the viewing room into the hallway toward the reception area and the conference room. "What about the girls?" Fisher asked McCay. "Are you going to talk to them today?"

"I hope so. I have to find out how old they are. If they're under 18, I need a parent in the room with me. I sure as hell don't want to step on any technicalities that could come back to haunt me."

Staton stood away from the conference room so he was not easily visible to the two girls who were huddled together on a single chair. Having overheard McCay as he approached, he tilted his head toward the glass wall and said, "John knows the girls. Wilhelmina Geist and Lydia Slocum. Lydia would be about 20. Not sure about Wilhelmina."

"Okay, then," McCay said, eyeing the girls. "I can speak to Lydia."

"Wait a Goddamn minute," Prado demanded. "What about a doctor?" She nodded in the direction of the conference room. "Look at them. They need to be examined, don't you think?"

"Thought of that," Staton said. "They've both been examined. We brought them here in an ambulance and had a doctor, a female doctor – thought of that too – give them a once over on the way."

Prado gave Staton a look. "A *once over*? Those two need more than that. God knows what he did to them. What kind of damage he did. What did the doctor find?"

"She said that other than the obvious" – Staton pointed at the girls – "emaciation and dehydration, they're as good as we can expect."

"What the hell does that mean?" Prado asked. "'As good as we can expect'? What about the complications" — she pointed at her head — "up here. I know all about those."

McCay interjected, "It means that as cruel as this is going to sound to you, Eileen, I need to talk to Lydia and try to get as much as I can while everything is fresh in her mind."

"We know it was Orin," she replied. "We know he is…was a fucking deviant. Why torture the poor girl into recalling everything for us?"

"We have every reason to believe it's Orin and…." He held up a hand to stop Prado from interrupting him. "We'll be able to prove it was him when we do a complete forensics run-through. I don't doubt that, but we need Lydia to confirm it; to fill in some details. And I need to get some information from her for my own purposes."

"*Your own purposes*?"

"I need to do what I do, Eileen," McCay said determinedly. "I need to understand what we're dealing with."

Prado took a deep breath. "I get that, but she survived years locked in a basement dealing with whatever he put her through and you really think her mind is strong enough to pick at? And that's ignoring all the physical damage. How could she possibly be okay enough to give us anything useful?"

"This is going to be hard to listen to especially with those two broken souls sitting ten feet from us. And without a doubt, they'll never be able to slip back into our world like nothing happened to them, but many victims survive harrowing conditions and come out the other end, if not always whole, at least together enough to help us put the bad guys away. Elizabeth Smart survived because of her religious faith and love of her mother. It gave her the strength to survive rape and torture. I was involved in the case of Bobby Joe Long who killed ten women. One of his victims suffered years of sexual abuse by her grandmother's boyfriend and said that prepared her to deal with Long. She figured he, like her abuser, was likely to get angry if she fought him. So she didn't. She went so far as to flatter him and tell him she'd be proud to be his girlfriend. He let her go and that was the end for him. But the one who really sticks out is Colleen Stans. She was held for seven years and spent most of that time tied up and stuffed in a box the size of a coffin that fit under her kidnapper's bed. She survived by going along to get along and eventually escaped. These people did what they had to do to survive." He nodded at the conference room. "They did the same. I need to know what they know."

"You're going to have a problem prying them apart," Staton said. "They refuse to be separated. To get them clean, we had to let them shower together in our locker room."

"Have you called their families?" McCay asked.

"They're on their way in. Wilhelmina is Ida Geist's younger sister, so she also survived with Orin all those years."

Prado's eyes' saucered. "She's the 'Willie' that Gretchen told us about?"

"She is," Staton said, nodding.

"Orin's trophies…well, among his trophies were this first two victims," McCay said. "This is a first for me. Living, breathing trophies."

"And you're comfortable going in there," Prado said, her irritation still close to the surface, "and poking and prodding at that poor girl?"

"No, of course, I'm not comfortable," McCay said. "I'm never comfortable *prodding and poking*, as you put it, but if we're going to learn how to stop the monsters that do this sort of thing" – McCay pointed at the girls – "we have to deal with a shitload of unpleasantness. And I'm going to need you to put a lid on your reservations and help me. I can't go in there without a woman. You lead. Introduce me and I'll take it from there."

***

McCay went to the far side of the conference table across from Lydia. Prado pushed away a chair between her and the girl and sat a distance removed. "My name is Eileen and this is Bob. We're with the FBI. We'd like talk to you for a few minutes."

Lydia looked at them impassively. Hair wet, thin, and combed flat to her scalp, she looked very small and vulnerable. Her eyes bugged from an emaciated face. Her cheekbones looked like they might poke through paper-thin skin; her pallor was gray; lips almost purple; and with the overly-large uniform shirt hanging on her shoulders, she was barely more than a stick figure.

"Why'd you take Willie away?" she asked, her eyes showing a spark of life as they darted from Prado to McCay. "I ain't sayin' nothing 'til you tell me where she is."

"She's just down the hall a few rooms away," Prado said with a glance at McCay.

"Why'd you take her away?" Lydia's eyes darted from Prado to McCay, back to Prado.

"We'd like to talk to you and you're over 18. Old enough to talk to us if you'd be willing to do that."

Lydia's eyes went blank.

"We brought in some food for Willie," Prado said. You hungry?"

Lydia looked right through her. "When can I see her?"

"Real soon," McCay said. "I just have a few questions for you. Okay?"

Nothing but emptiness came back to him from Lydia.

"Do you know how long you were kept by Orin?"

She shook her head and McCay pointed at a calendar on the wall above the bureau.

She shifted her focus without moving her head. Tears spilled from her eyes, but she showed no emotion. She wiped her cheeks with the shirtsleeve.

"You and Willie are very brave. Few people could have done what you did."

"I didn't know it was that long," she said without inflection. "Just went from minute-to-minute, I guess."

"How are you feeling right now?"

"I really don't know." She blinked as the tears streamed down her face, which never changed expression. "I dreamed so much about not being there I'm not sure I'm not still there."

"You're not," Prado said.

Lydia looked down at the table and slowly brought her hand up from her lap. She brushed her fingers across the table and pressed her fingers on it.

"Would you mind if I asked you a few questions?" McCay said softly.

She shrugged. "Go ahead. I'm not sure what I can tell you. I haven't thought through any of this. Never 'llowed myself to think on it when I was in it. Never seemed like a good idea. There's nothin' much churnin' up here," she said with a wave of her hands over her head.

"I'm not a psychologist, Lydia, so I can't explain what you're feeling, but I can tell you I've talked to a lot of people like you who were victims of very bad things, and your being numb, which I think is what you're describing, is normal."

She looked up at McCay. "I don't think I'm much looking forward to not being numb."

Prado reached out to comfort the girl. Lydia pulled away and sat straight in her chair. "Ask what you want, then I want to see Willie."

"How did you and Willie manage to stay alive?"

"We just kept breathin.'"

"That you did." McCay carefully considered his next words. "Orin brought a lot of girls to that basement, then took them out and they never came back. But he kept you and Willie. Why do you think that is?"

Lydia dried the last of her tears and let her hands fall into her lap. "We did whatever he asked. We talked to him. We tried to make friends with him." She began to rock backward and forward. "Orin's a bad person, but he has a soul." She shrugged. "I don't have any other way of sayin' it. He's evil for sure, but there is somethin' there we found we could touch when we needed to keep him from hurtin' us too much."

"You feel bad for him?"

Lydia's eyes flashed causing McCay to push back slightly in his chair. "No, I hope he rots in hell. You asked how we kept livin'. He was human enough so we could talk to him about some stuff like… oh, like his house. He was really proud of his house. Maybe like three times he brought us up from the basement and would show us what new thing he built. I remember when he finished the porch, he showed it to us." She wagged a finger. "Not that he took us outside or nothin', but he let us look out the window a coupla times."

"He never took you outside?"

"He did once. After he killed one of 'em, he wanted us to help him put her in the pond. He also wanted us to clean up in the pond. We never had a shower or bath. He'd fill a bucket with water sometimes and pour it over our heads. No soap."

"Did he put her in the pond?"

"Didn't see him do that."

"Where did he keep you before he built the house?"

"That burnt out hole in the ground, but it wasn't like a long time or nothin'. He musta been building that house and was almost finished. The basement in the new house seemed like a palace after that other place." Lydia smiled, a reaction so foreign, she looked surprised by the tic. "Funny how you can go from somethin' real bad to somethin' still bad and think it's a lot better. We was sleeping on the floor in the burnt-up place. Was full of burnt up wood and papers and ashes. We was breathin' in all that stuff and it made us both sick." She stopped as if considering her next words carefully. "You asked before if he ever let us out. Like outside. I guess it was twice, not once. When he took us to the new basement would be another time. He let us wash off in the pond before we went into the new place." She turned her head away from McCay and the tears began to roll down her face. "When we came out of the pond he told us it was where he put Ida."

"Did Orin tell you anything about what he did with the other girls?"

"If you're askin' me if I knew he killed'em, yeah, I figured he did. What else was he gonna to do with'em? But he never said that."

"No, I'm asking if he told you *where* he took them. *What* he did with them?"

Lydia gave McCay a look. "He did what he did with us, only worse. They died and he put them in the pond, right?"

McCay decided not to keep going down that road and asked, "Do you know how many girls there were all together?"

"I didn't keep count. I couldn't think 'bout that stuff. I was jus' tryin' to stay alive. I went into my head to forget 'bout stuff, so there could have been girls I don't even know was down there." She looked around the room and back at McCay, holding her eyes on him. "You asked about me survivin'. I think that's the way it happened. I just went away in my head." She leaned toward McCay. "I'll sit with you as long as you want and you can ask any kind of question you want, but you gotta promise you won't do this to Willie. I ain't heard her say more'n a word in a long time. Maybe like a year." She looked at the calendar. "I don't really know what a year is anymore, but, like I said, it's been a long time. She can't tell you more'n what I can even if she did talk, but if you make her try, she's gonna shatter like glass."

Prado took a deep breath and exhaled a whimper.

McCay assured Lydia, "I promise I won't talk to Willie, and I'll tell Marshal Staton and Sheriff Esper what you said about her."

Lydia nodded and returned to McCay's question. "I do remember some of them. Ida. Alice Moore 'cause she is the only Black person I ever met. Rochelle Lee 'cause we went to high school together. That girl Dina 'cause one of the other girls told Orin her name."

McCay listed: "Ida. Alice Moore. Rochelle Lee. Dina Rounds and the one who knew her. That's five."

"There was others. There was Gretchen. She was with me, Willie, and Ida when we went to the pond and got grabbed by Orin. He musta' found her and killed her later."

McCay drummed his fingers on the table. Lydia obviously had not seen Gretchen the night before. He quickly considered telling her what happened when she was taken, then thought better of it. To what end? Tell her that her friend escaped and never said a word, leaving her in hell? That might trip the wire and blow-up Lydia's fragile hold on sanity. He moved on. "Why do you think Orin took the girls from the basement when he did? Did they make him angry? Or maybe it was something that happened during the day that caused him to take them away. Like he was worked up about something, or maybe lonely?"

"I already said, I didn't spend a lot of time thinkin' 'bout this kinda stuff. I was there sometimes, and not there a lot. In my mind, I mean. I think there was times he just seemed to want to beat on us and make us do stuff with him. Other times one of the girls would say somethin' that made him mad and he'd go off on them. One of the girls called him all kinds of names and talked about his burns. Dina, I think. He beat her to death right there. Other ones would also make him mad for not doing what he wanted, like if he wanted them to blow him, or if he wanted to fuck them in the ass, and they fought instead of just shuttin' up and doin' it.

"I saw he wanted them to obey him. He wanted to make us be like his slaves. If they all woulda jus' done that, maybe more woulda made it through." She sat silent a moment. "But I don't know for sure. There was times it seems he came down into the basement all pissed off already and just had to have someone to beat on." Lydia shook her head. "I can't say for sure what it was all about."

"Did he ever talk about his family? About his sister or about Ken Plough?"

"All the time. I knew his sister Miss Crystal, and everyone knew Ken."

"How well did you know them?"

"No one wanted to know Ken. You stayed away from him as much as possible."

"Do you know he's dead?"

"Yeah, Orin said somethin' 'bout that."

"Really?" came out of Prado almost involuntarily.

McCay asked, "Did Orin talk much about that?"

Lydia shrugged. "No, just that Ken was dead and they was never going to find out who did it."

Prado asked, "Did he say why he thought no one was going to find out?"

Lydia shook her head. "No, but sometimes he laughed 'bout Ken being killed, which I thought was weird 'cause I knew they was some kind of relations, but he had us in a basement, and was doin' all kinds of things to us, so him laughin' 'bout Ken being dead wasn't so strange."

"What else did he say about Ken being killed?" Prado asked and felt a pang of guilt about scolding McCay for doing exactly what she was now doing.

"I really didn't pay much attention. I was always tryin' to go to sleep or drift off in my mind. He did go on 'bout how they was too smart for people in town."

McCay gestured for Prado to go on. "*They* were too smart?" she asked. "Are you talking about Crystal and Orin?"

"Don't know. I'm jus' sayin' what I heard. He said they was too smart for anyone to find out anything."

"They? You're sure he said 'they'?"

"Yes, ma'am, he said 'they.'"

"Find out what?"

Lydia shrugged. "Don't know."

"You said he talked about his sister? What did he say about her?"

Lydia stared ahead, worked her jaw, and squinted as if churning to recall. "He talked 'bout his sister buggin' him all the time, and how it wasn't right her always raggin' on Ken even though he sometimes laughed 'about Ken bein' dead. Jus' part of all the shit he used to say."

"He talked to you and Willie about this? About his sister and Ken, and no one knowing what happened?"

"Not so much *with* us, more like with hisself, and we was there. He would make hisself mad by the things he was sayin', and lotsa those times he would beat on one of us, or take one of the girls outta the basement. He could also get all worked up talkin' 'bout how someone ignored him, or said somethin' he thought was disrespectful. He was full of anger." Lydia again surprised herself with a smile and pulled it back as fast as it came. "Guess I really didn't have to say that last thing 'bout him bein' angry a lot."

Prado reached toward Lydia who did not recoil this time. "You're one of the bravest people I have ever met. You and Willie both."

McCay asked, "Do you know what a serial killer is?"

"'Course I do," Lydia answered sharply. "A person who kills lotsa people. Like that guy Manson."

"There are a number of different kinds of serial killers and Orin was among the worst of the worst. You found a way to survive and what you've told me is going to help us learn more about what these people do, what makes them do those things, and how we can stop them. Thank you."

McCay realized he had lost Lydia mid-declaration. She was half out of her seat when he sensed the door to the conference room opening. Lydia bolted toward the door and enfolded a much smaller girl in her arms. Behind them, a woman who looked like Lydia might have in a quarter century, absent this trauma; beside her a bald man built like a refrigerator with legs.

The two girls clung to each other, oblivious to anyone around them. The woman put her arms around Lydia and Willie and the three shook with sobs. The man walked around the scrum and approached McCay and Prado, who stood together.

"I want to thank you for saving my girl," came out of the block of humanity. "God bless you."

McCay shook his head. "Those two girls saved themselves, sir."

"Are they going to be okay?"

Prado asked, "Did anyone explain to you what happened to them?"

"We talked to Marshal Staton and Sheriff Esper."

"Like I said, they saved themselves. They're very strong." McCay could not bring himself to offer anything more.

Prado and McCay walked into the hallway where they met Fisher, Esper and Staton. McCay asked, "What about Willie's parents?"

"Willie's parents left Oletha about two years ago," Esper said. "The girls' mother was never right after she lost her girls. Or thought she lost both of them. Neither was Mitch, the father, but he could at least function. But things got so bad with his wife that he had to take her back to her parents. I haven't heard anything since. We're trying to find them." His eyes filled and he turned away from the others. "I don't know how that's going to turn out."

"God," Prado croaked through a closing throat, "I hope I never have to do anything like this again."

***

McCay, Prado and Fisher stood shoulder-to-shoulder in the cramped viewing area looking through the two-way mirror at Crystal who was facing them. Staton sat across from her. Esper stood in the corner of the room next to the door.

"Leo knows his stuff," McCay remarked. "Having John behind Crystal has to be making her uncomfortable."

As if on cue, Crystal turned and looked at Esper.

"When you're uncomfortable," McCay continued, "you're not relaxed and you can't keep your thoughts straight."

Prado jabbed Fisher with her elbow and winked. "Sound familiar."

"Is what she's telling them consistent with what she told you back at the house?" McCay asked.

"So far," Prado answered.

"Still," Fisher offered, "there are lots of problems with her story. Orin brings a gun with him to say goodbye to his sister? What's with that? And then shoots at her and misses? He was a decorated sniper."

McCay grunted and watched as Staton and Esper secured the final seconds of the timeline from Crystal.

"Well, based on what Lydia told us, Crystal is full of shit."

Fisher jerked his head in McCay's direction. "What?"

"Yeah, I was going to fill you in on that," Prado said.

"Really," Fisher answered, "and when were you planning on doing that?"

"Right now," she said and gestured to the door of the viewing room.

The three retired to the conference room where McCay and Prado reviewed their conversation with Lydia. Prado concluded with, "Translating what Lydia told us, Orin had some real problems with his sister, and I'm thinking that's why he went to see her. To confront her before he took off. I don't know what he expected was going to happen, but it sure as hell didn't go his way."

"Wait," Fisher demanded. "Back up. *They* were too smart? *No one was going to find out*? Lydia said that?"

Prado and McCay nodded.

"Shit, yeah," Fisher responded. "It was Orin." He fell against the back of his chair. "He killed Plough."

"He might have pulled the trigger," McCay agreed, "but that wasn't his game. He had his own thing going on and wouldn't have gone beyond that. He had no reason to. He was taking care of his needs and killing Plough wasn't part of it. Didn't do a thing for him."

Prado nodded. "It was Crystal, and that raises all kinds of questions."

"Not 'why,'" Fisher said. "Plough was an equal opportunity asshole and I imagine Crystal had had enough."

Prado sat back in the chair and shook her head slowly. "Was that really enough? And why the civil rights claim? How much do Tricia and Lurleen know?"

"Lydia is ground zero for us," McCay said, "but I can tell you from experience nothing she told us is going to be considered adequate enough to detain Crystal so we can try and get answers to those questions."

"Why?"

"Lydia was held captive by a serial killer for nearly four years and experienced the most horrible things, things that would warp anyone's mind." Before he could get any pushback, McCay raised his hand. "Those women I told you about whose testimony convicted their attackers were not initially believed. Two woman escaped from David Ray Vaughn, the Toy Box Killer. One of them even had her throat cut. She couldn't make the police believe her because she'd been drugged and was hazy on crucial details. One of Dahmer's victims made it out of his apartment and into the street where he was found stark naked. The police returned him to Dahmer despite what he told them. Remember, we're dealing with things that most people just can't wrap their heads around."

"There's the other girl, Willie," Fisher said. "She can corroborate what Lydia told you."

McCay shook his head. "She's nearly comatose."

"Staton will give us some leeway on this," Prado insisted. "We can ask him to hold her until we take our shots. Maybe we can get her to give it up."

"I'm sure he'll give us time to try our hand," McCay said, "but we have to consider all the possible ramifications of what we do, and the first one is if we don't do this just right, if we push too hard, Crystal will lawyer up. And if we use what Lydia told us, we give away who our asset is and the game is on to rip Lydia apart. She won't ever be any good to us. But I have an idea. Where's Lurleen?"

"She's next up," Prado said. "Why?"

"Crystal's the ringleader," McCay said, looking at Prado. "It will be interesting to see how closely she hews to Crystal's story."

Prado bolted toward the door of the viewing room, trailing the words, "Ira, play along with me."

***

"Perfect timing," Prado said as they walked into the hallway and crossed paths with Esper, Staton and Crystal. "Sheriff, Marshal," she acknowledged them. "I have just a few questions of my own for Crystal, if that's okay."

Crystal turned toward Esper and Staton and raised her eyebrows in question as if expecting them to object.

"Sure, go right ahead," Staton said, reached back and opened the door to the interrogation room.

"Please," Prado said, ushering Crystal to the side of the metal table facing the mirror. "This will only take a few minutes. I just have a couple of things I want to clear up for myself." She sat opposite Crystal and, with her eyes, guided Fisher to a corner of the room behind the table

"I told'em everything I know," Crystal said as she sat. "Same stuff I already tol' you."

Prado smiled ingratiatingly. "And we'll be exchanging notes with them." She took a legal pad from a stack sitting to one side of the gun metal gray table and pulled her chair close so her knees were touching Crystal's, who pushed away from the table.

"I thought you all was lookin' into the killing of Ken and all that stuff?"

"We are," Prado confirmed.

"Is this 'bout that?"

"It is, and more. Now," Prado said, making a show of centering the pad in front of her, clicking her pen, and checking that it was working by scribbling on the pad. "You said Lurleen came over to your house this morning like she did every morning, right?"

Crystal lifted her eyes to the mirror. "You know all this."

"Just bear with me. She comes over and tells you about the girls in the truck. Is that right?"

Crystal hesitated before nodding.

"But Orin already told you what he was doing. You knew he'd been kidnapping, torturing and killing girls before Lurleen said anything about the girls, right?"

Crystal stared at Prado, her expression wary.

"You learned that *before* Lurleen came over, right?"

Crystal cocked her head slightly. "What're you gettin' at?"

"I'm just trying to clear up a few details I'm confused about. Just so we're on the same page. Okay, then Orin told you what he was doing, but when Lurleen told you about the girls in his truck, you said that surprised you, right?"

"Findin' out they was in the truck right outside my house was a surprise, yes."

"But you killed him before you knew about those two girls. The ones in his truck."

Crystal shook her head slowly. "I shot Orin because he was gonna kill me."

"Why was he going to kill you?"

"'Cause he was fuckin' nuts. 'Cause he told me 'bout them girls and I said I was gonna tell you all." Crystal scowled. "You know all this so why're you askin' me the same stuff again?"

Prado raised her hand, index finger extended. "I appreciate your patience. This will only take a few more minutes, I promise."

"If you two are supposed to be investigatin' what happened to Ken, why are you askin' these questions?"

"We help each other with our cases," Prado responded pleasantly. "And we think there might be a link between them," she said, couching it as an afterthought, and went on. "Did Orin ever exhibit any violent tendencies that would explain why he did what he did? I'm referring to what he did to the girls."

"You was the ones who told me 'bout some woman he was supposed to've killed in Canada," Crystal answered. "It seems to me he was jus' nuts. Don't that answer your question?" She waved her hands. "But let's put the brakes on this for a minute. You said there is a…a what was it? A 'link' 'tween everything. What link? What're you talkin' 'bout?"

"Frankly, Crystal, we're not sure, and that's what we're trying to figure out." Prado wrote on the pad, the only sound in the room was her scribbling. "Okay," she said declaratively, and looked up. "Orin comes over to your house. He tells you what he's been doing. You tell him you're going to tell us. He threatens to kill you so you kill him.

Then Lurleen comes over and tells you about the girls in the car? That about it?"

Crystal nodded.

Prado wrote extensively and slowly. She considered what she had written and, eyes still focused on the pad, she asked, "It doesn't really make a lot of sense that Orin would drop by your house to say goodbye, does it? I mean only for that reason."

Crystal squinted and turned her head slightly as if trying to understand what Prado asked. "What?"

"Orin has kidnapped and killed at least half a dozen girls and he shows up at your house. Why would he do that? Wouldn't he have been better off just getting the hell out of Dodge and calling you later if he felt the need to say goodbye?"

"I tol' you why he said he came over. That's all I know."

"Okay, he came over to say goodbye, and while there he tells you about the girls. Right?"

"Yeah, for the thousandth time, that's right."

Prado leaned in. "There was no *other* reason why he would want to talk to you? Nothing else at all?"

Crystal's eyes widened and she inhaled audibly. She looked away from Prado and shifted in her chair.

"Crystal," Prado said sharply. "Did you two talk about anything else?"

"No, and unless you got anything else, I want to leave. I need a cigarette."

"You've been very cooperative, Crystal. Special Agent Fisher will show you out." Prado made a point of holding up a hand to stop her before she was fully out of her chair. "Oh, one final question. Did Orin mention he had killed Frankie Hebert and another man right before he came to your house?"

"Yeah, he did. Sorry, forgot that."

Prado pulled back her head in surprise. "Really? An oversight?" she asked dramatically. "You simply forgot to mention that Orin told you he killed two men right before coming to your house to say goodbye?"

"There was a lot of shit goin' down."

"Anything else you're forgetting to tell us?"

"No," she said harshly, pushed herself up, and walked toward the door.

"If you think of anything, you know where to find us."

As they started through the door Prado called out to Fisher, "Bring Lurleen in."

Prado let Crystal and Fisher get a few steps into the hallway before she came to the door and said, "One more thing." She walked toward them. "A number of times when we came to see you, Lurleen was there, but Tricia wasn't. But almost every time we went to talk to Tricia, both you and Lurleen were with her. Is there any reason why Tricia was cut out of some conversations?"

Crystal did not turn around to answer. "Lurleen lives like a mile from me." Walking away, she added, "She's over my house all the time."

***

Prado was standing as Fisher guided Lurleen into the room. She pointed the woman to the single chair facing the mirror. Fisher leaned close to Prado and whispered, "Tricia is here," then backed away and stood behind Lurleen.

Prado smiled and looked across the table. "We know this has been tough on everyone in your family. I know how close you, Crystal, Tricia and Orin were. Well, how close you *are* with Crystal and Tricia."

Lurleen's eyes darted around the small room. She turned and looked at Fisher.

"We just have a few quick questions for you," Prado said as she carefully centered the legal pad and pen in front of her. "We had a nice conversation with Crystal and we'll be speaking to Tricia right after we talk to you. We need everyone's help to find out exactly what happened and why."

"Orin came over to Crystal's and was gonna kill her. She killed him first," Lurleen declared.

"It's the details we need," Prado said.

Lurleen scowled, releasing the softness of the jawline. "I woulda thought the Marshal and John were gonna be talkin' to me."

"Here's the thing, Lurleen," Prado said, working hard for a look of sincerity tinged with a hint of confusion. "They asked us to talk to you because they heard some things from Crystal they thought might compromise how they dealt with you. That's why we ended up talking to Crystal." Prado shrugged. "To double check a few things."

Lurleen hesitated before asking, "What're you talkin' 'bout?" She brushed away a lock of yellow curls that fell across her brow, which she wrinkled in concern. "What'd Crystal say?"

Prado smiled ingratiatingly. "She told us a few things that while not pointing directly at you as someone who knows more than you've said so far, at the very least left us with the impression that you might not have told us everything you do know."

Fisher fought unsuccessfully to suppress a smile. This was worthy of the Abbott and Costello "Who's on first" routine. His admiration for Prado soared.

"She said I was responsible for somethin'?" Lurleen asked and turned to look at Fisher who went straight-faced. "Is that what you're sayin'?"

"Are you?" Prado asked, adding a hint of surprise in her voice. "Responsible for something?"

"No," Lurleen responded angrily. "I ain't. But what'd she say?"

Prado knew she had planted a seed of doubt. Now to nurture it. "She said she had to shoot Orin, who was going to shoot her, and you came over and helped her."

"So?"

"How did you help her, exactly?"

Lurleen placed her hands on the table and entwined her fingers. She waited a moment before offering, "She called me and I came over. I saw those girls in the truck and I went inside where Orin was lying on the floor of the kitchen."

Prado smiled knowingly. "She called you and you went right over?"

Lurleen nodded.

"And you saw the girls in the truck on your way into Crystal's?"

"Yeah."

"And you told her about them when you got inside, right?"

"Yeah."

"And that was the first she knew about them. So, she was surprised by that information?"

"That's what I been sayin'," she answered irritatedly. "How many more ways you gonna ask this same stuff?"

"See, here's the problem. Crystal said she and Orin got into it because she threatened to tell us about the girls." She stared at Lurleen. "Orin must've said something about the girls before you got there."

Fisher walked up behind Lurleen and leaned on the back of her chair. "Your timelines are different."

"I tol' her 'bout the girls in the truck. I don't know what Orin tol' her."

"Okay," Prado said pleasantly. "One final thing. What did she say when she called you?"

Lurleen glanced over her shoulder at Fisher who was still leaning on the back of her chair. "You mind?"

"Not at all," Fisher said backing away.

Prado smiled at Lurleen. "So, what did she say when she called and asked you to come over?"

"That she had to kill Orin and she needed me to come over."

"I thought you two had a standing date every morning. Why'd she have to call you to come over?"

Lurleen looked down at the table and took a deep breath. "We do have coffee almost every morning. There's times when I have things to do and can't go over. She wanted to make sure I did go this morning."

"To summarize then, she called you to come over. She didn't know about the girls in the truck until you told her, but you think Orin must have said something about them, and that's what led to the shooting."

Lurleen placed her hands on the table and studied her fingers. "Yeah," she said with a hint of a question in her voice. "That's mostly what happened."

"Mostly?" Prado said insistently. "Or exactly?"

"Shit, I don't know if it's *exactly*. That's about how it happened. Ain't that how Crystal said it happened?"

"Tell us about Orin," Prado responded. "You've said he could get crazy. What do you mean by that?"

"You're shittin' me? You know what all he did with those girls. Kidnappin'em and stuff. Don't that strike you as crazy?"

"How did this craziness affect you and Crystal, or Ken, or the kids? I mean personally. Crystal had some things to say about all that."

"Whatever she told you is the way it was," Lurleen said wearily.

"I want to hear what you have to say about it."

"He could get nuts. That's 'bout it."

"Crystal said she was surprised to learn what he had done, but you don't sound like it surprised you at all."

"'Course it surprised me. Getting' mad and actin' up is one thing. Kidnapping and killin' a buncha girls is 'nother."

"He must have done something violent that caused you to think he was crazy, as you describe him. Did he ever threaten you?"

"No."

"Did he ever threaten Crystal?"

"Not that I know of."

"Did he ever threaten Ken or do anything violent to him."

There was a moment of hesitation before, "No, he and Ken got along good."

"You're telling us Orin didn't have a problem with Ken burning down his house and practically killing him?" Prado's voice got sharper and louder. "He had no problem with Ken making him do all the dirty work for him. Like hauling stolen livestock?" She opened her eyes wide and pointed at Lurleen. "Despite burning down the house, the scars that it left on Orin, and him being under Ken's thumb, Orin never said a harsh word about Ken? Is that what you're saying?"

Lurleen looked toward the door and then at the mirror. "What the hell is goin' on here? You asked me 'bout what went on this morning. I tol' you. All this other shit is…well, I don't know what the hell it is."

"Did you know Orin was a suspect in a murder in Toronto?"

Lurleen stared at Prado. "No."

"Does that surprise you?"

"Not now that I know all this other stuff."

"Did you know he was a sniper in the Canadian army?"

Lurleen looked away from Prado. "No."

"You never talked to him about his time in Toronto?"

"All I know is he went there."

"One final question. Why do you think Orin would go over to Crystal's? Wouldn't it have made more sense for him to take off and then call to say goodbye?"

"I don't know," Lurleen said, exasperation in her voice. "There's no accountin' for crazy I guess."

"Unless, of course, he wanted to talk to her about something else." Prado pulled her chair closer to the table and waited a short beat before asking, "Do you think he might have wanted to talk to her about anything else? Could that be why he went over?"

"I don't know. Now, unless you got anything else you want to talk to me 'bout, I'm leaving."

"Why would Orin kill Frankie Hebert?"

Lurleen jerked straight up in her chair. "What?"

"He killed Frankie Hebert and another man who came to his house immediately before going to Crystal's. Why do you think he'd do that?" Seeing confusion wrinkle Lurleen's face, Prado pressed. "Crystal didn't tell you Hebert went by Orin's and Orin killed him and another man named Butch. She never mentioned that to you?"

Lurleen did not answer the question, saying only, "Orin was a crazy SOB. I ain't surprised if he did it."

"Okay, better question. Why do you think Frankie and the other man went to Orin's?"

"I don't know."

"Do you think Crystal knows?"

Lurleen shook her head.

"Orin kills two people, puts the girls in his truck, drives to Crystal's to say goodbye rather than leave right away. Does that make any sense to you?"

Before Lurleen could respond, Prado smiled broadly at Lurleen. "You've been very helpful. Thank you."

As she did with Crystal, Prado waited for the woman to get a few steps toward the door before stopping her. "I'm sorry, but I have one final question. A number of times when we visited Crystal, you were there, but Tricia wasn't. But almost every time we went to talk to Tricia, both you and Crystal were with her. Is there any reason Tricia was cut out of some conversations?"

"She wasn't cut out. I live a mile or so away from Crystal. We visit a lot."

Prado held Fisher back and let Lurleen walk into the hallway before following her and asking, "Would you show Tricia how to get back here so we can talk to her?"

"What's the deal with asking her about Crystal knowing why Orin killed Hebert and the other guy?" Fisher asked.

Prado said, "Just causing trouble. Stirring the pot."

***

Prado and Fisher were standing when Tricia walked into the room. "We appreciate your agreeing to talk to us."

"A Course."

Prado pointed to the seat opposite her as Fisher took up his position near the door. "What brought you here?"

"Lurleen said you wanted to talk to me."

"No," Prado said with a broad smile. "I mean why did you come here to Maryville, to the station?"

"I heard what happened and wanted to see how Crystal was doing."

"Not Lurleen?"

Tricia squinted. "What?"

"Not concerned about Lurleen?"

"Course. Came to see 'bout her too."

"Well, that was very thoughtful. I'm assuming you've heard about Orin and the allegations about his involvement in the kidnapping and killing of a number of young women. Girls, really."

Tricia nodded.

"Surprised?"

"Shocked is more like it. Is that what you want to talk to me 'bout?"

"That and a few other things." Prado made a production of reading the notes on the legal pad, and scribbled a few additions, before asking, "Whenever we visited with you, Crystal was there. I know you called her a couple of those times and asked her come over, and she was already there with you a few other times when we came by. Did she ask you to call her whenever we wanted to talk to you? Did she want to be there every time?"

"Wasn't like that. She and me and Lurleen are almost always together. Ken liked it that way so we could watch the kids and be with him. He was a big family man. Liked us all to be together."

"We've heard the same thing from Crystal," Fisher shoehorned in. "Those exact words."

Tricia turned toward Fisher. "Well, that's the way it was."

Prado continued, "I can understand and appreciate that. I even admire the way the three of you get along so well. Not very common with most wives and ex-wives."

Tricia smiled. "It worked good for us."

"Even after Ken was gone?"

"'Specially after that. We needed to support each other."

"Based on what I know from visiting you, and from talking to Lurleen, it was Crystal who insisted you all should continue doing that."

Tricia made a face. "No, we just did it."

"But Crystal was the driver. The one who made sure you did it."

"We woulda done it anyways."

"Okay," Prado said, "but how does that explain all the times I was at Crystal's, but you weren't there."

"But Lurleen usually was," Fisher added.

"What're you sayin'?"

"What we're saying, Tricia, is Crystal didn't seem to want you with her all the time, but she definitely wanted to be there when you met with us."

Tricia took a moment before answering, "We didn't spend every waking minute together."

"I'm not talking about every waking minute. I'm talking about those times when we met with you and Crystal was almost always there, usually with Lurleen. Or, like I said, when we'd go and talk to her but you weren't with them. I'm trying to understand." Prado let her hands slide across the table toward Tricia and gestured with open palms, asking very deliberately, "Why did she insist on being there when you talked to us, but she didn't need you there when we talked to her?"

Tricia shook her head and shrugged. "Don't know. I just know we was together a lot and I wanted her with me when you all was askin' questions. It made me feel more comfortable."

"Sounds to me like Crystal didn't trust you to tell us what she wanted you to tell us," Prado said and did not wait for a response before moving on. "One more question for you. Why do you think Orin went to Crystal's to, according to her, say goodbye rather than… ?" She stopped mid-sentence and asked, "You do know Orin was over at her house to say goodbye because he was planning on leaving and he had two of the girls with him?"

Crystal raised her shoulders toward her ears as if heading off a shiver. "Yeah, she told me."

"Why do you think he'd go by there rather than just leave and then call? He was concerned we wanted to talk to him, which we did, and yet he felt the need to stop on the way out of town. Doesn't make a lot of sense, does it?"

"He was her brother. They was close and I guess he wanted to say goodbye in person."

"They were close? Until about three or four years ago, she didn't know whether he was alive or dead. She left her family to be with Ken, who burned down her house, and Orin was badly burned. *Close*? Really?"

"She was making up for lost time, I guess. All I can tell you is they was together a lot since he got back."

"So, he goes over and tells her some truly awful things, and he's expecting she'll be okay with that and she'll let him go on his merry way?" Prado asked, an edge to her voice. "Is that what you're saying?"

"I'm answerin' your questions best as I know how."

"Did you know Orin killed Frankie…?"

"Crystal tol' me. And the other guy."

"Why do you think he did that?"

Tricia's body went limp. "I don't know," she replied, almost in a whisper. "I don't know 'bout most of this stuff." She looked beseechingly at Prado. "We almost done. I don't feel so good."

"Almost. One more question. Did you know Orin was a sniper in the Canadian army?"

"No."

"And a very good one. Earned all kinds of medals and commendations."

Tricia stared at Prado. "That's good, right?"

"As long as he isn't shooting at you."

No light dawned in Tricia's eyes that Prado could detect.

"You said you came here this morning to be with Crystal," Fisher said. "To see how she was doing? To be supportive?"

Tricia nodded.

"Crystal called you, right?"

Tricia nodded.

"Thanks for your patience," Prado said and stood.

Fisher said to Prado as he ushered Tricia from the room, "This time you follow my lead. I'll be right back."

***

"We have a few final questions," Fisher said to a very displeased Crystal who he followed into the interrogation room.

She slammed her purse on top of the metal table, announcing loudly, "I was the one who got attacked and defended myself from a crazy, sick fuck." She stood next to the table. "I been real cooperative, but you're makin' me feel like I done somethin' wrong."

Fisher pointed at the chair. "We appreciate your patience and understand how physically and emotionally drained you must be. I admire the way you've handled yourself and only have a few more questions, I promise, then it's all over. Please," he said, pointing again to the chair, "have a seat."

"I'll stand," she declared. "I think maybe I need a lawyer."

Prado, just inside the doorway, looked at the mirror and nodded knowingly.

Fisher feigned surprise. "Why would you need a lawyer? You haven't done anything wrong. You were almost the victim. But you can have a lawyer present any time you want."

Crystal plopped down on the chair. "Let's just get this shit over with."

"Thank you," Fisher said, and taking a leaf from Prado's playbook, spent a moment reviewing what she had written on the legal pad before asking, "Why didn't Orin rebuild the house Ken burned down? He had the foundation and the basement to work with. Wouldn't that have been easier than starting from scratch?"

"First off, Orin didn't build it. Ken built it with Orin's help. Second, Ken was building it for me," she said forcefully, "and I didn't want it too near where the other one was."

"Everyone thought Orin lived with you."

"He did live with me for 'bout six months, 'til the house was built, which was 'bout three years ago."

"No one knew it existed. Was the house supposed to be a secret?"

Crystal shrugged. "I don't know what everyone thought. In case you ain't noticed, we don't have a lot to say to people 'round here and they don't speak to us much, 'cept to accuse us of stealin' or sayin' we're threatenin' them for one reason or 'nother."

"You said Ken was building the house for you. How did Orin end up living there?"

"Too long of a story."

"Give us the short version."

"Ken wanted to build me a house back on the pond where I grew up. He talked about rebuilding our old place but I said 'no', not right there. Too many bad memories. He found a place on the other side of the pond that he liked 'cause it had a…a, uh" – she made a dipping motion with her hand – "kinda downhill from a high spot down to the pond." She looked at Fisher then at Prado. "Now, this is gonna sound strange to you, but he wanted to build like a bunker-type place where he and the rest of us could go if things got bad."

"What does that mean? 'If things got bad.'"

"He was certain someone, actually lotsa people, was gonna one day try'n kill him." She rolled her eyes. "Which they did. Anyway, he wanted someplace we could go 'til whatever got'em angry, passed." Crystal shook her head. "Don't ask me to explain it. It never made any sense to me."

"And did he?" Prado asked. "Build a bunker?"

"Yeah, and then filled in 'round it and made slope natural-like to the pond so you didn't know nothin' was there."

Prado, standing in a corner near the door, glanced at the mirror, raising her eyebrows in a "Are you believing this?" expression.

Fisher asked, "Did you ever see the bunker?"

Crystal shifted in her chair. "No, after Ken was killed, Orin said he was 'fraid it might cave in, and he didn't need it, so he filled it in with dirt." She jabbed a finger on the top of the table. "That was supposed to be my house."

"You got screwed," Fisher said. "How did that happen?"

Crystal's face was now the color of a ripe apple. "Don't matter." She folded her arms across her chest and looked away.

"Another short version," Fisher said encouragingly.

"I pissed him off. I asked for more money for me and the kids."

Prado pushed herself away from the wall and walked around the table to face Crystal. "And he wouldn't give it to you?"

"Fuck, no. He never gave us all that we needed." Crystal took a deep breath and forced a smile. "He took care of us okay, I guess."

"But you thought you deserved more?" Prado questioned. "Given all I heard you did for him, I'd agree."

Crystal did not respond.

Prado reached for words to restoke Crystal's anger. "So, he gave the house to Orin? Just because you asked for a few more dollars for your kids?"

"Can you fuckin' believe it? It was supposed to be my Goddamned house," she said with an anger that raised her out of the chair. "If anyone crossed him, he was one mean son-of-a-bitch."

"Did you really need the money for the kids?" Fisher asked.

"Or maybe you felt it was way past due," Prado added. "Due for all those years of protecting him and doing exactly what he asked."

"It was for me and the kids, but, yeah, I deserved it. I deserved whatever I wanted from him. And I told him so, and said if he didn't help me out a little more, I might not be so accommodatin'."

"Accommodating?"

"Keepin' him from gettin' in trouble." She shook her head. "And that's all I gotta say."

Prado leaned on the table. "Did he abuse you?"

She stared intently at Prado. "Abuse me? Is that what you call it?"

"Did he rape you?"

"He took what he wanted."

"Tricia too?"

"By the time he got 'round to her, he'd calmed down some. She was lucky. Didn't hafta deal with half the shit me'n Lurleen did." She squared her shoulders and pushed away from the table. "We done here?"

She was up and out of her chair before Prado and Fisher could respond. As she disappeared through the door, Fisher smiled at Prado and whispered, "I put Tricia in the viewing room."

***

McCay, Staton and Esper crowded into the interrogation room. "That was artful," Staton said to Prado and Fisher. "I'd like to be a fly on the wall when they compare notes. The paranoia should be electric."

"Except with Tricia," Fisher said. "I don't think the lights are all on with her, but I did try to jump start some brain cells."

"The big bonus was the bunker," McCay said. "Now we know how that came to be." He directed himself to Prado. "It wasn't an Orin creation. He inherited it and made it his own."

"I'm thinking all three of them are looking at each other with suspicious eyes," Staton said. "Especially Lurleen. I'm sure you managed to convince her that we" – Staton pointed at Esper – "heard something squirrely from Crystal."

Prado smiled broadly. "That was the plan. Do you really think it worked?"

"I would've left wonderin'," Esper said. "'Specially after you told her about Frankie and Butch. She's gotta be asking herself why Crystal didn't tell her 'bout that, and what else Crystal hasn't told her."

"Ironically, that omission by Crystal has no bearing on anything," McCay said. "I think she just honestly forgot about it with everything else going on."

Fisher crowed, "Yes, sir. Anything to plant those seeds of doubt and suspicion."

McCay winked. "Oh, they've been planted."

"A real-life version of the Tell Tale Heart," Fisher said.

Esper screwed up his face in question. "What?"

"A short story by Edgar Allan Poe about a man who commits a murder, buries the body under the floorboards of his house, and pretty soon thinks he hears the dead man's heart beating. The guilt overwhelms him. I'm betting Lurleen begins to hear Ken's heart beating. Crystal is a hard case. I'm guessing she feels fully justified doing what she did."

McCay agreed. "She's not going to crack."

"By the way," Fisher said, "we're all in agreement that Crystal pushed Orin into killing Plough, right?"

"I think that's a safe bet," McCay said. "There's a lot of anger there. The house. Not getting her fair share. And Ken was definitely a brute."

"But we'll need a tell-tale heart to break the case," Prado said. "I agree Lurleen's the weak link in this. My play would be to wait a few months and bring her back for some more questions." She nodded at McCay. "You hit it right on Crystal lawyering up. If we continue to press them now, she'll do it and then we've lost them."

Staton said, "We can't hold them on what we have now anyway."

Prado continued, "Let some time pass and hit Lurleen up again. Press her on why Orin showed up at Crystal's. She was rattled when we pointed out the discrepancies between her story and Crystal's. By then the guilt should be gnawing at her."

"I'd also press Lurleen on what she knows about the sniper rifle," Fisher suggested. "I'm guessing they talked to Orin about getting rid of it."

"Orin wouldn't have gotten rid of that rifle," McCay said. "Being a sniper was the one thing he did well in his life and the rifle is a souvenir of that success. It's around somewhere."

"There's one thread hanging out loose that we haven't mentioned," Esper said. "That second round of shots. Crystal's gun is a .38. A revolver."

"That follows," McCay said. "A coup de grace from her makes sense. She'd want to be sure he was dead, and it gave her an active role in the revenge she so clearly wanted."

"How is it no one saw her?" Fisher asked. "How could she have walked up to the truck, shot Plough, and walked away without anyone seeing her?"

"The chaos," McCay answered. "From what I've heard…." He turned toward Esper. "It was chaotic. People dropping to the ground, then running away. No one was taking roll call."

"About right," Esper agreed.

"Crystal knew when Orin was going to take his shots, and she timed her follow up, and left," McCay said. "Did the autopsy recover any slugs?" he asked Esper.

"Ken's wounds were so bad from the first shots, the second rounds musta gone straight through. They weren't in Ken. After I found out there was a second weapon, I went back to look for whatever I could find in the area." He shook his head. "Nothing."

"What about the pickup?" Fisher asked. "There had to be something there, right?"

"Crystal sold it."

"You didn't impound it?"

"She came and got it while I was sorting through everything else."

"And sold it that fast?"

Esper nodded.

"To who?"

"Some guy upstate."

"And that's it?" Fisher asked. "No follow up?"

Staton stepped in. "We had no probable cause for a search warrant to get the bill of sale, if one even exists. And we still don't have probable cause."

A knock on the door interrupted the conversation. Officer Laydon apologized as he stepped into the room. He handed Prado a piece of paper. "Tricia Plough asked me to give this to you."

Prado read it and let her hand drop to her side. "Well, our job here is done," she said to Fisher. To the others, "And yours is to be continued. Tricia" – she said, waving the note – "is dropping the civil rights suit. Says she just wants it over with." She read from the page: "It's time to move on for the sake of my children. We need to let Ken rest in peace. Thank you for trying to help us out."

"I didn't see that coming," Fisher said, taking the note from Prado.

Prado shook her head. Not angry, but with a great deal of frustration in her voice, she said, "This is all Crystal. She convinced Tricia to drop the whole thing, and she sure as hell wants us out of here as soon as possible. If you needed any more proof that we're bumping up against stuff she doesn't want us nosing around about" – she jabbed a thumb at the note Fisher was studying intently –"this is it. But there's nothing holding us here."

"I'll be joining you," McCay said. "This is a done deal from my end. And it's the quietest one I've ever worked on. I see no reason to make any noise about it. I'll be urging my friends in Washington to keep it that way. I always hated giving these people a platform. The Bundys, the Raders, the Jespersons, they thrived on the notoriety. Maybe we can keep this where it belongs. In the dark.

WEDNESDAY

Prado and Fisher crossed the street heading toward Jill's. Fisher stopped and looked up and down the pitted road. "Looks smaller than I remember it," he said with a laugh. "Feels like I'm revisiting some place I left years ago even though we've only been here three weeks." He caught up with Prado who was waiting for him in front of Jill's.

She conducted her own review of the surroundings. "We've been through more than three weeks' worth of carnage. Messes with your head. I know."

As she pushed through the door into the diner a line of familiar faces turned in their direction. This morning, most were smiling.

Jill was waiting, a coffee urn in her hand. "Heard you all was leavin' us."

"That old reliable 'tin-can express'," Fisher said as he slid into the booth.

"We are," Prado confirmed. "Tricia has decided to drop her claim. No reason for us to darken your door any longer."

Jill filled two mugs and slid them to Prado and Fisher. "But you truly don't know that one of us didn't kill Ken, right? Least ways I ain't heard you have."

Prado said. "We have a pretty good idea it wasn't" – she hooked her fingers – "'"one of you."'"

"And you're okay with leavin' things undone."

Prado took a sip of coffee. "Sometimes you just have to move on."

Jill nodded as she was forming her next thought. "Do you know more'n when you first walked in here?"

"Boy," Fisher said, "that's an open-ended question. We know a lot about some things we had no idea we'd get dragged into, and not quite enough about things we were planning on closing out."

More nodding from Jill as she scooted across the bench seat next to Prado. "You're sayin' you do have an idea 'bout who killed Ken."

"Yes," Prado conceded, "that's what I'm saying."

Jill considered Prado for a moment. "I'm guessin' if it was worth stayin' on 'til you knew somethin' for sure, you'd be stayin'."

Prado smiled her answer and took a sip of coffee.

Jill stood and wiped down the table. "Seems like everything is as good as we can expect. Better, I suppose. Ken's gone. Orin's gone. Looks like that's where it ends."

Prado handed Jill a paper bag. "Your clothes. Washed and folded. Thanks."

FOUR MONTHS LATER

"You there Marshal?" McCay's voice came through the conference console.

"I'm here along with John," Staton said. "How about Eileen and Ira?"

"We're here," Prado responded, "and very curious about why you wanted to speak to us."

"But first," said Fisher, "how do you like being the heroes who took down the Oletha Monster? You and John have logged more time on the tube lately than Oprah."

After a moment of silence, Esper said, "I could've lived without it, 'specially the Oletha Monster part. That's embarrassing."

"It wasn't us who loosed the dogs on you," McCay said. "I have no idea how that happened."

Staton offered, "Someone around here couldn't keep their mouth shut, I'm guessing."

"Which is ironic in so many ways," Fisher offered.

"But the Oletha Monster is a little over the top," Esper said. "Now that's all anyone knows about Oletha."

"The media needs a catchy nickname to draw attention to its reporting," McCay said. "I haven't heard a word about Plough, so I guess that's an upside."

"Not so," Staton said. "We've had documentary and movie people all over both of us about Ken and how Karmic justice might've come home to roost in the form of a serial killer since the town covered up a murder. Really stupid shit, especially since Orin started way before Ken was killed."

"Why let the facts get in the way of a good story," McCay volunteered.

"A good story that would be totally scrambled if it got out that Orin also killed Ken," Fisher said with a strangled laugh.

"Did you find any remains of the other girls?" Prado asked.

"No," Staton answered, "and not for a lack of trying. We combed the Woods, but it's 20 acres. And once the media started in on us, they were tromping around out there for weeks. Contaminated everything."

"What about the pond?" Fisher asked. "Behind Orin's house."

"We looked," Staton answered. "No luck. It's been a long time. Whatever might be there has melted into the mud and silt."

"Anything new on Crystal? Any closer to getting that resolved?"

"And that's why we wanted to speak to you," Staton said. "Things have played out pretty much as you predicted, Eileen." A moment of quiet was filled with a buzz from the phone connection. "Well, maybe a little differently. John can bring you up to speed."

"I got a call the other day, three days ago to be exact, that the house Orin lived in, the one where he held those girls, was on fire. Folks have been talkin' for a while 'bout tearing the place down, but not 'bout burnin' it down. Anyway, because it's pretty isolated there was no way the fire department could do much. No fire hydrant or anything out that way. After the place pretty much burned to the ground, we found a body inside the house. This morning it was identified."

"It was Crystal, right?" Prado blurted.

"Yeah," Esper said, "it was."

"Tricia," Prado declared. "Tricia did that."

Staton said, "It sounds to me like you've been thinking about this."

"I have," Prado replied. "The day we interviewed all of them, we talked about one breaking loose. Either Lurleen would come clean, or the light would dawn for Tricia. I initially thought it would be Lurleen. That she'd chew on what we said and worry that Crystal might throw her under the bus. Then, the more I thought about it, I decided Tricia would be the one. That she'd stew over what we said and figure it out. Realize she was the odd one out all along, and Crystal kept her out of the loop for a reason. She didn't trust her. Sounds like she figured it out and did something about it. Have to say, though, this is not how I thought things would go."

Esper said, “It’s been coming for a while. ‘Bout a month back everyone noticed that Lurleen was drivin’ around in a brand-new Ford pickup. One of those real fancy ones, a step-up cab, four doors, panel of lights on the roof, reinforced bed, over-sized tires and everything. Bushwhacker I think they call’em. And she and Tricia started goin’ everywhere together, without Crystal who was spending more and more time in Dummy’s, and even at Stacy’s over in Maryville. Folks swore she was turning tricks. Her house was getting rundown and all.”

“Tricia held the purse strings,” Prado said thoughtfully. “Ken left her everything. She must have cut Crystal off.”

“Yeah,” Esper agreed, “that’s what everyone was thinkin’, but no one ever got the full story. Lurleen and Tricia never said anything ‘bout it. Truth is they never said anything about anything. People said they haven’t said two words to anyone in months. They keep to themselves. Even pulled their kids outta school and are teaching’em at home.”

“Have you questioned Tricia and Lurleen about Crystal?” Fisher asked.

“Course, we did,” Esper answered sharply.

“And?”

“And they are each other’s alibi.”

“Twenty-four/seven?” Prado asked.

“Yeah, they’re livin’ together. When I talked to’em they said it saved’em money and makes it easier to watch the kids.”

“Did you confirm that?” Fisher asked.

“The best we could.”

Staton added, “Lurleen is selling her house.”

“Where does that leave things?” Prado asked.

“There’s more,” Staton said, “and this is especially for you, Eileen.”

Prado looked at Fisher and answered, “It better be real good with a lead-in like that.”

“It is,” Esper responded. “With Crystal’s death being suspicious, we got a search warrant for her house and....”

“And you found the C14,” Prado spit out.

“You’re on a roll,” Staton said with a laugh

"We found the sniper rifle," Esper confirmed. "Surprised the hell outta me that she had it. Well, that she had it to begin with and never thought to get rid of it."

"Did you confront Lurleen about it?" Fisher asked. "See if you could push her into saying something?"

"We did. She said she didn't know anything 'bout it."

"She's tougher than we thought," Fisher offered.

"I even took a page from your book," Esper said, "and made sure Tricia was in the viewing area…"

"With me," Staton said.

"…when I questioned Lurleen. I talked 'bout how it might be Orin who killed Ken, and Crystal was the person who put it all together. I was expecting her to push back, or, at least, get real nervous and twitchy, but she was cool as a cucumber. Just sat there and listened. Didn't deny a word. Only said she didn't know anything 'bout the rifle or Orin and Crystal bein' in cahoots 'bout Ken."

"Did you say anything about Crystal being motivated by anger about the house and wanting more money?" Prado asked.

"Yes," Staton said. "Lurleen pleaded ignorance and Tricia didn't bat an eyelash through the whole thing. She watched, and then the two of them left the station together. Arm-in-arm, literally. Two peas in a pod."

"They're all each other has," Prado said. "They've closed ranks and are moving on, the hell with everybody else."

"I have another take on it," Staton said. "I think Lurleen told Tricia everything. She took a chance and laid it all out. Probably convinced Tricia that she was dragged along unwillingly by Crystal. Either Tricia was outraged Crystal would play her like she did, or she really loved Ken. Whatever, she had a lot more cold in her than any of us thought."

"So, the loose ends are tied," Prado said.

"They are," Staton agreed. "What goes around comes around."

Complete Profile of Orin Truville Schneiderman ("the subject")

1) The subject is a Caucasian male born November 13, 1992 in Oletha, Iowa.

2014 Radford/FGCU Serial Killer Database: Serial Killer Database annual statistics report indicated that for the decades 1900–2010, the percentage of white serial killers was 52.1% while the percentage of African American serial killers was 40.3%.

MY NOTE: Census results for Oletha, Iowa report that the population is almost entirely Caucasian (99.99 percent). Iowa Workforce Development's Migrant and Seasonal Farm Worker (MSFW) outreach program states that a negligible number of migrant and/or seasonal farm workers are employed by the region's growers.

2) The subject was the victim of a house fire when he was five years old during which he was badly scarred.

The Development of Serial Killers — A Grounded Theory Study by Meher Sharma: Theories about the etiology of serial killing can be generally broken into two groups: biological perspectives and psychosocial perspectives (Siegel, 2005). Biological perspectives include brain abnormalities, genetic predispositions and other factors, whereas, the psychosocial perspectives generally revolve around mental disorders, childhood trauma, and social learning related influences.

And...

Allely et al. (2014) concluded that there exists a complex interaction between predisposing neurodevelopmental complications (such as head injury), stressful and/or traumatic environmental incidents and serial killing. They stressed that neurodevelopmental problems were not a single factor etiology for serial killing, and said there exists an interaction between neurodevelopmental and environmental factors such as sexual, psychological, or physical abuse, leading to an individual being prone to becoming a serial killer.

3) The subject had an unstable home life in which domestic violence was the norm. His mother murdered his father, and he was shuttled from one foster home to another before he found a stable environment.

Frequencies Between Serial Killer Typology and Theorized Etiological Factors by Leryn Rose-Doggett Messori: Burgess et al. (1986) believes that the budding serial killer would be born and raised in an ineffective social environment, defined as difficulty with attachment due to caretakers either ignoring, rationalizing, or normalizing "various behaviors in the developing boy or, through their own problems (e.g., criminal behavior or substance abuse), and support the child's developing distortions and projections." People important to the child do not provide the required safety, support, and nurturance, rather becoming non-protective or imposing adult responsibilities onto the young child. This "ineffective social environment" then supports the deviant child's distortions of the world and others as uncaring. It is proposed that formative events would arise in the child's life that also have an impact on the developmental trajectory. The model's concept of formative events refers to three contributing factors that can occur to help perpetuate the future serial killer's distorted view of the world and others. This usually occurs through a trauma (physical or sexual abuse), which frightens the child and shapes their thought patterns.

The Development of Serial Killers — A Grounded Theory Study by Meher Sharma: Research on the psychosocial causes of serial killing points to the likelihood that childhood experiences – particularly abuse, loneliness and abandonment – lead serial killers to commit their crimes. Mackey and Immerman (2004) claimed that the presence of a father or a father-figure during childhood prevents/ reduces violent and aggressive behavior during adulthood; Holmes and DeBurger (1985) suggested that most serial killers are born to parents out of marriage, presumably increasing the rate at which the killers were raised without one of their parents. Hickey (1997) found that among a group of 62 male serial killers, 48% faced some kind of rejection by either parent or another important person in their life. Apart from rejection, other psychosocial factors such as childhood humiliation (Hale, 1994), neglect, early adoptions, and abandonment during childhood (Whitman & Akutagawa, 2004) have been found to relate to serial murder. These unstable and unhealthy relationships may result in the incapability of forming emotional attachments during childhood.

Identification of Psychosocial Factors in the Development of Serial Killers in the United States by Tiffany Brennan: The prevalence of abuse in serial killers has been found to be greater than the general population. In this study, the data confirmed what has been found in previous research; 56% of the serial killers had documented or known childhood traumas. For example, Keith Hunter Jesperson's father drank heavily and he would witness his father putting women and kids down constantly (Krueger, Justice, & Hunt). [He] almost molested by a neighbor at age 11, he claimed he was raped at age 14, his dad shocked him in a greenhouse, and was beaten after being blamed for his friend's wrongdoings (Krueger, Justice, & Hunt). He experienced a lot of traumatic experiences in his childhood that affected him for the rest of his life and took it out on his victims. Another example is of Rodney Alcala who experienced abandonment by his father at a young age (Rodney Alcala: Dating Game, 2017).

4) The subject was bullied in school, and according to interviews with various classmates (one cited herein), failed to establish any meaningful attachments.

Frequencies Between Serial Killer Typology and Theorized Etiological Factors by Leryn Rose-Doggett Messori: A study by Smokowski, Evans, and Cotter (2014) found that the experience of chronic bullying (in rural adolescents) was associated with "higher levels of anxiety, depression, and aggressive behaviors as well as lower levels of self-esteem and future optimism than non-victims." All serial killers grow up to become aggressive, albeit with different motivations for the aggression. While this current study was descriptive in nature, it seems important to note this finding as it is the only etiological factor examined that the majority of serial killer case histories endorsed as being present.

Identification of Psychosocial Factors in the Development of Serial Killers in The United States by Tiffany Brennan: It was found that the majority of all types of serial killer experienced negative aggressive acts by peers, and that these proportions were not statistically different across typologies (ranging from three fifths to three quarters of each typology) is a substantial and important finding.

MY NOTE: Former classmates of the subject were unanimous in their recollections of a chronically shy boy whose appearance was off-putting to his classmates. Given his size and athletic abilities, he did have some success on the school's rugby team, but even this was limited by his own inability to create friendships and by his shunning by teammates off the field.

Classmate Joi Lansing Turner recalls that "He didn't seem to know how to talk to anyone. The one time I tried to make friends, he got mad when I wouldn't let him walk me home after school. He slapped some books out of my hands and if the janitor hadn't come along, I think he would have hurt me. I stayed away from him after that."

5) The subject committed sexual battery on three different girls when in high school.

Serial Murder—Pathways for Investigation, U.S. Department of Justice, Federal Bureau of Investigation: A large percentage of offenders had an arrest record; however, 78% had a record at the time of their first murder versus 88% that had a record at the time of their last murder. At the time of arrest, the leading categories of offenses:

Assault/battery offenses (12.9%)
Theft/larceny offenses (10.6)
Sex related offenses (9%)
Burglary (8%)
Drug offenses (6%)

U.S. Department of Justice, Office of Justice Programs, Bureau of Justice Statistics: Those convicted of murder (36%) or felony assault (35%) were the next most likely to have had an active criminal justice status when arrested. Fifteen percent of murderers were on probation, 13% were on pretrial release, and 8% were on parole. Nineteen percent of those later convicted of assault were on probation when arrested, 11% on pretrial release, and 6% on parole.

MY NOTE: In addition to the reported sexual battery, it was reliably reported that the subject was involved in theft, burglary and drug offenses after returning to Oletha from Toronto.

6) The subject was in the Canadian Armed Forces and served in Afghanistan as a member of a six-man sniper team with the Sniper System Project (SSP). The Canadian team received praise for its extreme long range shots and for killing a significant number of and combatants.

Identification of Psychosocial Factors in the Development of Serial Killers in the United States by Tiffany Brennan: Castle and Hensely (2002) suggest that the military may be a location that serial killers could gain exposure to killing. The exposure to brutalization and desensitization to violence that begins in boot camp could aid in the classical conditioning used by the military to assist budding serial killers to begin to "associate violence with pleasurable 28 consequences."

And…

[S]erial murderers that are later classified as organized are more likely to have been in the military than disorganized serial murderers. Having military experience was split in the 15 case histories determined to be lust-oriented (53% not present; 47% present) and the seven categorized as power-oriented (43% not present; 57% present)

Sociological and Psychological Predispositions to Serial Murder by Katie Marie Krueger: It should also be noted that while the majority of the serial killers did not serve in the military, the percentage of those that did was statistically significant when compared to the military service of the general population. Therefore, military experience might also be considered a pre-dispositional factor to serial murder.

MY NOTE: The subject's team commander Master Corporal Leonard Duggan described the subject as "an excellent marksman but a lousy soldier" who received a number of commendations for his success as a marksman, but was discouraged from re-enlisting. Duggan said it was his evaluation of the subject as "not being a team player" and "a loner who often disappeared for days at a time to the point of being reported as AWOL on more than one occasion" that influenced the SSP not to encourage the soldier to re-enlist, and to actively discourage him from doing so when he requested the paperwork to re-enlist. Duggan also said that no spotter wanted to work with the subject who was "belligerent," "disrespectful," and "just plain unlikable." When he was asked if he thought the subject might have been operating on his own and even against those not deemed the "enemy," Duggan did not hesitate to say "that was always my concern."

Referencing the studies above pointing to the likelihood that "military experience might also be considered a pre-dispositional factor to serial murder," it is clear that the offender in the events under investigation is an organized killer. He exhibits five of the seven phases associated with organized serial murder (phases 6 and 7 have yet to be confirmed for this particular subject) as developed by psychologist Joel Norris:

1. Aura Phase

The first phase serial killers experience is withdrawal from reality. It may go unnoticed by those closest to them, but life has lost all meaning for the killer. Their senses are heightened. Violent fantasies begin to form, and they feel the urge to act on them.

2. Trolling Phase

This is the phase in which the killer starts to search for their victim as well as looking for a place to commit the crime or dump the body. This phase can last for months or just days, until the would-be serial killer has found the perfect victim.

3. Wooing Phase

This is when the killer sets out to gain the victim's trust to put them at ease before attacking them. They may present themselves as charming, wanting to help – or harmless and in need to help themselves. This phase is experienced by only the most organized serial killers.

4. Capture Phase

In this phase, the killer reveals his true sadistic self. The victim becomes incapacitated, whether knocked unconscious or restrained or trapped somewhere.

5. Murder Phase

This is the phase where the murder takes place. Organized killers often chose to kill their victims slowly, causing them much suffering and torture before they die. Disorganized killers are more likely to kill their victims instantly and commit further acts, such as necrophilia or mutilation, on their corpses.

6. Totem Phase

In the totem phase, the thrill of the kill begins to dissipate for serial killers. To keep some of the excitement, they will often take a souvenir from their victims, such as the clothes they were wearing or newspaper stories about the crime. These serve to remind the killer of the moment they made their warped fantasy real.

7. Depression Phase

The final phase in the cycle. The anticlimax causes a depression in the serial killer who comes to feel that his fantasy was not properly fulfilled. Some may even kill themselves in this phase. Those who don't, will soon begin to experience the violent fantasies of the aura phase and the cycle begins again.

7) The subject is a person of interest in a murder in Toronto committed prior to returning to Oletha, where he lives with his sister Crystal Truville and performed various odd jobs for Kenneth Plough. These events, and others, created stress and anxiety in the subject's life.

Frequencies Between Serial Killer Typology and Theorized Etiological Factors by Leryn Rose-Doggett Messori: Organized offenders are also thought to kill primarily after stressful life events. They plan the murder with order and control to regain a sense of control or to expel the stressful feelings. The crime scene tends to reflect this level of planning and precision.

And…

Whitman and Akutagawa (2003) quote an article published by Douglas and Olshaker in 1999 that states: Being able to dominate, manipulate and control a victim, to decide whether the victim lives or dies, or how that victim dies, temporarily counteracts, for some, their feelings of inadequacy and speaks to the other side of the psychological equation. It makes them feel grandiose and superior, as they believe they are entitled to feel. In other words, raping and murdering sets the world right with them (as cited in Whitman & Akutagawa (2003).

The Development of Serial Killers — A Grounded Theory Study by Meher Sharma: Bundy speaking of himself in the third person: "[W]e can see that this kind of person, because one of the primary reasons he did this ... uh, committed the murders ... was a search for a release of stress or feelings of low esteem or anger, hostility, resentment, whatever ... it was channeled for some reason toward women. Young women ... and in a particular way." (Michaud and Aynesworth) "Well, we talked again, about... we have to go back to the root causes of the person - the causes we can identify in trying to determine why any individual would undertake to kill persons in this way. And we said that this person was reacting inappropriately to stress from his own environment. We're talking about stress as an umbrella label for any number of things. Uh, stress in his personal life. Let's say, a financial situation ... uh, his own sense of self-esteem and fulfillment. The failures in his life ... other forms of anxieties."

And…

Moreover, serial killers seem to operate cyclically, and as evidenced by previously mentioned data, presumably kill while they are facing some kind of stress. Whether it was being constantly exposed to violence and crime (for Richard Ramirez), or the stress/trauma experienced by the loss of an important relationship (for Ted Bundy and Gary Ridgway), these three individuals resorted to serial killing. For example, both Bundy and Ridgway admitted to killing as a coping mechanism - to relieve stress and vent frustrations or rage. On the other hand, Ramirez turned robbery and violently sexual murders into his career. This study's data suggests that these serial killers internalized their stress and/or trauma, and externalized the symptoms as evidenced by their actions; harming and killing people to relieve feelings of frustration, stress/trauma, and loneliness, and to experience power. In order to relieve themselves, they killed, felt elevated, and went on with their lives. When they were faced with more stress and were unable to cope in healthy ways, they engaged in killing more people, wanting to feel the same or a higher level of elevation. This addictive cycle continued until they were caught. As Simon (1996) and Giannangelo (1996) suggested, a serial killers' need for stimulation increases as evidenced by an increase in the rate of his or her killings, reflecting a compulsive and addictive pattern of behaviors.

MY NOTE: The subject has lived in a state of anxiety throughout his life. From his earliest childhood being a burn victim to growing up early in life in a home characterized by domestic violence to being removed from his parents' home and shuttled from foster home to foster home to being shunned in school, and in other instances throughout his life. Although I have no hard evidence of precisely what his relationship is with his sister or was with Mr. Plough, I have gained some insight into these relationships from my interactions with people who know all the parties and saw them interact. I think it's safe to say that both his sister and Mr. Plough dominated the subject and controlled him thereby creating another level of anxiety in his life.

8) The subject had little to no control over his life due to his feelings of inadequacy and his rejection by others.

Frequencies Between Serial Killer Typology and Theorized Etiological Factors by Leryn Rose-Doggett Messori: Power/control-oriented killer. Serial killers within this category murder to exert control over the victim. While it has been debated that many of the serial killer typologies achieve a secondary gain by having control during the act of killing, this type of serial killer's narcissistic need for power and control constitutes the primary gain of the killing (Pollock, 1995). It is the serial killer's need to exert ultimate control, the power of life or death, over the victim that fuels his or her continued desire to repeatedly kill.

<u>The Development of Serial Killers — A Grounded Theory Study by Meher Sharma</u>: For example, Special Agent Bill Hagmaier from the Behavioral Science Unit, after interviewing Bundy, said the following to Michaud and Aynesworth: He [Bundy] said, that after a while, murder isn't just a crime of lust or violence. "It becomes possession. They are a part of you. After a while, when you plan these, that person becomes a part of you and you are forever one." He [Bundy] said that even after twenty or thirty that it's the same thing, because you're the last one there. He [Bundy] said, "You feel the last bit of breath leaving their body." And he [Bundy] said, "You're looking into their eyes and basically a person in that situation is God! You then possess them and they shall forever be a part of you. And the grounds where you kill them or leave them become sacred to you, and you will always be drawn back to them."

And…

"I think we see a point reached - slowly, perhaps - where the control, the possession aspect, came to include, within its demands, the necessity ... for purposes of gratification ... the killing of the victims ... Perhaps it came to be seen that the ultimate possession was, in fact, the taking of the life. And then purely ... the physical possession of the remains ..." (Michaud and Aynesworth, Ted Bundy Talks about Himself section).

9) The subject has suffered rejection by women.

<u>The Motivation Behind Serial Sexual Homicide: Is It Sex, Power, and Control, or Anger? by Myers, Safarik, Husted and O'Toole:</u> The authors provide theoretical, empirical, evolutionary, and physiological support for the argument that serial sexual murderers above all commit their crimes in pursuit of sadistic pleasure. The seeking of power and control over victims is believed to serve the two secondary purposes of heightening sexual arousal and ensuring victim presence for the crime.

<u>Serial Killers: The Mechanism from Imagination to the Murder phases by Nicola Maliza</u>: As the years pass, the future killer's reliance on fantasy only increases. It continues to substitute for real feelings of control, and as a vent for anger, and also comes to compensate for feelings of low self-esteem and feelings of general failure (FBI, 1985).

And…

Essentially: "sexual homicide is an act of control, dominance and performance that is representative of an underlying fantasy embedded with violence, sexuality and death."

And…

The child will create a personal imaginary world and will project the hostility and hatred that the child has experienced in the real world. In fantasies any individual can imagine the self to be immense and without limits. The main difference between a criminal and a normal subject is that the former believes to have some sort of divine right to satisfy his fantasies, without moral or legal restrictions (Norris, 1988).

The Development of Serial Killers — A Grounded Theory Study by Meher Sharma: Loneliness and the need for power/ control have been common themes in the lives and crimes of … serial killers. Loneliness experienced by most serial killers can be counted as a contributing factor to the motivation of controlling victims (Ramsland, 2006; Martens & Palermo, 2005).

10) The subject has characteristics identified with serial offenders.

Sociological and Psychological Predispositions to Serial Murder by Katie Marie Krueger Butler: The analysis of the data revealed that a majority of the serial killers shared six characteristics. These factors included: being of the male gender, having abandonment issues likely brought on by the desertion of someone close to them, education level – particularly being a high school dropout or being a college dropout, being employed in a blue collar job, and having a prior criminal record. While not every serial killer in this sample has all five of these characteristics, they do share a majority of them.

Identification of Psychosocial Factors in the Development of Serial Killers in the United States by Tiffany Brennan: There is a combination of both sociological and psychological factors that are common among serial killers. Serial killing is present across all demographics. The presence of mental illness, criminality, childhood trauma, substance abuse, military involvement, and parental mental illness are all risk factors for serial killing. There are also patterns between motives and types of victims; all of the serial killers examined chose their victims for a particular reason whether it be revenge, hatred, pleasure, power, or money. They all chose victims that they know will be unable to defend themselves and that they could have control and power over, and they all gained something from their killings (Ioana, 2013).

Serial Murder—Pathways for Investigation, U.S. Department of Justice, Federal Bureau of Investigation: Only 25% of (serial sexual murder) offenders were married and 65.6% were employed either full time or part-time. Forty-five percent of offenders were either renting or owned their own home. The majority of offenders (64 .1%) had a high school diploma or higher educational level; with 39.1% having some college education. At the time of the first murder, over half (56.5%) of the serial sexual offenders had a prior arrest record as compared to other serial offenders (21.7%). Twenty five percent of serial sexual offenders had prior military service as compared to other serial offenders (7.6%).

ADDENDUM

The MO, signature and forensics indicate a single organized offender is responsible for the Maryville/Oletha murders. The victims are all young girls who were sexually assaulted and disposed of at a similar location.

Identification of Psychosocial Factors in the Development of Serial Killers in the United States by Tiffany Brennan: The serial killers examined killed for a variety of reasons including revenge, hatred, pleasure, money, etc. but overall the motive for killing was to gain something. They all had a type of victim and the motives remained the same. Serial killers may pick their victims based on something symbolic to them such as killing someone that looks like the person that abused them (Ioana, 2013).

Pocket Guide to the Crime Classification Manual. A Standard System for Investigating and Classifying Violent Crimes by JE Douglas, AW Burgess, AG Burgess, RK Ressler - 1992 - ncjrs.gov: Crime scene characteristics for organized killers are noted to show planning and control prior to and during the criminal act, targeting of a stranger for the victim, personalization of the victim, use of restraints, and ability to transport and hide the body after the murder is complete.

Serial Murder—Pathways for Investigation, U.S. Department of Justice, Federal Bureau of Investigation: In this study, 329 of the 480 victims were killed by an offender who was sexually motivated. Female victims comprised 85.4% of these victims, male victims were 14.6% of this category.

The age range of the victims:

- *8 to 13 years (3.3%)*
- *14 to 29 years (47.4%)*
- *30 to 45 years (35.0%)*
- *Over 45 years (9.4%)*
- *For sixteen of the victims, their age could not be determined.*

The racial breakdown of the victims:

- *White (52.0%)*
- *Black (38.9%)*
- *Hispanic (6.1%)*
- *Other (2.4%)*

The specific disposal sites:

- *Outdoor public areas (72.6%)*
- *Victims' residences (14.6%)*
- *Offenders' residences (2.4%)*

The causes of death:

- *Strangulation (51.6%)*
- *Blunt force trauma (13.7%)*
- *Stab wounds (10.6%)*
- *Gunshot wounds (7.6%)*
- *Undetermined (9.1%)*
- *Other (0.6%)*
- *Unknown (4.9%)*

In 75.1% of the cases, the victims were found nude or partially nude.

We are pursuing a dangerously impaired individual who is a power-control oriented, serial sexual sadist. He lacks empathy of any kind and will continue kidnapping, torturing and killing young women and girls until he is caught or killed.

Serial Killer: The Mechanism from Imagination to the Murder Phases by Nicola Malizia: The serial killer does not stop of his own accord. Unless prevented, the serial killer will kill again and again (Holmes & De Burger, 1988). Each successful murder exhilarates the killer, both confirming and reinforcing the act.

Simply put: serial killers tend to increase their killings; it appears they have to kill often to maintain their equilibrium. The fantasy and psychic high that they obtain induces bold and more frequent attacks, sometimes with a complete disregard of risk (Geberth, 1990).

And…

This is, in certain respects, no different from the alcoholic using their drink of choice as a coping mechanism. Just as addicts tend to fall into a downward spiral, until all else in their lives centers around the addictive substance, the serial killer's life begins to revolve around fantasy. The revolution becomes so dominating that eventually fantasy becomes the center of the serial killer's life. And just as the heroin addict's need for a fix may drive him to steal, the serial killer's obligation to the fantasy drives him to murder. In short, the cycle of the serial killer is no different from the cycle of any other addict, the end result of murder being functionally the same as the heroin addict's theft.

The UNSUB is most likely local and not a transient given the number of killings happening in a relatively short period of time in and around a single point.

Geographic Profiling of Serial Murderer, Gary Ridgway, to Assist Law Enforcement in the Apprehension of Future Serial Murderers by Rachel Neldner: *Rossmo (2000) found American serial murderers generally encountered targets at an average distance of approximately 22 km (13.662 miles) and left their victims' bodies on average of approximately 34 km (21.114 miles) from their home location. A breakdown of Rossmo's (2000) results indicated residence-to-crime distances were shorter than 20 km (12.42miles) for 46% of his sample. The results show the residence-to-crime distance distribution follows a decay pattern, whereby the likelihood of disposing of a body decreases as the distance from the murderer's residence increases, and furthermore the median and average distance from the murderer's residence to the body recovery locations are roughly 8 km (4.968 miles) and 30 km (18.63miles) (Snook et al., 2005).*

Geographic Profiling by D. Kim Rossmo: Offenders "consistently in neighbourhoods they personally know well or are very similar in physical, social and economic characteristics to their home (Brantingham & Brantingham, 1995, P. 13). Familiarity with, access to, and departure from a scene affect an offender's target choices (Beavon, Brantingham & Brantingham, 1994).

A nod to Leo Staton and John Esper.

The Development of Serial Killers: A Grounded Theory Study Meher Sharma: Bundy said (speaking in the third person): "In his readings and in his observations and what have you - in his fantasy world - he'd imagined for some reason people disappearing all the time. He was aware of how people dropped out and became runaways and whatnot. In devising his scheme, he'd taken the somewhat unrealistic conclusion that under the correct circumstances he could select any person as a victim and that there'd be virtually no attention paid to that person's disappearance. People disappear every day. It happens all the time." (Michaud and Aynesworth, 1999, p. 326)

Reference Sources

The Killer Across the Table: Unlocking the Secrets of Serial Killers and Predators with the FBI's Original Mindhunter
John Douglas and Mark Olshaker
Dey Street Books

The Anatomy of Motive
John Douglas and Mark Olshaker
Simon and Schuster Inc.

Hunting Humans
Dr. Elliott Leyton
John Blake Publishing Ltd.

Angel of Darkness
Dennis McDougal
Grand Central Publishing

I'll Be Gone In the Dark
Michelle McNamara
HarperCollins Publishers

Whoever Fights Monsters
Robert K. Ressler and Tom Shachtman
St. Martin's Press

Murder in the Bayou
Ethan Brown
Scribner

In Broad Daylight
Harry N. MacLean
Dell

Serial Murder: Multi-Disciplinary Perspectives for Investigators
Editor: Robert J. Morton
Supervisory Special Agent
Behavioral Analysis Unit-2
Federal Bureau of Investigation

Serial Murder: Pathways for Investigation
Robert J. Morton Supervisory Special Agent, National Center for the Analysis of Violent Crime Federal Bureau of Investigation
Jennifer M. Tillman Crime Analyst, National Center for the Analysis of Violent Crime Federal Bureau of Investigation
Stephanie J. Gaines ORISE Research Analyst, National Center for the Analysis of Violent Crime Federal Bureau of Investigation
2014 Radford/FGCU Serial Killer Database
M.G. Aamodt
http://maamodt.asp.radford.edu/serial killer information center/project description.htm

The Development of Serial Killers: A Grounded Theory Study
Meher Sharma
https://thekeep.eiu.edu/cgi/viewcontent.cgi?article=4722&context=theses

Frequencies Between Serial Killer Typology and Theorized Etiological Factors
Leryn Rose-Doggett Messori
https://etd.ohiolink.edu/!etd.send_file?accession=antioch1471990999&disposition=inline

Identification of Psychosocial Factors in the Development of Serial Killers in the United States
Tiffany Brennan
https://digitalcommons.salemstate.edu/cgi/viewcontent.cgi?article=1216&context=honors_theses

Sociological and Psychological Predispositions to Serial Murder
Katie Marie Krueger
https://digitalcommons.butler.edu/cgi/viewcontent.cgi?article=1040&context=ugtheses

The Motivation Behind Serial Sexual Homicide: Is it Sex, Power, and Control, or Anger?
C. Myers, M.D.; David S. Husted, M.D.; Mark E. Safarik, M.S.; and Mary Ellen O'Toole, Ph.D.
https://www.academia.edu/30556345/The_Motivation_Behind_Serial_Sexual_Homicide_Is_It_Sex_Power_and_Control_or_Anger

Serial Killer: The Mechanism from Imagination to the Murder Phases
Nicola Malizia
https://m.scirp.org/papers/74772

Crime Classification Manual: A Standard System for Investigating and Classifying Violent Crimes
J E Douglas; A W Burgess; A G Burgess; R K Ressler
https://www.ncjrs.gov/App/Publications/abstract.aspx?ID=137386

Geographic Profiling of Serial Murderer, Gary Ridgway, to Assist Law Enforcement in the Apprehension of Future Serial Murderers
Rachel Neldner
http://www.gis.smumn.edu/GradProjects/NeldnerR.pdf

Geographic Profiling
D. Kim Rossmo
https://www.amazon.com/Geographic-Profiling-D-Kim-Rossmo/dp/0849381290

The following serial killers are mentioned in *A Wretched Creature.* Information is from *Wikipedia* unless otherwise indicated.

Charles Frederick Albright (born August 10, 1933) is an American murderer from Dallas, Texas who was convicted of killing one woman and suspected of killing two others in 1991.

In 1988, Rhonda Bowie was found stabbed to death in north Oak Cliff. Years later, between December 1990 and March 1991, Mary Lou Pratt, Shirley Williams and Susan Beth Peterson's bodies were found in Dallas. All had been shot in the back of the head and had their eyes removed. Police connected the crimes, and Charles Albright, a carpenter from north Oak Cliff, was arrested in March 1991 and charged with capital murder in the slayings.

https://www.dallasnews.com/news/2017/11/01/flashback-the-eyeball-killer-stalked-murdered-four-oak-cliff-women-in-1991/

In more than 20 years of studying serial killers, FBI Agent Judson M. Ray testified in Albright's trial that he had never seen anything like the "precision cutting" used to mutilate three Dallas prostitutes. "What was interesting to us was the method in which these victims, these body parts, were taken," the FBI agent said. "In my professional opinion, it's doubtful that you would have more than one person that deranged living in this city.

http://maamodt.asp.radford.edu/Psyc%20405/serial%20killers/Albright,%20Charles.htm

David Richard Berkowitz (The Son of Sam) born Richard David Falco; June 1, 1953, pleaded guilty to eight separate shooting attacks that began in New York City during the summer of 1976. He killed six people and wounded nine others by July 1977. Berkowitz claimed that his neighbor's dog was one of the reasons that he killed, stating that the dog demanded the blood of pretty young girls. He said that "Sam" was his former neighbor Sam Carr, and Carr's black Labrador retriever Harvey was possessed by an ancient demon that commanded Berkowitz to kill. In 1978, Berkowitz was sentenced to 25-years-to-life in prison for each murder, to be served consecutively.

https://en.wikipedia.org/wiki/David_Berkowitz

Berkowitz on his first killing: "You just felt very good after you did it. It just happens to be satisfying, to get the source of blood… I no longer had any sympathy whatsoever for anybody. It was very strange. That's what worried me the most. I said, 'Well, I just shot some girl to death and yet I don't feel…' They were people I had to kill. I can't stop and weep over them. You have to be strong and…you have to survive." (Elliott Leyton, *Hunting Humans: The Rise of the Multiple Modern Murderer*, Carroll & Graf; 2nd Revised edition, 2003)

Paul Kenneth Bernardo (born August 27, 1964), also known as **Paul Jason Teale** is a Canadian serial killer and serial rapist. Bernardo is known for initially committing a series of rapes in Scarborough, Ontario, a suburb of Toronto, between 1987 and 1990. He subsequently committed three murders with his then-wife Karla Homolka; among these victims was her young sister Tammy Homolka. After his capture and conviction, Bernardo was sentenced to life imprisonment and was later declared a dangerous offender unlikely to be released.

Bernardo scored 35 out of 40 on the Psychopathy Checklist, a psychological assessment tool used to assess the presence of psychopathy in individuals. This is classified as clinical psychopathy.

https://en.wikipedia.org/wiki/Paul_Bernardo#:~:text=Paul%20Kenneth%20Bernardo%20(born%20August,Toronto%2C%20between%201987%20and%201990.

Jerome Henry "Jerry" Brudos; January 31, 1939 – March 28, 2006, was an American serial killer and necrophile who committed the murders of at least four women in Oregon between 1968 and 1969.

Brudos had a fetish for women's shoes from the age of 5, after playing with stiletto heeled shoes at a local junkyard. He reportedly attempted to steal the shoes of his first-grade teacher. He also had a fetish for women's underwear and claimed that he would steal underwear from female neighbors as a child. He spent his teen years in and out of psychotherapy and psychiatric hospitals. While incarcerated, Brudos had piles of women's shoe catalogues in his cell—he wrote to major companies asking for them—and claimed they were his substitute for pornography.

https://en.wikipedia.org/wiki/Jerry_Brudos

Brudos began collecting trophies. In one instance, he cut off the foot of a victim and stored it in a freezer using it to model high heels he had collected. In another instance, he hoisted the body of a victim with a pulley in his garage and had sex with the corpse on multiple occasions. He cut off her breast and made a resin mould of it and used it as a paperweight.

https://allthatsinteresting.com/jerry-brudos

Theodore Robert Bundy, born Theodore Robert Cowell; November 24, 1946 – January 24, 1989, was an American serial killer, kidnapper, rapist, burglar, and necrophile who assaulted and murdered numerous young women and girls during the 1970s, and possibly earlier. Shortly before his execution and after more than a decade of denials, he confessed to 30 homicides that he committed in seven states between 1974 and 1978. The true victim count is unknown and could be much higher.

https://en.wikipedia.org/wiki/Ted_Bundy

In Bundy's 1979 trial for the murder and attempted murder of co-eds at the Chi Omega Sorority at Florida State University, the jury deliberated for less than seven hours before convicting him. Trial judge Edward Cowart imposed death sentences for the murder convictions. (Bundy v. State, 455 So.2d 330 (Fla.1984) Archived September 16, 2012, at the *Wayback Machine.* Retrieved July 21, 2011 and Bundy v. Wainwright, 808 F.2d 1410 (Fla. 1987) Archived April 7, 2012, at the *Wayback Machine.* Retrieved July 21, 2011)

Describing his attitude on life and murder: "I'm as cold a motherfucker as you've ever put your fucking eyes on. I don't give a shit about those people."

http://crimelibrary.tumblr.com/post/16042970803/some-of-ted-bundys-notorious-quotes

Richard Trenton Chase (The Vampire of Sacramento), born May 23, 1950, committed suicide December 26, 1980. He killed 6 people in the span of a month in Sacramento, California. He drank his victims' blood and cannibalized their remains.

Chase granted a series of interviews with Robert Ressler, during which he spoke of his fears of Nazis and UFOs, claiming that although he had killed, it was not his fault; he had been forced to kill to keep himself alive, which he believed any person would do. He asked Ressler to give him access to a radar gun, with which he could apprehend the Nazi UFOs, so that the Nazis could stand trial for the murders. He also handed Ressler a large amount of macaroni and cheese, which he had been hoarding in his pants pockets, believing that the prison officials were in league with the Nazis and attempting to kill him with poisoned food.

https://en.m.wikipedia.org/wiki/Richard_Chase

"Jack the Ripper" terrorized the Whitechapel district in London's East End from August to September in 1888. He killed at least five prostitutes and mutilated their bodies in an unusual manner, indicating that the killer had a knowledge of human anatomy. Jack the Ripper was never captured, and remains one of England's, and the world's, most infamous criminals.

https://www.biography.com/people/jack-the-ripper-9351486

The "From Hell" letter (also called the "Lusk letter") is a letter that was posted in 1888, along with half a human kidney, by a person who claimed to be the serial killer known as Jack the Ripper. It is addressed to George Lusk, the chairman of the Whitechapel Vigilance Committee. It reads (misspellings included): "From hell. Mr Lusk, Sor I send you half the Kidne I took from one woman prasarved it for you tother piece I fried and ate it was very nise. I may send you the bloody knif that took it out if you only wate a whil longer signed Catch me when you can Mishter Lusk."

https://en.wikipedia.org/wiki/From_Hell_letter

Keith Hunter Jesperson (Happy Face Killer) born April 6, 1955, murdered at least eight women in the United States during the early 1990s. He was known as the **Happy Face Killer** because he drew smiley faces on his many letters to the media and prosecutors. Many of his victims were sex workers and transients who had no connection to him. Strangulation was his preferred method of murdering, the same method he often used to kill animals as a child.

After the body of his first victim was found media attention surrounded a woman who falsely confessed. Jesperson was upset that he was not getting any media attention. On a bathroom wall hundreds of miles from the scene of the crime, he drew a smiley face and wrote an anonymous letter in which he confessed to the killing and provided proof. When that did not elicit a response, he began writing letters to the media and prosecutors.

While Jesperson has claimed to have killed as many as 185 people, only eight murders have been confirmed.

https://en.m.wikipedia.org/wiki/Keith_Hunter_Jesperson

Edmund Emil Kemper III, born December 18, 1948, murdered 10 people, including his paternal grandparents and mother. He regularly engaged in necrophilia and claimed to have consumed the flesh of at least one of his victims, but later retracted this confession. He is known for his large stature and high intelligence, standing 6 feet 9 inches tall, weighing over 250 pounds), and having a reported IQ of 145, characteristics that left his victims with little chance to overcome him. Found sane and guilty at his trial in 1973, he requested the death penalty for his crimes. However, capital punishment was temporarily suspended in California and he instead received eight life sentences. Since then, Kemper has been incarcerated in the California Medical Facility.

https://en.wikipedia.org/wiki/Edmund_Kemper

Describing his approach to murder: "One side of me says, I'd like to talk to her, date her. The other side says, I wonder how her head would look on a stick."

https://www.psychologytoday.com/us/blog/wicked-deeds/201403/the-real-life-horror-tale-the-twisted-co-ed-killer

Todd Christopher Kohlhepp (born March 7, 1971) is an American serial killer convicted of murdering seven people in South Carolina between 2003 and 2016.

Shortly following Kohlhepp's arrest, authorities in Spartanburg County discovered a number of seemingly joking product reviews for various items such as padlocks, shovels, tasers, and gun accessories on retail website amazon.com written by a user known simply as "me." One review written for a folding shovel, read, "keep in car for when you have to hide the bodies and you left the full size shovel at home...does not come with a midget, which would have been nice."

https://en.wikipedia.org/wiki/Todd_Kohlhepp

Randy Steven Kraft (The Scorecard Killer, The Southern California Strangler, The Freeway Killer), born March 19, 1945, murdered a minimum of 16 young men between 1972 and 1983. Kraft is also believed to have committed the rape and murder of up to 51 other boys and young men. He was convicted in May 1989 and is currently incarcerated on death row at San Quentin State Prison in Marin County, California.

"To have something like this take place in our society, I [...] I think I've sent eight or nine individuals to their death in my courtroom before. I can take all those aggravating circumstances in those other cases and they don't match Mr. Kraft's record. I just can't comment. If anyone ever deserved the death penalty, he's got it coming." Judge Donald A. McCartin passing the death sentence upon Randy Kraft November 29, 1989.

https://en.wikipedia.org/wiki/Randy_Kraft

Leonard Lake, born October 29, 1945, and Charles Ng, born December 24, 1960, were a pair of serial killers, rapists, abductors, robbers, and family annihilators believed to be responsible for as many as 25 murders.

Lake and Ng targeted women but were not hesitant to abduct entire families. After killing the men and children to get them out of the way, they would hold the women captive in a custom-built room in a bunker at Lake's ranch, tie them up and torture and rape them, video-taping each other while doing so.

Lake killed himself, and Ng is on death row at San Quentin.

Lake on one of his video tapes: "I want to be able to use a woman whenever I want. And when I'm tired or bored or not interested, I simply want to put her away, lock her up in [her cell], get her out of my sight, out of my life."

Ng's work time chant: "No, gun, no fun. No kill, no thrill. Mommy cries, baby fries."

https://criminalminds.fandom.com/wiki/Leonard_Lake_and_Charles_Ng

Robert Joseph Long (October 14, 1953 – May 23, 2019), also known as **Bobby Joe Long**, was an American serial killer and rapist who abducted, sexually assaulted, and murdered at least 10 women in the Tampa Bay Area in Florida during an eight-month period in 1984.

https://en.wikipedia.org/wiki/Bobby_Joe_Long

"It was like A, B, C, D. I'll pull over. They get in. I'd drive a little way. Stop. Pull out a knife, a gun, whatever. Tie 'em up. Take 'em out. And that would be it. And the worst thing is I don't understand why. I don't understand why."

https://www.oxygen.com/mark-of-a-killer/crime-news/bobby-joe-long-classified-ad-rapist-florida-serial-killer

Thomas Donald Bruce McArthur (October 8, 1951) was raised in Toronto, Canada. Between 2010 and 2017, a series of men disappeared in Toronto, Ontario, Canada. In January 2018, investigators obtained evidence connecting two disappearances to Bruce McArthur, a 66-year-old self-employed landscaper, whom they arrested on January 18, 2018. Police say that they found evidence in McArthur's apartment leading to homicide charges and that they found the dismembered remains of several men in planter boxes at a residence where McArthur stored landscaping equipment.

McArthur and many of his alleged victims were active on online dating apps for men who have sex with men, where McArthur stated that he wanted to meet submissive men. By April 18, McArthur had been charged with eight counts of first-degree murder in the deaths of missing men, most of whom had been linked to Church and

Wellesley. On January 29, 2019, McArthur pleaded guilty to all eight counts in Ontario Superior Court, and was subsequently sentenced to life imprisonment with no parole eligibility for 25 years. McArthur is the most prolific known serial killer to have been active in Toronto, and the oldest known serial killer in Canada.

https://en.wikipedia.org/wiki/2010%E2%80%932017_Toronto_serial_homicides

Herbert William Mullin (born April 18, 1947) is an American serial killer who killed thirteen people in California in the early 1970s. He confessed to the killings, which he claimed prevented earthquakes. He noted that there were no earthquakes during his killing spree, and felt vindicated when a Mw 5.8 earthquake hit the area soon after his arrest. In 1973, after a trial to determine whether he was insane or culpable, he was convicted of two murders in the first degree and nine in the second, and sentenced to life imprisonment.

Mullin is noted to have had interactions with Edmund Kemper, another serial killer active in the same area and at the same time as him; the two shared adjoining cells at one point. Kemper recalled "Well, [Mullin] had a habit of singing and bothering people when somebody tried to watch TV. So I threw water on him to shut him up. Then, when he was a good boy, I'd give him some peanuts. Herbie liked peanuts. That was effective because pretty soon he asked permission to sing. That's called behavior modification treatment."

https://en.wikipedia.org/wiki/Herbert_Mullin

"We human beings, through the history of the world, have prevented our continent from cataclysms by murder. In other words, a minor natural disaster avoids a major natural disaster." —Herbert Mullin

https://criminalminds.fandom.com/wiki/Herbert_Mullin

Dennis Lynn Rader (BTK Killer/BTK Strangler stands for "Bind, Torture, Kill"), born March 9, 1945, murdered 10 people in Sedgwick County, Kansas between 1974 and 1991. He sent letters describing the details of the murders to police and local news outlets before his arrest. After a decade-long hiatus, Rader resumed sending letters in 2004, leading to his 2005 arrest and subsequent guilty plea. He is currently serving 10 consecutive life sentences at El Dorado Correctional Facility in Kansas.

https://en.wikipedia.org/wiki/Dennis_Rader

From one of the notes (including misspellings) Rader sent to reporter Cathy Henkel at the Wichita Sun: "When this monster enter my brain, I will never know. But, it here to stay … Society can be thankfull that there are ways for people like me to relieve myself at time by day dreams of some victim being torture and being mine. It a big compicated game my friend of the monster play putting victims number down, follow them, checking up on them waiting in the dark, waiting, waiting … Maybe you can stop him. I can't. He has areadly chosen his next victim."

http://www.greensboro.com/btk-killer-held-wichita-captive/article_3cb95474-9ca3-5733-bd7c-9a83a0b7be90.html

Ricardo Leyva Muñoz Ramírez/Richard Ramirez (Night Stalker), February 29, 1960 – June 7, 2013, was a sex offender and serial killer who murdered 13 people. His highly publicized home invasion crime spree terrorized the residents of the greater Los Angeles area, and later the residents of the San Francisco area, from June 1984 until August 1985. He used a wide variety of weapons, including handguns, knives, a machete, a tire iron, and a hammer. Ramirez died of complications from B-cell lymphoma while awaiting execution on California's death row.

https://en.wikipedia.org/wiki/Richard_Ramirez

When convicted and sentenced to death, Ramirez told the court: "I am beyond your experience. I am beyond good and evil, legions of the night – night breed – repeat not the errors of the Night Stalker and show no mercy… I will be avenged. Lucifer dwells within all of us… See you in Disneyland." (Peter Vronsky, Serial Killers: The Method and Madness of Monsters, The Berkeley Publishing Group, New York, New York, 2004).

David Parker Ray (November 6, 1939 – May 28, 2002), also known as the Toy-Box Killer, was an American kidnapper, torturer, rapist and suspected serial killer. Though no bodies were found, he was accused by his accomplices of killing several people and suspected by the police to have murdered as many as 60 women from Arizona and New Mexico, while living in Elephant Butte, New Mexico.

He soundproofed a truck trailer that he called his "toy box," and equipped it with items used for sexual torture. Ray sexually tortured and presumably killed his victims using whips, chains, pulleys, straps, clamps, leg spreader bars, surgical blades, and saws. It is thought that he terrorized many women with these tools for many years, while living in New Mexico, with the help of accomplices, some of whom are alleged to have been several of the women he was dating. Inside the torture room, along with numerous sex toys, torture implements, syringes, and detailed diagrams showing ways of inflicting pain, there was a homemade electrical generator, which was used for torture. A mirror was mounted in the ceiling, above the obstetric table to which he strapped his victims. Ray also put his victims in wooden contraptions that bent them over and immobilized them while he had his dogs and sometimes other friends rape them. He has been said to have wanted his victims to see everything he was doing to them. Ray often had an audio tape recording of his voice played for his victims whenever they regained consciousness.

https://en.wikipedia.org/wiki/David_Parker_Ray

Gary Leon Ridgway (Green River Killer), born February 18, 1949, was convicted of murdering 49 women and girls in the state of Washington during the 1980s and 1990s (he claims to have murdered 71), making him the most prolific serial killer in U.S. history. Most of his victims were alleged to be sex workers and other women in vulnerable situations, including underage runaways. The press gave him his nickname after the first five victims were found in the Green River before his identity was known. He strangled his victims, usually by hand but sometimes using ligatures. After strangling them, he would dump their bodies in forested and overgrown areas in King County, often returning to the bodies to have sexual intercourse with them. As part of a plea bargain, wherein he agreed to disclose the locations of still-missing women, he was spared the death penalty and received a sentence of life imprisonment without parole.

https://en.wikipedia.org/wiki/Gary_Ridgway

Regarding the number of women he murdered: "I killed so many women I have a hard time keeping them straight."

https://www.inspiringquotes.us/author/9467-gary-ridgway

Maury Troy Travis (October 25, 1965 – June 10, 2002) was an American murderer and suspected serial killer who committed suicide in custody in St. Louis County, Missouri, after being arrested for murder. Travis was named in a federal criminal complaint for the murders of two women. At the time of the murders, he was a hotel waiter and on parole for a 1989 robbery. While Travis claimed in a letter to have murdered seventeen women, some authorities were doubtful; others thought he may have murdered up to twenty women.

https://en.wikipedia.org/wiki/Maury_Travis

When police began combing through Travis' home they didn't just find an apartment with a few bloodstains, they discovered a full-on torture chamber. In his home was a cabinet full of implements that he used to bind his victims before choking them to death, and a stun gun that he sometimes used to subdue his victims. One of the most horrific details is the amount of blood spatter that investigators found on his walls. Apparently, after a victim bled out on his walls, Travis would repaint them in order to hide the evidence of his crimes. Judging from the coats of paint on his wall, this kill - paint - kill again cycle happened many times.

In a sadistic twist to Travis' crimes, he filmed almost everything that he did in his torture chamber. In many of his home movies, Travis brings back a woman, smokes crack with her, and either has consensual sex before allowing them to leave or he brutally tortures and murders them. His worst crimes were captured on a VHS tape labeled "Your Wedding Day," which featured footage of Travis reenacting BDSM fantasies before strangling women to death. After viewing the tape, Police Chief Joe Mokwa ordered that everyone who saw the footage had to undergo psychological counseling. He told ABC News, "They'll give you nightmares."

Before ending the lives of each of his victims Maury Travis made sure that he completely mentally devastated them. On the tapes recovered from his home police saw that Travis would tie up his victims and cover their eyes with duct tape before berating them. His favorite thing to discuss was how the women had abandoned their children. In one video he shackled a woman to a bed and made her say, "You are the master. It pleases me to serve you."

After Travis brazenly sent a letter to the local paper with a map leading investigators to the body of one of his victims, the police managed to figure out exactly who he was by tracing his IP address. The map he sent the police was clearly printed from Expedia, so the police contacted the website and discovered that only one person had looked at a map of West Alton within the previous week.

Not only had the online map only been viewed by one person, but that same person zoomed in and enhanced the image until it looked exactly like the map that was sent to the paper. After that the police took the IP address, 65.227.106.78, to Microsoft and tracked down who owned that specific address. It belonged to someone with the screen name "MSN/maurytravis."

https://www.ranker.com/list/maury-travis-facts/jacob-shelton

David Russell Williams (born March 7, 1963) is a British-born Canadian convicted murderer and former colonel in the Canadian Forces. From July 2009 until his arrest in February 2010, Williams commanded CFB Trenton, Canada's largest military airbase and a hub for the country's foreign and domestic air transport operations.

An investigation and subsequent confession showed he had been breaking into 82 women's houses to steal underwear (including little girls'), later escalating to sexual assault and two counts of rape and murder. He was formally charged by the Ontario Provincial Police, pursuant to the Criminal Code, with two counts of first-degree murder, two counts of forcible confinement, two counts of breaking and entering, and sexual assault. Another 82 charges relating to breaking and entering were later added. On October 21, 2010, Williams was sentenced to two life sentences for first-degree murder, two 10-year sentences for other sexual assaults, two 10-year sentences for forcible confinement, and 82 one-year sentences for breaking and entering, all to be served concurrently.

Williams had been described as an elite pilot and "shining bright star" of the military. He had flown Queen Elizabeth II and the Duke of Edinburgh, the Governor General of Canada, the Prime Minister of Canada, and many other dignitaries across Canada and overseas in Canadian Forces VIP aircraft.

https://en.wikipedia.org/wiki/Russell_Williams_(criminal)

Statement by Williams: "Your Honour, I stand before you, Your Honour, indescribably ashamed. I know that the crimes I've committed have traumatized many people. The families and friends of Marie-France Comeau and Jessica Lloyd, in particular, have suffered and continue to suffer profound, desperate pain and sorrow as a result of what I've done. The understandable hatred that was expressed yesterday and that has been palpable throughout the week, has me recognize that most will find it impossible to accept. But the fact is, I very deeply regret what I have done and the harm I know I have caused so many. My very sincere hope is that my detailed confession on the night of Feb. 7, my full co-operation with investigators since, and ultimately my guilty plea earlier this week has, in some, way served to temper the very serious harm I have caused my victims and their families and friends."

http://www.ottawacitizen.com/news/williams+tearful+plea+forgiveness+falls+deaf+ears/3705505/story.html

Author Biography

John David Bethel is the author of award-winning novels, *Unheard of* and *Holding Back the Dark*. Other published novels include *Little Wars*, *Capitol Evil* and *Hotel Hell.* He has also been published in popular consumer magazines and respected political journals.

Mr. Bethel spent 35 years in politics and government. He served in the Federal Senior Executive Service as a political appointee where he was Senior Adviser/Director of Speechwriting for the Secretaries of Commerce and Education; Editorial Director for the U.S. Small Business Administration; and Assistant Administrator for the U.S. General Services Administration's Office of Communications and Citizen Services. Bethel also worked as press secretary/speechwriter to Members of Congress.

Mr. Bethel is a senior consultant for a number of prominent communications management firms, including Burson Marsteller and The Wade Group.

He graduated with Phi Beta Kappa honors from Tulane University and lives in DeLand, Florida.

For sales, editorial information, subsidiary rights information or a catalog, please write or phone or e-mail

AbsolutelyAmazingEbooks
Manhanset House
Shelter Island Hts., New York 11965, US
Tel: 212-427-7139
AbsolutelyAmazingEbooks.com
or AA-eBooks.com
www.BrickTowerPress.com
bricktower@aol.com
www.IngramContent.com

For sales in the UK and Europe please contact our distributor,
Gazelle Book Services
White Cross Mills
Lancaster, LA1 4XS, UK
Tel: (01524) 68765 Fax: (01524) 63232
email: jacky@gazellebooks.co.uk

Thank you for reading. Please review this book. Reviews help others find Absolutely Amazing eBooks and inspire us to keep providing these marvelous tales.

If you would like to be put on our email list to receive updates on new releases, contests, and promotions, please go to AbsolutelyAmazingEbooks.com and sign up.

CPSIA information can be obtained
at www.ICGtesting.com
Printed in the USA
BVHW091812100522
636630BV00008B/710